MONA LISA

Books by TIFFANY THAYER

Thirteen Men   1930
Call Her Savage   1931
The Greek   1931
Thirteen Women   1932
Three-Sheet   1932
One Woman   1933
Kings and Numbers   1934
Doctor Arnoldi   1934
The Cluck Abroad   1935
One-Man Show   1937
Little Dog Lost   1938
Tiffany Thayer's Three Musketeers   1939
Rabelais for Boys and Girls   1940
33 Sardonics (Ed.)   1946
Adult's Companion (Ed.)   1948

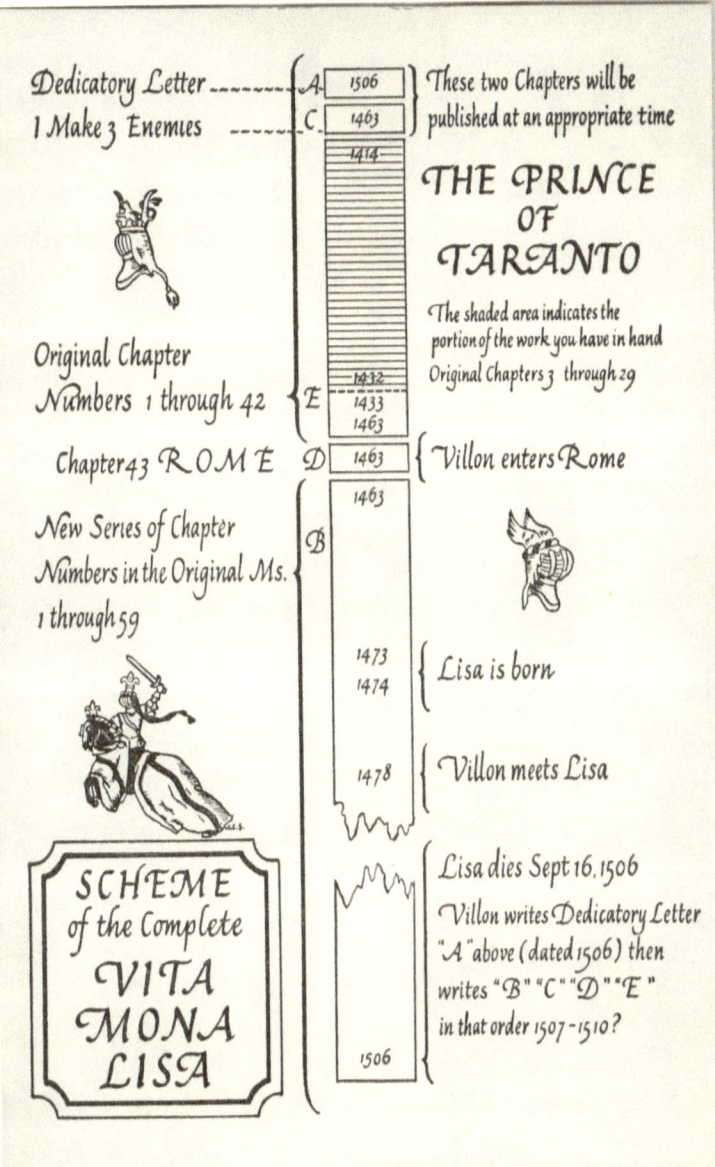

Dedicatory Letter ------- A. 1506 } These two Chapters will be
I Make 3 Enemies ------- C. 1463 } published at an appropriate time

1414

THE PRINCE
OF
TARANTO

The shaded area indicates the
portion of the work you have in hand
Original Chapters 3 through 29

Original Chapter
Numbers 1 through 42 { E 1432
1433
1463

Chapter 43 ROME D. 1463 { Villon enters Rome

1463

New Series of Chapter
Numbers in the Original Ms.
1 through 59 B.

1473
1474 { Lisa is born

1478 { Villon meets Lisa

Lisa dies Sept 16, 1506

Villon writes Dedicatory Letter
"A" above (dated 1506) then
writes "B" "C" "D" "E"
in that order 1507-1510?

SCHEME
of the Complete
VITA
MONA
LISA

1506

MONA LISA

THE PRINCE OF TARANTO
VOLUME ONE

TIFFANY THAYER

CUTTING EDGE

ISBN-13: 978-1-962896-80-1

Published by
Cutting Edge Books
PO Box 8212
Calabasas, CA 91372
www.cuttingedgebooks.com

To
Kathleen

CAVEAT CRITICUS

I F THE Ms which commences publication in the next chapter is not the first and only major prose work of François Villon, I have been swindled.

No one, I think, can deny that the MS is a major work of prose. It runs to no less than 45,669 leaves, which could not be printed in fewer than 14,823 pages of such a book as this one. That ain't *minor,* if you'll pardon the expression, and if it's poetry, I'll eat every leaf of it. The question, whether or not François Villon wrote it, is, perhaps, not so easily settled.

The MS stands me $149,000 in round numbers, to date, and it was obtained from a one-eyed archivist plying his trade in a tomb at Sarno, which is about twenty Italian miles from Naples, the other side of Vesuvius. I do not give the name of this ghoul, because he admitted that the MS was stolen, and I should not like to make any trouble for him if the work is authentic.

Sixteen years ago I would buy any bit of writing or printing offered to me on the subject of Mona Lisa, the painting or the sitter, because it had been suggested that I was just the lad to find out what made her smile like that. Your memory probably doesn't go back so far, but sixteen years ago there was a popular American superstition to the effect that I knew more about women than any other articulate male since Solomon and before Kinsey. We need not go any deeper into that. I mention it only to explain what led me to Naples. Lisa was born there, and I thought I should start looking for the meaning of her smile in the atmosphere where she acquired it. The atmosphere might have changed somewhat in 465 years, but not greatly, I think. It is still quite a town.

In Lisa's childhood, Naples was "rollicking".

"... the busy streets of rollicking Naples." *Staley*

Its Queens had been "amorous".

"... Lorenzo de Medici ... boasted descent from the jovial founder of the family fortune ... remembered in legend as one man to whom the amorous Neapolitan, Queen Giovanna la Superba, refused her favors." *Loth*

I pass by Monsieur Loth's use of the quaint old phrase, "refused her favors"—a presumed reference to the familiar back-breaker—without comment, but it may be useful to you to know that in the MS which follows shortly, Villon refers to this Queen as "Joan II, that royal whore". In all, Naples had four Queens named Joan (or Joana, Juana, Giovanna), each of them called "Superb", two before Lisa's time, one who gave the child a pair of diamond earrings in return for a favor, and one, a baby, with whom Lisa played as if she were a doll.

A bastard was on the Throne when Lisa was born.

"... When Alfonso died, in June 1458, Calixtus (III, Alonso Borgia) refused to acknowledge his son Ferrante as the heir, on the score of his illegitimate birth, and claimed the kingdoms of Naples and Sicily as the property of the Holy See. In a conversation with the Milanese ambassador, he spoke of Ferrante as a little bastard whose father was unknown." *Mathew*

Your particular attention is called to the use of the word "father" in this context. It would not have mattered in the least if Ferrante's *mother* had been the only one of his parents who was "unknown", but when the Pope threw doubt upon the bastard's *father* too, that deprived Ferrante of any vestige of claim to Naples. Still, he was on the Throne.

"... Naples was the city of ancient pleasure; the sirens lay in its waters, and the satyrs played in the sun. Its women had as a heritage tricks of desirousness, pagan arts learned in the days of Tiberius." *Taylor*

It was a place of "dark deeds".

"... Leonora (Duchess of Ferrera) and her two little daughters set out for Naples, under the escort of Nicolo da Corregio, to be present at her father King Ferrante's second marriage with the young Princess Joan of Aragon, a sister of Ferdinand the Catholic ... Beatrice was too young to realize the rare degree of culture which had made Alfonso's and Ferrante's court the favorite abode of the Greek and Latin scholars of the age, too innocent to be aware of the dark deeds which threw a shadow over these sunny regions, where the strange medley of luxury and vice, of refinement and cruelty, recalled the days of Imperial Rome." *Cartwright*

It is careless in Madame Cartwright to refer to Ferdinand (the sometime sponsor of Columbus) as "the Catholic" at the time of Ferrante's second marriage, 1477. The title, "the Catholic", was not given him until 1492, when Rodrigo Borgia, P. P. Alexander VI, conferred it specifically to honor Ferdinand for ending the Moorish reign in Granada. It is less careless than stuffy of the lady-writer to attempt to palm off the bride upon us as "a sister of Ferdinand". If the girl had been that King's full and legitimate sister, she never would have been given in marriage to Ferrante of Naples. Even as a bastard half-sister of Ferdinand, she was considered by her family to be much too good for her husband.

Naples was "the most vicious of courts".

"... It was not long before Donna Sancia (d'Aragon) caused herself to be freely gossiped about (in Rome). She was beautiful and thoughtless; she appreciated her position as the daughter (illegitimate) of a king (of Naples). From the most vicious of courts she was transplanted into the depravity of Rome as the wife of an immature boy (the Pope's son)." *Gregorovius*

These squibs are quoted quite helter-skelter, and not to teach you history, but only to give you the taste of Naples, which is more or less the same as you would get from holding a handful of dirty pennies in your mouth. The dates on the coins do not matter, nor the identity of the profiles in copper, but the poisonous acridity on your tongue and palate should be rather more than memorable.

The King exercised "the utmost oppression and cruelty".

"... The refusal of Calixtus III (Alonso Borgia) to recognize Ferrante had forced that able but crafty and brutal prince to reconquer the kingdom (of Naples) for himself. Having accomplished this, he had maintained his power for over thirty years by the utmost oppression and cruelty. Not only were his opponents treacherously entrapped and ruthlessly destroyed, but the fiendish monarch frequently pleased himself by keeping some of the most troublesome of them in cages, like captured wild beasts, in order that he might gloat over the sufferings to which he subjected them. He exhausted his people by ruinous taxation; and as he condescended to trade on his own account, his avarice even went the length of accumulating stocks of corn, oil and other merchandise, and then forbidding his subjects to sell their stocks until he had obtained a scarcity price for his own." *Fyvie*

Dice were not taxed in Naples. (An item of exemption which concerned François Villon particularly.)

"... The great Alfonso, who reigned in Naples from 1435 (?) onward, was ... brilliant in his whole existence ... fearless ... mild ... generous ... affable ... modest notwithstanding his legitimate royal descent ... a crusade was preached, as a pretext for taxing the clergy; the Jews were forced to save themselves from conversion (to Christianity) and other oppressive measures by presents and the payment of regular taxes; when a great earthquake happened in the Abruzzi (1456) the survivors were compelled to make good the contributions of the dead. On the other hand, he abolished unreasonable taxes, like that on dice ... Ferrante, who succeeded him ... was equaled in ferocity by none other among the princes of his time. Restlessly active, recognized as one of the most powerful political minds of the day, and free from the vices of the profligate ..." *Burckhardt*

I don't know what *Herr Doktor* Burckhardt regarded as "the vices of the profligate", but for your information Ferrante fathered eight or nine bastards, and the Villon MS (if I may call it that) shows us the young Lisa playing with those of her own age in the royal nursery, and calling Ferrante "Grandpa", although no blood kinship is implied.

If Ferrante was "Alfonso's" son, he had a mulatto half-sister.

"... Leonello (d'Este, Marchese of Ferrara) ... had also had a lawful wife, herself an illegitimate daughter of Alfonso I of Naples by an African woman." *Burckhardt cites Sanudo*

Naples produced "obscene" books.

"... Antonio Beccadelli, surnamed Panormita (Secretary and biographer of Alfonso I of Naples), was ... the author of *Hermaphroditus,* a collection of epigrams surpassing in obscenity the worst productions of ancient times ... [Lorenzo] Valla goes far beyond the previous attacks of the Humanists on the monastic life. His predecessors ... under the guise of stories, held up the excesses of individuals to scorn. [Valla's] attack is of a more radical character; he assails the monastic life in itself ... strikes at the very root of the religious life in general ... With equal audacity and venom, Valla turned his arms against the temporal power of the Papacy, in his pamphlet, *On the falsely credited and invented Donation of Constantine* ... It will be seen that it is Valla, not Machiavelli, who started the often-repeated assertions that the

Popes are to blame for all Italy's misfortunes ... Valla was not alarmed by the attacks of theologians on his daring opinions, for King Alfonso of Naples was his firm protector." *Pastor*

In Naples was much hatred.

"... the Neapolitan barons ... hated Ferdinand [same as 'Ferrante'] on account of his cruelties. Not until 1462 [should be 1464] was he freed from the Angevin claims to his throne; and during the succeeding twelve years he was engaged in plots and plans which allied him with the Milanese Sforza and the Florentine Medici, and enabled him to maintain his authority in spite of the disaffection of his subjects. Everything was accomplished by dishonesty and treachery; neither in Ferdinand, nor in his allies, nor in Pope Innocent VIII, did a spark of honesty exist." *Clement*

"... Never was any prince more bloody, wicked, inhuman, lascivious, or gluttonous than he [Alfonso II, son of Ferrante]. Yet his father was more dangerous, because no man knew when he was angry or pleased; for he would betray men in the midst of his entertainments and caresses ... Both father and son had ravished several women; they made no conscience of sacrilege, nor did they retain the least respect or obedience for the Church. They sold their bishoprics, as that of Tarento, which the father sold for thirteen thousand ducats to a Jew ... In short, it is scarce possible that any prince could be guilty of greater villainies than they were." *Commines*

It was a pretty place, too.

"... The very names of Parthenope, Posilippo, Inarime, Sorrento, Capri, have their fascination. There too the orange and lemon groves are more luxuriant; the grapes yield sweeter and more intoxicating wine; the villagers are more classically graceful; the volcanic soil is more fertile; the waves are bluer and the sun is brighter than elsewhere in the land ... Naples, where, according to Pontano, 'nothing was cheaper than the life of a man'." *Symonds*

Quite a town, Naples. A visit seemed to be indicated if only to find out "who did what, and who paid whom"!—and there Lisa was born—not in the city itself but at the Villa Posilippo, a few miles outside the gates, overlooking the Bay. The house is no longer there, and the MS purports to tell how it was demolished.

2

I should hate to be hanged for it either way, if this MS be valid or not, but I can find no fault with its facts. A good many sacred cows have their udders lopped off by the swish of the writer's quills, as sharp as his swords, whoever he was, but in every case where the text is at variance with received opinion, I have been to extraordinary pains to investigate the discrepancy, and not once have I been able to refute a statement as it appears in the MS. Knowing that any friend of mine has found a better place to bury his nose o' nights than between the musty pages of some history book, filled with the lies men have agreed to tell about the past, I have winnowed this matter thoroughly, and what I have Englished out of the obscurities of some twenty-two languages is the juicy part that those other fellows thought better not to mention in our mother tongue. The books on this subject which they gave you in school were intended to cover up what we have here, and most of the books you have read about these times, since you left school, have been written by women who could not tell a fairy from a Harvard man if Krafft-Ebing, Havelock Ellis and Freud were all in the room with anatomical charts and pointers.

Some half-dozen short stories, one-act plays, and longer, and one lorn novel written by a preacher, have had for their theme a love affair between Lisa and Leonardo da Vinci. Ignorance could hardly be profounder.

Not from any spirit of scandalmongering, but simply in the interest of getting behind the smile that came from his brushes, I dutifully report that Leonardo was, from his apprentice days in Verocchio's studio to the end of his life, a practicing homosexual, exclusively. With his own hand—the left—he wrote:

"The act of procreation and everything that has any relation to it is so disgusting that human beings would soon die out if it were not a traditional custom and if there were no pretty faces and sensuous dispositions."

That, I submit, is not normal, any more than his constant companionship with pretty, frizzled, prinked and perfumed boys was normal. He was never without one—and the *squabbles* they had!

Twice, in Florence, he was arrested on charges of paiderastia (sodomy to you), involving artists' models (male, more or less), and the only way he beat the raps was by intervention of the kinsmen of some of the others involved. One was a Tornabuoni, as was the mother of Lorenzo the Magnificent, and the other was a bastard of the Rucellai family. By sheerest coincidence, and no other connection, because Lisa was still living in Naples, so, too, was Lisa's mother a Rucellai, legitimate however.

3

We all had a lucky break in 1761, when the young Edward Gibbon was rounding off his Oxford schooling with a year or so in France, and stopped to take inventory of his equipment for a life-work. He actually stood with a coin in his hand—a farthing from home—and said: "Heads, I shall write the *Decline and Fall of the Roman Empire*; tails, I shall write a history of the expedition of

Charles VIII (of France) into Italy (1494), with critical researches into that king's title to the crown of Naples."

Gibbon tossed the coin—and we won. That is to say, it came down heads, but that was a near one, wasn't it? Suppose *he* had got wind of this Villon MS!

I can call it nothing else. After working with the material so long, I accept it as authentic, although that bare statement is likely to give you goose flesh, unless you are the editor of the *London Times Literary Supplement*. If you are that, then, certainly, you will miscarry.

No literary event since Theodore Dreiser slapped the face of Sinclair Lewis, in pique at Red's attainment of the Nobel Prize, is so likely to set the reading world on its ear as the appearance of a prose memoir by François Villon which he did not begin to write until he was about 75 years old. The learned of every land could hardly be more astonished (not to say outraged) by the finding of the Log of the Ark, kept in Father Noah's hand, with daily entries of latitudes, longitudes and relative humidities. The relative humidity was 100 per cent for forty days and forty nights, if I know my Bible, but—let that pass.

Every right-minded and well-ordered human who has paid any attention whatever to the poet-murderer, sometimes called "the Beloved Rogue" (starring John Barrymore), sometimes "the Vagabond King" (starring Dennis King), and so on, knows that when Villon was exiled from Paris, 1463, for a list of crimes as long as a stave, he was a very sick man.

All too readily almost everybody has assumed that because he was sick he crawled away and died within the year, harried to his graveside, at age 32, by a complication of consumption and syphilis, a multiple syndrome diagnosed modernly from the symptoms of his poems. This always has been a gratuitous assumption, founded upon nothing but silence, because from the time Villon's sentence of exile was recorded, until today, not a single scrap of documentary evidence has been found to indicate what became of him. The model and archetype of romantic scapegraces, the most fascinating of rollicking roisterers and gallows-birds—who chanced also to be a genius—simply disappeared, leaving the world a picture of himself as a gaunt, starveling, scald and scarred Tomcat, aprowl in midnight alleys, and a handful of verses of such quality, grace, power, color, melody, verity and virility that one cannot name a baker's dozen of poets to be compared with him in all time and in all tongues, and one of those, a Lesbian.

True, Our Master Rabelais has recorded a conversation of Villon in the Royal Privy with King Edward V of England, supposed to have taken place after the exile.

4

Master François Villon, being banished France, fled to him, and got so far into his favor, as to be privy to all his household affairs. One day the King, being on his close-stool, showed Villon the arms of France, and said to him, "Dost thou see what respect I have for thy French kings? I have none of their arms anywhere but in this backside, near my close-stool."

"Odd's life," said the buffoon, "how wise, prudent and careful of your health, Your Highness is! How carefully your learned Doctor Thomas Linacer looks after you! He saw that, now you grow old, you are inclined to be somewhat costive, and every day were fain to have an apothecary; I mean, a suppository or clyster thrust into royal nockandroe: so he has, much to the purpose, induced you to place here the arms of France; for the very sight of them puts you into such a dreadful fright, that you immediately let fly, as much as would come from eighteen squattering *bonassi of Paeonia.* And if they were painted in other parts of your house, by jingo, you would presently conskite yourself wherever you saw them. Nay, had you but here a picture of the great oriflamme of France, odds bodkins, your tripes and bowles would be in no small danger of dropping out at the orifice of your posteriors.— But henh, henh, *atque iterum,* henh.

> A silly cockney am I not,
>> As ever did from Paris come?
> And with a rope and sliding knot
>> My neck shall know what weighs my bum.

"A cockney of short reach, I say, shallow of judgment, and judging shallowly, to wonder, that you should cause your points to be untrussed in your chamber before you come into this closet. By'r Lady, at first I thought your close-stool had stood behind the hangings of your bed; otherwise it seemed very odd to me you should untruss so far from the place of evacuation. But now I find I was a gull, a wittal, a woodcock, a mere ninny, a jolt-head, a noddy, a changeling, a calf-lolly, a doddipole. You do wisely, by the mass, you do wisely: for had not you been ready to clap your hind-face on the mustard-pot as soon as you came within sight of these arms, mark ye me, cop's body, the bottom of your breeches had supplied the office of a close-stool."

In another place The Master has repeated a popular rumor of the day, indicating—by the way and in passing—that Villon fell among players, folk who, in that pre-Hollywood era, had fewer rights before the law than either whores or Jews, and that the writer traveled, perhaps as an actor-manager, at least as far as Brussels.

Master François Villon, in his old age, retired to St. Maixent, in Poitou, under the patronage of a good honest abbot of the place. There, to make sport for the mob, he undertook to get the *Passion* acted after the way and in the dialect of the country. The parts being distributed, the play having been rehearsed, and the stage prepared, he told the mayor and aldermen that the mystery would be ready after Niort fair, and that there only wanted properties and necessaries, but chiefly cloaths fit for the parts: so the mayor and his brethren took care to get them.

Villon, to dress an old clownish father greybeard, who was to represent God the Father, begged of Friar Stephen Tickletoby, sacristan to the Franciscan friars of the place, to lend him a cope and a stole. Tickletoby refused him, alleging, that by their provincial statutes, it was rigorously forbidden to give or lend anything to players. Villon replied that the statute reached no farther than farces, drolls, antics, loose and dissolute games, and that he asked no more than what he had seen allowed at Brussels and other places. Tickletoby, notwithstanding, peremptorily bid him provide himself elsewhere if he would, and not to hope for anything out of his monastical wardrobe. Villon gave an account of this to the players, as of a most abominable action, adding that God would shortly revenge Himself, and make an example of Tickletoby.

The Saturday following he had notice given him that Tickletoby, upon the filly of the convent (so they call a young mare that was never leapt yet) was gone a-mumping to St. Ligarius, and would be back by about two in the afternoon. Knowing this, he made a cavalcade of his devils of the *Passion* through the town. They were all rigged with wolves', calves' and rams' skins, laced and trimmed with sheep's heads, bulls' feathers, and large kitchen tenter hooks, girt with broad leathern girdles; whereat hang'd dangling huge cow-bells and horse-bells, which made a horrid din. Some held in their claws black sticks full of squibs and crackers; others had long lighted pieces of wood, upon which, at the corner of every street, they flung whole handfuls of rosin-dust, that made a terrible fire and smoak. Having thus led them about, to the great diversion of the mob, and the dreadful fear of little children, he finally carried them to an entertainment at a summer-house, without the gate that leads to St. Ligarius.

As they came near the place, he spied Tickletoby afar off, coming home from mumping, and told them in macaronic verse,

> *Hie est mumpator natus de gente cucowli,*
> *Qui solet antquo scrappas portare bisacco.*

"A plague on his friarship," said the devils then; "the lousy beggar would not lend a poor cope to the fatherly Father; let us fright him!"

"Well said," cried Villon; "but let us hide ourselves till he comes by and then charge him home briskly with your squibs and burning sticks."

Tickletoby being come to the place, they all rushed on a sudden into the road to meet him, and in a frightful manner threw fire from all sides upon him and his filly foal, ringing and tingling their bells, and howling like so many real devils, "Hoh, hoh, hoh, brrou, rrou, rrourrs, rrourrs, hoo, hou hou, hho, hho, hhoi. Friar Stephen, don't we play the devils rarely?"

The filly was soon scared out of her seven senses, and began to start, to funk it, to squirt it, to trot it, to fart it, to bound it, to gallop it, to kick it, to spurn it, to calcitrate it, to wince it, to frisk it, to leap it, to kick it, with double jerks, and bum-motions; insomuch that she threw down Tickletoby, though he held fast by the tree of the pack-saddle with might and main. Now his straps and stirrups were of cord; and on the right side his sandal was so entangled and twisted, that he could not for the heart's blood of him get out his foot. Thus he was dragged about by the filly through the road, scratching his bare breech all the way; she still multiplying her kicks against him, and straying for fear over hedge and ditch; insomuch that she trepanned his thick skull so, that his cockle brains were dashed out near the Hosanna or High-Cross. Then his arms fell to pieces, one this way and the other that way; and even so were his legs served at the same time. Then she made a bloody havock with his puddings; and being got to the convent, brought back only his right foot and twisted sandal, leaving them to guess what was become of the rest.

Villon seeing that things had succeeded as he intended, said to his devils, "You will act rarely, gentlemen devils, you will act rarely; I dare engage you will top your parts. I defy the devils of Saumur, Donay,

Montmorillion, Langez, St. Espain, Angers; nay, by gad, even those of Poictiers, for all their bragging and vaporing, to match you."

Even before the Villon MS came to me both these parables were generally conceded to be fictions. Albert Jay Nock (of revered memory) found the anecdote of the close-stool told 200 years before Rabelais, in a version wherein John is King of England, and the arms of France are extolled as a physic for Englishmen by a *jongleur* named Hugues le Noir. Also, D. B. Wyndham Lewis, who has written a loving biography of the Packman of Rennes, says—"Both are almost without doubt fantasy." Rabelais merely embroidered them to augment his income (as Cure of Meudon), even as these words are put down here to sweeten mine.

Now we learn—from the MS—that Villon never went to England and that he revisited St. Maixent in Poitou only briefly, after he had become master of her household to the Signora Elisabetta Gherardini della Gioconda, whom the world now calls *Mona Lisa*.

The shock will subside as you read the text, for the explanation of the cutthroat's survival is simplicity itself, his long silence as naturally consequent upon his interim occupations as twilight after sunset, and so too the series of events which led him, ultimately, to commemorate the life of a woman whom, Villon says, "I never possessed or even wished to."

After taking a good solid look at the painting, I'm afraid a good many of us are inclined to agree with him in the letter of that unwishfulness, but that is not quite what the writer meant. There is more to life than mere sex (I am told), and more things to know about a woman's smile than a man can learn by kissing it. Villon never felt Lisa's comither applied to himself because she was *ae* five when he first saw her, and he was past forty, but he was not the only male who met the lady—nor was Lisa the only woman born in the Renaissance. Every man to his taste, there is somebody here for each.

It is a good deal to ask, and I don't suppose my request will be granted, but if you can consider the matter calmly, you should appreciate that this relationship of two celebrated immortals is not even a coincidence. The only cause to marvel at it works the other way around. The coincidence is that intervening generations have conferred separate celebrities and immortalities upon two people who bore this relationship to each other quite naturally and completely unaware of what their posterity was going to make out of them. Villon was not VILLON to Villon: he spits upon his own verses. As a matter of fact, if he had died when most people think he did, *circa* 1463, he never would have seen his poems set in type, because the earliest printed edition known was not impressed until 1489.

Nor was Lisa in the least enigmatical to herself: whether she grinned, smirked or smiled, wept or laughed outright, she always knew very well why she did it, and the mystery of the one, like the fame of the other, has been imposed by the rest of us along with personalities tailored to the tastes of the tailors.

That Villon survived was due directly to Robert d'Estouteville, sometime Provost of Paris, who had saved him from the gallows before this—as the poet says, "on ten or more occasions"—and at the last the nobleman saved the miscreant one more time, sending him to Rome, into the household of Robert's cousin, Cardinal Guillaume d'Estouteville, the only member of the Sacred College who was richer than the Vice-Chancellor Rodrigo Borgia.

Hot rivalry between the Cardinals d'Estouteville and Borgia on the score of their incomes was barely hidden by the loose Consistorial etiquette of that day, because d'Estouteville certainly would have been Vice-Chancellor of Holy Church instead of Borgia, had not Pope Calixtus III been Rodrigo's "uncle". Both men wished fervently to be Pope, and the Vice-Chancellory was highly regarded as the steppingstone to Saint Peter's Chair, inasmuch as it carried the keys to the treasury of the Apostolic Camera.

The Gaul, d'Estouteville, employed Villon as "spy and pick-lock, cut-purse and pimp", offices demanding as much anonymity and obscurity as the wit and skill of a practitioner of those arts can possibly command. Hence the long silence—now happily filled in.

That is, perhaps, the greatest value the MS has. Although the writer set out to "minute down this memoir of my Madonna's life", and calls his book by her name, when he began to leaf over the pages of his memory, searching for the earliest beginnings of their association, he inadvertently—but almost perforce—gave us a fairly complete chronicle of his own life and adventures as a political spy through that period of time when the world as we know it today was being born. As a matter of fact, the main body of the narrative begins about sixteen years before Villon himself was born, but let us consider such technicalities at another time.

5

Inevitably the world will marvel that one who was so fine a poet should now be revealed as the possessor of a magnificent prose style as well, powerful, moving, trenchant, full of color, crackling with phrase, wit, wisdom and humor, not to mention a rare gift for narrative and characterization perhaps never before equaled. Factual events come from this man's hand more exciting than any fiction. Story follows story at a pace that leaves Shahrazade sounding like Uncle Don. Here are a thousand and ten novels, and more characters than Balzac and Zola invented in their aggregate lifetimes, yet, there is no confusion. As hero follows hero through the plots and counterplots which made the Renaissance so lush and lusty, each salient figure or group of figures pertinent to Lisa's story emerges from the welter of slaughter and corruption, individually unique, unmistakably identified, impressed indelibly in memory without apparent effort. Frankly, I couldn't have done it better myself.

You cannot explain this amazing feat by saying that most of the persons named in the MS were flesh-and-blood men and women whom Villon knew. His achievement is no less spectacularly successful in presenting people he did not know and in relating their crimes and their loves to his own.

He was helped by the sensational nature of his Neapolitan material. It is the very special quality of those effluvia which gives his work its unique sweet-and-pungent charm. Those tidbits about Naples which I quoted earlier are as far as nice people have cared to go in writing on our topic, but if you will slip on asbestos mittens and clip a clothespin on your nose you will find the truth about the place a full forty times as gripping as any fiction you ever read. In a word of one syllable—Wow!

My role as translator and paraphraser has probably tended to increase the resemblance of this personal history to romance, and critical opinion will be divided whether that has helped or hindered the work to find its proper place in the world. Persons of a staid or billious turn are likely to bewail the evil chance that put a MS of such colossal significance into the hands of one so irreverent, flippant and congenitally facetious as myself, recalling that this same era has inspired two gentlemen and one lady to write polite semi-fictional classics.

Dmitri Merejkowski gave us *The Romance of Leonardo da Vinci,* which perforce included Lisa, and related some of the same incidents which Villon comes to, in time.

George Eliot wrote *Romola*, also naming many of these same people, including—notably—Lisa's Rucellai kinsfolk, but George Eliot was not aware of their relationship.

Charles Reade wrote *The Cloister and the Hearth*, which ends at just about the time Villon's Roman span begins, so that not many of the same people appear in both books, but Reade—like Eliot and Merejkowski—employed numerous historic figures as persons of his drama, so that the association—not to say comparison—between these three well-known oldsters and Villon's Vita Mona Lisa is quite natural and not invidious. Not only are all four books about the Renaissance, but look how *long* they are!

Villon's and mine, if you'll forgive the boast, is the longest. It is not as polite as those other three, because we are neither ladies nor gentlemen. In fact, I am of such a raffish sort that I have lived the happiest sixteen years of my life inside the dirty hide of this homicide, my collaborator. The affinity has become so close that when a traffic cop gives me a hard time my reflex is to reach for my sword.

So—I offer my condolences to readers who deplore our lack of dignity. No Charles Reade, George Eliot, Merejkowski or Edward Gibbon would have done for this job. The material is just too hot for a housebroken writer to handle.

6

Not the least of the work's values is the insight it gives us into that portion of Rodrigo Borgia's life which previously had been almost blank. The character which all good Christians have been taught to abhor as Pope Alexander VI, the father of Don Juan, Lucrezia and Cesare Borgia (to name no more), is well enough known and familiar to all, since he has been the whipping-boy and scapegoat for the Church ever since he died in 1503, but the years which Villon spent in greatest intimacy with Rodrigo have not been filled in until now by a competent observer. Villon had just the eye for it. One must allow for his prejudices, to be sure, especially as they favor his patron d'Estouteville and the Signora Giaconda, and one must remember that the writer was 75 years old before he took time out from "politics", as he practiced that "painted process", more often than not with quickflashing steel, and sat down to record this chronicle from memory. Sometimes he forgets. Sometimes he may muddle a blood-line which entitles a friend to a fortune, the way he makes it come out, but you yourself know Philadelphia lawyers who are doing that every day. These are human frailties, peccadilloes, flyspecks upon a performance which stands alone and unmatched among the books of the world.

It is as if Casanova had written *War and Peace!*
It is as if Benvenuto Cellini had written the *Decline and Fall!*
It is as if François Villon had written the *Life of Mona Lisa.*

MONA LISA

CHAPTER ONE

BEDSIDE CONVERSATION BETWEEN Kings and Queens is not easily come by, unless you hide under the bed a good while before Their Majesties retire and lie very still, rather to the right side, that is more under the Queen, lest the King's hand-groping for his thunder-mug—catch hold of your sword hilt instead. Giovantonio Del Balzo-Orsini had taken these precautions. Although only 18, he was really a man, and he had learned all the tricks of palace life as it was lived in Naples under his stepfather King Ladislaus.

Giovantonio was not listening to the royal panting through morbid or prurient interest in his mother's wifely duties but solely to hear what was said about himself, whether he was to be invested Prince of Taranto, his patrimony from his real father, or created Duke of Calabria and adopted as Ladislaus' son, and heir to the Regno. The King had promised the one or the other when he married Marie-Luise nee d'Enghien-Bourbon, a widow with four children, and His Majesty would have promised a great deal more than that to annex Taranto, and Marie's County of Lecce, to the Crown: but nothing was being done about keeping the promise that the youth under the bed could see, and he was getting damned impatient for an income of his own.

The King was fresh back from Rome that day, returned especially to mount the Queen, who remained ungravid to the disturbance of affairs of State and the King's peace of mind. Aside from that, Ladislaus had every reason to be pleased with himself.

Newly victorious, he had remained affable throughout the home-coming celebration tendered by the Neapolitan tradesmen, but he had pointedly ignored Giovantonio's expectant hints when they met on the Mole. Ladislaus was a past master of the brush-off, and a genius at finding excuses for delay in this particular matter. The latest had been delivered just before he marched upon Rome, and it amounted to an indefinite postponement, in the King's words. "We shall discuss your affairs, my son, after I have pounded some sense into one of the Popes."

Three or four Popes were practicing simultaneously at the time: he was a poor King who did not have one of his own: but Ladislaus Anjou-Durazzo had preferred to put his money and his faith into good Commanders of heavy-armored horse.

Only one of the multiple Popes lived in Rome, and that was the one Ladislaus went to reason with at the head of his per-suasive army. This particular Holiness had not tarried to hear the King's arguments but had run like a frightened fallow-deer, thereby revealing his guilty conscience. He had been dickering with a distant cousin of Ladislaus—Louis II Duke d'Anjou—who wished to be King of the Regno in Ladislaus' place.

Clearly that debate was pertinent to the ambitions of the youth under the bed and so he had waited as patiently as his eager nature permitted while his stepfather captured the Eternal City and declared himself "King of Rome". Giovantonio could not quarrel with a minor procrastination that increased his potential inheritance so greatly, but his heart misgave him whether Ladislaus was acting in good faith. If he were, why had he not conferred Taranto as an interim income before he went away?

The activity topside, over young Del Balzo-Orsini's head, was calculated to cheat him of the ampler settlement via adop-tion, by providing Ladislaus with an heir of his own making, but judging from the sound of it no more was being accomplished on this occasion than ever had been in the past.

"You DO something," His Majesty complained to the snooper's mother.

"I, Milord?" Marie's voice was pleasant, her tone completely innocent.

"*You*, Milady. You close something up. I think you do it purposely too, so that boy of yours can be King."

Ah! Giovantonio had been pretty sure that they sometimes spoke of him in bed, but his mother never had intimated that she was giving him a leg up in this way, or even that she knew how. At 18, the Prince of Taranto (although I call him that without the King's sanction) had no more than five or six years' fornicating experience, and he had fathered only one bastard that he knew, so that he was not yet an authority upon a woman's powers whilst coupling. Could a woman, indeed, "close something up" at will, and thus bear or not bear at discretion?

Marie-Luise denied it. "I do not. I cannot," said she. "I should not know how."

Young Taranto grasped his sword so tightly his knuckles turned white, quite ready to roll out to his mother's defense if the King abused her.

"Then how is it you were able to bear Taranto four children—and cannot give me even one?"

Men, men, men! Eh? The deficiency never is theirs. Marie-Luise might have asked why neither of his two earlier wives and none of his scads of mistresses ever had been taken pregnant by him either, but she kept a diplomatical silence rather than precipitate a duel between her men-folks, which must certainly be fatal to one, and probably would kill them both. Besides, in her heart, Marie-Luise sympathized with her husband's predicament. He was absolutely the last male of his line, and it is a sad thing to see an illustrious family terminate in sterility. His branch of Anjou had reigned in Naples for one hundred twenty-five years.

"Answer me," said the King. "Why is it?"

"I do not know, Majesty. O, truly, I try."

"Well, don't *cry* about it!" Ladislaus flung out of bed. "You know I can't stand your tears."

Marie-Luise did cry a little, but not enough to draw her son out of hiding. Giovantonio watched the King's bare feet poke around for his sheepskin slippers. The boy pushed one of them out a bit so Ladislaus would not have to look under the bed.

"Giovantonio would make a good King," said his mother, "better than Louis d'Anjou—if anything should happen to you."

"Nothing is going to happen to *me*," the King boasted, "and if it should—Louis II never will be King of the Regno. The Barons would rather have Joan than him."

"They would rather have Giovantonio than Joan—if you would sign the articles of adoption."

"Joan will not hear of it."

"Then marry him to Joan."

The eavesdropper almost betrayed his presence by groaning. Joan was Ladislaus' only surviving sister, a widow past forty, with no more offspring than her brother. She had kept herself so fully occupied, from her tenderest years, that neither leisure nor room for childbearing ever had afforded. Currently, with the milita absent in Rome, Joan was on a starvation regimen, sleeping with a single company of the King's light-horse and one Pandolfo Alopo.

Alopo was the most recent addition to Joan's stud, an upstart from the Latrine district of Naples, but Giovantonio felt indebted to Alopo regardless of his mean extraction because he had appeared just in time to save the strapping young Taranto from Joan's draft.

Once was enough for Giovantonio, when he found out what Joan expected of him. Strong as he was, the way she liked it taxed every thew and sinew. That position has been illegal in all Christian countries from the earliest times, but the King's sister set herself above the Law, in this as in all things else, and completely disregarded her obligation to her House. The caper has never yet produced an heir, and it never will. Messer Durandel was required to take the dirt road whilst the right fist came around in front and lost itself well up the wrist. "How many fingers was that?" asked Joan, and Taranto realized that his labors were quite hopeless.

Alopo, on the other hand, was such a contortionist and so energetic that he made nothing of hopping back and forth, and front to back, like a conger eel, so that any little fellow just starting out would have been run down and tramped on in an hour.

As long as the Joan-Alopo *status quo* continued at this salubrious pass, to speak of marrying Giovantonio to Her Voracity was simply borrowing trouble. The lad swallowed his groan, but if he had possessed a knitting needle he would have jabbed it up through his mother's mattress as a warning to change the subject. Any man in his proper senses would have preferred Taranto free and clear to the Crown with Joan attached, even now that Rome had been added to the Regno.

"Joan swears she never will marry again," Ladislaus sighed as he buttoned his shirt. "If *you* can convince her to take the boy I have no objections. Meantime, I'll send Atra Bilis to blood you, and we'll try again when he's done."

"Try again—tonight?" Marie-Luise quavered in mild alarm.

"Why not tonight?" the King barked. "I've got to get back to Rome."

"No reason—dearest Majesty lover husband—no reason. Come back! Do, do come back! I die until you do."

Ladislaus was at the door by that time. "I shall return," said he: but by the oddest chance he never did. He went out of that room and spoke to Atra Bilis, his surgeon, sending him to blood the Queen, and as soon as the medico was thus engaged the King got into another bed with the doctor's daughter.

Now this child was vastly more ashamed of not having given her sovereign a son than ever his wife was, and she had consulted her father, how to hold the King's affection in spite of her barrenness.

"I'll give you some salve," said the physician, a bitter type and no mistake, because he really fixed them up.

The girl had this stuff ready for Ladislaus' visit, and—in the nick—she put a dab where he would be likely to get some of it on him.

"What is that?" quoth the King.

"It is Blessed Balm of Gilead," the child gushed passionately, "and if you come to me now you will never love any other woman but me."

Sure enough, that was the way it worked. It set them both afire with a burning itch that spread from their privates all over their bodies in a running blister that oozed a poisonous yellow water which carried the contamination to every part it touched.

The girl died first, being of weaker constitution, but Ladislaus did not live more than six hours, and expired of his agony.

Hubbub is hardly the word for those six hours in Castel Nuovo, and nobody behaved quite rationally, unless it was the widow Joan when she got there.

The Prince of Taranto crawled out from under the bed when the first frantic summons came for the leech. The Queen ran to see what Ladislaus was howling about, but Signor Atra Bilis— better informed—did not follow her. He faced Giovantonio with a fanatical gleam in his eye and solemnly intoned, "The wages of sin is death."

The youth did not realize until later that the surgeon had sacrificed his own daughter as an instrument of retribution, but he was quick enough to comprehend that the man before him was the King's assassin, and—as such—a very handy fellow to have around. The two started to leave the Castel together, Giovantonio intending to get possession of the citadel of Taranto before anybody there learned what had happened. Blame his habits of thought and his immaturity for assuming without consultation that his mother's authority as Queen would continue, certainly until after the funeral. If he had doubted that, he would have stayed to protect her, but as things were, the entrance of Joan with Alopo only made the boy hasten to get out of sight. Marriage with Joan was now the only hope left him for making himself King, and that was too much to pay, but he could fortify himself in Taranto and defy Joan to take it from him.

Sneaking through the stable to get their horses, Atra Bilis and the scion of Del Balzo-Orsini came upon the Prince's cousin Raimondo Orsini, Count of Nola and Chamberlain to the dying Ladislaus. Raimondo had four or five of his personal staff with him and they were strapping bulging panniers on sumpter mules.

"Eggs?" asked Giovantonio, and the others burst out laughing. They had the Crown, a good many of the incidental jewels, and lashins of gold coin from the royal treasury.

"The wages of sin is death," Atra Bilis told the retiring Chamberlain, and that Orsini turned to his cousin with a grimace. "Let's leave *him* here," said he.

Raimondo was several years older than Giovantonio, but not so wide in the shoulders; still, together they made a pretty pair of champions, too formidable to be stopped by the Castelan, who was not there anyway. Everybody was buzzing around the King's apartments, stealing whatever came to hand.

"Let's get him out of town, at least," said Taranto, referring to the surgeon. The Prince was still young enough then to feel gratitude for the favor Atra Bilis had done him.

They took the road to Andria, where another cousin, Guglielmo Del Balzo, was Duke. He was the eldest of the three (and the most substantial in money and men) but his features were those of a cherubic child who has just been surprised.

"The King is dead," the cousins told Guglielmo, but did not add, *Long live the Queen!*

Duke Andria provided an armed company for Giovantonio's use, and the trio of budding knights—still haunted by the fanatical leech—moved swiftly upon Taranto. No battle was joined, but they worked the stratagem of assembling the town officials and richest burghers, the former adherents of Giovantonio's father, all favorable to his son, and through them inveigled the Captain of the King's garrison to step out of the citadel and have his head split.

That particular action does not do Giovantonio a great deal of credit, because the Captain's loyalty could have been bought for one of the golden collars stolen from the Castel, but—we all make mistakes—and as soon as he was set up practicing Prince of his rightful patrimony, his management of such affairs grew firmer and his prestige rose higher and higher with rarely a setback.

The psalm-singing leech and filicide, out of tenderness for his immortal part, went to a local priest in Taranto and confessed not only his own garland of sins but those of the cousins too, especially Count Nola's possession of the Crown by pilferage. Luckily the boys had followed Atra Bilis into the church, anticipating the fanatic's weakness, and as the supplicant and the confessor left their privacy they faced a ring of pointed instruments.

Not to desecrate the holy place, Giovantonio directed Nola and Andria to make their incisions in the surgeon outside on the porch, and Giovantonio himself gave the priest the choice of taking the ultimate journey in company with the penitent or becoming chaplain to His Highness as Prince of Taranto and absolving the cousins from everything.

The priest accepted the appointment, like a man of rare good judgment, and his second duty was to bury Atra Bilis.

That was the real beginning of Taranto's career as a diplomatist, and both his titled cousins acknowledged his leadership from that day forward. Under his guidance, Andria and Nola sent out their lieutenants to unite all their kinsmen, Del Balzos and Orsinis, in defense of Giovantonio's claim. If Joan Anjou-Durazzo wished to wear her dead brother's Crown, she must apply for it by sending the Prince his investiture with Taranto.

The boys were toasting their *coup,* a bit prematurely, with a bevy of local beauties, all volunteers with flowers in their hair, when one Ettore Pappacoda arrived—steaming with sweat—from Naples, to say that Joan with her light-horse and the low-born Alopo had got the jump on everyone.

Assuming the style of Queen Joan II without any man's let or lief, that Majesty had locked up the widowed former Queen Marie-Luise together with her three younger children in a donjon-keep. Then she had executed Ettore Pappacoda's father—who had been Seneschal to Ladislaus—and conferred his staff, title, emoluments and perquisites upon her darling Alopo.

The three youths swayed a little as they received this shock from their orphaned friend, for they were high in wine. Then with one voice they demanded to know—"Where was the Grand Constable?"

The Strong Man of Naples, Serjianni Caracciolo, Duke Melfi and Grand Constable of the Regno—highest ranking Minister in Ladislaus' Council—was the only man Joan feared. She was afraid of him for several reasons, political as well as personal. As Grand Constable he knew the ropes which sailed the ship of State, and Joan had not the remotest notion which line led to what. As a Caracciolo he was head of the most numerous family in the Regno, and some of his kinsfolk were married to all the wealthiest of their Baronial peers. Lastly—and even more pertinently—in refusing to lay finger to Joan amiably, Serjianni had laid on his whole hand in a rude shove that would have spilled her to the floor if others had not supported her. Serjianni—of all men—might have been expected to prevent Joan's outrages now. Was the Grand Constable, then, executed too?

"He was still alive—still in office—when I left Naples or I never could have got away," Ettore told them. "Serjianni sent to warn me that Alopo had ordered my arrest without a warrant—without a charge—no laws are being observed. Alopo is the Law."

"And Mother—in gaol." That, of course, was the sobering nub of the news to Giovantonio, and his hot blood boiled up a score of devices for freeing her and his sisters and small brother, each frantic plan more futile than the last.

"And what became of my mother's ladies? Are they with her in prison? One of them bore me a child—Maria. Where are they? Where is my baby?"

"I do not know," Pappacoda confessed lugubriously. "I didn't stop to ask many questions. I'm sorry, Gian."

The Prince beat his forehead with the heel of his hand.

Count Nola commiserated Ettore on the loss of his father, who had always been a good friend to the Orsini, guiding his first steps in the King's Council. At the same time Nola called for congratulations upon his own foresight in escaping—and with the Crown. "SHE will go down the entire list of Ministers putting in her own men—except Serjianni, perhaps. I got out just in time."

Their merrymaking was quite broken up. The wenches were neglected in another part of the citadel as the four confederates sat down to face responsibilities and problems in tactical judgment far beyond their years. If strength and courage alone had been sufficient for their ends, that round table might have been matched against any other that could have been assembled, but of experience they had not enough amongst them in the aggregate to fry a small fish. Only Nola ever had sat in Council, and his voice there, as mere Chamberlain, never had been heard even when it was raised. The Lord High Chamberlain was no higher than thirteenth among fifteen Ministers, so that he, like his companions—except Giovantonio—had but one cure for the disagreeable, and that was draw and thrust. The baby-faced Guglielmo Duke Andria was especially eager to lead a raid upon the prison to spring Taranto's family.

"We haven't enough men to hold our own walls and get Mother out too," the Prince demurred. Their properties of Nola, Andria and Taranto were days apart, and the confederates did not yet know if the Barons of intervening lands would support Joan II or not.

"Joan can't mount our walls without an army," Andria argued. "Her militia is in Rome—and she won't call it home until the Council at Constance elects a new Pope. Even if she wanted to—Serjianni is too smart to let her release that grip on the Vatican."

Taranto acknowledged that sagacity, IF Serjianni kept the upper hand. Joan had stepped into luck up to her knees, finding herself in command of Rome just when she would need a bargaining advantage to obtain Sacred Oil for her Crown.

Practically every Christian nation was sending delegates to Constance in Switzerland with the intention of allaying the Church scandal by reducing the number of Popes to a single one, a new one, agreeable to the majority assembled. Ladislaus had instructed his delegates to Elect Cardinal Oddo Colonna, a friendly neighbor whose family estates lay between the old border of the Regno and the city of Rome. As that border had now been moved to include Rome, the Cardinal and all the Colonnas were—nominally and for the nonce—subjects of the Regno.

If Oddo Colonna was Elected, he—as a born Roman—would certainly wish to bring the Holy See out of Avignon, back to the banks of Tiber, but he couldn't do that now without Joan's sanction. She had him on the hip.

"But suppose Louis II d'Anjou Elects *his* man in Constance," Giovantonio bewared his lads. "Louis II is Count of Provence— and Avignon is in Provence—and there's nothing that brings so much money to local tradesmen as having a Vatican in the vicinity. Louis will be paying high prices for votes in Constance, and if his man wins, Louis II will be King of the Regno. He never stood a chance while Ladislaus was alive, but now—he's a male, and Joan is a female, as we have good reason to know—that will affect the voting in Constance. Lots of those Cardinals don't think women should rule. Some of them are as fanatical as Atra Bilis and wouldn't put Holy Oil on Joan's head any more than they would put Holy Water on her tail. Does anybody know if Joan has ever had Cardinal Colonna?"

The others turned to the former Chamberlain, as most likely to know. Raimondo Orsini was himself the son of a Cardinal, defunct, and he had kept up a friendship founded in the nursery with Antonio Colonna, eldest son of Cardinal Oddo. The classic animosity between the Roman Orsinis and the Colonnas was never so marked in the Neapolitan branches of the Orsini family, and Raimondo had often crossed the old border to hunt with his childhood playfellow.

"I'll ask Antonio the next time I'm up there," said Count Nola amiably. "But whether Joan has had him or not, Uncle Oddo would make a good Pope for *us,* and I think we should let him know we're on his side."

Agreement was unanimous.

"I might even take a sack of gold—and carry Antonio to Constance," Count Nola continued, almost musing. "We could buy some votes—and Antonio will speak for us—to his father."

"Will Antonio go?"

Nola nodded confidently. "I've never heard him say no to anything. He's a very agreeable fellow. The question is, do we want to go over to the side of Louis II? It will take a long time to get your family out of prison that way."

"I know how to get Her Majesty out of prison," baby-faced Andria put in. "I will capture Alopo—and set that as the price of his ransom. Joan will empty the prisons to get her buck back."

"I'm for trying both, if you are with me," said the Prince. "You, Raimondo, carry Antonio Colonna to Constance—and Elect Cardinal Oddo if you can. You, Guglielmo, take your men to Naples—and see if you can catch Alopo. Go incog, and don't get caught yourself.

"You, Ettore, are already a fugitive, even more than the rest of us. You stay here and hold the fort for me. I put you in command."

Asked the other three—"Where are *you* going?"

"I am going to Rome—to treat with Sforza and the Caldoras. Joan can't hold The City if her Captains desert her—for us."

The boys had a drink on that, then several more, but the question returned again, if their cabal was to support Louis II d'Anjou for King or merely to force Joan to do them justice all around.

"One of us should find out where the Constable stands on Louis II," the Pappacoda warned. "Serjianni has saved me—this time—but he won't do it again if we go against him."

The Constable never had looked upon Giovantonio Del Balzo-Orsini as anything but a pup, and one not too likely to grow into a dog of more than average distinction. Serjianni had not favored adoption for the Prince, and as for the taxing of Taranto, if he had been asked to name the man for it he could have thought of no one better qualified than himself. Acquisition was Serjianni's guiding star, and grab, clutch and hold were his strength, so that his position in the question of Joan versus Louis II would depend upon which of the rival Angevins offered him the larger pieces.

"He will not speak man-to-man with me," the Prince of Taranto admitted, "but I do not know a better policy than his for us to follow ourselves. If Aunt Joan will meet our demands I am for her—if not—then *viva* Louis!"

They drank to that, and began to article their demands in writing.

Item—that Marie-Luise nee d'Enghien-Bourbon be freed, and with her the children, Caterina, Maria and Gabriel Del Balzo-Orsini.

Item—that Marie-Luise be reconfirmed in her County of Lecce and granted a pension equal to half the privy purse she had enjoyed as Queen.

Item—that the Princess Caterina Del Balzo-Orsini, *ae* 16, be sent, at the expense of the Crown, in a style suitable to her station, to her affianced, Tristano Chiaramonte of Palermo in Island Sicily, that is Sicily *ultra* Pharum: her marriage portion, as contracted, to be paid by Joan II.

Item—that Giovantonio be confirmed in his possession of Taranto and invested Prince of that State.

Item—that Raimondo Orsini be reconfirmed in his County of Nola and reinstated Lord High Chamberlain, with full pardon for his crimes, adequate safeguards for his person, and freedom from the Royal Exercise.

Item—that Ettore Pappacoda be confirmed in his inheritance of his father's residuary estate, real and personal, and that Ettore be indemnified for the cruel, unreasonable and unwarranted execution of the former Seneschal, by payment of 50,000 ducats: that Ettore and all members of the Pappacoda family be accorded adequate safeguards for their persons and guarantees against molestation without cause.

"How about *freedom from the Royal Exercise?*" asked Count Nola who was doing the writing. "Will you have exemption too?"

"It will just make her angry if we all shy at her altar," said Ettore with an air of making a personal sacrifice for the common good. In solid sooth, he never had been bidden to the Awful Couch, being sallow of complexion, pitted by the pox, and—all in all—the least prepossessing of the company. "Leave it out—and if I'm called to serve I'll make my own arrangements."

The bottles had gone around a good many times by then, and the boys were finding more cause for laughter than the seriousness of their screed called for. "We might as well make it good," said Nola. "We aren't going to get what we ask for anyway."

"We'll get it," Taranto hooted, "or Aunt Joan won't get her Throne! You, Guglielmo, what do *you* want from Her Majesty?"

The Duke pursed his cupid's bow. "I have everything," he minced in mockery. "Just say I want to keep it."

"How about your aunt's suit against Serjianni?"

"You will just antagonize him."

"These demands are not made of the Constable. We are addressing the Queen."

"Well, SHE doesn't dare to antagonize the Constable."

"She is shoving Alopo down his throat."

"I am removing Alopo."

"Ah—if you are able to remove Alopo—Serjianni will be our best friend."

"Not friend enough to give up Avellino to us."

"Louis II will give Avellino to your aunt—to get us on *his* side."

"Not if it means losing Serjianni—Louis won't."

Thus early in his diplomatical career Taranto found himself riding a tiger. At issue was the taxing of the very rich County Avellino, which the Del Balzos had wrested from the Filangieris in the time of the Normans. With his eye always cocked for the main chance, Serjianni Caracciolo, then only Duke Melfi, had married the last of the Filangieris, thereby wedding their ancient claim.

Showing no regard for her husband's avarice, the Filangieri woman died without producing an heir to her nebulous and troublesome dot. Anyone less grasping than the Strong Man of the Regno would have charged off the loss and looked for another heiress, but not Serjianni. O, he married again, a Caldora girl who brought him a handful of little pieces near Melfi, but he also refused to let go of Avellino.

By Del Balzo reckoning Avellino belonged to Alix, the matriarchal dowger of their clan, the oldest woman alive, who was also Baroness des Baux in Provence, where her allegiance was to Louis II d'Anjou.

Alix Del Balzo had outlived all her heirs except this chicken Guglielmo who had already seen the old lady's will and knew that he was to have the Barony des Baux *and* her claim to Avellino, if she ever died, which was beginning to be doubtful.

The case was being tried in the courts, and the late Ladislaus had been impounding the taxes pending judicial decree, thus keeping his Grand Constable and the Del Balzos, both, on their best behavior, like children before Christmas. The accrued tax was estimated to make a pile of gold pieces as high as Vesuvius, and potentially it was almost as explosive.

"If Joan doesn't give that money to Serjianni he will break her in two," said Andria. "And if Louis II doesn't give it to him—Louis won't reign very long either. The only way *I* will ever get it is by storming Avellino."

"Then we'll storm Avellino," boasted the Prince, and the cousins clinked goblets around. "But first—storm Alopo—take that pig prisoner and I'll see that you get Avellino. *Item*—Raimondo! Write it down. *Item*—Duke Andria to have Avellino! What else do you want? How about marrying my little sister Maria?"

"I should be delighted!" crowed cousin Guglielmo, refilling his goblet.

"How much dot? Don't stint yourself. This is on Queen Joan!"

They wrote down 200,000 ducats, saying Queens should not be niggardly.

"Call in the girls!" someone shouted. "Let's ask them what *they* want!"

CHAPTER TWO

R IBALD THEY WERE, but determined too, and when the Castelan came to say that ten of Joan's officers had come to arrest Pappacoda and Count Nola, the boys went whooping down to the drawbridge, buckling on their swords as they ran.

"Lower the bridge for them," Giovantonio shouted. "Lower in the name of the Queen!"

Alone, the four ranged themselves under the portcullis and beckoned with broadest swings of their arms to the ten grim horsemen who would not set hoof to the planking. "Come in! Come in!" the Prince called. "Come in—we're having a party."

The Captain of the tiny force, inadequate even for parly, called back, "Send Their Highnesses over here—with the Crown—then I'll come in and talk."

"Why, what are you afraid of?" Taranto mocked the Queensmen. "Would we dare lay steel to Her Majesty's officers?" He drew his sword as he spoke, and started across the drawbridge toward the Captain. Behind him, Nola, Andria and Ettore also drew, and fell into step, advancing without armor upon ten in mail. The gesture was not nearly as brave as it sounds, because just inside the citadel gateway were upwards of a hundred soldiers ready to sweep out to their masters' rescue, but it looked good.

A crowd of Tarantine townsfolk had assembled to see how their new Lord handled his affairs, and those who were not armed with blades or cudgels had bricks, stones or jagged jugs in their hands. If any bay leaves are to be awarded here for spunk, let the Queensmen have them, for they—under orders from afar—were deep in hostile territory, completely surrounded, outnumbered, and dependent for their lives upon the whim of a new-fledged Prince in his cups. Still, the picture of four young fellows—hatless—causing ten helmeted Sergeants of the Queen to retreat before them had its dramatic aspects and the rabble loved it.

The people began to hoot and whistle as the barbed horses backed up, and the insults increased with each step. The first rock to fly caused the officers to break in panic for the town gates, and with that they became targets for every kind of missile a city street provides. The rain on their breastplates was like a tattoo of skillets but the clangor did not match the resounding huzzahs for the boys, more particularly for Giovantonio. He was the Tarantines' kind of man, a hero to their taste, and from that hour until his death he could do no wrong.

Every chance favored the increase of his legend, for the city gates had been closed, and when the Prince saw the horsemen turn there, at bay, and ready to sell themselves only at frightful cost to the locals, Giovantonio called a halt and sent Nola back for the *Items*. "We'll give these fellows something to carry to their Queen. Joan would be wroth with them if they returned empty handed."

While he waited for that mischievous document, Giovantonio made a speech, his first one of record, to "his" people. Standing on the back of a wain, he had them in tears for the fate of Marie-Luise, but hastened to hold back their vengeance from the Queen's officers. "You must not harm these men!" His voice rang like doom's tocsin. "For if you do, you never will see your mistress my mother alive again. Let them go. Let them carry my ultimatum to Her Wickedness the Queen, and if her reply does not give us satisfaction—I shall know what to do."

Thus, extempore, and almost by chance, those reeling demands went off to Naples, and when the fumes of their party had been slept away, the quartet asked each other what they had done and if they could make good their threats.

"We can," said Taranto, "and we will, if I have to go back and marry Joan myself. But let's try every other way first."

"Only tell me this," Guglielmo of Andria worried. "Did we leave in the *item* about Avellino?"

"We did," said Taranto.

"Then if Serjianni sees that document we are dead men."

Not so, said the Prince, for he had not divulged quite all his assets to his cousins. It is knowing just a little more than his confederates that makes a leader a leader. "Not so," the Prince repeated, "but I will change places with you. I shall go to Naples and you to Rome. The danger to me is not so great, and it is my mother, not yours, who wants freeing."

Andria protested, but Taranto overrode him, and outlined the other man's Roman duties. He was to speak first with Antonio Caldora—son of Count Aversa—whom Ladislaus had suspected of traffic with Louis II d'Anjou. "I don't know what evidence my stepfather had. He intercepted letters to Aversa from Provence, but I never saw them. Ladislaus was having both Caldoras watched, to find out if the father was in it too."

The lands of County Aversa extend to the sea, where Louis could land troops almost within sight of Naples. Besides that, the elder Caldora was military Governor of Capua, for the Prince of Capua in his minority, and Capua adjoins Aversa, straddling the main roads from the north, which made it the key to Naples if the invader should come by land—say, from Gaeta or Rome.

"A trap is set for the Caldoras," the Prince went on, "but I don't know its secret. The King was tight lipped about it. He never told Joan. She suspects nothing. He never told Serjianni—because of his wife. The Duchess of Melfi is Count Aversa's daughter. Serjianni may be in the plot. I shall certainly *say* that he is—and accuse him to the Queen if he tries to interfere with me before I can kidnap Alopo.

"So, you see, I shall be perfectly safe in Naples, but *you* must beware that the deadfall set for the Caldoras does not come down and crush you. Will you go?"

"Of course I'll go," Andria pouted, "but you could do it better."

"I can't be everywhere at once. Speak first to Antonio Caldora, as a friend. You have a legitimate interest in Louis II. Quite aside from Avellino, are you not heir to Baux in Provence? See one or both of the Caldoras before Sforza knows you are in Rome, because he is their superior and they resent his command.

"Make them offers. Say that you have nothing to gain by this Queen's success—but be sure that you know the way out of the place before you open your mouth.

"They will listen because they are both veterans of Joan's bed—and Sforza too, when you come to him—and every one of them fancies that he would make a better Seneschal than this snipe she has picked out of the gutter.

"If the Caldoras have direct communication with Louis II, they will let you know it by-the-way. Find out if Serjianni is committed with them—and let me know at once. Tell them that you can remove Sforza if they will swear to hold Rome in Louis's name until Constance gives us a new Pope."

All the cousins, and Ettore too, hung upon every word. They had only awe for such fertility, so much insight into men, prescience of the future. They did not ask by whose authority Giovantonio committed them to Louis's cause, although the topic had been moot at last mention. They did not examine their own judgments, if this was the best possible course, or if they should wait to hear how the Queen received their demands. The only question was put by Andria ... "How do I remove Attendola Sforza? He knows how much Rome is worth now. Why should he give it up?"

"You tell him that I have come to terms with Serjianni. That I am marrying Joan—to free my mother—and that when I am crowned King I am pledged to strip Sforza of everything Ladislaus gave him and hand it over to the Constable. Say that I am giving Avellino to Serjianni too. That is why you have broken with me and turned to Louis II.

"That will send Sforza to Naples as fast as he can ride, and I shall have prepared his reception. But don't send him unless you're sure the Caldoras are with us. If they won't hear you—don't trust you, or you them—take the other tack. Undermine them with Sforza and get yourself appointed to command in San Angelo. Whoever holds that arsenal holds Rome."

"You make it sound very easy, Cousin." Andria wagged his head. "But how——"

"Why, where is Sforza's boy Francesco?"

"In Tricarico," Count Nola supplied, "under the eagle eye of Sforza's sister."

"There you are, Cousin," said Taranto blandly, but Del Balzo echoed, "Where?"

"From Rome you send a demand to Tricarico, calling for the delivery of the boy, and you sign it *Caldora Count Aversa*. Then subtly inform Sforza—so he discovers it. I leave that to you."

Conduct of the Papal Election in Constance was as freely delegated to the judgment of Raimondo Count Nola, and the defenses of Taranto, to the judgment of Pappacoda, but when the time came for parting the Prince offered one more blanket advice. "Wherever we go—any of us—we must spread the word to our people to withhold all remittances to the Crown. Lie, delay, makeshift, do anything—so Joan gets none of our money; no tolls or taxes or revenues are to be paid for anything.

"Now go!—and let us all keep Ettore informed where we are. I give you this for our signet and countersign—it is a pledge— *Cousins and brothers!*"

They kissed each other, and kissed each other's swords, in a kind of childish play-acting which still had a binding effect, and then they disappeared—as nearly as possible—in disguises which might have fooled Alopo but never Serjianni.

Giovantonio took only four men, in addition to his squire, and all dressed like well battered soldiers, without a sign of distinction or designation of rank (unless you count the jewel-encrusted hilts of Taranto's daggers; his gold sword and scabbard was left at home in favor of a less shiny one, borrowed). The four were all older, by years, than their master, postgraduates of a terrible school. Outwardly they were made of whipcord and bowstring, greasy hair and steel links. Of their guts, you shall see that they had aplenty, but of hearts, they had none at all. Tomaso, Riccardo, Erri and Quito—named for Saints, the most obscure— they were chosen, over twenty volunteers just as tough, for their semiliteracy. Tomaso, Riccardo and Quito could read, a little, and Erri could sign his name.

The squire was younger, a Luxemburgian protégé of Marie's, hight Aloys, a gift from the former Queen to her son on his sixteenth birthday. He was a novice who had not killed anyone yet, and as such the butt of the soldiers' japes, but he took their jesting in good part and promised to show them a trick with a hole in it when the need arose.

Leary of ambush by forces from Naples, they went a course like a hound's hind leg, choosing their roads so well that they avoided any encounters, and looking so troublesome in and of themselves that most countrymen along their way took pains to avoid them. Six footloose soldiers in a clutch always means trouble to village maids and innkeepers, so that only the hardier among those met would risk a spoken word upon topics of common bruit, but those who did talk revealed a strikingly uniform and growing preference for Louis II d'Anjou for King. This was true not only of locals but of wagoners from town and porters from castles who echoed the views of their betters, reflecting a desire formed spontaneously and without any help from the Caldoras. Numbers held for Louis II simply because Joan was a woman. Others—themselves women—spoke for the outlander because Joan was the kind of woman she was, by them called "unnatural". Some reasoned that Joan had no other heir and no nearer kin than Louis, so that when she did die of her excesses—which must occur soon—he would be King anyway. The taxpayers could avoid the expense of one Coronation by giving Louis the Crown in the first place. That would be the end of heir trouble for a good while, too, because Louis already had three legitimate sons.

Every move Joan had made since assuming the title (and she called herself Queen of Rome too) had cost her a lot of friends. The imprisonment of Marie-Luise, the execution of Pappacoda, and the deprivation of all but a few of the Council, had turned at least thirty of the wealthiest families against her—and Alopo was doing the rest.

Although the post of Seneschal is outranked by the Grand Constable and at least nine other Ministries in the Regno, its distinguishing attribute and one unique duty provide the incumbent with the most aggravating of powers and make him potentially the most fertile source of trouble, jealousy, animosity and vendetta at Court. The Seneschal is the official master of ceremony and protocol. He arranges the seating or the standing or the marching order for processions—in relation to the sovereign—and thus he is arbiter and dictator of rank and precedency in practical daily usance, and not only as applied to his colleagues of the Council but to the Barons of the Regno and outland visitors, be they Envoys, Orators, Kings, Popes or Pashas.

Obviously, Alopo and this niche in life brought out the worst features of each other, and before Taranto and his little troop entered Naples they had heard the new Seneschal's murder predicted five-several times. In Naples, the date for it had been set and the assassin had something on account.

"We don't want to kill him," Taranto whispered to his men as—afoot—they hugged a wall in the deeper shadows of an alley that was black to begin with. "He's no good to us dead." They were reconnoitering, merely, planning their movements, weighing possibilities. "If we can catch him on the Lungo, we can bring him through here. We must have an extra horse."

"We need more men," said Tomaso. "Five and a half can't do it."

Aloys, the fraction, gave his critic an oral fig, soft, but not soft enough. The passage they were in led directly to the Lungo alongside the moat of Castel Nuovo, and the Lungo was better patrolled under Joan's regime than at any time within memory. Sentinels by fours paced the length of it, from the Mole to the Piazza, within sight of each other, within easy hail. The alarm of one man brought twelve.

The one man who heard Aloys' little *brrrrrup* whistled sharply, thus closing that end of the alley. Three of the sentinels lowered their pikes as the fourth went only a step along the street to take a torch down from its sconce. Unaware that eight more men were coming on the double—four from the left and as many from the right—the Prince did not order retreat, but drew.

More astounded than dismayed, Tomaso did likewise, but repeated his previous warning. "We need more men!"

"Not yet," Taranto whispered. "Wait for the torch. I want to see their faces." Giovantonio's logic was utterly Neapolitan. If he knew even one of these warders by sight—could call one name—he could bribe the lot. The Tarantines were masked, so they were not necessarily announcing their identities the first night in town, not even if swords must be crossed. The gambit had merit. The chance was worth taking. It might have saved a world of trouble, had it been successful, but it went contrariwise.

The torch revealed no familiar features but, instead, what appeared to be an army just arrived, too many to bribe, too many to combat. No choice remained but to run for it. They ran: but Aloys, aware that if he survived, the jest would be that he had been fleetest away, undertook to show his mettle by running slower than any, and gaping back over his shoulder.

The passage was no wider than four men could span, elbow to elbow, and Tomaso was keeping the tenderling company in the rear rank, so to say, when the foremost of their pursuers heaved his pike ahead with a mighty force, at the level of a man's knees. It struck both men—Aloys and Tomaso—and the novice was more nimble. He stumbled but he did not go down, whereas the older soldier did.

At a time like that, the concussions by impetus, the crashes and collisions, occur in such rapid sequence that no principal to the melee has time to think or to weigh his actions. The Prince and the other three did not know what had happened until it was told them—after. They heard someone go down, and then two or three more, and louder, tripped up by the first, but they did not know it was Tomaso, and the speed of their flight carried them some way before they could stop to see.

The jackass who had pitched the pike was capsized by his own handiwork. He crushed the breath out of Tomaso, tumbling over him. The next two guards after him—one bearing the flambeau—joined that scramble, without their volition but by sheer velocity, and the torchbearer was the first man Aloys ever killed. No longer a virgin, the squire gave himself the pleasure again, upon the person of a pikeman standing up, and he was engaged in his third affair before Giovantonio had got back to the real battle site.

Tomaso had broken the neck of one assailant in the gutter, by twisting his helmet to the left whilst his knee held the man's cuirass toward the right. That done, and the torch gone out from the shock of its fall, Tomaso groped here, there and everywhere searching for his sword, sending such volleys of curses at the Queensmen that I shouldn't be surprised if one or more succumbed to them.

Riccardo and Quito were not idle either, and neither was very hard pressed. One to the left and the other to the right of the Prince, they hewed and jabbed, as befit the moment, each calling out the sum of his score to the other—"Three!" "Four!" "Four!" "Five!"—and so on. Not quite all the guardsmen they felled actually died of their wounds. Some lay down at the merest scratch and rested until the fight was over.

Taranto was not so prodigious a slayer that night as a hero should be. He got only two—but they were big ones. He was too much concerned for Aloys to do his best. That Luxemburgian child had to be pulled away or he would have died of exhaustion.

In the darkness the dead or otherwise prostrated could not be counted, but when opportunity came to tote up, they estimated a round nineteen. Larger fields have been won with fewer casualties. In fact, it was the narrowness of the theatre of War and the heaped up corpses and facsimiles that gave the smaller force the victory. No more than four—really three-exchanges could be in progress at one time, because the Tarantine valor and skill prevented any of the Queen's reserves and re-enforcements from getting behind the defenders' front line. Guards kept pouring in from the Lungo end of the alley all the time, but they only got in each other's way, and they durst not throw any more pikes, for fear of bashing their own men.

The tumult had drawn a multitude of women and other night-crawlers of the street to the opposite end of the alley—*the way out*—but few partisans of the Queen and her Seneschal were among them, and no military or Blacklegs or catch-poll Sergeants. Still—to prevent surprise from that quarter—Erri had held a station there throughout the encounter, fretting and bouncing in frustration at the evil chance which kept his sword dry. Yet, in the end, he saved his companions and justified the vigil, because some of the guards, unable to enter the fray from the Lungo end, eventually made their way around the buildings and were descending upon the Tarantines' rear when Erri saw them coming and shrilled the alarm.

Only the press of noncombatant curious prevented a second front, which could hardly have failed to reduce the little force of six. The women *et al* conspired at it to impede the progress of the Queensmen, and Erri covered the pell-mell retreat of his tired but skin-whole companions down a reeking street of steps and away.

MR. THAYER INTRUDES

This "King of Naples" business threw me at first—although I have known several "Queens of Chicago". They were different. "The Kingdom of Naples"—also called "the Regno"—was a lot more than a city. It took in the whole foot and ankle of the Boot and went a good way up the calf. It was the continental half of "the Two Sicilies". French writers always call Louis II d'Anjou "King of Sicily", meaning King of the island, Sicily *ultra* Pharum, and of Naples, Sicily *citra* Pharum. Italian writers apply the same titles to *their* entries in these bouts, but you can always tell the fighters apart by the color of their trunks.

The name "Italy" does not occur in the MS until Machiavelli uses it in Chapter 42 or thereabouts. He is the first politician in this book to think of "Italy" as what we call a *nation*. The Boot was all cut up into semi-sovereign States, but Naples was the only Kingdom.

They called some of the pieces Republics—like Florence, Venice, Siena—but you had to be a real-estate owner to vote, and unless your grandfather had owned that same real-estate, you couldn't run for office. After Villon gets to Florence he admits that the "citizens" never totaled quite 10 per cent of the population, so you can see how "Republican" vox pop was.

The writer never gets on a soapbox, but his class consciousness comes out in little ways, especially when he mentions "the People" or "the commonality". The People of Genoa and Bologna were forever trying to set up Republics. Piombino was a Principality.

I didn't know any of this stuff when I started checking up on the MS, did you? Well, it will not only help you follow the *cousins and brothers* as they chop their way up, but it will come in mighty handy if you are ever on a quiz program.

Milan was a Duchy

Urbino—a County

Mirandola—a County

Ferrara—a Marchesate

Mantua—a Marchesate and then there were the States of the Church, which were at the disposal of the Pope—more or less.

I say, "more or less," because practically every County in the Papal States had been taxed by its strongest local family or House for a good many generations, the title passing from father to son, or to nearest of male kin, and this practice had become so much the habitual order that the well-born maintained their inheritances in primogeniture as an inalienable "right", and even the suckers who supported these overlords by paying their tyrannical exactions, entertained a perverse sense of loyalty to those Houses and none other. It was as if the cows of New York State should refuse to give down their milk to any but members of the Borden family, yet each new Pope attempted to substitute members of his own family, or politically potent friends, for some of these local "heirs", and the consequence was the endless turmoil which keeps spattering these pages with blood on a family versus family basis.

I was jesting in earnest, or not really jesting at all, at that point in the introduction where I indicated that Edward Gibbon came within an ace of writing this book instead of his *Decline and Fall.* He even started to block it out, and the sum total of his thinking on the subject occupies seventeen pages in volume two of his *Miscellaneous Works,* London, 1796.

Gibbon wrote those seventeen pages in French, and they are dated, *A Beriton, le 14 Avril 1761.* The piece is titled *Recherches Critiques sur le Titre qu'avoit Charles VIII, a la Couronne de Naples,* which is translated, Critical Researches concerning the Title of Charles VIII to the Crown of Naples.

A great deal of ink was spilt on this subject and the case was tried in numerous courts to justify the invasion of Naples in 1494 by Charles VIII of France, and the topic concerns us particularly because Elisabetta (Lisa) nee Gherardini *della* Gioconda was a resident of Florence when Charles VIII marched into the city. There, in a few words, you have the classic understatement of all time, that Lisa *was a resident.* Mama mia—wait till you read it!— in Book Three, perhaps.

Gibbon was a smart boy to give up the idea. He chose the easier assignment. To do the job properly he must have begun in 1250 A.D., with the Emperor Frederick II Hohenstauffen. I had to do that to verify the Villon MS, but you may relax. I am not going over it with you. Our text covers only the last phase of the struggle, leading directly to the French invasion which Lisa lived through.

We learn, quite incidentally and by the way, how Charles VIII—a Valois—came into his shaky title to a claim which, through more than two centuries, had inhered to the House of Anjou.

At the opening of the MS the contest is between two branches of the Anjou family, the senior branch headed by Louis II Duke d'Anjou, and the cadet—but incumbent—branch headed by Ladislaus Anjou-Durazzo. Upon the death of Ladislaus, Joan II complicates the struggle by being a woman. No woman could legally succeed to the title of Anjou—or of any French peerage—but the precedent of Queens in Naples, the Two Sicilies, and in Aragon, was well established.

In the foregoing chapter, and indeed throughout the work, I have taken the liberty of misusing the term "Vatican" as invariably meaning "the Papal residence", whether that residence be in Avignon, Rome, Florence or elsewhere. Properly, the only Vatican is that on the hillock in Rome, and in the original MS any number of terms are employed for the various Papal palaces as the pontiffs were chased hither and yon, but I have rendered them all "Vatican", as more readily understandable to the present generation.

Although he had his eye on posterity, setting out to raise Lisa above her enemies, Villon was writing for his contemporaries, and so he is prone to assume that all literate persons will know pretty well what he is talking about. The upshot and outcome of the events he chronicles were still being lived by the scions of these same Houses, and in much the same way. The same motivations were common to every breast, the same animosities prevailed, and Schism was ever just around the comer, so he never had to pause and explain himself or analyze the palpable. Thus he gallops through the master plan of the Prince of Taranto as if its purport were only too obvious. Unfortunately, not everyone can now fill in his elisions out of personal experience, and so a second look may be helpful.

As I understand it, when Ladislaus employed Sforza to go against Rome, the King demanded, as surety for the Commander's loyalty in the field, possession of Sforza's bastard Francesco, then about 12 *ans.* At first the boy lived in the King's household, but success had given Ladislaus greater confidence in his *Condottiere,* and the taxing of Tricarico was conferred on Francesco. He was permitted to live there with his aunt. The King's death made the lad's position most precarious, and Taranto was not the only Lord who saw Francesco's hostage value.

Ladislaus had left Attendola Sforza in supreme command at Rome, in possession of the fortress of San Angelo, also known as Hadrian's Tomb, that great cheesebox which the Popes used for an arsenal. Under Sforza were two Caldoras, Giacomo Count Aversa and his eldest son Antonio. All three men had been pressed into the Exercise by Joan before it had attained to Royal status, and now that she pretended to the Crown each of them might hope to oust Alopo as her favorite.

Taranto instantly recognizes the value to Joan of her military occupation of Rome, and just as quickly realizes the value to his party of pitting the Caldoras against their superior officer, Sforza.

Further, as is clearly implied, Sforza, as supreme Commander of the militia, has been in rivalry for power with Serjianni the Grand Constable, who is married to one of Giacomo Caldora's daughters. If those two giants can be induced to throw rocks at each other, all currently vested authority and military strength will be weakened accordingly, and the potency of the Tarantine cabal increased in proportion.

That is the Prince's purpose in sending his cousin Guglielmo Duke Andria to Rome, the while he baits a trap in Naples to bring Sforza within reach of the Constable's jealousies.

The street broil with Alopo's defenders, meaningless of itself, prevents Taranto's strategy from fruiting in season, but the game is young, the stakes are high and the prize is to the strongest.

CHAPTER THREE

T HIS EPISODE, which elevated the Prince's squire to manhood and won him the affection of the others, had the further effect of increasing the Queen's watch upon all approaches to Alopo, and of practically confining him indoors. The chances of kidnaping the Seneschal were reduced almost to nil, but the conspirators—by ones and twos for safety's sake—persisted in spying out his habits in search of the opportunity.

At the same time Giovantonio, going dirtier than his men for the sake of his incog, set out to find the sweet Lady Maria who had made him a father. Former friends did not know which of Her Majesty Marie's Bedchamber had been permitted to attend her into prison, but Joan was no Barbarian to deny attendants to a former Queen, and popular bruit was that Marie-Luise and her family were enduring no hardship whatever save the confinement itself. A certain tower apartment was assigned to their use, and her own cooks and maids were still with her. Logic said that the Lady Maria and her infant of the same name were in that tower too.

Unfortunately that was an *inner* tower, and logic—as often as not—is an awful liar, so that Taranto was a sucker for tips and rumors from utterly unreliable persons who knew somebody who had seen a resemblance, here or there or yon. He would follow any page or punk who whispered, "Wanna find Maria?"—and he followed one too many.

Against the city wall near the Posilippo gate was a hovel that climbed for three floors up the masonry, and it looked like any other hen roost at twilight. Women, of uninteresting age and no figures, yacked at each other in the doorway, three or four of them, barnacled with babes.

The slippery little devil who had led Taranto thus far darted between the ample skirts of these shapeless lumps and beckoned from the first stair-step inside for Giovantonio to follow.

The women stopped speaking and gave the Prince and Aloys the hostile eye, a most unnatural thing, because both youths— even begrimed—always drew glances of quite another character, and especially from women so plain.

"Wait for me here," the Prince directed his squire—and followed the imp inside.

The slattern dames turned all to inspect the Luxemburgian, left behind to the mercies of their curiosity and to the ravages of their brats. The strength which had made him so formidable in a midnight alley against an army melted to a nerveless jelly as small females climbed his legs as if they were trees, and plucked at his weapons with hands only half as big as flowers.

"Get down," said Aloys weakly, trying to brush them off. "No, no. You will hurt yourself. Go away."

"Why should she go away?" One mother took umbrage, and another said, "You're nothing but a baby yourself." She was disengaging a suckling as she spoke, and offered her still dripping dug to the man. "Are you hungry? Take din-din."

"Make him take din-din," said another sow, and the children took it up. "Make him take din-din! Make him take din-din!" they screamed, and pounded Aloys with twenty insignificant fists in rhythm with their demand, as the lusty brazen one—who had a reputation among her sisters as a prankster—tried to put the funny brown button of it into his mouth.

Even if Giovantonio had called out for help, Aloys could not have heard him for the din about *din-din,* but the Prince had no opportunity to cry out. The misbegotten guide to disaster led the Highness who should have known better through a door toward a bed where something lay bundled. That was the last Taranto knew for some time. He never saw clearly what was bundled on that bed until it was himself, very thoroughly trussed.

A splitting pain at the back of his skull informed his carelessness. A woman named Maria, but only by coincidence, was mopping his face and neck with a wet rag that stank vilely. The Prince spat violently as the noxious cloth passed over his mouth, and struggled to sit up. Nobody but this nurse, hare-lipped and dour, was in the room with him, and when she observed his convulsive awakening she bade him lie still, and she went out.

This place was neither Heaven nor Hell, so he must be Alopo's prisoner, Taranto reasoned, and asked himself, simultaneously, how he could have been such a fool, and if Aloys were taken too. Then, for a longer time than is conscionable, he lay planning how he should face his low-born captor, whether with scorn and pride, or in conciliatory vein, weighing his chances for escape either way. At the moment his arms and legs felt dead, so tightly was he bound, and the hemp went more than once around the bed. He could not see his blades. Their empty scabbards were still on his person.

The Prince must have dozed, for when he opened his eyes again, two people were in the room. One was the Great Serjianni Caracciolo—Grand Constable and Strong Man—the other, his assassin called a secretary. Taranto covered his surprise with a gasp of relief. With a peer, a gentleman knows better how to deal, and in dealing with this glutton for power, lands and wealth, the term of the Prince's captivity would depend solely upon the terms of the promise required. What would Serjianni ask for—in addition to Taranto?

"Ah, good Uncle!" the Prince groaned. "How did you find me?—but cut these cords before you answer. They are killing me." By calling the Constable *uncle* the Prince hoped to flatter the fellow. They were not actually related even by marriage.

The Strong Man—whose physique rhymed well with his attainments and ambitions—could play-act too, when he chose. In mock solicitude he leaned over the youth to inspect his bindings, murmuring, "Who has done this terrible thing to you, Highness?"—but he did not draw his own misericordia to cut the ropes nor tell his man to do so neither.

"I do not know, Milord. Do, please, release me. I have fainted twice from the pain of it."

"Wounded too? The dastards! Who would dare? You, the Queen's son!"

"Cut! Uncle! Cut! Will you not cut me loose? Then we can talk. I cannot describe this agony."

"But where is the wound?"

"You delay."

"I? Delay?"

"Your Highness—I do not understand—and I shall not try to, until you release me. I shall not say another word until you cut my bonds."

Serjianni turned to his man. "A chair."

A rickety piece to sit on was found, and the Constable settled his fat arse upon it gingerly … "Now," he puffed. "Some things I do not understand any better than you, my son. If you are the Queen's prisoner, for instance, I shall have to obtain Her Majesty's permission to let you go."

Taranto's eyes were fired, but he did not speak. Serjianni's subterfuge was too thin, nor was he solicitous to be believed.

"You are not in Naples in your own identity. You are ill clad, unkempt—in disguise, in short. Against whom are you here?"

No answer, but the boy ground his teeth. Against whom, indeed, with his mother held prisoner!

"Was that not your party—who killed three guards—"

"*Three!?*" The word popped out in spite of him. The Tarantines had counted nineteen, from memory.

"There, now," said Serjianni, "you have broken your oath not to speak, so you may as well answer my questions. Why have you come to Naples in disguise?—against whom? ... Speak, Highness. You are beyond rescue. Nobody knows where you are, and your men are all taken too."

Giovantonio did not believe that, but he made no answer.

"I know you are forming a cabal of your families, and the Pappacodas, and the Chiaramontes. How many men can you put into the field? If you are strong enough—I might join you." The Constable rolled his eyes owlishly, and waited, but he received no answer.

The contest here between their two wills was enormously unfair. The Prince, in truth, was barely conscious from being so cruelly bound. Still the Strong Man's anger rose in proportion to the other's stubbornness. From his pocket Serjianni draw Taranto's "demands" upon the Queen and slapped the parchment with contemptuous fingers. "You want Avellino—for the Del Balzos—eh? How do you propose to get it? ... Do you expect Alopo to give it to them? ... Or will you make love to the Queen? ... Perhaps you mean to marry her. Is that your bridegroom's attire?" Between each question and the next Serjianni gave his prisoner time to speak if he would. "Queen Joan must marry someone, you know ... Someone capable of winning back the Barons she has lost to Louis II ... Someone of my choice ...

Do you know anyone strong enough—with whom I could do business?"

"Yes!" the Prince shouted, "but until you release me I never will speak."

The Constable leaned over the bound man intently. "Speak— and your mother may start for Lecce—or Taranto—tonight. *Speak!*"

The room, the world, the moon-face lowering over him, shimmered, faded, almost slipped away from Giovantonio. Nothing remained real to his sight or other senses save indomitable determination. After a few moments of utter silence, the Constable gestured his man to the bed, and spoke surlily. "You cannot get away. My guard fills the building—the street. Don't try to get away, Highness."

The ropes fell off Taranto's wrists, his ankles, his waist, sawed by a blade which would not hesitate to puncture an unarmed man, prone and paralyzed. No immediate change was apparent in the Prince's perceptions. His ears rang, his head pounded, his sight was unclear and wavering, but Serjianni's boast did not carry conviction to the fluttering consciousness on the bed. The Prince knew well how delicately balanced the real power seesawed that day in Naples, and reasoned that the Constable would not have risked attracting Alopo's attention to his movements by a great stir of his personal guards outside this hovel so near to a city gate. The boy believed his tormentor was lying, and his misty mind resolved upon a leap for the door instantly he was free. Alas, when he tried, the only result was a kind of abdominal spasm, a bending at the waist, followed promptly by collapse. His arms and legs would not move.

"Be so good as to chafe my wrists, Antonio," he begged the secretary. "I cannot lift either hand."

The Constable's man looked to his master for sanction, but Serjianni shook his head. "You will recover soon enough. You are unbound now. Let us speak as friends ... Get wine, Antonio."

Through the slits of his drooping lids the Prince watched Antonio open the door, and saw dimly—outside in the corridor—three men-at-arms, swords bare and at ready. "You do me too much honor, Milord," said the Prince wryly ... "Wine," said Antonio to those outside.

Serjianni ignored Taranto's sarcasm and launched at once, in his crude version of diplomacy, into the pressing need for Joan II to marry before the Council at Constance named the new and only Pope. "You and I could accomplish great things together," the Constable leered. "I might relinquish Avellino to your cousins—for such an agreeable King—if I got something better. Shall we say—Salerno?"

The income of Salerno would be, roughly, twice as large as that of Avellino, but Giovantonio was paying scant attention to the Constable's words. The boy could feel the blood returning, tingling, to his members, but he lay very still, as a ruse, and when wine was brought he continued his pretense of helplessness, requiring Antonio to hold the cup to his mouth. Then he said, "If I ever marry Aunt Joan, Milord, you shall have Salerno and Avellino too—and Taranto and Rome as well."

The Constable raised both hands a little, to ward off so much generosity, but the Prince went on. "That is to say, I am not the man to be the Queen's consort—"

"She is mad for you!"

"She is mad for you too, as far as that goes, but you have not given in."

"I am a married man—with a family. I have no royal blood. You have. Your Highness Mother is a cousin of Louis II——"

"A cousin in the thirty-second degree!"

"She is, nonetheless, descended directly from Saint Louis of France. We can make much of that. The Barons will acknowledge it. The new Pope must honor it. You are, in solemn fact, a cousin—however distant—of Louis II d'Anjou, and by the same token, of Charles VI of France."

"Yet you did not hesitate to lay hands on me in violence."

"Only to save Your Highness from yourself."

"You did not hesitate to keep me bound—to force me to deal with you."

"Only because your blood was hot. Now that you are cool, see how well we get along. I can make Your Highness King."

"You cannot make my Highness King. The husband of Aunt Joan never will be anything but a stick wrapped in ermine, and a breed-bull. But I give you another cousin of my mother's—who has already offered himself, even before Ladislaus died."

"A Bourbon?"

"Jacques Bourbon Count of Marche ... If Antonio will hold the cup for me, I propose a toast to His Highness Jacques Bourbon as the next King of the Regno."

Again the Constable's loyal killer consulted his master's wishes, before the toast could be drunk, and Taranto took advantage of their interchange to test if he could move. He could.

"Give him the wine," said Serjianni, "but I cannot drink that toast. If the Count of Marche ever offered to marry Joan, why was I never told about it?"

"Because my stepfather suspected Your Highness of sympathy for Louis II," said Taranto distinctly. "You and the Caldoras have been closely watched, Milord. I have letters enough to behead you—all three—if I were King."

The Great Serjianni sat as motionless as the brash boy on the bed. Not even by a flicker of an eyelid did he betray his true reaction to that awful charge. As the Prince read

Serjianni's immobility, it meant that letters capable of beheading the Constable-under certain circumstances—actually existed, as in fact they did, but Taranto did not have them in his possession, and Serjianni was pretty sure his adversary was bluffing.

This game was for the highest stakes in the world, for the power to make and unmake Kings and Queens, which is a greater thing than wearing a crown, and for control of Holy Church by means of a halter on the Pope, which is superior to sweating under the Tiara. Each of the players was aware of his need for the other, in alliance, but neither wished to enter agreement on the short side, and the circumstances were particularly irksome to the Strong Man, in that he was forced to lock horns politically with one who—only the day before—had been a mere whipper-snapper.

Out of his greater experience, the Lord Constable spoke at last, saying, "I cannot vouch for the Caldoras, but only for myself. You, Milord, have no letters of mine shewing me traitorous to my King. Every man has good right to look to his fortune and guard it against eventualities. I have done no more in this way than Your Highness, in occupying Taranto. I am not committed to Louis II, and if your letters indicate that I am, they are forgeries. Let us speak more about the Count of Marche. Will Your Highness' party support him?"

"I should have to ask my associates. They will be easier to bring around than Aunt Joan. She has already refused to have him."

"She was not Queen then."

"She is not Queen now—until a Pope anoints her."

"For all practical purposes she is Queen. Married to another descendant of Saint Louis—and supported by yourself and me—she will be Queen. No Pope could refuse to bless her. How much difference is there—in consanguinity—between Louis II and Jacques Bourbon?"

"I shall have to ask my mother. Would Your Highness be pleased to transport her to Lecce? You and I could confer with her there—without Alopo's interference. My Majesty mother would be of great assistance in bringing Cousin Jacques to the Regno."

"So she would!" Serjianni agreed, more enthusiastic than he was. "A pity I have not access to Her Majesty. I should not know how to release her." Words, merely, to conceal the Constable's awareness that by releasing Marie-Luise, her children, *et al,* he would be sacrificing his grip upon Taranto. Serjianni would sooner have freed the Prince in person than let his mother leave the tower.

Giovantonio cut through the obfuscation at a stroke. "Your Highness will have to exert yourself in that way," said the Prince, flexing the fingers of his left hand, which the Constable could not see. "My mother—my family—and I must all be quite free, and united, before Cousin Jacques is sent for." The boy's tone was not particularly insolent, but the brave presumption of that demand, made from the depths of his helplessness, touched the spring of the Strong Man's resentments and brought him to the bedside in a leap.

"You dare to dictate to *me!* You threaten to have my head! You tell me what I must do? You—you——"

By chance, the Constable's rising so abruptly had sent the rickety half-chair tumbling into a dark comer behind him, where—in a pile of offal—a family of rats had their nest. Disturbed, they scurried and the big papa rat took a course which crossed Serjianni's line of vision. By chance, too, rats were just about the only thing that this Caracciolo was afraid of. Demons and Queens, he cuffed about, and you have seen how little terror he felt for a paralyzed lad, but rats gave the Constable the screaming-meemies and he could not control it.

Gibbering, jouncing, in a kind of ague, both hands trembling around his quivering lips, the pretender to Avellino and to King-making power teetered on his toes, little better than an idiot, a revolting sight to see.

"R-r-r-r-rats!" he screamed. "R-r-r-rats!"

His cry brought the three men-at-arms bursting through the door, and set them and Antonio to stabbing the shadows all around the room, whereupon the Prince of Taranto jumped off the bed and ran about halfway to the corridor. Liberty was only three more steps away but he had no legs to run with. He folded at the knees, buckled and went down, and then a strange thing happened. Serjianni, recovering somewhat his presence and his strength, entirely forgot the relationship between himself and his prisoner, forgot his animus, and valiantly lifted Taranto up in his arms and carried him to the street, to save His Highness from being devoured by those ferocious beasts.

CHAPTER FOUR

IN FAR-OFF CONSTANCE, Raimondo Orsini Count Nola and Antonio Colonna surprised Antonio's Cardinal father by dropping in for dinner. Cardinal Oddo laughed at their hasty-hearted politics which called for quick decisions. "Bless you, children, the Council can't Elect a new Pope until the present Popes resign—and none of them wants to. It's going to take time. But—stay here with me. We're going to have a fire. We're going to burn John Hus."

The Cardinal enjoyed their stories about the Prince of Taranto, however, and said that if their young friend succeeded in getting the former Queen Marie-Luise out of gaol, he could then move on to get Sforza out of Rome, and when that was done, the Prince might have his choice of Antonio Colonna's sisters for wife, with a dot large enough to show the Church's appreciation of these services rendered.

"Our cousin, Duke Andria, is moving Sforza out of Rome," said Nola, as if the transportation were to be upon rollers. "We are authorized by the Prince of Taranto to say that Your Lordship—as Pope—will be able to enter the true Vatican at your convenience."

Out of tenderness for their sensitive feelings Cardinal Oddo did not laugh outright. A laugh at youth's too-great confidence can ruin it forever.

Like themselves, the Colonna was seriously considering Louis II d'Anjou for King of the Regno, and entertaining that candidate's offers. "Louis is not only directly descended from a Saint," said the Cardinal, tousling his son's hair, "but he would do great things for you, Antonio. What Counties in the Regno would you like to have?"

"How many?" asked Antonio, which made his father glad. "There speaks a true Colonna!" said the Cardinal, "but you had better take your titles one at a time."

"Then I'll take Salerno first," said Antonio, thereby setting his wishes against those of Serjianni Caracciolo. Sooth, the lad could hardly have named any taxing in the Regno without conflicting with the Constable's personal desires, but you mark the coincidence that Serjianni had already mentioned the port of Salerno to the Prince, so that now the *cousins and brothers* cabal was directly at variance with the Strong Man on two important incomes, Salerno and Avellino.

In his report to Ettore Pappacoda, for transmission to the Prince, Count Nola jested about the daughters of Cardinal Oddo, none of whom, he wrote, was big enough. *So tell Giovantonio he need not hurry to Paliano to make his selection. Anna, the eldest, is only 11, Caterina 8, and Vittoria 4. Vittoria would be my choice. Antonio recommends Caterina. Anna is too severe.*

Jesting aside, if the Prince does think well of this offer, let him be reminded that for convention's sake these little ones are known as daughters of Lorenzo-Onofrio Colonna Duke Paliano, and my gossip Antonio is called Paliano's son. This courtesy will become even more important if we succeed in making their "Uncle" Oddo Pope, and the chances are excellent.

CHAPTER FIVE

I N ROME, Guglielmo Del Balzo Duke Andria was making even swifter progress, and Joan's army was helping him. The enlisted men were in open revolt for their pay, and Joan's income was so much curtailed that she could send nothing. The City itself was in such a sad sorry state that little was left to steal. Starvation stalked the lower orders and even the priests were fasting on feast days.

The cherubic cousin had no difficulty conferring with the Caldoras, father and son, who were on the point of abandoning their commands because their commands had abandoned them. Less Protean double-dealers might have been disturbed by these turns and twists of uncontrollable events, but not Count Aversa or his son Antonio. Their garrisons in Aversa and Capua were made up of their own men, paid up to date and not given to whimsy.

"Our position is quite unique," said the father, in his crisp way of speaking. "Others must come to us. We need not go to them. You have come to us. We honor you and your cousins. We consider your offers. But we do not rely upon you—or upon Queen Joan, or upon Louis II, or even upon my son-in-law, the *Great* Serjianni. We rely upon ourselves." Aversa was a tight-knit, smallish fellow, with a trimmed black beard which needed no dye to keep its years from showing, and Antonio was an exact replica, more like a twin than a son.

"Today I am Governor of Capua. Tomorrow I shall be Prince—and Antonio shall have Aversa—in my lifetime, at once. My ultimatum will be presented to Her Majesty. I leave for Capua in the morning. We do not care what Sforza does. He will find his match in Serjianni. Those two will keep each other fully engaged. Depend upon it."

Young Del Balzo saw the logic of that. If the jealous rivalry of the Constable and Sforza deprived Joan of military support, she would have no choice but to turn to the Caldoras, and the Principality of Capua would be a small price to pay.

"Precisely," said Count Aversa distinctly. "And Louis II is equally dependent upon alliance with us. I take you into our confidence, Highness. You will convey this to the Prince of Taranto at the earliest. He may inform Louis II or not, as he pleases.

"Queen Joan will invest me Prince of Capua, as I ask, because there is much evidence that the present Prince—Rinaldo, who is four years old—is truly the son of the late King Ladislaus. Indeed, the King's only child."

"We can prove it," put in Antonio as Duke Andria gasped, but the speaker's father corrected him with an amplification. "We can prove that Rinaldo *is* Ladislaus' son—or that he is *not* Ladislaus' son—as best suits our convenience. Nobody else can prove the one or the other, because the boy is in my custody and nobody else knows where he is ... You may tell that to the Prince of Taranto. He and Louis II will wish to take it into their reckoning in approaching us for a landing area."

Guglielmo was ashamed to have been caught napping, to have betrayed his shocked surprise at this gambit, but he could not call back a gasp that had been gasped, or narrow his saucered eyes. This was the curse of a baby face and a guileless heart, but he still had a pretty wit. Smiling them fair, he puffed his cheeks like a *putto,* and asked, "Will the price be the same either way?"

The humorless Caldoras refused to discuss anything so vulgar as price, so prematurely, but if the Barons wished to make Rinaldo King, over all other contenders, Count Aversa—as lifelong guardian of the child—would expect to be Regent until the sovereign came of age.

When Guglielmo sat down alone to retail this encounter to Ettore Pappacoda—by cipher to the citadel of Taranto, as arranged—he took a calmer view of this bastard in tender years. Even if Rinaldo were offspring of Ladislaus, which was dubious, the boy had no party. He was a threat to nobody but Joan, and only to her conscience, an entirely supposititious entity. Further, before the Queen would raise Caldora to be Prince of Capua, she would demand custody of her purported "nephew". So Duke Andria wrote: *The Caldoras are at such loose ends they are eating little children.*

The next day the Caldoras left Rome, and the only troops remaining faithful to Joan were two of Sforza's garrisons, the one holding San Angelo, inside The City, the other, Ostia, at the mouth of Tiber on the coast, both under command of lieutenants. These officers parlied with Duke Andria freely, even glibly, vainly trying to conceal that Sforza was already gone to Naples to contest the sway of Serjianni and Alopo by marrying Joan himself.

Cousins and brothers! Andria's mission to Rome was thus accomplished, in all but one detail. He had not put himself in position to command the Seven Hills for Louis II. Accordingly, he set up host to all Sforza's hungry officers, and hired the best cooks and the prettiest whores, paid five prices for meat and wine, made himself a second Lucullus.

To Pappacoda he wrote:

This is costing more than Rome is worth, but I can guarantee Giovantonio that if he attacks after dark not one captain will be found with his clothes on or able to stand on his feet.

CHAPTER SIX

THAT ASSURANCE MIGHT have been encouraging if it had reached Giovantonio in good season, but all these letters were long delayed, and—interim—to speak of the Prince "attacking" anybody was bitterly ironical.

Whilst Pappacoda took his ease and his sport in Taranto, honored by the natives as their hero's agent, and never challenged in his stewardship even by the Queen; and whilst Count Nola, as the feted guest of the Colonnas in Constance, watched Holy Church attempting to heal itself around the embers of John Hus; and whilst baby-face Andria lolled in his private fleshpots, to "take" Rome through the belly of the military—where was their leader?

Tomaso, Riccardo, Erri and Quito never gave up the search. Day long and night long they covered Naples, peering high and prying low, looking at every found corpse, as diligent to find Aloys as the Prince, and Aloys they found. He was dead, washed up out of the Bay where the Constable's guard had flung him wounded. The jeweled fish of those enchanted waters had nibbled the corse, but not so much that Tomaso did not recognize the boy, and over the blue, bloated body of the Luxemburgian, the grim and hard-bitten four pledged themselves to vengeance. "I—*I* shall trail the Constable's guts through every street of the town," Tomaso swore. "I shall chew up his eyeballs—like grapes—and spit them in his face."

Until then the four had not connected the Constable with their master's disappearance, but after they buried Aloys they filed solemnly past Caracciolo's palace. They were not permitted to pause in that street. No one was. The Constable was guarding his prisoner at least three times as carefully as Joan was guarding Alopo.

The Tarantines saw nothing whatever to substantiate their conviction, but at the end of that single, superficial reconnaissance they knew the Prince was inside. Almost without words they apportioned perpetual surveillance four ways, so that one or more of Serjianni's gates was under their eyes at all times. The vigilance of his guards matched theirs exactly, never relaxing, and Serjianni's soldiers—all from Melfi—were incorruptible within the range of the pooled assets of the four.

Several months of that futility brought out Tomaso's old plaint: "We need more men." They had not seen Giovantonio at any window. They had not been permitted within a long stonesthrow of the Constable's person. "We need sixty men," said Tomaso, in one of his less laconic moments.

Erri rode to the citadel in Taranto. Quito went to the town of Nola. Riccardo set off for Rome to find Duke Andria. Only Tomaso remained in Naples, tailing the Constable, walking endless hours around and around the Caracciolo palace, but Opportunity—the jade!—continued to flout him.

Serjianni had no reason to dread a Nemesis so weak, so ignorant. In the absence of their master those sturdy souls lacked any means to correlate events, to add two and two. They had not even the benefit of the meager intelligences being assembled in the citadel at Taranto, because Giovantonio had not told them how or where his messages were to be received in Naples. So that their keenest observation of the Constable's activities had not revealed his intentions or taught them what to expect.

On his own—to demonstrate his independence of his guest-prisoner—Serjianni had summoned Jacques Bourbon to Naples to become King. The former Queen Marie-Luise had not been consulted in this any more than had her son.

By the strictness of Taranto's incommunicado, Serjianni caused numbers of the cabal to assume that Giovantonio was dead, among them Artuso Pappacoda, brother of the former Seneschal and uncle of Ettore. Through Artuso—thus deluded— the Constable bound a majority of the Barons to the support of Jacques Bourbon, with the argument that Jacques was the perfect compromise between the present ravages of Alopo and the expense of a War on behalf of Louis II.

Almost in passing, with his left hand, Serjianni trapped Sforza into prison, and—all in all—quite justified his nickname, the Strong Man: but the Prince of Taranto was not dead, and as time passed his heart was tempered, now by heat, now by coldest cold, tempered and hardened and hammered into an instrument of devastating hatred for his captor, an irreducible stone of steel resolve to have his revenge upon Caracciolo in spite of Hell and all the gods.

Not to make his confinement any more rigid, as well as to spare his mother reprisals, Giovantonio concealed the virulence of his emotion even when the Constable's pride of achievement caused him to boast of his *coups*. Sometimes they played chess or tric-trac, and frequently supped or breakfasted together, not as friends—be it said—but without recriminations or outbursts of dire, prophetic fizzing. Taranto was mastering self-control, and only when he was alone did he thrash his arms and flail the air in token of the future.

By this restraint Giovantonio kept himself better informed than he would have been otherwise, and from the fluctuations of the Constable's moods he was able to guess much that went unsaid. It was a great lesson in patience to the Prince, too, and that was hardest for his disposition to bear. Less than half Serjianni's age, Giovantonio could afford to wait, but it was torture to be confined so closely at a time when every morsel of outland intelligence held such vital personal significance.

Queen Joan was receiving proposals of marriage from second-sons of reigning monarchs all over the world, from England, France, Cyprus, Aragon—the latter especially inviting because it offered a chance of regaining Island Sicily for the Crown of the Regno. Ladislaus had lost the island to Aragon in one of his Papal dickers, and the superstitious commonality held that Naples never would prosper again until the Two Sicilies were reunited.

Joan saw her chance to become a popular idol and to break Serjianni's power over her at a stroke, if she could communicate with the King of Aragon without the Constable's knowledge. "She is trying to send letters through your Chiaramonte friend," Serjianni gloated to Giovantonio. "I have intercepted three. Her Majesty suggests that the King of Aragon confer the crown of Sicily *ultra* Pharum upon his son Juan before their marriage." The Constable could not help laughing. "That would make her Queen of the Two Sicilies—and give her the armies of Aragon to defend her—from *me*. Do you think Chiaramonte would be agreeable to that?"

Giovantonio had not a sword to stick with, so he could not but swallow such taunts. For a truth, the Prince could not guess how Tristano would receive that move from Joan, but hardly a question a man might ask concerned his plans more deeply. This Chiaramonte was the betrothed of the Prince's elder imprisoned sister. He was the Chiaramonte of the *items*, the richest Lord on Island Sicily, the greatest single asset the creaking cabal had counted on for its revolutionary operations. If Taranto's brother-in-law-to-be was now backing Juan d'Aragon for King of the Regno, this was the time for Giovantonio to know it, before his party dissipated itself in division favoring either Cousin Jacques Bourbon or Louis II d'Anjou.

"I suggest that Your Highness send me to Palermo," Giovantonio suggested. "I could learn a great deal in a very short while, face to face with Tristano."

"So you could. So you could," Serjianni agreed, "if I were fool enough to trust you."

"How can you distrust me—with my whole family in the tower? Would I bring execution upon my mother? Would Chiaramonte permit me to bring execution upon his bride—or to alienate her dot?"

"I am not given to execution upon women," the Constable frowned darkly. "I shall trust you as soon as Jacques Bourbon marries Joan. Not before. When they are married—I have pledged you—your sister shall marry Chiaramonte, and have her dot from the Crown. Every article of your demands shall be granted—excepting Avellino—as agreed."

Although Serjianni said "as agreed," he should have said, "as dictated," because Taranto had no voice in the terms of the so-called "agreement". By the Strong Man's concession, they divided the *item* Avellino, the cash accumulation to be paid to the Del Balzos in quitclaim for their title which Serjianni would retain: this, and all other articles to the one-sided arrangement, contingent upon Del Balzo-Orsini support for the Jacques Bourbon regime.

"I trust you will not try to get to Palermo—or even out of this house—until I give you lief," the Constable warned. "You could not get away in any case, but if you so much as try, I will put you in irons for the rest of your life, and bring your mother's head to you for company."

Even so quickly the Man so Strong had overcome his scruples against assassination of females, and Giovantonio never doubted that he would be as good as his word. Accordingly, the Prince postponed his heart-to-heart talk with the money-man in Palermo, but he was able to get a letter out of the palace to Chiaramonte through the girl he was sleeping with, a *femme de chambre* named Giovanna.

Nobody paid much attention to Giovanna's goings and comings, she being more than a little fey, and terrified by her own shadow. She had one other advantage as a messenger too, delighting in the illusion that the Prince was the Angel Gabriel and herself the custodian of his horn. They made a great thing of that, putting it away, well out of sight, so she wouldn't be tempted to blow it. As the Prince said afterwards, "I don't know what I should have done if I hadn't had Giovanna."

The maid carried the letter to the shore, where boatmen by dozens were ever ready to sail to the ends of the earth for a ducat, but Giovanna had no money. She shewed them the writing on the outside of the packet and said that the Lord named there would pay on delivery. The ruder of the boatmen made uncouth noises at that, which threw the girl into a temper. She stamped and raged and threatened them with the Wrath of Holy God, because the missive had been written by His favorite Angel.

"O!" said one, brighter than his fellows. "I will take it, then. Why didn't you say so in the first place?"

The letter changed hands amidst the hoots of the skeptics, but that mariner knew what he was doing. Before the goggling eyes of the others he pushed his shallop out into the drink, set his sail and took the letter to Palermo. The rest of the sailors were dumfounded at the time, but you should have seen their faces when he came back, much later. I must not get ahead of myself, but let me say, that when that one boatman died—ripe in years— he was independently wealthy, on the fortune he founded by that voyage.

Encouraged by the successful launching of his first letter, the Prince gave Giovanna another, this one to be left in a certain bakeshop in Naples, whence it would find Artuso Pappacoda, the uncle of Ettore.

"You are the most wonderful Keeper of the Horn that Gabriel ever had!" Giovantonio praised his helper. "I never shall part with you!"—and to give his appreciation tangible form he gave her a child too, his second.

As the *femme de chambre* increased in girth, Taranto's hopes grew too, and the longer he lived with the notion of an Aragonese consort for Joan, the more attractive the prospect became. Confined with his dream, he doted upon it, and not only because of his sister's alliance with one of Aragon's richest subjects but even more for the disaster it would bring to the Great Serjianni.

Still, no replies came to either of the Prince's letters, and his gaolor-host increased the tension by staying away from his own palace. Serjianni was too much occupied with his machinations for the Queen's frustration ever to leave Castel Nuovo those days.

The Constable's choice for bridegroom had got as far as Venice under his own power and at his own expense, but there he waited for Serjianni to send galleys to fetch him the rest of the way, the cost to be defrayed by the Crown.

It was not the money but the delay that overturned Serjianni's digestion, and the longer he dwelt upon the threat of an Aragonese alliance the worse his heartburn tasted. He sent galleys to Jacques out of Manfredonia, and two days later was apprised by his spies that Joan II had slipped one over on him, herself sending a Doctor of Laws and a frater out of Gaeta, directly to Catalugna, to sign her marriage contract with Juan d'Aragon. Serjianni's rage was classic, picturesque, and—above all—active.

Both seas, then, supported rival wedding parties simultaneously. Somebody was going to be embarrassed.

"It will not be me," said the Constable, ungrammatical in his fury, and he strode into the Queen's apartments ready to enforce his will with the full power of both lungs, but Joan—anticipating this visit—had absented herself, and only Alopo was there, surrounded by a bodyguard sufficient to the defense of his person. That precaution was highly advisable when Alopo was at his Ministerial duties, because he created more enemies for the regime with every stroke of his pen.

"Where is Her Majesty?" the Constable growled, and the Seneschal snapped right back, "She is hiding from you."

"Hiding her guilty conscience. What do you know about this embassy to the Aragonese?"

"I say it is a lie."

"Do you tell me *I* lie?"

"I say that Your Highness has been lied to. The Queen has no guilt to hide—but goes in fear for her life—because you deprive her of any defense, turn all her friends against her or throw them in the keep."

"Sforza is a traitor!"

In sooth the charge which held Sforza was one of technical treason, in that he aspired—e'en plotted—to marry the Queen himself.

"Can you say *traitor* after putting Caldora up to his filthy tricks? The word should choke you," said Alopo, safe in the bosom of his bodyguard.

Nobody, until then, had accused Serjianni of complicity in Caldora's demands for Capua, and the charge as stated was baseless, but the Constable saw his own best advantage in permitting the suspicion to remain.

Caldora, unprompted by any adviser other than his own ambition, had given the Queen his reasons, in writing, why he should be invested Prince of Capua. His words were—for *the defense of the Regno and Your Majesty's Throne, for the purpose of punishing the presumption of the pretending Prince's mother, who dares to allege that her child was fathered by Your Majesty's former brother, the King.*

Although veiled thus in innuendo, that was a palpable threat, and so long as Joan and Alopo thought that Serjianni was party to it, they would not be granting Caldora the investiture and hence could not command his proffered arms in the Queen's defense. In a word, Her Majesty was helpless—in a military way—which was exactly what the Constable wanted.

"Where is the Queen?" the bully roared again. "Has she gone to the summer palace without *you?*"

Alopo shrugged in a supercilious way, more than ordinarily aggravating because his airs were so recently acquired, and returned his attention to the papers on his table without deigning to reply.

"O, thou impudent maggot," said the Constable, gaining better control of himself, "when I crush you I shall step so hard you will not even leave a grease spot." Then he turned a scornful back on the Seneschal and his staff of poltroons, and went to commence Queen Joan's humbling more in his wonted manner.

First, he sent express to his father-in-law in Capua, commanding him—rather—to be the first to greet Jacques Bourbon as King, and to lay his plea for the Capuan investiture in the lap of the new Majesty. Jacques's itinerary would land him at Manfredonia in ten days or so, and if Caldora captained the escort of honor across the Boot to Naples the pair could arrange between them for the disposal of the pretended bastard of Ladislaus.

Next, Serjiani ordered assembled a complete household staff adequate to attend Joan's needs in her villa—maids, cooks, grooms, waiters, pages, Major-domo and all—some drawn from Castel Nuovo, and some from his own palace, but all notably faithful to the Caracciolos.

Awaiting the arrival of this troop, the Constable dictated two letters in the Queen's best style, the one countermanding her instructions to the special Aragonese envoys, and calling them home, the other apologizing to the King of Aragon for any annoyance her abortive diplomacies had caused him.

"Affix your seals," he instructed the scrivener, "but we shall not sign them. Just bring your pens and ink-horn—and come with me."

The Queen was in her summer counting house, counting out some nameless yokel she had called in from the barn. On these occasions, unless the man was most extraordinary, when he was ushered out, the exit shown to him was always the roof. There a priest heard his last confession and he was required to jump. Time had been when Joan dictated this procedure for those of her common soldiers whom she pressed into boudoir service, but Serjianni had put a stop to that before she decimated the army. "You're at liberty to make Sforza jump, and I'll help you," the Constable had said at that time, "but no more enlisted men. By God, if you're going to be Queen of Rome you've got to save enough infantry to hold it."

Arriving this day at the villa, a more sensitive man must have been touched by Joan's wishful gesture toward her own defense. At the gate, the Constable's way was barred—for the length of time consumed by one wave of his hand—by ten or twelve of the Palace Guard, of which company Serjianni was titular Commander. So that, the invasion was accomplished without loss of sweat or blood, and while the Strong Man berated and lambasted Joan in the parlor, the new staff pushed the old out of the house.

Only two of the Queen's Ladies had the strength to push back, the one, Covella nee Ruffo, wife of Marzano Duke Sessa, the other, Caterinella Alopo, the Seneschal's sister. The Alopo girl could not have defended herself, but Covella weighed nearly three hundred pounds, every pound well-born, so domestics durst not touch her. She picked up the younger, more normal woman under her arm and practically carried her as far as the door of the Queen's parlor. Voices came through very distinctly.

"Don't you call me a bitch!" screeched the royal bitch. "I will not marry any damned Bourbon flunky of yours. He is a frog!—and you are a toad! You just wait until I tell Alopo what you called me."

"Unless you do what I tell you," Serjianni returned, "you will never see Alopo again. Sign these letters."

Joan read the screed of apology to King Ferdinand of Aragon only to the point where she was represented as excusing herself by saying that Prince Juan was too young at 18 to marry a woman of 47.

"Why, damn your soul," the beldame cursed, "that's why I want him. You just don't want me to have a child. You want to keep everything topsy-turvy here so you can use the Crown for a football."

"You may have as many children as you like by Jacques Bourbon."

"So that *you* can go on bullying me—and them. I will not do it. Jacques Bourbon shall not touch me."

The Queen's rising anguish was too much for the Duchess of Sessa to bear. She was no more afraid of the Strong Man than of the little peas you ate this morning, and she had sent him about his business more than once before this when he had abused Joan. In fact, an old feud between Covella and Serjianni's mother still festered in the folds of the Ruffo woman's flesh, and she welcomed every opportunity to denounce her enemy's son. Setting the mountains of her weight arolling, the Duchess bore down upon the Constable's guard like an avalanche picking up a kerchief, and would have gone through the door whether it opened or not. By good luck it did open just in time to avoid being torn from the hinges, and Caterinella Alopo was sucked along into Joan's presence by the Ruffo after-draught.

"Get out, you blood-sweating Behemoth!" the gallant Serjianni bawled. "This doesn't concern you. Nothing concerns you. You are fit only for elephants!"

"You are fit only to sweep up after elephants!" the Duchess retaliated. "Stop abusing my baby!"

"Get out of this room," Serjianni foamed, in a rictus of rage. "Get out or I'll have you thrown out!"—a palpably impossible threat.

Caterinella Alopo had her arms around Joan who took as much comfort from that as if the girl had been the Seneschal. Thus defended, the Queen appealed to her Constable's higher nature, choking out each word. "Why do you hate me so?"

"Why do *you* hate *me?*" the Constable countered.

"I do not hate you. I love you. I want you. I have always wanted you—but you have struck me—and would again. You are the cruelest man I have ever known."

The eyes of all three women underlined that charge with burning shafts of accusation.

"Send those two away," the Caracciolo commanded.

"I will not!" said the Queen, and there they were, the irresistible force and the immovable object.

An immensely exaggerated symbolic significance attached to the act-of-kind in the contest between this unquenchable female and the man who held her in complete contempt. Joan's fierce desire, in this one instance, was a more powerful urge than lust. It had become the paramount necessity of her existence to bend his mighty will to her own in that one most personal particular. Serjianni was only vaguely aware of that lashing insistence driving her from within, but a corollary symbolism strengthened his resistance out of all proportion to the importance of the deed. This Superba was not repulsive, as Junoesque women go, nor even through the eyes of Caracciolo's prejudice was her way of life so loathsome that it could account for his inveterate aversion. More times than he cared to remember, continued resistance to her onslaughts had not seemed worth the effort, but the cumulative effect of his repeated victories had been to imbue the mundane, commonplace struggle with a mystical connotation not unlike the shearing of Samson's hair. Serjianni, at the time of writing, was utterly convinced that he must sustain the struggle, for if he ever succumbed to her he would lose everything, tangibles and intangibles. Verily, Serjianni knew that if—by any means—Joan ever got his drawers off, he would drop so low in his own esteem that he would elect to exit by the roof, like an enlisted man or a swineherd.

"Let them watch us," Joan said huskily. "Let Covella and Caterinella watch you plant your seed in me—and I'll sign your letter."

Serjianni shook his head. "I'd rather forge your name," he said.

"I'll have your head for it," the Queen flared.

"Then who will do your thinking for you? Take my head and you will be swept off the Throne like a fly."

"Send Alopo to me."

"Sign."

"Will you send him—if I sign? Will you free Sforza?"

"Free Sforza?—so you can marry *him?*"

"I never would marry that peasant. I am giving him Caterinella."

The Alopo girl thrust out her breasts in a gesture half defiance, half pride. *This,* she seemed to say, *is what Sforza is getting.* For good measure, then, she stuck out her tongue at Serjianni, and entirely within himself he conceded that it made a nice package. Nor was Serjianni averse to the match. It had the advantage of estopping Joan from marrying the great Commander, but these three women were no more to be trusted than Sforza, and—once he was released—where was the assurance that the Queen would not take her Lady's place at the altar? "Marry Caterinella to Sforza *in prison,*" the Constable offered, "and I will let him out."

"Agreed!" Joan snapped. "Take her with you now. See them married—and send them back to me."

"Sign first," Serjianni insisted, extending a dripping pen, but Caterinella Alopo struck it to the floor, sobbing, "*Not* in prison. I will not be married in prison!" They were some time in getting her quiet.

With utter bad faith on both sides, a solution agreeable to all was not worked out in an hour, but as evening approached Serjianni made concessions rather than risk remaining overnight. He agreed to present their proposals to Attendola Sforza for signature in his cell. If he signed, in the presence of Churchmen of Serjianni's choosing, the Constable agreed to loose him for a proper wedding in the Cathedral.

Joan, for her part, agreed to set her name to the recall of the Aragonese envoys when she had in hand the contract signed by Sforza. To tempt the *Condottiere*—and to make Serjianni boil—the Queen assigned the taxing of Manfredonia and several small pieces to Caterinella for her marriage portion.

On those terms, and on a schedule indecently speeded by the Constable's urgent necessity, Sforza got a shapely young wife, but Serjianni saw to it that no money was paid over, no revenues from Manfredonia, and he kept the bridegroom so bobtailed as to armed men that Sforza could not take possession of any of his new titles. What honeymoon the couple had was spent in a hill village which Ladislaus had given to Sforza's eldest bastard on his twelfth birthday, and there they would have stayed the rest of their lives if Serjianni had his way.

In retaliation Joan decreed the Constable's baton forfeit to Sforza, and commanded Caracciolo to deliver it up, but Serjianni paid no more attention to the command than to the decree, and vice versa.

The only way to distinguish between Serjianni and God, for the moment, is by reference to the Constable's father-in-law, that tight little Caldora with his trim black beard. Even he obeyed Serjianni in the letter of his orders received, but he concealed something from the Strong Man at the same time. God was watching, however.

As directed, Count Aversa set out to meet Jacques Bourbon, but since the Principality of Capua had not yet been assured to him, and he could not rely upon the generosity of the Barbarian newcomer, he took characteristically independent means to safeguard his future. He carried the child-Prince of Capua right along with him, as far as Foggia. Only a few of Caldora's retinue were aware who the little boy was, and nobody in Naples—certainly no one at Court—was aware of the transfer. The gentlefolk in Foggia who took in the youngster for rearing were given to understand that he was a bastard of Caldora's.

So much arranged neatly, the schemer who fancied he had one or more advantages over all factions, including the Constable's, proceeded to Manfredonia, and there he greeted

Jacques Bourbon as "Majesty", bent the knee, kissed the hand, and asked to be made Prince of Capua. The request was taken under advisement, just as Caldora had feared it would be, and the quasi-royal procession started for Naples.

Couriers kept Serjianni informed of the party's progress as he worked against time to obtain Joan's consent to marry Jacques immediately he arrived, but the professional gamblers of Naples would give no better than even money on an issue so nip and tuck. Serjianni's tactic was cruelly coercive. Joan had not seen a man in a week. Even male domestics were supplanted by women, and the females obeyed Her Majesty only at their own whim. Alopo was no help to her. Although in nominal command of Castel Nuovo since the Constable's demotion, the Seneschal's authority was completely flouted and even his own sleeping quarters were virtually under siege. The Queen's sole companion, comfort and source of strength was the great hulking Covella Duchess of Sessa, but between them those two generated a perfectly fabulous fortitude, and, at the last, Serjianni saw that they must be separated or Jacques Bourbon would have had his journey in vain.

Thorny and onerous, the duty fell to Marzano Duke Sessa to go to the villa and bring away his wife. "Are you not her Lord and master?" Serjianni inquired, not without bitter humor.

"I am her Lord," Marzano conceded, "but Covella's master has still to be found. Is Your Highness recommending that my Duchess be brought away by force?" Sessa was no weakling, but an able General, currently commanding the largest body of Neapolitan arms, but the strategies of domestic warfare were too subtle for him.

"No scandal!" said Serjianni. "Persuasion, yes, but no physical violence. The new Pope might say that we had forced this marriage upon Her Majesty."

Hampered so, Sessa's sortie upon the villa accomplished less than nothing. Covella and Joan doused him with slops and pelted him with tiles from the roof, to say nothing of their curses, refusing even to parly until the Queen's sovereign dignity should be restored.

Sessa came back to the city with the novel theory that a little more lenience was indicated rather than any more stringency. "Joan would marry the Devil to please you if you'd get into bed with her—just once."

"Never!" said the Strong Man, and he ordered all the candles removed from the Queen's villa.

Apparently, going taperless was harder to bear than any previous restriction, because that brought a plea for truce. Joan was ready to talk business.

Elated, Serjianni sent word to his Archbishop to bring the marriage contract to the villa. Jacques Bourbon was only two days away. The Queen's signature would hardly be dry before she must stand at the altar. Victory seemed within his grasp, and the Constable, gloating to Duke Sessa, waved an expansive, gracious hand. "Send your men out to catch three sailors and an acrobat for Her Majesty. We'll take them along as a peace offering, eh?"

The chase after conscripts—who soon learned what they were wanted for, and scattered everywhere, spreading the warning to the able-bodied—made such a stir that bruit of the Queen's capitulation penetrated even to Alopo. He could not but take it glumly; his string was running out, but one fair chance remained for him to catch the end of it. Was he not now brother-in-law to the world's greatest fighting man, Sforza? Together they could make a very strong case for presentation to Jacques Bourbon. Between them they commanded the royal residence in Naples and the city of Rome, not to mention the Queen's good will, which Serjianni never could buy with a gift of seamen and tumblers.

Disguising himself and a few of his faithful, Alopo waited until Serjianni was on the road to see Joan, then he slipped off to Sforza's honeymoon bower in the hills to pick up his new brother-in-law and intercept Jacques Bourbon with a recital of their merits as allies.

Unfortunately, for them, they had not many soldiers at the moment, and they made the mistake of underestimating Caldora, who had a great plenty, and who had the advantage of several days of conversation with Bourbon before they got to him.

Alopo and Sforza presented themselves as the grand procession moved out of Benevento on the last leg of its march, and they committed their second great blunder the moment they opened their low-born mouths. They addressed Jacques Bourbon as "Highness", merely, as Count of Marche, instead of as "Majesty", King of the Regno. Steel was drawn, and the two were in chains before you could have said *paternoster.*

The Pretender was not quite a fool, you see, and this was his most sensitive point. He assumed the position that he came to the Throne of the Regno by right of inheritance rather than by marriage to Joan, and every outward show of homage was required to give that dream substance. The marriage was agreeable, perhaps even necessary, but by playing his blood-line straight Bourbon made himself less beholden to Caracciolo for his elevation.

Caldora had communicated Bourbon's kingly conceit to Serjianni so that he could marshal his diplomatical rebuttals, but a further quirk of Bourbon's, in the same vein, had not appeared in those crisp despatches. The first persons Jacques Bourbon had asked after by name when he landed at Manfredonia were the former Queen Marie-Luise and her son the Prince of Taranto, his beloved cousins, but Caldora had neglected to warn Serjianni of that portentous affection. This neglect was no oversight, nor stupidity neither, nor yet a mark of friendliness toward Taranto, but purely and simply a calculated attempt to weaken the Constable's position the while Caldora strengthened his own.

At town after town along their way the sleek little double-dealer, playing both ends against the middle, professed the greatest astonishment that Taranto was not among the greeting party, but an incident in the capture of Alopo and Sforza caused Caldora to face up to the impending consequences of his actions, and his past temerity began to frighten himself.

In the scuffle to make the two men prisoners, along with their meager retinues, only the redoubtable Attendola Sforza had dared to draw in his own defense. Alopo had dropped on all fours, surrendering to circumstance: and the merest accident had prevented Milord Aversa from being the hero of the occasion. Not Caldora but one of his Captains—one Giulio-Cesaro di Capua—had the honor of disarming Sforza, and for that Jacques Bourbon bade the man dine at the royal table.

In Caldora's view, as the officer's employer and master, the net of this achievement should have brought himself the investiture with Capua out of the new sovereign's spontaneous gratitude, and the fact that it did not shewed only too clearly that all his boot-licking across the country had failed to endear him to Bourbon. On the other hand, these events would be reported to Joan, eventually, and she would not follow this Barbarian's lead in singling out a mere Captain for her (negative) attention. The onus for this affront to Alopo would be laid, entire, upon Caldora's head—and there went the taxing of Capua, out the window.

Only one day from Naples—only one day from an accounting with his irascible son-in-law—Caldora decided, belatedly, that he had better keep peace in the family if he could. Accordingly, the courier who carried news of the grand capture into town carried, likewise, the brief intimation that Jacques Bourbon was expecting to find his blood-kin in good health and the best of spirits.

A fine time to worry Serjianni about the state of Taranto's *spirits!* Ten thousand details of the reception already had Caracciolo on the jump, and if Joan Superba found out what had happened to her darling Alopo, the work of a full year would be to do over again. The secret would not keep long. Naples was already drunk and delirious in honor of Bourbon's coming, and when the masses heard that the Barbarian was bringing them Alopo the Seneschal, trussed and ready for the spit, their rejoicing laughter spiraled up toward Heaven higher than Vesuvius' plume. Pressed as he was, Serjianni could not go himself to make peace with his prisoner, but he spared his secretary Antonio for that office and primed him what to say. "My compliments to the Prince. The tower is opening even sooner than I promised. Remind His Highness of our agreement. His family was not to be released until Joan was married—but I wish to be generous. I will not even wait for Bourbon to get here.

"Assure him—reassure him—that his mother, sisters, brother—and his own child and its mother too—are all on their way to him, as quickly as they can be moved. Let him prepare to receive them.

"Blame the Queen. Say that I had to get her consent. Will he believe that?"

"I shall swear to it—on Your Highness' word of honor," said Antonio bravely.

"Better swear on the Crucifix—if you must swear," Serjianni advised. "The Prince may not have a very high opinion of my honor."

Bourbon's party was expected before nightfall, and an hour was appointed early next day for a private audience—just for the Prince and the former Queen Marie-Luise—and places the most honorable at the royal nuptials were being reserved for them as the new King's nearest of kin.

To polish off this miracle of reformation Serjianni added his regrets at being unable to attend Taranto's family reunion. His palace was theirs, however, and everything in it, to be regarded as their home as long as they would stay. The household staff was to be so instructed.

Antonio, the one-time captor of the Prince, became more and more nervous as he emptied this cornucopia under Taranto's steady gaze. The role of fairy godmother was new to the cut-throat, and each gift he poured tended to restore the normal contrast between their stature and status. As the Prince was freed, his former strength flowed back into his person like wine into a jug, but the tongue that conveyed his freedom faltered and halted, its owner drained of the little borrowed power the captivity had lent him, so that when Giovantonio said—without smiling—"Bring me my arms"—Antonio flung himself on the floor, crying, "Mercy! Highness! I never harmed you. Mercy! I was always your man."

"Get up," said the Prince. "I'm not going to kill you. Get my sword—so I'll know I am free."

"You are free, Highness." The varlet bounced to his feet. "You are free—and I am your man. Command me! I give you my soul."

"Just a sword," said Taranto. "Your soul wouldn't cut curds."

The alarmed man was no coward, and his protestations of devotion were not all gas, as witness, that instead of leaving the palace then, at a gallop, as he easily could have done, he came back with a sword and something in dagger form which he presented to the Prince. They were not Giovantonio's instruments, but they had points and edges, and, when they were buckled on, Taranto's chest expanded a full handsbreadth. "A man without a sword is only half alive," he said. "Now tell me what this means.

What has frightened Milord Melfi?" By employing Serjianni's lesser title the stature of the one-time Constable was further reduced, even in the eyes of his own retainer.

Still Antonio would not call Serjianni "frightened", but only more eager than usual to assure himself strong friends, and the bravo went on to give the Prince as full an account of events then forward as his penetration enabled. Perhaps the biggest surprise Duke Melfi had received in connection with the outlander's arrival was the numerousness of his train. Jacques Bourbon was reported by Count Aversa to have brought along a complete Bedchamber and Council of French-speaking nobles from Marche, Castres, Luxemburg, France and Lorraine, no less than fifty such, all out-at-heels but nonetheless set upon taking over the governance of the Regno in fact. "Milord Aversa provided them with whores at every stop along the way, but the French would rather talk business!" Antonio made that incredible point with a gesture comprehending the hopelessness of dealing with such people. "All they care about is incomes, taxable counties, and our order of precedence."

Slily the Prince said, "So? I am beginning to understand. Serjianni means to make me Seneschal—to rid himself of these headaches."

"Your Highness' Lord Cousin will have brought his own Seneschal—if I understand Count Aversa's despatches—but Your Highness knows so much better than I."

"On the contrary, I know nothing," said the Prince, very wary of a trap but trying all he could to catch the other's drift.

"My master looks to Your Highness' cabal for assistance."

"I have pledged it to him." Taranto bit off the resentment consequent upon that pledge, lest he say too much, but Antonio was wagging his head. "The assistance may be needed against your Lord Cousin the King, and especially if Her Majesty Queen

Joan learns—before her wedding—that Alopo and Sforza are in the donjon of San Vincenzo."

"I am flattered," the Prince said sharply, frowning hard upon the secretary's swarthy features. "Until Serjianni sent you here today, he has been treating me as if my assistance were beneath contempt. Now that he sees trouble ahead he wishes to use me and my mother for pawns. My compliments to His Highness, but he never shall learn what side I am on by a trick so crude."

For a moment Antonio looked as if would weep. "My master does not know I am saying these things. If he finds out, I am a dead man. I mean only to warn Your Lordship. My master has had private dealings with Messer Artuso Pappacoda—for the support of your cabal without Your Highness. What shall I do to convince you?"

Not a trace of emotion stirred any feature of Taranto's attentive face, for he was not yet ready to trust this vis-a-vis despite his apparent candor, but the revelation of a communion betwixt Serjianni and the elder Pappacoda could explain why the letter, left so long in that certain bakeshop, had not been picked up. It could explain why no reply ever had been returned from Chiaramonte in Palermo, why none of Giovantonio's comrades or *cousins and brothers* had been able to find him or to communicate all these dreary months.

No bitterness or condemnation of anyone entered the Prince's pondering, but rather a sense of relief. Artuso Pappacoda was the bridge in Naples over which all elements of the cabal must pass, and if Serjianni blocked that bridge, or blew it up, or kept it so well guarded that none durst approach, then nothing but silence was to be expected, and the very quiet was a testimonial to the conspirators' good sense.

Whether the silence meant that Serjianni had won over Pappacoda could not be determined indoors, and not from the speech of Antonio either, with any certainty. The gambit here was to put the man off—but without offending him—until the broad light of a clearer day could penetrate these confusions.

"The friendship between the Caracciolos and the Pappacodas has not been broken for many generations," said Taranto evenly. "I should be greatly surprised if either Bourbon or myself could come between them."

"As Your Lordship pleases," said Antonio lowering his head. "I meant no harm."

Illumination had gone no deeper than that, and no arrangement had been entered into between the Prince and the traitorous daggerman for the transfer of future intelligence, when the liberated prisoners arrived, and in the hurly-burly of greeting, Antonio disappeared.

Not just once but a score of times Giovantonio's entire family rushed into a mass embrace, a tangle of arms and legs, a nuzzling puzzle of smacking mouths and a very river of joyous tears.

Daylight was failing as the party came in but Marie's features were recognized by some watchers outside and her name was added to the songs of the populace celebrating Alopo's downfall. In the once forbidden streets surrounding the Caracciolo palace the old restraints and restrictions had quite collapsed under pressure of the jubilation. Fickle Naples—with wonted perversity—was singing, dancing and lighting red fire because one of its lowliest sons, who had ascended the heights, was now tumbled down and superseded by an ultramontane they never before had seen or heard of. Where else on Earth is novelty and innovation so greatly loved for its own sake? The canaille who had known Alopo as a boy, as one of themselves, formed a frolicsome serpentine, chanting the praises of Serjianni for putting their upstart brother into a donjon cell.

More restrained as to exuberance, but no less exultant inwardly, Tomaso, Riccardo, Erri and Quito—also reunited—stood in that same street, where their master had been so long confined, and with them were two well-born, Duke Andria, come incog from Rome, and Artuso Pappacoda. Between them, these six commanded about ninety men, dispersed along the approaches to the palace, loitering, at ease, but heavily armed.

The bakeshop letter, so long neglected, had been retrieved just five days before, on the same day—in fact—that Jacques Bourbon landed and met Caldora in Manfredonia. Its contents was utterly outmoded by the fact of Cousin Jacques's arrival, but its salubrious service was to confirm the suspicion that Giovantonio was alive on the other side of the Constable's walls. To a man—except for the sage Pappacoda—when they read that letter, the rest were for a frontal attack upon the Melfi palace gates instanter, but Artuso's intimacy with Serjianni's affairs—not to say, troubles, and mounting—gave his advice the prestige needed to hold the others back from day to day.

The motley composition of the miniature army—gathered from four quarters, and a few at a time—had preserved it from special notice. Practically every Baron of the Regno was in town to greet Bourbon, each with his suite, escort or guard, of from ten to fifty fighting men. Nobody heeded the twenty Tarantines, twenty Nolans, thirty Andrians, and Pappacoda's smaller company. Nobody observed that their fraternization was quieter or more purposeful than that of other very similar groups.

Hay had been made, as a matter of fact, among the other Barons, since the baby-faced Del Balzo and Artuso got together, and if they had elected to storm the palace, the nucleus of the cabal's force could have tripled itself magically by accretion of new allies.

"One of us must go inside," Andria insisted for perhaps the fifth time since Antonio had come out. "Giovantonio must be told we are here. It will change all his plans. He thinks he is helpless. He is far from helpless. By God, we could take the city."

Perhaps the Duke's enthusiasm exaggerated their strength a little: after all, at least twenty members of the Caracciolo family were scattered here and there about town: but the picture was very pretty. Only one stone wall was keeping Taranto unaware of this power assembled to his need and awaiting his command, and Pappacoda could pass through that wall at will.

"I shall go in soon," Artuso promised.

"You have been saying that for five days," Del Balzo expostulated. "Soon! Soon! I could milk an ax sooner!"

"If we had attacked five days ago—Queen Marie-Luise would still be in the tower," Pappacoda said calmly. He was twice the age of Duke Andria and thus more accustomed to waiting for the blunders of more impetuous men to determine his course for him, but the natural impatience of young Del Balzo would no longer be denied. To his mind the future of the cabal never before had been so bright, and the music in the streets, the celebration, could well have been for the conspirators. Its stridency, rising in volume and rhythm, exactly matched Andria's fever and paced his coursing blood. Finger by finger he marshaled his reasons for immediate council of War with the Prince.

"We have a letter from Chiaramonte." Tomaso had the mariner in tow. "Would you have Serjianni come home before Giovantonio has read that letter?"

"Serjianni will not be home this night." Artuso was certain of that. "If the French won't have the women he's provided, they will keep him talking until daybreak."

"They may send for the Prince."

"They may."

"Before Giovantonio speaks with Bourbon he must know that Cardinal Colonna has offered him one of his daughters to wife."

"I have not seen that letter," said Pappacoda.

"You have not seen it because it is in Erri's head—committed by rote—and if Erri drinks another bottle he will forget it—or jumble it up. If I drink another half-bottle I'll forget how I planned to take Rome. Will you not be reasonable? Aunt Marie would not be in there if we were suspected. Go in, Artuso! You will meet no resistance."

Whether by this logic or the pounding of the drums, or the sentries getting drunker than Andria by the moment, Pappacoda was persuaded. "I will go in at midnight," he decided.

"Go now—or I will," the Del Balzo insisted.

"No," said Artuso. "Now they are kissing. Let them finish kissing—then I will go in."

MR. THAYER INTRUDES

LET US HOPE I am not going to make a habit of this, but you may skip these interruptions if you wish. The kissing and killing go right on without me.

What strikes at least this one modern reader at this point is the contrast between *summits* then and now. In a day so authority ridden as the present, when every breath we draw is dictated by some well-intrenched vested power, imposed or delegated, it is difficult to adjust the mind's eye to the glare of the absolute freedom reflected in these pages. A continuous effort is required to keep alive the realization that, on these upper levels, where the principals of this narrative moved, one had no appeal from the willful acts of others, however frustrating or painful. They had

Law enough—and to spare—for controlling the lower orders, but in the sense that I am remarking, even petty tradesmen had better sources of redress—in civil courts, however corrupt—than their so-called sovereigns.

Not to spread these cogitations too thinly, Joan's predicament is an example. What could be emptier than her assumed title of Queen if she could not choose her own consort?—and she could not. She was completely dependent upon the whims, jealousies and greeds of her Ministers, Barons and Courtiers, or upon the same qualities in her contemporary fellow monarchs, almost all of whom were as hard put to it as she was to keep themselves on their hotseats. Just nowhere on Earth was there authority capable of maintaining itself in an administrative capacity over any territory larger than a village.

Joan's own expressed preference for an Aragonese Prince for a mate is probably the most politic move she made in her life, but—because it would have made her independent of him—Serjianni frustrated her aim. Perhaps she could have appealed to Mother Church, over her Constable's head, if God's House had been in order, but under prevailing circumstances she had nowhere to turn.

The world as we know it today was not yet born. *Catalugna* was the common designation for the entire Hispanic peninsula, that is, *Iberia,* or what we know as Spain and Portugal. Strictly speaking, *Catalugna* was the single province on that east coast, of which Barcelona was the capital, but the name applied—by extension—to the then independent States of Aragon, Castile, Leon, Valencia and all the rest, collectively.

"France" and "Germany"—as such—did not exist any more than did *Italy* or *Spain.* You noticed that Jacques Bourbon's train of office-seekers came from Marche, Castres, Luxemburg, France and Lorraine, all almost equally independent States, as were Anjou and Provence, Bretagne, and—especially—Burgundy. "France" was but the lie, hardly more than Paris and environs, and although these lesser Lords had their titles from the King of France, allegiance was of the loosest, and the Duke of Burgundy pretended to even fuller independence by honoring the Holy Roman Emperor as his suzerain.

What we call *Germany* (East and West) was then the Holy Roman Empire, a sad and vestigial remnant of what it had been. The "Emperor" was no more than Kaiser of a single Germanic province, a poverty-stricken eleventh or less among his fellow Princes, but he still clung to the prestige of certain Ghibelline traditions which his friends found useful in their Wars with each other for pitting against the Popes. Not only in Burgundy but south of the Alps too—in Milan, Mirandola, Mantua and Ferrara—the Emperor reserved the privilege of allotting the crowns or coronets, and the Houses in possession of those places generally conceded him the right, the while they sniggered at his patched pants.

As a court of appeal for Joan, however, the Emperor was quite useless—and England did not amount to a hill of beans.

We are not informed by the text what the attitude of Louis II d'Anjou may have been toward Serjianni's selection of his cousin Jacques Bourbon to reign with Joan, but I don't think Louis liked that much. One of the Popes had "Crowned" Louis II King of the Two Sicilies just before the turn of the century, and he clung to the title as long as he lived.

Probably the arrangements for Bourbon's sortie into the Regno were made behind Louis's back. He was a pretty busy man, what with trying to Elect a French Pope at Constance and to keep the Curia at Avignon, between whiles governing Paris, fending off the Duke of Burgundy's unremitting efforts to snatch away the imbecile King Charles VI, and raising arms to send against the British in Normandy.

Undoubtedly Serjianni's eagerness to have Bourbon's marriage consummated speedily and without scandal was as much to have it over, *fait accompli,* before a new Pope was Elected and before Louis II found the leisure to object, as for any reasons nearer home.

One marvels, too, at the long-sustained faith these highly intelligent people felt for the institution of marriage as a reliable political instrument. Theoretically, once a marital knot was tied between Houses, the two families became one, and the weal of either was the weal of both, but the failure of that spiritual cement to hold was a common daily occurrence. Statistics are not available, but I venture that the troth failed of this purpose as often as it succeeded, and still they persisted—against all reason—in trusting vast weights to a bond so frail.

You see the folly of such reliance at its most flagrant in the relations of Serjianni and the elder Caldora. Just because Serjianni had taken one of Caldora's daughters for wife, the Strong Man assumed the loyalty of the other, a fellow who grew a beard because he durst not trust his hand with a razor near his own throat, much less the hand of a barber.

I have the advantage of knowing the Caldora story to the end, but even at this juncture I should think it would have been obvious to a politician of Serjianni's keenness that his father-in-law was in fact his rival for place under Bourbon's rule, and that nothing but the accident of Alopo's capture had caused Caldora to reveal the newcomer's overweening fondness for the former Queen and her son.

Verily, as Villon is wont to say, if Alopo and Sforza had not stumbled into captivity, Serjianni would have remained unwarned, and Caldora would have denounced him roundly— but secretly—to "King" Jacques.

This is stated in full knowledge that the Caldoras—son and father—had previously dealt with Louis II d'Anjou for his accession in the Regno. The point is that Louis II was too busy to come and Jacques Bourbon was already there. The Caldoras were nothing if not expedient.

CHAPTER SEVEN

B ETWEEN KISSES, inside the palace, the Lady Maria caused baby Maria to show Daddy how she could talk. Giovantonio enjoyed that, but could not make out one word until the women translated for him. "*Mon papa* is Lord Highness the Prince of Taranto by the Will and Grace of God." Once he knew what was being said Giovantonio understood it very well.

What the others said was of no moment. They were free. They thanked God for it, and they looked to Giovantonio for instruction how to begin the new life. No other family ever had been so blest in its head, its eldest son and brother, as theirs. They idolized him and vied for his glances and caresses.

Wryly ironical, the Prince informed his mother of their scheduled private Audience. "We shall be told where to stand— and which way to walk—at the wedding and at the Coronation. Serjianni is trying to rush Joan through both ceremonies before she finds out that Alopo and Sforza have been locked up, but you and I shall not stay for either function."

Not stay? The younger heads clustered close as the Prince continued, quietly, to his mother. "You and I will hear them out, tomorrow, and pretend to agree to everything, but while we are at our Audience, Caterina and Maria will pack up here and get ready to ride for it—swiftly—the instant the Audience is over. We shall not sleep here tomorrow night. You, Gabriel, will see to the saddling. The *femme de chambre*, Giovanna, will help you. She is with child by me and will ride with us."

Gabriel—only 12—swelled with importance. If the Lady Maria was less pleased to learn, in this offhand way, about her low-born rival, she gave no sign.

"We'll ride directly to Nola," the Prince continued. "We can get there before anybody knows we are gone. Nola is garrisoned against Joan's confiscation, but I have the password. You will be safe there—while I raise an army and find out what my cousins have been doing. We'll see which way the frog has jumped by that time."

Marie-Luise took her son's hand in prideful compliance. "We shall do exactly as you say. You are Taranto now. Your father would be proud of you."

Only the sisters Princesses Caterina and Maria let their disappointment show. They had been dancing with each other for a year, and had been looking forward to the wedding and Coronation balls as a welcome break in the monotony of that. Princess Maria sighed, that she was not even betrothed, and those ballrooms would be full of potential husbands. Princess Caterina took her sister's part, saying that to run away would be an affront to Cousin Jacques. "He will take offense and refuse to pay my dot—and *you* will have to take it out of your own purse."

Big brother put an arm around each of the girls and assured them they should have dancing enough under happier auspices. As for offending their cousin, a fig for that, because Serjianni, restored as Constable, would be doing Jacques's reigning for him, and if Caterina's marriage portion were not forthcoming out of the Royal Exchequer, Jacques and Joan might whistle for the Crown itself, which was hidden safely in Taranto. "As for *your* bethrothal," the Prince went on, kissing the Princess Maria's nose, "how would you like to marry your cousin Guglielmo and be Duchess of Andria?"

"I'd *love* it!" the child exploded.

"That's just what *he* said when I asked him," Taranto beamed. "So that's all settled. Guglielmo is in Rome now—"

Cousins and brothers! If the speaker had looked out the window at that moment he could have seen the top of Andria's head as the Duke pushed Pappacoda across the street toward the door.

Under the new dispensation a butler announced his caller to the Prince, and that started up the clappings and kissings all over again, to Pappacoda's vast embarrassment. The mouth, by his lights, was for eating and speaking—an occasional tipple and sometimes to spit with—but this rubbing of it, one against another, was a silliness suitable only for retarded children. No matter, they kissed him anyway, and when they found out Guglielmo was near, he was sent for to absorb what Artuso did not want, which the Del Balzo did with profoundest relish.

Tomaso and the waterman were called in then, and Riccardo, Erri and Quito. They all knelt to their Queen, but were pulled quickly up by the Prince who must feel if their bones were still whole—and then he counted noses.

"Where is Aloys?" No more natural question.

The four veterans looked this way and that, but finally at Tomaso. "In Holy ground," said the soldier. "The Constable's Guards threw him into the Bay—too much hurt to swim."

"That day!" Taranto recalled. "The day I was taken."

The comrades nodded. That was the day.

Account for it as you will, that casual disposal of a tow-haired page, an outlander of no lineage, was Serjianni's blackest crime to date, in the record kept within Taranto's breast. Nothing else that Caracciolo had done to the Prince—not the assault upon his person, the overlong delay in freeing Marie-Luise, nothing, ever—had bitten so deeply or ached so hard or raised such venomous bile.

The youth's teeth clenched against an anguished blasphemy that would have shocked a marble image, and in that moment the Constable's gesture toward better relations was obliterated from Del Balzo-Orsini memory.

"That is all," Taranto finally said, hardly louder than a whisper, and he smiled into Tomaso's eyes. "That is all," a singularly worded pledge. "How many are we?" asked the Prince.

Pappacoda said, "Ninety—but up to three hundred—if so many are needed."

"Bring in only enough to loot this place—and wedge the gates—and hold the stable—so that we can leave at any time. When we go—we'll put a torch to it."

Andria had been whispering in the Princess Maria's ear, but he heard the word *torch,* and came out of the clouds for more mundane business.

The low-born four were ready to begin the looting without any other assistance, but Pappacoda demurred. He was under obligation to Caracciolo—"And so is my nephew Ettore. Neither he nor I would be alive today—I should not have a *denaro*—but for Serjianni. I am Your Highness' man in politics, and if that must make me an enemy of Serjianni, I am ready to fight him. But looting and torching—merely for revenge—without any clear advantage—will do our cause a vast injury. It would be a premature declaration of War. It would drive Barons from Your Highness into the Constable's camp. We are not ready for burning yet, Highness, if I may be so bold."

As the Prince heard the older man's conservative protest, he could not fail to recall the warning of the bravo-secretary Antonio, and that tarnished Artuso's sincerity a little. Sooth, what is the test of a man's words, whether they say what is in his heart? No touchstone appearing, Giovantonio took heed that as long as one Pappacoda was in possession of the citadel of

Taranto the time was not ripe to alienate that family. Softly and slowly was the watchword here. Vengeance must wait upon expediency. "No burning," he agreed, "and no looting—until I have Caterina's dower." The afterthought, delivered with unnecessary force, brought no protest from Artuso but only a broad grin of approval. "You will get that," he assured the Prince.

"There's nothing here worth stealing anyway," sneered Del Balzo, looking around the crudely furnished room, barren of art or adornment. "What does Serjianni do with his money?—bury it *all* in Avellino?"

Taking that opportunity, Giovantonio rehearsed the terms of the Avellino "agreement", which Andria heard with a mock-judicial air, and pronounced quite satisfactory. "I like to get money in *chunks*," said he, "and none of this knocking from door to door, *and will you be pleased to pay your hearth tax?*"

The Princess Maria laughed a good deal more than the jest was worth, a failing of little girls in love, but the mood of the entire company was exuberant. If not that night, when, then?

The letter from Palermo was produced, and the mariner rewarded. "Let us see what Tristano has to say," said the Prince, unfolding the parchment with a flourish, but before he had read the first page he regretted the mixed nature and the numbers of his council.

An overweighty problem was posed here, a problem in personal policy requiring the deepest consideration and not to be shared with soldiers, chits, or persons who felt obligation to Caracciolo.

The Prince broke off his reading abruptly and excused himself to visit the close-stool, going quite alone, not taking Guglielmo or even his mother with him. Marie-Luise was not good at puzzles to begin with, and this one required a seer.

Leaving out the sympathy, and the compliments, which were sincere and abundant, the Chiaramonte letter made plain that the writer was not backing Cardinal Oddo Colonna for Pope, and as the Prince lowered his drawers the look of it was that he could not accept the proffer of a Colonna bride and keep the Sicilian money-man as an ally too.

Which, then, should he choose?

Chiaramonte was all affection for the Aragonese rule in Island Sicily: persons of quality—like himself—had never had it so good: and the King of Aragon had his own Pope, styled Benedict XIII, whom he meant to keep no matter what decision was taken by the Council at Constance. To show what *he* thought of their Council at Constance, Ferdinand "the Just" of Aragon had not even sent delegates to sit in their deliberations. He was the only monarch of any importance who had the abdominal equipment to abstain.

That was the kind of King that Chiaramonte preferred, and he advised Giovantonio to break up Joan's marriage to Jacques Bourbon, to push her into union with Juan d'Aragon, to break off relations with Cardinal Colonna, and to put the cabal behind Benedict XIII, *bringing Serjianni along with him!*

"I would sooner bring Beelzebub," Taranto grunted, and the page in attendance stuck his head in to ask, "Did Your Highness call?"

"Not yet," said Giovantonio, and he whistled a little Tarantella softly to himself as he read the letter again, checking off the points of possible accord.

Too late, thank God, even to consider making an ally of Serjianni on the side of an Aragonese King for the Regno, but to stop Joan's marriage to Jacques Bourbon seemed a simple matter, from where the Prince sat. One had only to inform Joan where

Alopo was, and she would balk, even if she were already kneeling at the altar.

Giovantonio went on to grapple with Chiaramonte's more prickly suggestion—that the Prince renounce Cardinal Oddo.

"No, by God, I will not do it," Giovantonio burst out, and again the page appeared with the towel. "Now?"

"No. Go away," Taranto grumbled. "I'm just sitting here thinking."

It would not be fair to Cousin Raimondo Orsini who was working his brain to the bone for Colonna's Election, to switch entries on him now. Not only that, but now they had an investment in Oddo, and marriage with one of his bastards was a good way to recover that money whether the Cardinal got the Tiara or not. What other family—except, perhaps, the Roman Orsinis— had so many men under arms? Marriage with the House of Colonna would bring the Prince's fighting strength to a ponderable total, capable of challenging the Caldoras and Caracciolos united—unless they released Sforza from prison. Giovantonio was not brash enough to think he could whip the Maestro, but Sforza and Serjianni were not likely ever to agree again after the abuse the Constable had heaped upon the soldier. Holla!

Across Taranto's economic scheming flashed the dazzling possibility of himself—somehow—releasing Sforza and adding *him* to the cabal.

That beautiful vision was set aside to dwell upon at leisure. The more immediate need was for a firm and indissoluble bond with the next Pope, and the Catalan Benedict XIII stood not a Mongolian's chance of gaining the tithing of any people whatever except his own countrymen, the Aragonese. "Just" the King of Aragon might be, and the apple of Chiaramonte's eye, but in the struggle for the Papacy he was setting himself and his candidate against the whole of Christendom. They could not win, but the Colonna could.

Giovantonio pulled up his drawers with a snap, and brushed the page aside. His mind was made up, his plan of action formed. Instead of choosing between Chiaramonte and Colonna, he determined to keep them both. He would sign a contract to marry any daughter Cardinal Oddo would give him, as soon as that could be arranged, the youth of the girls notwithstanding, and he would visit Tristano Chiaramonte in person at once and win him to Colonna's side.

Chiaramonte had the reputation of a clear-headed, far sighted man. *Ergo,* he must see the wisdom of hoisting Cardinal Oddo to Saint Peter's Chair. What matter then whether Joan and Jacques Bourbon had been married or not? If they were, the Colonna as Pope would annul the union, and—in gratitude to the Aragonese—anoint Prince Juan King of the Two Sicilies, either as Joan's consort or on his own recognizances. A mere detail, that, which Giovantcnio, Chiaramonte and Juan d'Aragon would settle in conference.

Taranto re-entered the happy family circle beaming.

"I can see you feel better," quipped baby-face. "You got a load off your mind."

"I shall put a load upon yours, Cousin. You are to escort the ladies and my brother to Lecce, and see Gabriel put in charge. Then you will carry my mother to Taranto, and see her in full command. You and Ettore will then lead all the men who can be spared—and all you can recruit—to Rome. I trust you will be in possession of San Angelo before Sforza is released from gaol."

"You may rely upon it!" Andria promised, "if Sforza is kept in gaol long enough."

"If he is let out—treat with him—make him our friend. Don't waste your men fighting him." The Prince turned to Pappacoda.

"Will Your Highness attend my mother and me at our Audience with Cousin Jacques tomorrow? Will you bear Her Majesty's cloak?"

"You honor me."

"You will be very noticeably our only friend—alone. No one else will be with us."

Taranto's drift was not lost upon the older man. He was being asked to parade his colors under Caracciolo's nose. His loyalty was being tested. "All the greater distinction, Highness," Artuso smiled. "Her Majesty Marie-Luise and yourself are the King's nearest of kin."

"As we kiss the hand tomorrow I mean to leave the impression—especially with Serjianni—that I rely upon our Bourbon blood to keep us in favor, but I do not wish to deceive you. I would not have you expose yourself in this way—under any misapprehension. If possible—tomorrow—I shall bring away some portion of Caterina's dot, and if the sum is large enough I shall sail in the night for Palermo ... Does that alter your decision?"

"No, Highness."

"Serjianni will not like it."

"Serjianni will think that I am spying upon you in his interests," said Artuso. "All will be well."

Taranto flung open his arms, crying. "I kiss you!"

"Phuutt," said Artuso. "May I not bear the cloak without that?"

Then they dubbed the lucky waterman "Admiral" of his one-shallop navy, and—apart from the ladies—perfected details with him, and with Tomaso, Riccardo and Quito, how each should contribute to the sailing.

Erri was entrusted with the mission to Constance, and the rest of the night was spent teaching him what to say to Count Nola and Cardinal Colonna. The question arose, due to Erri's cup condition, if a cipher-letter would not be safer, but the soldier would have none of that. "I remember better drunk than sober," he boasted. "Hear me, now ... The Lord Prince of Taranto is the Cardinal's humble servant, and marriage to one of Your Serenity's *nieces*—don't say daughters—is the acme of his temporal desires.

"What the Hell does—the acme of his temporal desires—mean?"

"You don't have to understand it, just remember it," said Andria.

The Prince pledged that the Tarantine arms would bend the will of Joan II to the usance of Colonna as Pope, not only as applied to Rome but in Naples as well. To that was added a broad hint that Giovantonio had a workable plan for converting the Kingdom of Aragon, including Sicily *ultra* Pharum, to Colonna's tithing. Details were reserved for word-of-mouth conference, perhaps at Taranto's wedding.

All agreed that this last piece of bait was the subtlest diplomacy of the Prince's career, and the likeliest to succeed, because the main cause of delay in the deliberations at Constance was Aragon's stubborn abstention. A folly to call the Church "universal" while no Christians south of the Pyrenees were sending their contributions, and that issue was so vital that no less a personage than the Holy Roman Emperor was, even then, gone ambassador for the Council to the Court of Ferdinand "the Just".

Only fancy how proud were the Lady Maria, and the *femme de chambre* Giovanna, to mother children for a boy who so lightly undertook to accomplish what the Emperor could not do. Where was another such man in all the world? No Colonna bastard was good enough to wife him, but—his will be done. The Lady and the pregnant maid were more eager than he was to see the chit who would grow up to be their mistress, more curious to know what she was like. Giovantonio did not appear to care if she had six legs.

Nobody actually slept in the Caracciolo palace that night, but Giovanna turned down the counterpane for the Prince and the Lady Maria, and sweetly assisted at their reunion. Considering their long separation and their proven fertility in combination, one does not wonder that Taranto's third child was conceived before dawn.

In ample time for their Audience next day the former Queen Marie-Luise entered the street attended by her son and Pappacoda. They had not many jewels, and their raiment had been finer aforetime, but they carried off those deficiencies with a bearing that delighted the crowd. At sight of them, some people goggled an instant in disbelief, but when recognition was confirmed the vulgar huzzahs almost lifted the party out of their saddles. They were, moreover, well heeled by mounted men, and before they reached Castel Nuovo no less than ten Barons, and no pygmies neither, had joined their train, each with his little bodyguard.

Serjianni saw them coming, from a window in Castel Nuovo, and heard the cheers that followed them along the Lungo. Thus through eye and ear the conviction assailed him, that he—of all people—had made a mistake. The Prince of Taranto was a bigger boy than the Constable had taken him for. The Strong Man tried to push that thought aside. After all, this show of force was not unusual. If Taranto had not some following he would not be worth the trouble of palaver. The slightly sickish feeling in the pit of the Constable's stomach was the result of a hard night of bickering with four times as many greedy French as Bourbon had any right to bring with him. That was enough to put any man on edge.

Only his quick-bladed secretary Antonio was with Serjianni at the time, and together they watched the cavalcade as its heavy hoofs boomed on the drawbridge. "Where the Devil did he get that army?" the Constable muttered, not really expecting an answer, but Antonio said, "That's not the half of it."

"He has more?—in Naples?"

Antonio nodded. "His Highness has many friends." Serjianni did not hear the overtone, but the statement was made with a certain satisfaction.

"This looks more like an invasion than a private Audience. Tell the Castelan to staff the corridors for an emergency."

Watching still, after Antonio was gone on that errand, did not quiet the Constable's flutter: on the contrary. After the principals had passed into the Castel, a double file of the Tarantine arms and three or four of the Barons drew reign on the bridge and simply sat chatting, so that the span could not have been raised if it had been ordered up.

Serjianni had already explained to his puppet King how diligently he had kept trying to free Marie-Luise all these months. Now he hurried to join the "Majesty" before the Bourbon's kin could give him the lie. On the way Serjianni picked up the only two trusted henchmen he encountered and drew them along, one a cousin, Ottino Caracciolo, the other, Caldora Count Aversa. "Taranto has found himself an army," he told them. "Overnight! God knows what he has in mind. I've got to be standing beside the King's chair—on his right hand—when they come in. If any of those frogs try to squeeze between, you two give them the elbow." So soon was the Constable usurping the duties of the imprisoned Seneschal!

Less given to forms, the outland Highnesses did not understand the significance of the jostling but gave way to save their ribs, so that the tableau was arranged quite to Serjianni's liking—until the doors were opened. When the former Queen entered, Jacques, contrarily, refused to stay put but ran to embrace her, followed by his Bedchamber *en masse.*Not a man among them but had some claim to the attention of His Majesty's cousins. The Constable and *his* cousin—and his Caldora father-in-law—were left out of the picture.

Serjianni drew Ottino Caracciolo aside, whispering him down to the drawbridge. "See what those Lordships are saying," the Constable directed. "Remember every one who is there. Wait with them—stay with them until Taranto leaves—then go with him and keep me informed, where he goes, whom he sees."

Ottino never had been more than a watchdog for his potent cousin, and the habit of obedience was firmly fixed in the grain of him, but this day would see titles and offices redistributed on a scale hitherto unknown, it was no time for a Courtier to be out of Court, and Ottino found the courage to object. "I shall get nothing—as usual," he complained. "You already know who is down there."

"Do as I say," Serjianni hissed fiercely. "I'll see that you're not forgotten. Go!" The Constable walked away, ending the parly, and Ottino, reluctant and surly, with no hope whatever in the other's well worn promise, went to mount and mingle as directed.

Taranto did not see the Caracciolo leave the room, being too much occupied with his appraisals of Jacques Bourbon and his suite. A pity, perhaps, that the Count of Marche had not greater native abilities or more charm, but the Prince found nothing in him or in any there to inspire confidence. The Bourbon had a lanthorn jaw, a lower lip like a shelf, and a mincing, simpering manner which could not fail to remind Giovantonio how much finer a King he himself would make, if the price were not so high.

At once after their greetings, Jacques led the way to collation, seating Marie-Luise on his right and Taranto on his left.

The transalpine nobles crowded in next, with manners called "Barbarian", shunting the Constable and Caldora far below the salt. Pappacoda received this treatment too, but he had not the same reasons to resent it, and did not. He made a jest of it, saying *sotto voce* to Serjianni, "His Majesty wants a Seneschal—to replace Alopo—does he not?"

"Will you apply for the post?" Serjianni returned sourly. "Whoever is appointed will hardly survive the wedding, but—from appearances—your friends could get the staff for you if you wish it." The Constable did not yet truly suspect the depth of Artuso's attachment to the Prince or he would have concealed his annoyance. "Why did not His Highness bring his affiliates inside—to kiss the hand? I shall have to explain to His Majesty why so many of his Barons wait below, noncommittal. It is rude, embarrassing. What am I to say?"

Near the head of the table, too far away to be heard well, Taranto appeared to be saying as much as was necessary to make his position quite clear to the erstwhile near-King, and Jacques was nodding, comprehending, agreeing at a great rate.

"His Highness must speak for himself," said Pappacoda warily.

"He's doing that well enough," Serjianni growled. "How many men has he in Naples?"

"Very few of his own, but he has many friends. Am I wrong, Milord, in the impression that you are allied with Taranto? The Prince relies upon your good will."

"Is that why he has so many of his friends sitting on the drawbridge?"

"I believe nothing sinister is intended by Their Lordships' waiting."

"They are waiting to see if Taranto obtains all the concessions he wants. And if he does not—what will they do?"

"I do not know, Milord. The Prince relies upon your assurances that his wishes will be granted."

"And I rely upon *your* assurances that the Barons will support Jacques Bourbon. They must kiss the hand."

"Now, Milord?"

"At the King's pleasure—whether Taranto is satisfied or not."

"They will never bear arms against Taranto, Serjianni, and I never told you they would. When I got their pledges for you—some months ago—many of us thought the Prince was dead."

The Constable signaled for silence. He wished to hear what was being said at the other end of the table. By coincidence only, and not to be accommodating, Jacques Bourbon raised his voice. He could not do enough for his beloved kinsmen, he said, and granted the entire list of *itemed* demands as presented to the Queen. Lacking only the ability to perform his generosities, he instructed the Constable to provide the Prince of Taranto with whatever he required. "Particularly in the matter of our Cousin Caterina's marriage portion," said His Majesty. "That will endear us to the Chiaramontes. It can win us the other Sicily."

"Very good, Your Majesty," said Serjianni. "I authorize His Highness to use the Crown moneys already in his possession, for this purpose. And has Your Majesty arranged for the return of the Crown itself?" He was fast on his feet for a heavy man, that Caracciolo.

Taranto flushed purple. "I have neither the Crown nor any Crown moneys," he asserted. "I left the Castel empty handed."

"But your cousin Count Nola did not. He took half a barrel of other jewels too—quite enough for your sister's dot."

"I deny it—in his name—and in my own," the Prince lied stanchly.

The entire topic was news to Jacques Bourbon, but he could not make himself heard.

"Will you permit me to search the fortress at Taranto?" Caracciolo blazed, and the younger leather-lunged blustered in return, "Will you permit me to search your fortress in Melfi?"

"I will!" Serjianni thundered, rising. "Come now, or any time. Melfi is always open to His Majesty. But everybody knows where the Crown is—and I challenge Your Highness to combat for it."

Every man was on his feet at that, some elders crying, "Shame!"—but their makeshift sovereign had not the dignity to preserve any sort of order. "Is the Crown—then—missing?" Jacques asked of Marie-Luise. "Who is this Count Nola? Where is he?"

The Constable was quick to reply, not giving Her Highness a chance, "He is in Constance—conniving with Louis II d'Anjou to Elect a Pope opposed to us."

The King's suite jabbered so shrilly at that, no words could be distinguished, but Taranto pulled the royal ear close enough to hiss that a Pope favorable to himself was their Orsini cousin's aim. "He took the Crown with him to have it blest for Your Majesty," the Prince added. "But the Constable's pilferings have been piling up in Melfi for many years. With your permission I shall recover that money and jewels for you as soon as I return from Palermo."

A child should have known that these recriminations were retaliatory, but Jacques chose to believe his kinsman and began pounding the table with his goblet, screaming, "Silence! Silence! I will have silence!" In a little while he got it. "Hear our will, M. Constable, and do not interrupt us ... His Highness of Taranto is to sail at once for Palermo, and you are to give him all the cash he requires, and no more argument. How much will you need, Cousin, for a first installment?"

"Fifty thousand ducats," said Giovantonio promptly.

"For a *first* installment?" The Bourbon was more than a little stunned. Fifty thousand, in cash, would have bought the County of Marche from him at any time since he had come into it, but if this was the going rate in Naples, Jacques was not going to be a piker, with Joan's money. "Give the Lord Taranto fifty thousand ducats at once—*now!*" Jacques commanded, feeling every inch the King. This was something like.

"There is not so much money in the Castel," said Serjianni grimly. "Milord Taranto is robbing you."

"No more arguments!" shrilled the King. "Give him the money instantly! Who is King here? Do you set yourself above me?"

The question remained unanswered at the time, because the Strong Man had taken thought. He did, in fact, set himself infinitely above this descendant of Saint Louis, but immediate means to make his power felt were not at the table. This first day had got off to a bad start and wanted rectifying.

Swallowing his pride, Serjianni bowed low, saying, "Sire, I shall find what I can—and make up the difference from my own purse—but I beg your lief to run a course with His Highness of Taranto, or to suffer trial by ordeal with him, to prove which of us lies about the stolen Crown."

"Later, perhaps," Jacques conceded. "Get the money first. Pierre will go with you." Pierre was a bravo from Marche, with much the same duties as the Constable's Antonio. He had been standing behind Jacques's chair, as Tomaso stood behind Giovantonio's, as every other Lord's personal bodyguard kept "eyes-behind" for him. In addition to these worthies—running to nearly a hundred—about ten of the Palace Guard and an equal number of Capuan men-at-arms guarded the doors and windows of the collation hall, primed for emergency by the Constable's special order. Those at the wide main entrance stood aside smartly, with a breast-salute, as Serjianni went out followed by Antonio. By the time the King's Pierre reached that exit the soldiers had re-formed a solid wall of mailed manhood, and they did not move as Pierre approached. Some technicality of protocol—that was not the door for servants unless accompanied by their masters, or something of that nature—held the guardsmen motionless until Jacques Bourbon called out sharply, "Let that man pass at once."

Pierre was not delayed long, but long enough to serve the Constable's purpose. After Pierre passed through the door he was never seen again.

Until Pierre's exit, His Crispness Caldora of Aversa had not spoken a word since the collation began. He had heard as much as he could of Taranto's conversation with Jacques, but the trim little calculator had given no sign of interest or opinion. In sooth he was still sulking over Bourbon's ingratitude on the road, and felt put out that nobody had noticed his aloofness. He had stuck the hero Giulio-Cesaro di Capua with duty in the street to punish his presumption, hoping that the King would ask for the Captain and thus bring the issue to a head, but the Barbarian was not very observant.

The Count jerked to his feet, made a short, sharp bow in the King's direction and spoke with his wonted concision. "With Your Majesty's permission." He was asking lief to go, perhaps to watch the gold-gathering operation.

"Just a moment, Your Highness," Jacques replied, and took Taranto away from the table, leading him by the arm. "Tell me about this child—this little boy—whom Count Aversa is holding over my head. Is that a son of Ladislaus?"

"I think not, Cousin. My stepfather had no children that he was aware of, but Milord Aversa is acting in good faith. I commend him to you—more especially since Sforza is confined. Caldora is your finest Commander."

"Is it true?"

"He has also been a favorite of Aunt Joan. She relies upon him."

"Ah?"

"When she learns that Sforza and Alopo are both in San Vincenzo—she will turn to him."

"She will?"

"You will do well to bind Caldora to you, Cousin. Some token—of your regard—"

"He wants Capua—and with the title of *Prince.* That's no token."

"He is worth it. He will be worth two Capuas to you when Aunt Joan finds out where Alopo is."

"You know Her Majesty so much better than I. Advise me."

"When will you see her?"

"That is in the Constable's hands."

"Ah, too bad."

"Bad?"

"They quarrel so."

"Is it so?"

"Sex—you know."

"This is something to quarrel about?" Jacques Bourbon had a lot to learn.

"If you will be advised by me——"

"Yes, Cousin?"

"You will make Count Aversa Prince of Capua—at once—and send *him* to Her Majesty to arrange your first meeting."

"Without consulting the Constable?!" The bare thought froze the King's liver.

"Not a word to the Constable," Taranto admonished. "You must show him that *you* are the King."

"Aye. That is true."

"Aunt Joan will throw herself upon Caldora's protection—and your worries will be over."

That *ergo* was entirely unexpected to Cousin Jacques: some portion of the syllogism had fallen out along the way: but rather than appear stupid to this brilliant youth he permitted Taranto's infectious confidence to waft him over the obscurities and set him down in a flowering field where all problems solved themselves and even the serpents were friendly. "I'll do it!" said he, and turned to Caldora. "Milord Aversa, where would you go?"

Not knowing quite what to expect, the shifty one replied quickly. "To see Your Majesty's will executed."

"Splendid," said Jacques, "but first—come here. I have a surprise for you." He drew his sword as he spoke, and—all things considered—Caldora's compliance required considerable courage. Although he did, in fact, correctly interpret the King's gesture (and did, also, appreciate Taranto's part in recommending him for the benison), this rough and ready form of investiture was not usual in Naples, and Aversa easily could have been guessing wrong. Still, soldier that he was, he advanced, knelt, and bared his neck, and it is a pity that Bourbon did not chop his head off while he had him in that position. Instead, Jacques smote him lightly on the shoulder, and extemporized upon the God-given right and power "within us vested"—and so on—"I pronounce you Prince of Capua, you and your heirs male."

Just as the King-presumptive was uttering the very kernel of his utterance, Serjianni came back into the hall and heard it.

Now, as the Constable re-entered the room he was not carrying 50,000 in gold in his hands, nor was he attended by money bearers. He was quite alone. He had not been gone long enough to do more than issue orders, and his prompt return smacked of surveillance. He could not trust Jacques Bourbon out of his sight, and here, transpiring, was the event to justify his anxiety.

Considering that the deed in progress was bringing the taxing of Capua into the Constable's own family, and that hitherto he had appeared to favor this allotment, one might have expected him to be pleased, but he was not, and the distortion of his oversized features as he attempted to conceal that the jolt had shaken his teeth loose gave Caracciolo the strained expression of the southern end of a costive jackass … That another should be honored before him! That the King durst act without his sanction! That his already too independent father-in-law should have this material for greater independence added to him!

"What—" the Strong Man choked, "what—do I hear? Prince—of Capua!"

Jacques Bourbon's supply of courage was pretty well used up by then, but—reflecting that the ceiling had not fallen when he defied Serjianni the first time—he raised Caldora to his feet and kissed him on each cheek before he acknowledged the Constable's presence. That gave Serjianni time to screw on a stiff smile. "Now—if Her Majesty Joan will confirm it——" Serjianni began, but Jacques cut him short. "Where is the money for our Cousin Taranto?" he snapped petulantly. "Where is the fifty thousand?" Jacques would have liked to see so much gold all at one time himself.

"It is being put into a chest," said Serjianni with disarming deference, and walked toward Caldora with both arms outstretched to embrace him. "You are favored by our new master, Father."

Before Caldora would receive his kinsman's congratulations he turned back to Jacques protesting his unworthiness of so much honor from such a great monarch. The Bourbon ate it up.

The ultramontane nobles were no more than lukewarm in their amenities to the new Prince of Capua, inasmuch as his gain was their loss, but Taranto made his joy seem great enough to balance that deficiency.

Caldora could not so swiftly plumb the motives for Giovantonio's generous espousal of his interests, but connected it with Duke Andria's overtures, in Rome, to obtain Aversa as a landing place for Louis II d'Anjou. So much good will, certainly, was not tendered selflessly, but the beneficiary did not try to puzzle it out, knowing that Taranto's accounting would be presented for settlement in the sequel. While their faces were close Caldora whispered to the Prince, "I shall never forget this"—but no outward recognition of the youth's instrumentality informed the Constable of his guilt. Neither could Serjianni know that the Prince had suggested Caldora as the King's special envoy to Joan II, but the speed of these events flying out of his control made the Strong Man suspect everybody in the room of plotting against him.

Jacques drew the new Capua apart from all the others to give him his commission to Joan, and Serjianni all but walked between them to break up the tête-à-tête. As suddenly as that, the day's business had begun clamoring for the King's attention. "The Archbishop awaits Your Majesty's pleasure," said Caracciolo. "The Magistrates are here—the Presidents of the guilds—the Captains of the people—some of the richest merchants. Will Your Majesty not be pleased to open the public Audiences? Will you follow me?"

In so speaking Serjianni made the grave mistake of presenting his left side—and a vulnerable portion of his back—to the rigid soldier Tomaso, who was on oath to perform a certain ritual with the Constable's entrails, as well as to chew up his eyeballs and spit them in his face. A better opportunity than this to fulfill that vow would be a long while coming, but when Tomaso looked to his master for sanction of his unspoken desires, Taranto shook his head. The only fault the old soldier ever found with the Prince was this high-born ability to defer vengeance for the sake of gain.

"I will *not* follow you," Jacques snapped at Serjianni. "Where is the money?"

"It is being put upon mules—in the stable—Majesty. It will be ready whenever His Highness wishes to leave."

"I am leaving now," said Taranto, "if my cousin permits," he bowed, "and if my Highness Mother is ready. Your Majesty's Audiences are pressing—and my mission to Palermo cannot be performed too soon."

Followed, then, Jacques Bourbon's polite wish to keep Marie-Luise by his side, but her son advanced some eighty-three reasons why that should not be, and at length the quondam monarch bowed to Taranto's judgment. "Go, then," said Cousin Jacques, and added with a sniff, "You had best count the gold. If Milord Chiaramonte should find it short that would reflect upon our intentions."

The crudity of the insult was exceeded only by the accuracy of Bourbon's judgment, and the two together were of such force that Serjianni fairly strangled. "Does Your Majesty distrust me?" the Constable managed, between clenched teeth and lips drawn bloodless white.

"You will go to the stable with Milord Taranto—and see him satisfied," Jacques directed, and—turning to Caldora, "Your Lordship may go too—as I said?"

Caldora bowed low, and then everybody began bowing all around, and the French Lords edged into the Audience Chamber to safeguard their interests from the local supplicants for favors.

Still nursing his outrage, Serjianni took Caldora's arm and steered him into the corridor, speaking low, but speaking so vehemently and so fast that he spattered like a fountain.

Marie-Luise again took her place between her son and Pappacoda and thus those three followed the Constable to the courtyard gate of the stables. There—even as the Caracciolo had said that it would be—a heavy chest was suspended from shafts between two mules, and it was so thoroughly bound, strapped and tied that its appearance alone discouraged investigation. More or less in charge of the ironbound coffer, Ottino Caracciolo sat his horse near the head of the lead mule. Ottino was an over-tall but pallid effigy of all the Caracciolos, a man who never looked quite comfortable in an upright position but the perfect model for the recumbent knight to be carven on all their tombs.

While the rest of the party waited for their mounts to be brought up, Serjianni ignored them and spoke privately with his watchdog cousin, and Taranto knocked and tapped here and there on the chest, as if the sound would tally the gold pieces for him. By the thumps one must have accounted the box well filled with metal, but whether with produce of the mint or with scraps of iron and worn out spurs was left to the imagination. Just then Antonio—Serjianni's Antonio—came up and presented the key. The secretary was expressionless, and he did not speak, but as he put the key into Taranto's hand he twisted is slightly—about a quarter turn—against the Prince's palm at the same time staring with brazen fixity into His Lordship's eyes.

In the next moment, with his other hand, Antonio produced a receipt-in-blank, to be signed by Giovantonio, acknowledging the delivery to him of 50,000 ducats.

Antonio's gesture could not be construed as anything but friendly, in keeping with his manner and protestations of the previous day, and it could have but one meaning. It meant, *Open that chest now!*

By chance—or by a design which no one fathomed— Caldora's horses came out of the stable first, and a dozen of his soldiers with them. More adieus and compliments intervened then, and both the Prince and the Constable tried to learn the Commander's destination without the other's privity. Neither succeeded, with any certainty, and the new Prince of Capua rode his way, out of the courtyard and on to the drawbridge between files of Tarantines. Lacking instructions to impede his progress, the patchwork Del Balzo-Orsini army made no move to stop him, and most of the waiting Barons greeted their peer in passing.

When Caldora was gone, the Prince of Taranto held out the key of the strongbox toward Serjianni, saying, "If Your Lordship requires a receipt for the money, show me what I am signing for."

Suddenly the King's Audiences above stairs again exerted their imperative demand for immediate attention, and—quite ignoring his so recent demand for mortal combat—the Caracciolo put his arm around Taranto's shoulder, to say in cozening tone, "At a time like this!—take that chest down?! You would not ask it—while the Bourbon is giving away the Regno to his friends! I must go to him and save what I can."

"I will not ask it," Taranto agreed, "if you will bring another chest like that—with the money in it. Otherwise I shall carry this one to the Audience Chamber and open it before the King's eyes."

"The money is in it!" Serjianni lied. Nothing was in it but shard.

Taranto raised his hand in a gesture to the nearest of the Tarantine Captains.

"Well, then," said Serjianni quickly, "you should not have accused me of stealing. I meant only to even the score. This is no time for us to quarrel among ourselves. I will give you fifty thousand more—for the Crown. Take Ottino with you and let him bring it back to me. A bargain?"

"No," said the Prince. "The man who took the Crown had good reason to take it, and he will bring it back when the Pope decrees who shall wear it. But—Milord—*my*necessities will not wait so long. Order a chest with the money in it brought here at once—with the lid open—or prepare your soul for Hell. I shall not even trouble Cousin Jacques further. I can deal with you myself."

Serjianni looked well around the courtyard and decided not to tempt Fate. Raising his voice in command to Antonio—as if the secretary had made the mistake—the Strong Man boomed, "Take that chest back and fill it with gold." As the same time he reached for the key, but Giovantonio withheld it, repeating, once more, that flattest of negatives, "No ... You will leave this chest here, just as it is, and put the money in another. I shall take them both with me."

Nothing could move his determination, either, and the Prince did not deign to explain his fancy. To be sure, he was getting two fine coffers and four mules as boot in the transaction, but nothing so petty was in either's Lord's mind as they kicked that apparently piddling demand back and forth between them. Serjianni saw the Prince obtaining more or less permanent possession of evidence of the attempted double-dealing, and accordingly argued to keep it, but Taranto's sagacity went far beyond that, and he would not give in. "I will take two chests," he insisted, "and let the second one be as like the first as possible—except for its contents."

That was the gist of the youth's motive, two like chests would be interchangeable, as cats are in the dark, and Taranto's nimble mind was already picturing the courses those two boxes must take through the streets and out of the city. He was providing against the vicissitudes he surely would be put to before the right chest was aboard his one-vessel navy and on its way to Palermo.

Beyond any doubt, Serjianni would set men to recover the gold. Ashore, they would come as brigands, afloat, as pirates, and if they attacked in force, one or more boxes might have to be yielded to them.

By this foresight you may identify Taranto as a born leader of men, and by his persuasiveness, too. He said simply, "I have the upper hand, Serjianni. Do as I tell you."

Burning under the boy's manner, under the imperious command of his eyes, the Great Serjianni stood, flexing the fingers of both his massive hands as if they craved nothing so much as to strangle His Insolency Taranto. "I—I will go——and count the money——myself," the Constable choked.

"No!" said the Prince again. "Send Antonio. You wait here with us."

What could Serjianni do about it?

The Castelan of Nuovo was in the courtyard, only a few steps away, watching the interchange closely, but he was a Queensman, under no compulsion to obey a Lord whom Joan had stripped of Ministerial rank. Serjianni might be Bourbon's Grand Constable, but what that signified—in mercurial Naples—was very much in the air.

The Prince knew well that his advantage was but temporary, that the Strong Man's strength would return in a rush as soon as the thumb was lifted, but in his young confidence he trusted his acumen—if he could put his mother and sisters behind defensible stone walls, and himself get to Palermo with the money—whatever future stretched beyond that could be left to care for itself.

"Send Antonio," Taranto repeated, and Serjianni made such a gesture that Antonio disappeared back into the Castel.

Call it brave, or call it foolhardy, the Prince thus placed himself and his little troop in a possible pincers. Caldora was already outside the Castel, and could be summoning the rest of the Constable's family. Now Antonio was footloose inside, and quite capable of coming back with an array of the Palace Guard.

True, Caldora was freshly beholden to the Prince, and had said he would never forget the favor just received, but what bank will discount that kind of collateral? In a sense, too, Taranto had "spared" Antonio's life the day before, and—by the key in his hand—had a token of that bravo's appreciation, but how much reliance can a man place in a practicing traitor? Outside—the Regno's most notorious Baron Shilly-shally! Inside—a murderous brute in secretary's clothing, keen only in appraising a probable winner! The most random chance—the fall of a leaf or the stub of a toe—could have cut short Taranto's history in the next quarter-hour, yet that was the chance he took.

For what it was worth as a weapon of defense, Giovantonio said to Tomaso—openly, for all to hear—"His Highness Ottino Caracciolo will be riding with his. Attend him—now."

That was a frail reed to lean upon, only barely better than nothing. It made Ottino hostage for the good behavior of men over whom nobody in the courtyard could exercise positive control. It put the Constable's watchdog cousin in imminent jeopardy, liable to summary execution if a leaf should fall or a toe be stubbed.

Serjianni could not help but smile, first, because he wished nothing better than to have Ottino ride with the Prince, and, second, at the jejune logic which concluded that even the direst menace to Ottino could deter any action Serjianni had in mind. A more readily expendable cousin than Ottino would have been difficult to find among the Caracciolos.

In sooth the Prince did not overestimate Ottino's value as a hostage, but took possession to prevent him from riding with the alarm to more formidable allies of the family. "If Your Highness pleases," said Giovantonio to the Constable, "I shall carry Milord Ottino along with me. We can discuss the means for returning the Crown—as you suggested—and your payment to the Countess Alix Del Balzo for Avellino—as agreed?"

Mention of Avellino had the desired effect of completely infuriating Serjianni. "I will see every Del Balzo in Hell before I give them that money!" he flared. "You are going too far with me! By God, I'll break your Bourbon cousin's back before I'll take much more from you. Be warned! I have given you every opportunity to join with me—under this regime—but you have chosen to fight me. Look out for yourself, little boy. You are dealing with a man." Having delivered himself of that so deadly blast, the Man strode—a few strides—toward the archway into the Castel, fully intending to defy the whipper-snapper's edict which had held him in the courtyard thus far, but in the course of their debate, numbers of Tarantine horse-men had put their mounts between the principals and the stair, so that—to carry out his original intention—Serjianni would have had to leap over six mailed knights, and he was not Man enough to do that.

He called upon the soldiers to move aside, but not all under-stood him well, and some moved in as others moved out, so that the barrier remained impassable.

While the horses and Serjianni were executing this ballet, the grooms brought out the mounts for Taranto's party, and the Prince himself gave his mother a hand up, gallantly kissing her instep after she was in the saddle. Marie-Luise had said little on this visit to her former home, but speech was not the measure of her assistance to Giovantonio's designs.

Pappacoda did not mount at once, but stood somewhat back of his horse, making himself as inconspicuous as possible, hop-ing that the Caracciolos would forget he had been there—but the Prince would not have it so.

"Do get up, Artuso," he called out. "We shall be only a moment now." Indeed, even as he spoke, Antonio came with four slaves under the shafts bearing the second chest.

The Tarantine chivalry understood very well how to get out of the path of this burden, and when the way had been cleared for it, Serjianni took advantage of the opportunity to hurry inside to the King. He did not even look at the coffer as he passed it or throw back any bolts from his blazing eyes toward the victor. He took no leaves and gave no instructions. In solemn truth, he was too angry to speak.

While a second pair of mules was coming from the stable, the slaves put the box on the flags, and Antonio lifted the lid for Taranto's inspection. The gold pieces were in rolls, and the rolls neatly bagged, so the sight was not especially impressive. Giovantonio scarcely glanced at it, but made such a tactical gesture of faith in Antonio as must be remembered a lifetime. "Is it all there?" the Prince asked, reaching for the receipt-in-blank with one hand, and for the secretary's pen with the other.

"Yes, Highness. I counted it myself," said Antonio.

Taranto wrote his name.

Then the chest was put on two mules and secured, very like the other, and by the time the party had crossed the drawbridge, not more than six or ten of the most observant could have told which vessel contained the sweet, sweet stuff. The only way Taranto kept it in mind was by the mouse-colored Jennie of the gold-bearing team, but Pappacoda had a better device. "Just watch Ottino," said he. "The chest he is nearer is it."

"That touchstone is too reliable," said the Prince ironically, and set out to befuddle Ottino's judgment and to convey what plan he had to those directly involved. He rode first to Duke Andria, at the head of the escort, then back to the tail of the line, pausing to whisper only a moment to this Captain or that, by the way.

Slapdash and extempore, hardly one man knew what had been said to the others, and in that state of almost perfect confusion Andria reached Serjianni's gates, which were still propped open and in Tarantine hands.

The money-bearing column was halted, perforce, in a close-packed mass that blocked two cross streets and extended a third of the way back to where they had come from. All but the foremost were prevented from entering the Melfi courtyard by the press within waiting for the signal to ride out.

Obedient to their brother, the Princesses and their household were ready for the dash to Nola, and they greeted their cousin Guglielmo with cheers and a pretty outcry.

Andria cut them short by calling upon young Gabriel to help him clear space for the laden mules, and the squealing girls understood that Giovantonio had brought Caterina's dot. The tactic was to get both chests off the street for a time, beyond Ottino's purview, so that when—if ever—he saw them again he could not be sure which was worth following.

The soldiers, meanwhile, maintained the close formation which held Ottino, Pappacoda, and even Taranto himself, at the distance of the first street corner. The former Queen remained with them also, and Tomaso too, until both teams of mules had been inched through the press and disappeared inside Caracciolo's courtyard, guided by Riccardo and Quito.

To keep Ottino Caracciolo's mind off his worries, Taranto spoke to him gently about the Crown. "Your Highness understands that I do not have it with me ... It is in Constance—I think ... But then, you would not wish to carry it through the streets today—with only one groom to assist you."

A great skeptic, Ottino retorted, "I would carry it if I could get it, but you are not giving me the Crown. Nobody ever gives me anything."

The watchdog's discontent never had been so openly avowed before, but his grumbling smelled of the trap. "I shall speak for you to Aunt Joan when I see her," Giovantonio promised. "Perhaps she will make you Seneschal—after Alopo is executed."

Nobody had said that Alopo was to be executed, but Serjianni would hardly countenance any other outcome of the gutter-snipe's trial.

"If Serjianni executes Alopo," Ottino hazarded, "I would do better to leave the Regno than ask favors from Joan."

"Ask her now," Taranto shrugged, "before Alopo is executed. Ask to be made Castelan of San Vincenzo—so you can release Alopo for her."

"And have my skull crashed like an acorn by Serjianni?"

"You must make up your mind which will do the more for you," the Prince explained as if to a child. "Your cousin Serjianni will not have many incomes at his disposal, with all those hungry Frenchmen yawping for a joint apiece, but Joan needs friends—and Joan is still the Queen." Having said so much, Taranto motioned his mother forward in the wake of the mules, and himself made ready to follow, adding—by way of parting with Ottino—"Let us speak of these things when we meet again. My Majesty Mother is going a journey and I must put her on the road."

Lacking specific directions how to cope with such an emergency, and already aswim in novel conundrums too deep for him, the Caracciolo blurted, "Leaving Naples?—while her cousin is King?" This incomprehensibility impressed Ottino as equivalent to swatting one's fairy godmother with a sock full of *dreck,* and he concluded on the instant that Marie-Luise would attempt to carry the 50,000 away with her. Ottino was all but physically torn into three equal pieces. His instructions were to remain at the side of the Prince, his inclination was to stay with the money, but if the former Queen set off across country—with or without the gold—the Constable would wish above all things to know where she went. "Where is Her Highness going?" Caracciolo worried aloud.

"To Avellino," Taranto replied, "with Duke Andria, to recover the accrued taxes. Your Lord Cousin is releasing the money to Alix Del Balzo."

"In a pig's arse!" Ottino burst out. "I'm going to tell Serjianni." Suiting his action to his words, he sawed his horse's mouth this way, then that, but the beast could not possibly turn, being too closely hemmed in by lancemen.

"Talk it over with Artuso," said the Prince pleasantly, and flapped his reins. The soldiers made way for him to follow his mother.

Reluctantly Tomaso trailed after his master. For a time the opportunity to draw a little Caracciolo blood had seemed delectably near.

"What is his game?" Ottino demanded of Artuso Pappacoda. "Are you on his side—or Serjianni's?"

"I am trying to make them both of one side," said the other with complete candor. "This is no time for new factions to form. Taranto and Melfi must be brought together. I count on you to help me."

"*Help* you?—to reconcile fire and water—after this morning's business? You know that Serjianni will never forgive him. What's more, if that money is not carried to Chiaramonte, Taranto will find himself in a cell with Alopo and Sforza." Ottino spoke with a full, firm voice. No less than twenty of the Tarantine soldiers heard every word. "Will these men obey you?" Ottino went on. "Clear the way for me to follow those chests."

Pappacoda shook his head, but gestured toward the cross-street where were only a few curious bystanders, children, oxen, dogs and goats. "They might let us go that way——"

That move did not suit Caracciolo's purpose, for it would cost him his view of the main gate, so he kept his place but put his mouth near Pappacoda's ear to whisper, "Your nephew holds Taranto—and the Crown—does he not?" The implication was comradely. "We could put ourselves in a very strong position—with everyone—with Serjianni, Joan and Taranto too—if your nephew would admit us—or bring the Crown out, for a price."

Artuso pursed his lips to show how seriously he was considering the suggestion, but he made no comment.

"Queen Joan would do something handsome for us both—if we brought her the Crown," said the tempter.

"And something handsomer still if we brought her Alopo," Pappacoda agreed.

The soldiery were relaxing their vigilance as the two well-born spoke so quietly, and a movement forward was visible among the troop nearest the Melfi palace gate. Some of the men had passed that entrance and filled the street on the other side, as if awaiting a signal from within.

Inside the Melfi courtyard the great bustle of shifting and shuffling was almost over. The unhitching and rehitching of mules and horses had been so complicated that—in the end—the soldier Quito was the only man who could have taken oath where the money lay.

The mouse-colored Jennie was put between the leadshafts of a covered litter, but neither of the chests went into that carrier. Side by side, the chests were opened in a guarded stall, and the rocks and trash from the first one were put into the other, which formerly had held the gold. Riccardo sat watch on the empty coffer whilst Quito took the sacks of money away two at a time. Taranto did not concern himself with those details but went from one to another of his dear ones, instructing them what they must do if they never saw him again.

"I put you in the Virgin's keeping," said Marie-Luise, and the Prince adjured her to, "Watch over my Marias—and see Giovanna delivered of my son. I trust it will be a son."

"I pray so, my dear."

The others were praying too, all but the boy Gabriel, who found some new demand pressing for his decision and authority every way he turned. Despite that handicap, Andria at length arranged the marching order, Marie-Luise was assisted into the litter, the curtains closed, and the mouse-colored Jennie set in motion.

Then Giovantonio, and only Tomaso, led their horses through Serjianni's house to the kitchen, through the kitchen garden, and out a gate on another street, so that the Prince and his family left the palace at the same time, but going in quite opposite directions.

Not at all by chance, the side street where Taranto and Tomaso brought their horses, to mount, was the same one which Ottino had spurned a few moments before in favor of his view of the main gate, so that if the watchdog but turned his head to the left, he must see the Prince and his "eyes-behind" climbing aboard their chargers. For the moment Ottino was too engrossed even to blink as the mouse-colored Jennie, the litter, Duke Andria and all, filed out of the main gate and fell in behind the fore-runners of their escort.

"They have put the gold in the litter!" the Constable's cousin declared, but that was a very poor guess.

"Hallooo!" came a loud cry from up the street to the left, as Taranto waved a derisive hand over his head in farewell and gave his mount both spurs. He and Tomaso were away like two bolts from one catapult.

You ken Ottino's quandary. He could not follow Marie's litter and her son at the same time, and he durst not tarry to search his cousin's palace for the precious metal. Taranto's stratagem thus worked perfectly, and the Caracciolo bolted through the group of gaping curious townsfolk, electing to pursue the Prince, inasmuch as that course followed the letter of Serjianni's commands.

The soldiers raised a mighty shout and clangor, but did not in fact give chase, nor Pappacoda neither. They let Ottino go, as the Prince had said they should, and in only a moment Taranto, Tomaso, Ottino and his servant had all flown out of sight. Then the little army closed up the gap between itself and Marie's cavalcade, constituting itself her rear guard, brave and entirely adequate to her defense from all comers.

Pappacoda did not accompany that train but ceremoniously took leave of the former Queen, in the litter, of the Princesses, mounted, of Gabriel, Andria *et al.* Then he entered the Melfi palace, where only Riccardo and Quito remained with perhaps ten men guarding the chests.

No more given to extravagances than to kissing, still Artuso could not repress his appreciation of a plot so well executed. "Everything is working out perfectly," he grinned to the ruffian pair. "Your master is nothing less than a genius."

"A Lord to be proud of," they agreed, and Riccardo added, "Let us not fail him now."

The first chest filled with rubble was reslung between two of the royal mules. Then Pappacoda—with five or six men—escorted it out the gate in the heat of the day, in plain view of God and anybody else who cared to look. Going a slow pace, he followed the trail of Taranto *cum* Ottino, with the foreknowledge that the Prince was leading the watchdog to Queen Joan's villa.

At the breakneck rate those four had been going, they could have arrived there by this time, but the creeping chest bearers would not cover the same ground in less than an hour. That, too, was part of the plan.

After fall of dark, just before the city gates were locked for the night, Riccardo and the remaining soldiers—excepting Quito—toiled at like offices, with straining and sweating, upon the burden of the other shard-laden coffer out the Salerno gate and on to the Nola road, the same taken by Andria and the ladies. So that any emissary of the Constable who was not beguiled into attack upon the first chest might, with good reason, strike at the second.

The gold, meanwhile, was in the bottom of a donkey cart, covered over with garbage, and that small conveyance, with no guard whatever but only Quito to lead the donkey, was to carry the first installment of Caterina's marriage portion to the water's edge where Messer the Admiral would take it aboard his shallop, if all went well.

The Prince's reason for visiting Joan before he sailed was—Your Worships have guessed—to tell her where Alopo and Sforza were, but he knew that the guards and household staff which Serjianni had visited upon the Queen would not admit him, or deliver his message, hence the enticement of Ottino. Ottino could get in, and if he was feeling sorry for himself, put out with Serjianni at the time, Ottino might be tricked into conveying the intelligence, thus diverting the Constable's wrath—in this measure—from the shoulders of the Prince, already overloaded with that commodity.

With this in view, Taranto permitted his pursuer to overtake him about halfway to the villa, and as they pounded along the road, side by side, the Prince congratulated Ottino. "This is the wisest move you ever made," said Giovantonio. "It can make you Grand Constable."

"It's very kind of you to say so," the Caracciolo replied, "but how can it? Where are we going?"

"To the Queen!"

"O, no!"

"Certs. We'll fix his wagon."

"Whose wagon?"

"Serjianni's."

"How?"

"Joan will create a scandal at the altar."

"Break up the wedding?"

"Right."

"I don't understand you. Don't you want your cousin to be King?"

"No."

"Why not?"

"No power."

"The better for you."

"I can't fight the entire world—Serjianni now—later, Louis II—who also is my cousin—who has a better claim to the Throne." The even, rhythmic beat of their horses' pounding hoofs punctuated Taranto's catalog of reasons. "Louis d'Anjou is first cousin to the King of France. Jacques Bourbon is no closer than a fourth cousin in the male line. The new Pope will uphold Louis. I cannot fight them all."

"Are you for Louis, then?"

"Are you for me?"

"I shall know better tomorrow."

"Too late. I shall not be here tomorrow."

"No matter where you are—if Serjianni has not provided for me—I shall be your man tomorrow."

"I should be a fool to trust you until I know. Besides, what good will a title from Jacques Bourbon be to you unless the Queen confirms it? Be guided by me—and befriend Joan now. I pledge you this, on my honor as a Del Balzo and an Orsini, that I will support you and see you confirmed in any title or post Joan assigns you."

Fortunately, for the success of Taranto's sophistries, his victim had not been in the room when the Prince obtained a title from Jacques Bourbon for Caldora. Blown hot or blown cold, however, this compact offered Ottino very substantial advantages. Indeed, what had he to lose? If, by the proffer of his friendship, the Queen could be brought to utter a promise, Taranto was committed to its enforcement. Ottino saw no harm in trying.

They reached the gate to Joan's villa as Ottino arrived at that decision, and he stretched out his arms toward the Prince, saying, "I embrace you!"

"Splendid!" said Giovantonio. "And we shall both be forced to embrace Her Majesty before we leave the place. Come!—the countersign."

Ottino whispered to the gateman, and—once inside—his recognizances sufficed to open all doors for them until they reached Joan's own, the entrance to her sleeping suite, where she had retired with the Duchess of Sessa at the approach of these visitors, and barricaded herself with furniture pushed against the door. You may judge the condition of the poor creature's nerves when Superba shut herself off from four stalwart men. She thought Taranto had come to kill her.

"No so," they parlied through the keyhole. "Only let us in so we can speak in private. We have a plan."

"Tell your plan to Alopo—and let him bring it to me. I cannot believe anyone else. I have heard nothing but lies for six months," Joan replied from within.

"I have never lied to Your Majesty," Taranto shouted. "I have been a prisoner myself. I will have vengeance but not upon you. Your Majesty is blameless."

"I cannot trust you. Send Alopo."

"Tell her," whispered Taranto, and simple Ottino did so, putting his lips close to the keyhole so that servants should not hear. "Alopo is in San Vincenzo, Majesty. We need your help to release him—and Sforza too."

"Her Majesty has swooned!" said Covella the she-elephant. "Go away and stop torturing her."

"Open the door. We will help you revive her."

"Go away! You have done enough."

Then, nothing but silence from within for almost a quarter of an hour. To break in were not feasible and not likely to endear the intruders to Her outraged Majesty.

After they had pounded their knuckles raw, Taranto decided to try an approach through a window. Leaving the Caracciolo at the door, he went outside and found a ladder equal to the venture. Ascending, he tapped on the shutters, closed against the heat, and in a moment Superba peeked out, haggard in her misery. "Is it true, Gian?" she croaked. "Has Serjianni locked him up?"

"Yes, Aunty, and will have his head if we do not hurry," said the Prince most convincingly. "May I not come in?"

"You may come in. You are very handsome. You look very romantic on your ladder. You must always come in that way." She assisted him through the window and shut off his speech with a hungry kiss.

Twisting his face aside, Taranto said, "We must get down to business."

"Impetuous boy!" She pulled him to the floor atop her with two simple tricks of an accomplished wrestler.

"I mean to affairs!"

"Yours and mine."

"Of getting him out."

"I'll get him out. O!—the darling!"

"Will you not be serious?"

"Never more! O, what a proud fellow! Do you see where he goes?"

"I have seen it before, Majesty."

"Do you find it changed?"

"For the better, Majesty."

"Smaller, perhaps?"

"Perhaps."

"You comfort me greatly, Gian."

"It is my pleasure, Majesty."

"O, mine too! Just lie still now. There's no hurry."

"Time is of the essence, Majesty."

"Call me 'Aunty'. It's more incestuous."

"Aunty—"

"Yes?"

"We have much to do to get him out."

"Do you speak of getting him *out* when he is hardly in?"

"I mean Alopo."

"What is your plan?"

"To use Ottino. He has nothing."

"He deserves nothing. I have offered to make him Count of Nicastro—upon certain conditions."

"He did not tell me that. Upon what conditions?"

"That he help me—with Serjianni."

"Help you to get Serjianni *here*."

"Lie still. Yes, *here*. Why will he not come to me, Gian? Do I not make you happy?"

"Never so happy——"

"You like this?"

"Like this——"

"Not moving?"

"I never knew——"

"You don't want to go?"

"Never!"

"You don't want to leave me?"

"Never——"

"Is it hot, Gian?"

"So hot!"

"Do I burn you?"

"Like fire!"

"Will you tell Serjianni how I burn you—like fire?"

"Yes, Aunty, yes. I will do more. I will tell you how to get Serjianni—if you will make Ottino Count of Nicastro now—today."

"You know how?"

"I do."

"Tell me."

"Invest Ottino and I will speak."

The Queen raised her voice. "Covella!"

"Yes, Baby. I'm watching."

"Let in Ottino."

"Yes, Baby." The Duchess began moving the furniture away from the door in the anteroom.

Said Superba to Giovantonio: "You trust Ottino."

"No farther than this—that Serjianni treats him badly—and if you treat him well he is your man. Give him a pass to San Vincenzo—or make him Castelan—and Alopo and Sforza will be released."

"But I must have Serjianni before they come out. Afterward will be nothing but War."

"You may have Serjianni any time you wish, Aunty. Say no more about it in Ottino's presence."

The Duchess brought the Caracciolo to the door, caressing him with crude familiarity. "See how happy my baby is," she said. "I forgive you both for making her faint."

Ottino could see that Joan wore a pleased expression although he was looking at her face upside down. He would have liked to say something wittily befitting the occasion, but he never had been able in the past, and he made no history now. "Does Your Highness need any help?" he asked Taranto.

"Greater love hath no man," the Prince replied.

"Kneel down here," said the Queen, "and kiss my hand as Count of Nicastro. I invest you with it as of today, but the documents will have to wait until I can get the Great Seal back from your beloved cousin."

Elated, Ottino dropped to his knees, inarticulate with welling gratitude. "Majesty! Highness!—*me!*" he babbled, and began looking for one of the royal hands to kiss. Both were engaged at the moment, and Joan did not change their occupation, so that when the new Count did try to kiss them right where they were, Giovantonio said, "O, *thank* you, but that wasn't at all necessary."

None of this foolery could divert Joan's mind from her purpose of purposes. "Covella," she commanded, "help Count Nicastro to undress—outside."

"Outside?" The amazed Duchess was nonplused by this refinement of Superba's modesty.

"Outside," Joan repeated. "I'll call you back in a moment."

Ottino fairly soared out the door, buoyed by the sound of his new title.

"Now!" said Joan: and the Prince—purposely misunderstanding—dug in his toes. "No, no," his sovereign reprimanded. "Keep your bargain. I have done my part. How do I get Serjianni?"

"You must send a rat-catcher into San Vincenzo to catch fifty rats alive. So few will never be missed."

"Rats?"

"Serjianni is mortally afraid of them."

"Is he so?"

"Keep them in chests—in the passage outside your boudoir at Castel Nuovo. Get him there, by some ruse, set the rats free, and let your door be the only one that is unlocked. Believe me, he will fly into your arms for protection. The rest is up to you."

"And for this I gave away a County?"

"It is highly practicable. The sight of a rat robs him of all reason and strength. He has no will or resistance. I have seen him reduced to complete helplessness——"

"I do not question that, but unless I marry Jacques Bourbon I cannot get into my own boudoir. I cannot leave this villa. You give me a plan but no means to execute it."

"Ottino will help you. You have made him your slave."

"Ottino commands no men. I need an army."

"I give you Artuso Pappacoda. He has an army."

"An army crying vengeance upon me and Alopo!"

"Restore his brother's estate to him and Ettore and they will forget the past—as I have."

"Have you forgotten the past, Gian? Do you forgive me? Your family is free."

"I forgive you—everything."

"Do you, Gian? Is it so good? Do you like it? Is it hot? Do I burn you? Say again how I burn you like fire!"

"Like fire."

"Stay still. Stay still or you will leave me empty. I cannot bear to be empty."

"Ottino is here—and Pappacoda on the way."

"Pappacoda coming here?—in force?"

"Not in very large force, I am afraid."

"Large enough to take me away from these wretches of Serjianni 's and install me in town? My people hold Castel Capuano. Gian! Can you take me there? I'll restore the

Pappacodas. I'll do anything you ask if you will see Covella and me safe inside Capuano."

The Castel Capuano is a second royal residence within the walls of Naples, the breadth of the city removed from Castel Nuovo. Its name derived from its builder—some ancient Duke of Capua—but it had no present connection with that Principality or with Caldora's pretensions.

"Call Ottino," said the Prince. "I could not take you myself——"

"Covella!" called the Queen, "bring Milord Nicastro!"

The Duchess of Sessa never let her own pleasures delay obedience to the whims of her "Baby", so her enormous body filled the doorway in an instant, and she drew the fledging Count along with her. Their appearance was impressive, not to say unforgettable, because, after undressing Ottino—by Superba's order—Covella had gone on and undressed herself. The only article of apparel remaining upon either of them was a single riband, of a dark color, tied rather tightly—but in a pretty bow—in the midst of Covella's great right thigh. "Milord Nicastro was fixing my garter," said Her Mountainousness coyly, and lifted Ottino's fingers to her lips for a kiss of appreciation.

"He may continue," said the Queen, "if he can answer questions at the same time. Milord Taranto is going to help us get into Castel Capuano."

Two boons in one breath set Covella's entire body rippling with joy. "Happy day!" she sang out, beaming upon the Prince and guiding Ottino's hand down her belly at the same time. "Your Highness will never regret taking the part of two abused and defenseless women. God will bless you. Baby will bless you. I bless you, bless you, bless you."

More important to Giovantonio than Covella's profusion of blessings was the echo of his title to Taranto, spoken by Joan II.

This was the first time Her Majesty ever had applied that name to him, and the occasion augured growing confidence. It made the young diplomatist question his own diplomacies. Was he well advised to leave Naples at a time when both Cousin Jacques and Aunt Joan trusted him above Serjianni? Might he not better let them marry, and by playing one against the other make himself supreme? As many reasons pro as con teemed through the Prince's head, none honorable, but each laden with complications in the logic of probabilities for ultimate material gain.

Take the Royal Exercise for example. It did not seem so onerous today as it had in memory, the junction being more normal, less strenuous, if protracted, but there was the rub. What Prince of any self-respect could base his career as favorite upon the despotical and absolute dictation of a willom female? Stay still! Go fast! Roll over! Play dead! By the gods, a man should pleasure himself, call the tune, and beat the time.

Then, how dispose of Alopo? Regardless of promises, Alopo must not be freed and if he were not freed Joan's confidence would be destroyed and she would never again be tractable. On the other hand, if Taranto absented himself, ostensibly in the Queen's service, and stayed away until Alopo had been returned to his Maker, no responsibility could attach to himself, and he would be welcomed back into Naples eventually as the defunct's avenger.

Best, then, to go to Palermo as planned, keeping faith with Oddo Colonna in Constance, at least until one of the Cardinal's chits had been made Princess of Taranto. An abortive flurry on Joan's behalf now could cost Giovantonio that bride forever.

No more wavering! Avaunt vacillation! At the first opportunity the Prince would whisper the name of Juan d'Aragon into Joan's ear, reviving her hopes, steeling her to endure the ordeal of Serjianni's brutalities interim, even when the Strong Man's order sent Alopo to Hell: but this was the whisper which Ottino Count Nicastro must neither hear nor suspect to have passed. The coming of the Aragonese was too crucial a secret, too daring a dream, too devastating in its implications to be told to any man, least of all to a Caracciolo. In sooth it was too precious a thing to entrust to Superba herself, but the Prince saw no way to prepare Don Juan's bridal couch without informing the bride.

Lost in these cogitations, Taranto had quite forgotten where he was or what he was doing. He had called for Ottino and then fallen silent, eyes fixed upon the Count's childish entertainment of Covella's yearnings, watching without seeing. Neither the she-elephant nor her erstwhile swain noticed that conversation had languished, but the Queen observed it with wry amusement. Her pinkies began lightly to trace the outlines of Taranto's ears, their convolutions and recesses, but her smile was bent upon Covella's expression, growing ever more intense. When the Duchess' eyes rolled out of sight, Joan's hands contracted on the Prince's ears as if they were twin handles on a jug. That brought Giovantonio back to the present, and—aware of his lapse—he put the uppermost question to Ottino. "Would Your Highness be permitted to take Her Majesty with you—when you leave the villa tonight? Would you be stopped?"

"They can't hear you," said Joan huskily.

"Let go of my ears," said Taranto. "I can't hear myself."

Her grip did not relax. "Pretend you are floating," the Queen commanded, and, in fact, the man felt himself lifted, perhaps not quite as high as a bird.

"You said you wanted to get to Castel Capuano," the Prince complained.

"Float!"

It was a good deal to require of a man his size, but the only alternative appeared to be the loss of both ears, so he "floated".

Quick to learn, Giovantonio soon had the hang of it, and was actually beginning to enjoy it, when Aunty Perversity said, "Try again if they can hear. Ask about leaving the villa."

"Too late!" cried Taranto, looking toward the place their companions had been standing. "The Duchess has dropped dead—and Ottino is not to be found!"

They did find him, of course, some time later, enveloped and all but smothered in the superfluities of Ruffo flesh. Joan was not gracious about that, either. She had been saving Ottino for dessert. "That's the first time Covella ever betrayed me," mourned the Queen. "I don't know why I'm fanning her."

"O Baby!" said the Duchess, and again, with even more emphasis, "O, Baby!"

Joan could not remain angry with her only faithful Lady in Waiting, but turned upon Ottino, who sat, natheless still, propped against the wall, swigging a goblet of wine, and not unpleased with himself. "I told you not to play with Her Highness if you couldn't answer civil questions at the same time," said the Queen tartly.

"What was the question, Majesty? Let me try to answer it now," said Ottino, and his gaze trailed over the Lady Alp with a mountain-climber's affection for a peak he has scaled. Gone was his watchdog manner, gone the last trace of lackey subservience. By virtue of an unsuspected alchemy Count Nicastro had emerged from between Covella's thighs, a man reborn. The Duchess, for her part, looked no less happily on him, and—notwithstanding she was several times a mother—saw him in a light which never had shone upon her husband Marzano Duke Sessa.

This chance was more to Taranto's need than if the like impression had been left upon the Queen herself, because Covella's hatred for Serjianni was deeply ingrown, inexpungeable, whereas Joan wished the man no more vital ill than to be in love with her. A profitable day indeed, if it had put the team of Ottino-Covella into the cabal's service, and that was the look of it. Despite his Caracciolo blood, Ottino was dedicated.

"The question was—how large a force will be required to remove Her Majesty and the Duchess to Castel Capuano—tonight. Where are you likely to encounter difficulties? Here? At the gate? In town? At the Castel?" The Prince made the issue seem utterly personal, Ottino's bounden duty. "You know the Constable's practices. Can you pass through his guards—with Their Highnesses? I'm afraid a domino will not conceal the Duchess of Sessa's identity."

"I could pass them through," Ottino admitted, "but if I did, Serjianni would know at once that I have deserted him. I could be no further use to Her Majesty, nor free Alopo, but more likely would take his place on the gallows. Better to let me create a distraction in town—and Your Highness could ride in safely with no more than thirty men."

"Unfortunately I lack twenty-nine of having so many. My army is Tomaso, waiting at the foot of the ladder."

"You said Pappacoda was coming," Joan interposed.

"I'm afraid he has been delayed," said Taranto solemnly, walking to the window.

The view was toward town, and it included the highroad from a point half a mile away, but the contour of the land and the villa's trees hid the way between. Nothing more exciting than a flock of geese appeared in the distance but when Giovantonio looked straight down, Tomaso was coming up the ladder like a monkey. "Caldora——at the gate," he panted, "more than fifty—light horse. They have taken——Pappacoda——and one chest."

"Are they coming in?"

"The gatekeeper says no."

The Queen came up behind the Prince. "What is it?"

"The answer to your prayers," said Taranto. "An army for you—but this Commander will not be satisfied with a little County like Nicastro." He looked over Joan's shoulder and saw the great gams of Sessa spreading to receive another adjustment of her garter.

"Caldora!" Joan guessed.

"Caldora—with a hundred men. He wants Capua, with the prerogatives of a Prince. Give it to him, Aunty. Put yourself in his care. I am sailing tonight to Palermo. With Chiaramonte's help we'll restore your contract with Prince Juan d'Aragon. Don't marry before I get back—and I'll bring you the other Sicily."

The Queen held her features rigidly expressionless, but she could not check the twin torrents of brine that rolled down her cheeks and wet her breasts, still half unlaced from their frolic. "You would do all this for me," she said hoarsely, "but you do not want me for yourself."

No words the Prince had were adequate, but he gallantly took her into his arms.

"I am an unwanted woman, Gian, unwanted and unloved. Not even Alopo loves me. He climbed upon me—like a ladder." She turned her head to see what was going on behind her. "Look. Real desire. Something I cannot command. What is wrong with me, Gian?"

"I do not know. You *are* loved." He tried clumsily to kiss her, but Joan turned away ... "You are a noble liar," she said, then, grimly, "Must I give up Capua—to that black weasel Caldora?"

"He will protect you from Serjianni—until I get back."

"I can protect myself from Serjianni. Am I not to frighten him with rats?"

"Caldora will make that possible—by taking you to town."

"I don't think I wish to go to town with Caldora. I don't trust him. He's slippery—and his son is just like him."

"He is your only hope."

"Then, God help me."

Giovantonio leaned out the window. "Get our horses," he commanded, and Tomaso slid to the ground.

"You will leave me?" Joan's query was surprised and chiding at the same time.

"I have much to do to put myself afloat. Serjianni means to stop me." Pointing to the unequal combat on the floor—"Ottino was supposed to keep me from sailing, but now he is ours. I shall send Pappacoda to you. He is half ours—and you can win the rest. I command all the Del Balzos and the Orsinis, and ten more illustrious Houses have helped me today. My cousin, Andria, will hold Rome—if Sforza is not released. I am marrying a Colonna—whose 'uncle' will be the true Pope. I am going to fetch you the husband of your choice—and I have offered you Caldora's army. Dearest Aunty—what more can I do for you. I am not God."

"I need you near me ... See how happy they are ... And I am all alone. Come to me again now—before you go!"

"No! I cannot!" Taranto tore himself out of her grasp and put one leg out the window, feeling for the ladder with his toe.

Still Joan clutched his arm. "Tell me, then, does Caldora know your plans?"

"No one knows my plans but you—and you must not share them—not even with Covella. Above all, don't let Caracciolo know we are treating for Prince Juan again."

"No, no. I understand. Kiss me——"

The Prince was on the ladder by that time and might have got away, but in his make-up was the tenderness to comfort afflicted womankind. Besides, he had not gained his point for Caldora, and—consequently—had not gained for his own landing purposes that stretch of shoreline in Aversa. Giovantonio heartily disliked to leave that area fallow for cultivation by Louis II, so—for mixed reasons—he gave the Queen his mouth to chew upon a moment, then whispered against her lips. "Will you not speak with Caldora?"

"That is important to you."

"Jacques Bourbon has promised him Capua. If you do less, we lose him; you lose the only army you can command. Jacques has sent Caldora here to arrange a private meeting—behind Serjianni 's back. You can use that meeting to get to Castel Capuano."

Not because his logic had convinced her, or because she hoped for anything from Caldora, but solely because Giovantonio wished it, Joan gave in. "I can ... I will," she said. "Let Caldora come in. Sforza will keep him in his place—if Ottino can get Sforza out of prison."

"Do not doubt it."

"Right now I doubt everything but you, Gian, and God knows why I trust you."

CHAPTER EIGHT

ARANTO'S CONSCIENCE was a thing of steel, in the sense that it armored his desires against all shafts and arrows from without, so that Superba's parting words did not ring long in his ears. To be blunt, the Queen's tenderness, and his own momentary sympathy for her, had alike left his mind before he and Tomaso reached the villa gate. Small wonder, when you consider the enormity of ingratitude which must be dealt with in the roadway.

A scant two hours before, Caldora had said that he would "never forget" Giovantonio's intercession to obtain the taxing of Capua for him, but in that short space he had so far forgotten as to take into custody Artuso Pappacoda and one of the money chests. Belike the deed was by order of Serjianni, but not necessarily so. The lure of 50,000 in gold was ample to inspire Caldora's own initiative.

Crossing Joan's enclosed park toward the gatekeeper's lodge, Giovantonio asked Tomaso, "Has Caldora opened the chest?"

"What do I know, Milord?"

"It will make a vast difference."

"Aye." That it would! If Caldora already knew that he had been bilked, he was not likely to permit this defenseless pair to go their way unquestioned.

"Did you say he has fifty men?" The Prince was thinking aloud.

"Sixty," Tomaso replied tersely.

"We're outnumbered," said the Prince wryly.

They were outnumbered in the same ratio whether Caldora were operating independently or as Serjianni's agent, and in either case the aim of the majority would be to keep Taranto ashore until the gold was taken from him. No figment of prestige would hold his person sacred from their violence in the doing, for under the three almost co-equal "supremacies" then current in the Regno, any malefactor could find at least one authority to condone his acts of lese majesty against either of the others.

Caldora was at Joan's gate as an envoy of Bourbon, on a mission undercutting the Constable, but along the way he had acted agreeably to the Constable's wishes—in the matter of the chest— thereby providing himself with a defense if his perfidy should be discovered. Obviously, the only way for the Prince to assure himself of this ingrate's fidelity—the only way to reach the shallop and sail—was by appeal to Caldora's ambition, by convincing him that his greatest gain lay in Taranto's success, and that the Prince was invincible.

That was a large order for a fugitive attended by a single sword-hand, hampered by the necessity to keep his most powerful argument concealed. How tell a character so vile as Caldora that the secret of forthcoming Tarantine success was to be through betrayal of both his Angevin cousins to the Aragonese? The man would inform Bourbon and Louis II before Ferdinand the Just had agreed to the plan, and Giovantonio would be excommunicated by at least three of the Popes at once.

This much, however, would weigh heavily in Caldora's scales: the gift of Capua from Queen Joan—helpless as she was—had a vastly greater validity than the same investiture from Jacques Bourbon, and Her Majesty need not remain so helpless if the new Prince of Capua lent her his arms.

That, leastwise, was the heaviest artillery in Taranto's magazine, and if it failed to do his business he and Tomaso must ride like Hell.

The gate was still closed against Caldora's entry, and the contest between the Melfiman gatekeeper and the Commander had not yet got beyond the wordy stage, the guard defending his position with infinite volubility and Caldora doling out his syllables sparingly, as usual. "Open—or we will break down the gate," was the net of the demand, which provoked the other to a supplication of fifty Saints (by name), to witness that he came of a dutiful family for many generations (which he numbered), who never betrayed a trust, and on and on, to the ultimate effect that His Lordship could not come in unless he gave the password.

The harangue was passing through the wicket of the warder's lodge, and a handful of Serjianni's guards—no more than eight— clustered inside, fidgeting, listening, ready to skite themselves if eloquence failed to hold back the force in the road, when Taranto and Tomaso rode up. Only too clearly, an application to leave the place by that gate was untimely and would be denied. If the bars were let down for even an instant, the meager guard would be trampled over by the Capuans like so much grass. The gateman forsook the wicket to say so. "You can't go out, Highness. Forgive me or not—you can't go out. I call upon all the Saints to witness——"

Taranto dismounted, thinking fast, and thinking that the situation had its advantages. Here was the opportunity to question Caldora, take his temper, while a sturdy wall separated them. Let Caldora shew himself a reasonable man, and Giovantonio was ready to pass him the secret word which had opened the gate for Ottino: but if Milord Capua took the high hand, he would have to fight his way in, a feat impossible to accomplish before

Serjianni and Duke Sessa could get out from town with enough men to prevent it.

Cutting in upon the gateman's prayers, the Prince said sternly and loudly, "Her Majesty is expecting these Lordships. They come from the Constable. She wishes to see them."

"Her wishes ain't in my orders, Highness. If these Lordships be from the Constable they'd have the password. Trick after trick has been tried on me—but I know my duty. I come from a family that's served——"

The Prince entered the lodge and looked out the wicket, directly into the neat black beard. "Milord!"

"You here—Milord?" Caldora seemed genuinely surprised.

"I could not leave Naples until I obtained Her Majesty's confirmation—for you." As he spoke, Taranto tried to see around the sleek head, looking for Artuso Pappacoda or any of the Tarantines who had helped to shuffle the money boxes. "Her Majesty grants it—and I am the first to greet you as Lord Prince of Capua. I do so with my whole heart."

For what it was worth, judge as you will, Caldora was touched to his soul. "I am too overwhelmed to speak," quoth he, lowering his eyes like a maiden. "Does Her Majesty know that it was I who captured Alopo—and Sforza?"

Joan had called him a weasel without knowing that, but Giovantonio was not disposed to split hairs. "She forgives you," said he.

Caldora was still further impressed. "Nobody but Your Highness could have done so much—and how poorly I repay you."

Ah? Now it came!

Caldora beckoned to his right, and called, "Artuso!" Then he faced the wicket grimly. "Bad news, Highness," he said. "Milord Constable, to whom I gave my flesh in marriage, has cheated you."

That twist, so natural, struck Giovantonio dumb for a moment. He gasped—which looked like surprise.

"Aye," Caldora went on, bristling, "you have no dot for your sister, no money. He has given you a chest of stones! Here is Artuso. He shewed me. He will attest."

Pappacoda's lugubrious face appeared modestly at one side of the aperture, nodding sad confirmation. "Nothing but stones," he moaned.

Taranto bit his lip to keep from laughing, and Caldora's outrage continued building. "I could die of shame," he said. "This is the way my son-in-law pays you for all you have done for me. Who shall ever trust Serjianni again as long as he lives?"

Apparently Milord Capua meant to sweep past the great mystery, how the chest had come to be opened and the fraud revealed to him, so Taranto ignored that angle too. Frowning his frightfulest, Giovantonio avowed, "The King shall hear of this!"

"The *Queen*," Caldora suggested. "Let us tell the Queen. But these varlets won't let me in without their stupid countersign."

Taranto looked behind, at the gatekeeper who had drunk in every word. "Will you not open now, Messer Castelan? Their Highnesses have given me the countersign."

"I did not hear it, as God is my judge. They will have to say it to me. I know my duty——"

"Milord Capua just now said, *Bellasardabella*, as plainly as could be."

"I did not hear him."

"Then wash your ears."

"As God is my Judge, he must say it to me."

"Come, then, put your ear to the wicket."

The Melfiman leaned close.

"*Bellasardabella*," said Caldora.

"Damned if it ain't!" the astounded gatey burst out, and, to his men, "Take down the bars!"

Said Caldora, "Your Highness increases my obligation." He was moving away from the wicket, but Taranto called, "Milord!"

"Command me."

"You feel obligated to me."

"Everything I have is yours."

"If you will be so good as to convey that to your son Antonio—in Aversa——"

"Before I sleep!" Caldora Signed himself with a Cross.

"Some of my associates may be passing that way, and I should like to know that their reasonable requests—in my name—will be honored."

"Aversa is yours to command," said the weasel. "How soon may we expect your—your *associates*—to be passing that way?"

"May I not feel that they will be welcome at any time?"

"Any time," the other echoed, "as long as there is a Caldora alive."

The villa gates were opened then, and the Capuan army began moving in.

Taranto remounted and sat with Tomaso at the side of the path, waiting for the Commander and Pappacoda. When they came, Giovantonio indicated the little group of Serjianni's guards, afoot and shrunken into insignificance by the full-armored cavalcade. "May I suggest that Your Lordship have them tied up?" said he. "When that is done, you are in complete possession of the Queen. I trust you will treat her gently. She cannot be commanded—but may be led. She is expecting Your Highnesses."

"Are you not coming with me?" Caldora was disturbed.

"No," said Taranto, turning to face Artuso Pappacoda with narrowed eyes. "This scoundrel—this *thief*—has ruined all my plans. I cannot sail without that money. What have you done with it?"

Aware as he was that the Prince was play-acting, shamming, to throw Caldora off his scent, still those names were hard for Pappacoda to bear, and he colored, involuntarily, and clamped down his jaws in a bite so hard it would have cracked marble.

"I don't believe your lies about Serjianni," the Prince went on, "I counted the money myself. Where is it gone, you robber? Tell me—or I run you through." He made as if to draw his sword.

"Stolen, Highness," Artuso faltered.

"Stolen, where?—by whom? Who unlocked the box? How did you know only stones were in it? Answer me——" Again he bobbled his sword-hilt, and this time Caldora protested.

"Milord, I suspect Serjianni. He is the cozener. As you love me, do not kill your friend."

"Do you defend him, Milord?" Taranto blazed. "Then tell me where to find fifty thousand—*now*—this night—so that I may sail, for I cannot go empty handed."

"I have not so much in town," Caldora confessed, floundering with the novelty of these revelations.

"Of course not," Giovantonio snapped, "and so I shall have to wait. But mark you me, I shall learn the truth of this tomorrow. Messer Pappacoda! You will be pleased to attend me at midday—tomorrow—in the Constable's palace!" With that—as the last of the Capuan soldiers came through the gate—Taranto spurred around them and was off, closely followed by Tomaso.

The dodge was not ineffective, for it left the impression of a breach in the cabal, also, that Taranto would not sail that night because the money was gone; and it gave Caldora to ponder whether Pappacoda had purloined the gold or not.

The ethics of leaving his mother's cloak-bearer under so heavy a burden of suspicion never entered the Prince's mind.

The day was well advanced, the watch upon the water's edge was tightening by the hour. How many more such subterfuges might be necessary to elude Serjianni's vigilance?

The Prince headed toward Naples, and around the first bend in the road he let Tomaso come alongside. "If I were Caldora—that would not deceive me," Giovantonio said. "He will probably set men to follow us. So—let us pray—in San Lionardo."

The church and nunnery of that name already loomed on their right, at the place called Chiaja, which is only a little way outside the Posilippo Gate of Naples. Although religious in character, the edifice towered like a citadel, built on an island of rock, but accessible over a causeway wide enough to accommodate a wain. The church was a refuge for sailors and a sanctuary for all who were pursued or sore beset, an they came with contrite hearts. Since Taranto was not claiming haven, but entered only to pray, he did not examine the condition of his heart or inquire if Tomaso's were humble. They simply walked in, leaving their horses in plain view of any who looked that way either from the beach or from the Posilippo road on the bluff above. Even the Queen could have seen them if she had been looking, but her gaze was fixed nearer at hand.

Poor Pappacoda. What he endured for his Prince!

The day lacked but two hours of sunset, a span of some three hours until dark, but that is a long while to pray. In three hours the causeway could be flanked, covered and surrounded by Serjianni 's minions, ashore and afloat—and San Lionardo too. Delay would have been suicidal for the two supplicants, but they did not lose a moment. A single *Ave* and half a genuflection each disposed of their duties, as such, and Taranto led the way around the altar on a floor littered with straw.

Here evening had already come, and the dimness was punctured in only a few places by the smoking, yellow flames of blest candles consuming themselves before images. The Prince shuffled his feet, rather than striding, to avoid stumbling over sleeping derelicts, fugitives from who knows what man's wrath or whose laws. Some sat up, or crouched apprehensive, at this unwonted intrusion, informed by the Prince's bearing that he was not one of them. Not every Lord felt or acknowledged a proper respect for this sacred place or for its tradition of safety for the hunted. Under Alopo the catchpolls had dragged out more than one struggling penitent in spite of the priests' best efforts to stop them. One could never be sure of Divine Protection in Naples, where Infidels, Atheists, Pagans and Turks abounded.

"You," said Taranto to a husky chunk of flotsam, not unlike himself in size, "do you want a horse—as a gift? Have you a companion—who will ride with you? Do you want to get away? I'll give you money too."

Even this offer was none so great a novelty here as some gentlefolk may suppose. Politics, being the game it is, always dangerous and often lethal, not infrequently levels the orders of mankind. The big oaf in the straw did not leap at the chance, and neither did his neighbors start bidding for the dubious favor.

"We'll give you our clothing—in exchange for yours," the Prince bargained.

Some eight or nine men had come clustering when the overtures began, but the item of changing clothes only confirmed their native suspicion that they were being asked to volunteer as red herring. Horses, money and clothing would have to be defended at sword-point, and not even the murderers among them were accustomed to plying their trade face-on in knightly fashion. Neither had any of these riffraff the least interest in preserving one Prince rather than another.

"Not I," said the hunks. "There's no percentage." Others shook their heads or blankly stared.

"I'll get the priest," Tomaso suggested. "He'll make them change."

"No," said the Prince. "We'll swim as we are. Nobody can see what we're wearing under water."

"We can't stay under water four hours," the soldier objected, but he was overruled.

Weighted as they were by spurs, swords and daggers, Lord and man entered the water on the Bayside of San Lionardo, shielded by the church from surveillance ashore but in full view of the refugees, and of half a dozen churchmen, numbers of nuns in the cloister windows and a score of sporting urchins, who dove from the rocks and swam around the men, burdened by no more clothing than any other fish.

Taranto removed his cap in the water, and bade Tomaso shed his, making their heads indistinguishable from those of the boys, at very short distance, and thus they began seeking that one shallop, among the hundred there, which was the Tarantine navy. Tomaso had seen the vessel only once, Taranto, never, and from water level every hull of a size looked exactly like every other.

At first their young swimming companions jabbered myriad questions, answering each other when the men did not reply, where they were going, what they had done, who they were and who pursued them. Two of the lads had recovered the men's discarded caps, and put them on, so that nothing had been gained by throwing them away.

"Go back," said Taranto. "You will get us killed, and you are too young to have blood on your souls. Go back."

The boys were also too young to be swayed by adult logic or moralizing, and so remained near, swimming around, under and between the two grown-ups for the better part of an hour. Born to the Piscean element, the exercise wearied them less than walking, but Tomaso's strength began to flag.

They had swum around Uovo, the Castle of the Mystic Egg, and headed toward the smaller isle on which sate the masonry that was San Vincenzo, the royal donjon keep. Curiously, if Alopo and Sforza had been favored with cells boasting windows, the prisoners might have looked down upon the bobbing heads of two enemies whose potency, never yet very high, was at that moment in some danger of sinking altogether.

"With Your Highness' permission," Tomaso panted, "I think I shall float—a while."

"You have my permission," the Prince puffed back at him, "but let's see you do it."

Tomaso could not float, of course, which amused the small fry mightily. They, making no allowance for the steel their seniors were carrying, gave themselves fantastic pleasure in watching Tomaso go down.

"If you don't get to Hell away from us," Taranto threatened, "I'll cut your little kernels off!"

That was funny too, to the boys, but no vestige of humor remained in the soldier's plight. To the left of their course, the nearest shore was that stretch of beach where boats of all sizes, of all rigs, in various states of decay, were drawn up—if not gunwale to gunwale, still, cheek by jowl—and any one of them might be the vessel of the Admiral. Here—somewhere, some time in the night—the shallop would meet the garbage cart, but the finer details of those arrangements were no help to the swimmers. Whether their boatman would sail offshore until the appointed time, or sleep on the sand in the shadow of his tub, was no more likely one way than another. The adventurers were indeed at sea, and at least one of them might have died of it had not a homing oysterman sailed within their grasp.

The master of the craft came to beat the boys off his gunwales, but when he saw that they were men, fully clad and sodden, he called upon the Virgin (and the two sailors with him) to help the pair into the boat.

"Put about, and I shall give you my purse," said Taranto as the water ran out of his ears. "We have enemies ashore."

"And who hath not?" asked the delver for sea-fruit. "I have a mother-in-law at home."

"Don't take them," one of the rowdies called up from the water. "They have raped the Abbess of San Lionardo."

What special Devil is it who puts such maliciousness into the heads of innocent babes?

Tomaso, on his back among the bivalves until then, got to his knees, crying, "Go to!" and began pelting the urchins with oysters.

"Here, now!" The master struck down Tomaso's arm. "I've been all day finding them. Must I look twice?"

"Put about!" the Prince commanded, and pulled his purse out of his belt.

The mariner hefted it in his hand. "Soaking wet that would never carry Your Lordship to the bottom," said he, but even as he spurned the pay he ordered the boat about, as if heading back to sea. "I never forget a face," the oysterman explained. "Ben't Your Highness the Prince of Taranto?"

"When I'm dry—and to my friends," Giovantonio conceded.

"I never forget a face. I gave Your Highness the first oyster Your Highness ever sucked. Don't you remember—fifteen years ago? I've supplied the Castel with their shellfish since long before Your Highness was born," and the oysterman knelt on the day's catch to kiss the Prince's hand.

The vessel's arc, in turning, carried them close enough to the beach to reveal its tranquillity. No horsemen of any hostile persuasion, nor foot neither, could be seen right or left.

"What enemy doth Your Highness apprehend?" asked the master. "I am here every day. Is it the French King, now? A simple man cannot choose his party these days. Will Your Highness be pleased to guide me?"

"You must be of my party," said Taranto, clapping his hand to the oysterman's cheek. "I'll give you a King—" but with that he broke off, and began again. "Can you have the beach full of sailors tonight?—armed for trouble?—in my service? I will see them well rewarded—in time."

"I can't do that and keep Your Highness afloat too," the mariner said bluntly. "Somebody will have to pass the word ashore."

"Put about," said the Prince. "I'll take my chance ashore. How many men can you have?—dependable. The Constable is the enemy."

The oysterman whistled, low and long, looking to starboard where the school of younglings wriggled back toward San Lionardo like so many pollywogs. "The Constable—is it?"

"That makes a difference. That frightens you."

"I can't say it frightens me, Highness, but there's no denying it makes a difference. Not many would cross—Caracciolo."

"Thirty?"

"Perhaps ... There will be some killing?"

To the best of his ability, considering the meagerness of his own information, Taranto outlined the evening's prospects. When he came to name the boatman dubbed the Admiral, he could not even do that, but by the happiest chance the description sufficed. The man who had carried the letter to Tristano Chiaramonte was now notorious on the waterfront under the sobriquet of *Saint Gabriel.*

"Saint Gabriel!" the master discovered. "Why, *that's* his boat—right over *there!*" The oysterman pointed toward the opposite shore at the base of Vesuvius. "So that's what he's waiting for! Port! Port, boys," he called to the tiller. "We must put His Highness aboard San Gabriel's shell. By the Virgin, I'm glad *I* am not forced to sail to Palermo in that feast for woodworms."

Tomaso sniffed. "I'm glad that I didn't have to swim to it!" Even then the Tarantine flagship lay at such distance that it was not boarded for another half hour.

No matter. As the sun went down, Giovantonio's good luck fitted together with his foresight, and the chest which went out the Salerno gate, in the wake of Andria, Marie-Luise and family, drew off Serjianni's main force, so that the fishers and sailors and beach-mites who assembled to protect Quito's gold-laden garbage had nothing whatever to do but dance, play and sing, swig it and frig it till dawn.

CHAPTER NINE

THE MONEY SAILED—and was well received in Palermo by the Chiaramontes, who loved Giovantonio so much they would not hear of him leaving—ever. Let his family be sent for, most especially the bride, and let Time have its way with Queen Joan II.

On that one basic principle, of inevitable decay, the Prince and Tristano were in perfect accord, but their views, how they should assist the Fates from day to day, were widely divergent. Speedy decisions were the essence of Taranto's need, but his host—a more experienced tactician—swore that he could not move hand or foot, pending outland developments. Their differences were irreconcilable temporarily, but separation of their interests was unthinkable to both, so the Prince was forced to relax his impatience and inform the Queen—by cipher via Pappacoda—that he would be delayed.

Giovantonio explained to Aunt Joan that Chiaramonte would revive the negotiations to marry her to Prince Juan d'Aragon as soon as Ferdinand "the Just" had won his point in a prior dispute then pending between him and the Emperor *cum* the Council. Impossible to mix or mingle the two appeals, because the first one also looked toward territorial increase for Aragon, and the delegate-Electors at Constance were already calling the King, "Ferdinand the Octopus."

Ferdinand had agreed to abandon his Catalan Pope Benedict XIII if the Emperor could assure him that the Pope who came out of the Council at Constance would sanctify Aragon's claim to Corsica. That claim was opposed by the Corsicans themselves, and by the Banca San Giorgio of Genoa, as the largest holder of mortgages upon Corsican real estate, but Giovantonio could not even guess how Cardinal Colonna felt on the subject. What was more, the Prince was not going to ask the Cardinal such an embarrassing question until he had his Colonna bride.

The Emperor, on the other hand—still in face-to-face conference with Ferdinand—was writing to Cardinal Colonna and to every other candidate for the Papacy, attempting to elicit a uniform pledge from each, guaranteeing Ferdinand's satisfaction in Corsica no matter which of them was Elected. Not only was that the best means of breaking the deadlock but it was the only way the Emperor could get himself out of Perpignan. He was not a prisoner in any sense except that he could not leave, unless by undignified flight. Corsica, so to speak, was the price of the Emperor's ransom.

Taranto prayed that Aunt Joan would be steadfast in refusing to marry interim.

Alas, that cipher from Palermo did not reach Artuso until too late to shape an effective resistance. Serjianni, as usual, had been too fast for them.

As Caldora's troop moved into Naples through the Posilippo Gate—at dawn after the Prince had sailed—escorting Her Majesty, the Duchess of Sessa, Ottino and Pappacoda (with the stone-filled chest between them), they were confronted by Serjianni himself at the head of the Palace Guard. Duke Sessa and his eldest son by Covella—hight Marino Marzano—were of the Constable's party, and between *them* was the other chest, also filled with trash, which the Marzanos had recovered on the Nola road in the night. Disarmed, but still insolent, and not apprehensive for his future, the soldier Riccardo and his six Tarantine companions were distributed among the Constable's men-at-arms, in custody, but not bound, and entirely unmarked by battle for they had given up their box without a struggle.

The meeting of these two forces was sudden, as big a surprise to the one side as the other, and the presence of his son-in-law— so early up—shook Caldora's confidence. Even as the Queen's defender he lacked justification to strike the first blow, unless Serjianni demanded that Her Majesty be handed over, and nothing appeared to be farther from the Constable's mind. The Strong Man was weeping like a small child! He was weeping at first view, the tears were genuine and not shed for effect, moreover they flowed in greater abundance than the loss of a mere 50,000 of Crown moneys seemed to warrant. Caldora was thrown completely off balance.

"Woe, ah, woe!" the Constable sobbed, and—catching sight, first, of the she-elephant, then of the Queen—"Thank God you have brought her. Majesty—My Majesty—I must report that we have lost Rome."

In reality the Crown had lost nothing in Rome that it actually possessed a week or a month before. Sforza's men still held San Angelo and Ostia, as they had when Andria left The City. What the Constable meant was that Braccio da Montone, another *Condottiere,* had overrun the streets and occupied the bridges and walls, putting Sforza's garrisons under a state of siege.

"What else did you expect?" Superba snapped. "That is what comes of locking up our best Commander."

"Not I—but the King—ordered Sforza's arrest," said Serjianni, recovering some dignity, and went on, to Caldora, "Your Highness will prepare to march at once. We must get Braccio out of there."

"The Prince of Capua will remain with me," said Joan determinedly. "Sforza will drive out Braccio. Heed me."

Serjianni bobbed his head in mocking acknowledgment that he had heard, but he gave no sign that Caldora's new title, on the Queen's lips, had penetrated his consciousness. He spoke with a smile as he turned his horse to ride with Superba's party. "Your Majesty will wish to discuss that with the King. Sforza is His Majesty's prisoner, not mine."

"You will stop referring to this Barbarian puppet of yours as 'King'," said Joan. "There is only one Majesty in the Regno and that is mine."

Serjianni made no reply but rode straight on, and thus a clash at arms in the street was obviated. The defection of Caracciolo's kinsman and Pappacoda from the Constable's communion was neither openly revealed nor made an issue, for the nonce. At a sign from him, Serjianni's force wheeled and preceded the Capuans to Castel Nuovo. Under pressure of the Roman calamity, which required immediate and sovereign attention, the Queen and Caldora had no alternative but to follow; likewise Ottino and Pappacoda, although they both knew that Serjianni must be aware that Joan had been "escaping" at the moment of encounter. Whether they, personally, were suspected of conspiracy, or might lie their way out of it, could be revealed only in the sequel.

Artuso took substantial consolation from the strength of the Queen's position regarding Sforza. That Commander was indubitably the only man who could drive Braccio out of Rome, and Serjianni or Jacques Bourbon must release him for that purpose. Once that was accomplished, Sforza, at the head of his victorious army, would certainly require the Constable's baton from Serjianni, as already conferred by the Queen.

Even Covella was bemused into new confidence by Braccio's ambitious activities, and by the time the principals reached the drawbridge of Castel Nuovo she had—in fancy—sent Serjianni into a pauper's exile, and married her niece Polissena Ruffo to Sforza's son Francesco.

At the drawbridge Superba took occasion to address Caldora, even more pointedly, as *Milord Prince of Capua,* saying, "Your men will hold the bridge pending our pleasure. We may not wish to remain in the Castel." With that, she put her mount on the planks and swept regally into the royal dwelling.

Serjianni gave Caldora such a look as would have frozen the blood of a salamander. "Congratulations, Father," he said, with intentionally prophetic grimness—and followed the Queen inside.

In the courtyard, as Joan dismounted, Marino Marzano and the soldier Riccardo were screaming at each other, the high-born officer attempting to send the other, together with his six companions, to the donjon, Riccardo stanchly demanding to know the nature of their crime. "Have we stolen? Have we killed? Have we thought ill of the Queen? We did nothing but carry that chest full of trash—which the Constable gave to our master!"

"What is the trouble?" asked Her Majesty. "What have these men done?"

"They have stolen fifty thousand ducats from their master," said Serjianni. "Do not trouble yourself about them."

"But I do," said Joan, who already had the pith of this story from its prototype retailed by Caldora and Pappacoda. Tactfully, for the protection of her well-born defenders, she made no allusion to that earlier version but gave all her attention to this new one.

"Who is your master?" she asked the brave Riccardo.

"His Highness the Prince of Taranto, Majesty," the soldier sang out proudly, "and, please God, he has got clean away from them with every golden ducat of the fifty thousand. He is sailed in spite of the Constable—who filled that chest with rubbish."

"He lies!" cried Serjianni, Duke Sessa and Marino, all in one voice, and each went on to explain his own lie, in different words, raising a cacophony of shrill and incomprehensible pandemonium.

Superba waved their uproar aside and spoke softly to Riccardo. "I believe you," said she, measuring his physique with a practiced eye. "You are free to go about your master's business, but when it is finished come back to me. I have something to say to you."

"Gracious Majesty!" The Tarantines bent the knee. "They have taken our arms."

"Restore them their arms," Joan commanded Marzano the younger, "and hereafter know that the men of my nephew—Prince of Taranto—enjoy our special favor." Turning to Serjianni she commanded, "Give these men one hundred ducats each."

Never before had Caracciolo been so deeply humiliated.

"Hoho!" crowed Covella, not yet dismounted, because getting her off a horse was an undertaking second only to getting her upon one. "Hoho! That will teach you!" Then, moving closer to her son, she shook a stubby forefinger under his nose as if he were still an adolescent. "How many times do I have to tell you?—*never* do what your father says. You are getting more like him every day."

"Grr-r-row!" Marino growled, snapping with his teeth at his mother's hand, and laughing when she jerked away. Aside from his politics young Marzano was as likable a fellow as you could care to meet, sweet tempered and brave. "I'm sorry, Mother," he mocked her gently. "Father and I had the impression that the Principality of Taranto attached to the Crown. We did not know that Giovantonio Del Balzo-Orsini had been invested there. Now that we know—may I help you down?" He raised his arms as if to catch her as she leapt.

The process was none so simple. Eight hostlers generally participated, and more than one man had been ruptured in this service.

The Queen did not wait to see her Lady hit the ground or even to make certain that Riccardo and his men received their arms and ducats. Having spoken as the sovereign here, she assumed-most recklessly—that her will would be executed, and, reverting to her habits of the Alopo era, she headed for her own apartments, taking no cognizance of the change in her status or of any possible menace to her person.

Joan was right in this. No other approach to her problems could have served her so well. No other manner would have suited Superba, or pleased her adherents so much, or so greatly impressed Serjianni. He trailed after her, and Caldora after him, then Pappacoda and Sessa. Only Ottino held back, to be with his love, impelled by a sudden jealousy of her son Marino, with whom the newborn Count Nicastro now realized he had something in common.

When they were gone too, after the others, no one of consequence was left in the courtyard to see justice done Riccardo and company except Serjianni's Antonio. He had no orders from the Constable, how to deal with the situation, but he had heard the Queen say, *one hundred ducats each,* so—when the Tarantines had got back their stabbers—he led them into Serjianni's office.

"This is likely to go hard with me," said Antonio, counting out the money, "so I shall ask you to sign a receipt. Can you write your names?" Only Riccardo had acquired that art, so he signed for all, but in the doing, he seized Antonio's forearm with a grip not to be shaken, and said, "Ser Burser!—had you any part in the drowning of the Lord Taranto's Aloys?"

Antonio said he had not, since they were seven to one, and volunteered to prove his good will toward their master by acting the spy upon the Constable, in the Prince's behalf, as long as he held his present post, and after, an he survive it.

From a box the secretary took a seal, and on a parchment made its impress. Then from his head he plucked a hair, and shewed the Tarantines how to weave that in and out of punctures in the signet. "That will pass you through the strictest guards of Melfi—it will admit you to him or to me—wherever we are. It will give your Lord access to the Constable's most secret secrets if you use it right. Memorize the seal so you can draw it with pen—and—here!" With one mighty tug he tore out a handful of his own hair and folded it into the parchment like a letter. Holding that out to Riccardo, Antonio said, "I can do no more."

"This much more," Riccardo corrected him. "You can give me the key to the Grand Constable's cipher—if your heart is with us."

"I can. I will," said Antonio. "Come back—tonight, tomorrow—and I shall have it ready. I must not take the time now. We shall all wish to know what they decide about Sforza."

Granting the truth of that, the Tarantines kissed the traitor and left him, they to their horses, and he to the Queen's suite.

A great many words had been exchanged when Antonio reached the conference, but most of them ran in circles, so he had but a moment to wait before the debate began at its beginning again. The so-called King, Jacques Bourbon, had not yet made his appearance, having been seized by an aspen palsy the moment he knew Joan was in the Castel. His barber and his valet had to pursue him from place to place all over the dressing room to get him curled and clothed, and when he was at length presentable he would have run away had not his fortune-hunting

Bedchamber surrounded him in a body and practically carried him to Her Majesty's sitting room. *Voila!*

For his part, speaking sexually, when Jacques saw Joan for the first time he was pleasantly surprised, but speaking politically—which is the way Joan was speaking—the Bourbon could not overcome his awe. Like a cat in a strange attic, he was ready to jump out of his skin every time she raised her voice, and in order to be heard over Serjianni's bluster Joan had to do that frequently.

To cover his chagrin at the debacle of the twin chests, the Constable was demanding Giovantonio's exile. "I have evidence that he is a traitor to both Your Majesties, severally and united. He is consorting with subjects of Aragon, inciting the Aragonese to attack us. He hopes to put Prince Juan d'Aragon on the Throne of Naples—and if the Aragonese will not hear him, he will turn to Louis II d'Anjou. His Orsini cousin—who stole the Crown—is in daily consort with Louis in Constance. Our envoys report this to me.

"His Del Balzo cousin, Duke Andria, has approached Milord Aversa—I beg your pardon—His Highness the *Prince of Capua!*—for alliance, so that either of these invaders can land and come upon us through Aversa. Naturally my father-in-law denounced them—and reported their treason to me at once. But, deprived of Aversa for their landing, will they give up the expedition? Have they not Taranto itself—and Lecce—both gates open for your destruction?—Andria too—and Nola, right here on our doorstep. That is why they harass me for Avellino too. If the Del Balzos ever get Avellino, Your Majesties cannot even visit Taranto. I cannot get from here to Melfi! I say Giovantonio must be exiled—and this Del Balzo-Orsini conspiracy broken up."

"If you can prove your charges against the Prince, I agree to his exile," said Joan, "and I confer Taranto upon Milord Count of

Marche and Castres—if you can collect the revenues of Taranto for him. Now—let us return to the subject of Rome. You will have the Grand Constable and the Lord High Seneschal brought before me at once."

"I am Grand Constable, Majesty," Caracciolo corrected her in a voice that boomed like a rolling barrel, "and I will hold the baton in this hand until my dead fingers have to be broken from it one at a time."

"Speed the day!" the Duchess of Sessa interposed loudly. "That's the prettiest picture *you* ever painted."

Serjianni ignored the interruption. "I am Grand Constable, and it is only in that capacity that I will discuss the situation in Rome, or the case of Attendola Sforza." He turned to Jacques Bourbon. "Am I not Grand Constable, Majesty?"

To have Bourbon's "Majesty" consulted as superior to her own, or even as comparable with it, caused such a rush of blood to Joan's head that she could not see, but—even blinded—she remained aware that insults of this kind must be endured temporarily to get Sforza and Alopo out of prison. She could not speak, however. A rage so colossal never yet has been chopped up into words.

Jacques Bourbon managed to assent to Serjianni's pretensions, but in such a weak voice that he could barely be heard. He had brought along a Grand Constable of his own, from home, in the person of Milord Lourdin de Salligny, but this seemed a poor time to mention that. Somewhat wistfully Jacques wished that Giovantonio had not gone away, taking his strength and his clear head with him. Further, with a heart sunk low, the outlander faced the awful possibility that Serjianni's aspersions upon the motive for the Prince's journey might be justified. If they were, Jacques's position here—between the Devil, the blue sea, and Joan's pit—held more horrors than a hermit's nightmare, and the flight of Cousin Marie-Luise with her children, under Del Balzo protection, gave Serjianni's allegations a terrifying air of verity.

Jacques saw that he must choose a breast to lean upon, and he hoped he could select the stronger, but in the welter of ramified considerations he could find no firm basis for preference. Serjianni held the reins but Joan was the Queen, and either of them could withhold his Kingly honors if he sided with the other. Frustrate, he turned a vague gaze on Caldora. Only the day before, this man had appeared as a trusted friend of Taranto, but now he sat, reserved and noncommittal, hearing himself accused of betraying that youth. Even so, Caldora was the first Prince this Bourbon had created, and, as such, by the evidence there at hand, had demonstrated his gratitude by fulfilling his commission to arrange a meeting with Joan. Here she was. They were met. That had the look of faithfulness to Jacques, leastwise, it was the most reliable in that room, and so, silent decision was taken to lay his head on the breast of the weasel.

Serjianni, of course, was still speaking. "Attendola Sforza and Pandolfo Alopo have conspired against the Throne, committed high treason, and attempted your husband's life."

"He is not my husband yet," Joan shot out, "and unless you bring both men to me—he never will be."

"You have signed—"

"And I will tear up what I signed."

"You have sworn——"

"And I will abrogate my oath."

"You have lost Rome!"

"Send Sforza!"

"Marry Jacques—now—today—and I will send Sforza."

"Your word is no better than mine. Send Sforza first—and I will marry Jacques."

"Agreed!" Serjianni shouted, and shouted also to Antonio, "Bring Sforza to us—and send the heralds to announce immediate recruitment under the great Attendola."

"Bring the Lord Seneschal too," said Joan—but Serjianni's "NO!" shook the doors on their hinges.

"Bring Alopo!" screamed the Queen.

"No Alopo," Caracciolo countered.

"No Alopo—no marriage."

"Majesty—your word is no better than mine. I will hold Alopo until your vows have been made at God's altar—until, in fact, your marriage to His Majesty Jacques Bourbon is consummated in bed. Then I will give you Alopo—not before."

"I cannot trust you."

"You have no choice." Serjianni held up three fingers and counted his points upon them one at a time, while Antonio stood at the door awaiting the final outcome of the debate. "I will have Sforza brought to us—and the militia put under his command." That was finger number one. "When Sforza marches—you will marry—according to your contract and sacred oath." Finger number two. "The day *after* His Majesty has bedded you—Alopo will be freed."

"On one condition," Joan agreed. "I accept your terms if you will now—at once—remove your gaolor of San Vincenzo and install one of my choice."

"Whom?"

"Your cousin Ottino."

"O?" Serjianni looked at his watchdog as if he had never seen him before, neither him nor anything quite like him.

Ottino blinked under the scrutiny. He had not pictured his advancement being realized so publicly or in such a crucial interval. His hands strayed restlessly from his belt to the table and back again.

"Monkey business, Ottino?" asked his cousin.

Joan answered. "I have bound Ottino to me with the gift of County Nicastro. He is also to be Castelan of San Vincenzo—and he will see my wishes performed."

Count Nicastro raised his chin at that and dared to look Serjianni in the eye, but the Strong Man ruined the perennial poor-cousin's moment of triumph with a raucous, loud guffaw. "Nicastro!" the bully repeated between haws. "Now there is a fortune for you, Cousin! You have done well." Abruptly his forced mirth fell away and Serjianni leaned toward the Queen intently. "Agreed," he barked. "Ottino is Castelan. The rest shall be as we said, to the letter. Prepare yourself for the wedding, Majesty. I have much work to do." Rising, he called Pappacoda, Caldora and the Marzanos to him with a gesture, and left the room issuing orders right and left, not asking their lief of either Majesty, and ignoring the stipulation that Sforza was to be brought into Joan's presence.

Antonio was sent about the recruitment.

Duke Sessa, to call a full meeting of the Council.

Marino Marzano, to summon the Barons with their fighting forces for immediate march upon Rome.

Artuso Pappacoda, to the city of Taranto, to bring back his nephew Ettore and the Crown, and the tax-take too, if he could.

"And you, Father," Serjianni sneered to Caldora, "are made responsible for the safety of the Queen. By *safety* I mean that she is not to leave Castel Nuovo under any pretext whatsoever, and if she does—I shall hold you accountable. She is not to have any visitors from outside—neither males nor females—and most particularly none of those Tarantine ragamuffins who were in the courtyard before. She is to have no letters from Palermo. Bring any such to me."

"You excite yourself unduly, dear Son," smiled Caldora. "I never intended to do otherwise."

Then, in highest good humor, Serjianni carried Ottino to the office of San Vincenzo's Castelan, which was in Castel Nuovo, opposite that end of the long tunnel that connects the royal palace with the prison. That tunnel, well guarded inside and out, goes under land and under sea, hewn through rock and tufa, its length interspersed with iron doors or gates in six places, as I recall.

"Bring up Sforza," Serjianni commanded the Castelan, and that word was passed from guard to guard down the dank, dismal corridor which the Caracciolo never had trodden for dread of the pony-sized rats. "And now, Milord, I have good news for you," the Constable told the retiring Castelan, rubbing his palms together as he spoke. "I am sending you on a diplomatical mission—and if you bring it off to my satisfaction you are going up in the world."

The Castelan knew Serjianni so well that this bare announcement made him Sign himself with a hasty Cross, lest "up" meant as far as Heaven.

"You are to go to Constance—which you will find in the Switzer country—and there you will see the former Count Nola, Raimondo Orsini, who is living with Cardinal Oddo Colonna.

"Without the Cardinal's knowledge you will speak with Raimondo, in my name, calling him home to be reinstated at Nola with full pardon of Their Majesties Queen Joan and King Jacques, and—to make sure he comes—you will say that I offer him my sister Isabella for wife, with a marriage portion equal to his income from Nola in the year 1413—before taxes by the Crown.

"If that doesn't move him, offer a thousand more, then another thousand—up to five—and keep me informed of your progress.

"If you bring him back, you will be made my Castelan in Avellino."

"And if I do not?"

"If you do not—either leave him a corse or don't come back at all."

"I have always admired Your Worship's plain way of speaking. In these modern times it is becoming a lost art."

"No flattery, please. My cousin—Count *Nicastro*—will take over your duties here, while you are away. You will instruct him in them, shew him the ropes, and yourself leave Naples no later than tomorrow. Antonio will provide you with cash."

Back in the Queen's apartments, meanwhile, Joan had smiled upon Jacques's Bedchamber, if not upon Bourbon himself, and coyly professed herself unable to remember all their names. "You, for instance," she said, selecting one under 50 *ans*, "what is your name?"

The French part, including title, was rattled off too fast for her, but Milord Salligny finished the series with words only too clearly understood. "—and Duke of Salerno," he said.

"Duke of Salerno?" Joan frowned. "Salerno is a County."

"It has been advanced to a Duchy now, Majesty, and I have come into it," said Salligny quite unabashed. He looked more like a pawnbroker on the Sabbath than a Duke of the Regno.

"By whose authority?" asked Joan, ominously calm.

"By my authority," Jacques Bourbon squeaked. "My suite must be provided for."

The Queen studied her consort-to-be as if he had been a strange new kind of worm, and continued without speaking for so long a time that Jacques was constrained to continue his defense. His windpipe was very nearly closed by a nervous constriction, and his want of natural dignity was further beggared by the shrinking of his confidence under Joan's gaze, but still he retched out the essence of his rede in a flutey kind of gasp. "Your Majesty must know—is it not so? I come to the Crown by inheritance—not by marriage."

The theory was not new to Superba but this was the first time she had heard it from this cousin, and of him she was so contemptuous that it did not move her to raise her voice. "Does Serjianni know that you have given away Salerno?" she asked.

The Queen's deceptive mildness encouraged Jacques a little. "His Highness advanced some objections," he recalled, "but I held my position firmly. If I may say so, Majesty, it grieves me to see Your Majesty bullied by Milord Melfi, and after we are married I shall put a stop to it."

"Covella, darling! Do you hear? Isn't he sweet?"

The Bourbon colored a little, but bore on. "If Your Majesty and I agree together, Serjianni will be required to deliver up his baton and remain simple Duke Melfi."

"A Solomon!" Covella praised him. "But why leave him Melfi? Take that too."

"I'm sure one of these Hignesses would be glad for the taxing of Melfi," said Joan, looking them over again. "What other sweetmeats have you handed out?"

One old baldy was Duke Amalfi, a greybeard was Count Venosa, a third, with one foot in his tomb, was to be Count Celano, through his last days. Happily, all these incomes would be available for redistribution before very long, by intervention of the Reaper.

The cream of the jest had been skimmed by the time Caldora returned to announce, with a wink, his position as Joan's guardian. Her Majesty arose, making a gesture of dismissal of the French that spelled contempt in any language. "Out!"

Only the King had the hardihood to resist her authority, taking his courage from the physical presence of the first Prince he ever had created. Jacques wanted an expression from Prince Capua upon the charges against Taranto. Was it true that those cousins were dealing with Louis II d'Anjou?

"Not true," said Caldora.

"With the Aragonese?"

"Not true."

"Duke Melfi is only trying to frighten us?"

"Duke Melfi is afraid of Taranto—and will try to keep him out of the Regno as long as he can," the tight little man said crisply.

Jacques seized Caldora's hand impetuously. "We three must stick together—concert measures to get my cousin back. You, Milord Capua, are our strength."

"You honor me," said the weasel, withdrawing his forepaw with distaste.

"Has Your Lordship seen my Pierre?" Bourbon worried.

"No more have I!" Joan jested. "Shew us your Pierre!"

"He is gone—disappeared—not to be found," Jacques lamented.

"A thousand pities," mocked the Queen. "Then we shall not have any children. Whom do you suspect? When did you last see him? Did you feel no pain?"

This sort of badinage was the essence of humor to Covella, and each of the outlander's straight-faced replies made Her Enormousness jelly the more.

"Go and look for your Pierre!" Superba urged the smallwit. "Look among the sausages in the kitchen. Serjianni is not above a joke like that. He will serve your Pierre to us—fried. Go see! Go see!"—and she propelled Bourbon out the door, slamming it behind him.

Fire was in her eyes when she turned to Caldora, loosing her bodice as she spoke. "Not even to regain Rome would I marry such a ninny! You, Milord, must save me. Here!" She rubbed one bare breast into his beard. "I will do the talking ... Covella, undress me ... Dearest Prince of Capua, you must arrange to free me of Jacques Bourbon's presence. I don't care how you do it, so it is done before my wedding day. He likes you and trusts you. Take him hunting—and have a horse kick his head in. Cut his throat or push him out a window. I shall not rest until he is buried."

As Covella's fingers flew about their office, Joan's were unbuckling the weasel, but the Queen continued speaking, sometimes in tones so tender that an eavesdropper easily might have imagined that she liked the man.

"You are very clever at work like that—and you have an army to help you. An accident will be better than poison, but that I leave to you. Give me warning if I excite you too much. The past few years Your Highness has become more and more prone to the quick dribble. I excused you last night, but I want this to last until Sforza gets here. Nothing inflames him so much as jealousy. He will claw the floor. O, don't be frightened. I won't let him hurt you. I hope Serjianni comes with him. I'll make him watch if it's the last thing I do. Covella?"

"Yes, Baby."

"That might make a difference—to Serjianni—if we made him watch me with Sforza, feeling about him the way he does."

"You are much too beautiful to let Serjianni watch you with anybody," said the Duchess with wonted but perverse loyalty. "Serjianni is the one who should suffer the accident instead of that Bourbon clown."

"But, darling! We can't ask Prince Capua to make his daughter a widow—can we, Milord? No! I'll answer. Take the other one." She shifted the beard to the right.

"That upstart! Giving away half the Regno to his hangers-on! Salerno! Amalfi! Venosa! Celano! Celano! Celano! Do you like

Celano, Prince? You had better think about other things. Think how you are going to kill Jacques Bourbon so I won't have to marry him. And after he is dead, I want you to bring me your little protégé—what is his name?—Rinaldo! Yes. Bring me little Rinaldo—and if he resembles my former brother Ladislaus perhaps I shall adopt him. Don't stop to thank me. Celano! Celano! Celano!

"Louis II will be the only heir I have, after you have disposed of Jacques, and none of us want Louis for King, do we? I'll adopt Rinaldo, and name you Regent in my will. O! Stop! Hold back! O! Damn! You nasty old man, you dribbled—and Sfora's not here yet."

Caldora was covered with contrition.

In fairness to the weasel, however, one must admit that not even in his palmiest days could he have waited for Sforza. Attendola sat with his chains on all that day in Serjianni's office, refusing to march against Braccio da Montone unless it were made worth his while.

"I've heard these promises before," he told the Caracciolo. "You can't keep a promise. There isn't a straight bone in your body. You can't lie straight in bed."

Obviously, the *Condottiere* felt no awe for the Strong Man. Not only was the prisoner the better loved but, at the moment, he was a damned sight more urgently needed in the Regno's economy. "I want my wife, I want my son, I want possession of Manfredonia—and something more besides—or Braccio can keep Rome and welcome," said the chained giant.

"Something more?" said Serjianni, ready to defend his baton.

"You can stick your baton," said Sforza. "I can't play the Courtier—and won't; but if you want Rome—make it worth my while. Give me Benevento."

"Benevento belongs to the Church."

"That's why I ask for it. It's the Church that will be ransoming Rome. I want something of theirs, in my own name, to trade with. Braccio has Perugia, and the new Pope will let him keep it. Give me Benevento."

"It is not ours to give. If you want Benevento you must take it—at your own expense."

"But with Joan's arms."

"You will involve Her Majesty with the new Pope."

"With Joan's arms—and *before* I take Rome," Sfora insisted.

"Well—no!" Serjianni would brook no more.

"'Ihen put me back in my cell. I have been learning to read and write—with the help of the chaplain. A sissy sort of accomplishment—but fair enough pastime for an old man of a winter's evening. Can you read?"

"Certainly. I am reading all the time."

"Maybe if you didn't read so much you could take Rome back without my help."

"I will occupy Benevento for you—if you start for Rome within a week."

"Will you write that out for me?"

"Yes."

"And—Manfredonia?"

"I'll write that out too—and give you your wife."

"That leaves only the boy."

"You must leave Francesco with me—as a guarantee of your performance in good faith."

"I would rather trust him to the Turk."

It is a tribute to Caracciolo's diplomacy that he did not lay one alongside the prisoner's head. Instead, he stalked out of his office, leaving the *Condottiere* to mull upon his stubbornness for two hours.

That gambit had no effect upon Sforza. When Serjianni returned, the Commander was playing dice with his guard.

Caracciolo offered a second solution to their stalemate. "Put your son Francesco into Queen Joan's custody," he said.

Sforza pretended to be horrified. "Would you start that gentle lad on her treadmill before he is fifteen? You have no soul! No. Let Her Majesty fix an income upon Francesco and I will carry him with me to learn the art of warfare."

"He can learn warfare from Caldora."

"To retreat—yes—none could teach him better, but I want my son to know how to *win* battles."

Neither would give in—and while they argued vainly in search of compromise—Joan's impatience, frustration and growing suspicion were consuming her.

"Go and find out what is keeping them!" she commanded Caldora at last. "And send me two of your guards—big ones."

Two strapping volunteers came in, and so it seemed no time at all until the weasel was back with the amazing news that Sforza was refusing to be freed—unless his eldest son were protected from Serjianni.

Her Grampus the Duchess danced the first five steps of a saraband, hugging herself for joy. Here was her dream out, and nothing easier. "Now you watch *me!*" she said, and waddled to Serjianni's office. His guards had experience of Covella, and so drew aside. "Milords!" she cried, entering, "I bring you the answer to your prayers!" She enveloped Sforza, chains and all, and kissed him six-several times.

"Before God," growled Serjianni, "do you think he was praying for *that?*"

"Mind your manners when you speak to me, *Sardason*," the Duchess spat back. "I wouldn't help you to climb out of a shitwell if you were over your head and had sprained your ankle—but Baby wants Rome—and she must have it. Attendola, pudding-pie, let me send Francesco to my brother in Montalto. He has a daughter just Francesco's age—or a little younger—the most beautiful child you ever saw, hight Polissena, who wants a husband. An only child—my brother's heir—she brings Montalto in dot. And you know how long this turdonstilts would last if he stuck his nose into the Ruffo country."

Crude as Covella's logic was, it was serviceable.

"I would agree to that," said Sforza, "if it pleases Serjianni."

"Nothing that is *Ruffo* is pleasing," the Caracciolo rasped, "but for Her Majesty's sake I accept it. Guard!—strike off these chains."

Five days later Sforza marched out of Naples with the finest army he had commanded in many years. He marched as "Duke of Benevento", a defiance which Holy Church could not answer until it had a new head.

The day after that, Joan II Anjou-Durazzo, called Superba, Queen of Naples, "the Two Sicilies, Hungary and Jerusalem" (sic), was wed to Jacques Bourbon, former Count of Marche and Castres. The black weasel Caldora had failed her.

As always when he bungled an assignment, Caldora blamed someone else. The actual stroke had been delegated to that Captain of his who had once taken Sforza prisoner, Giulio-Cesaro di Capua, and when the fatal moment came, G-C had mistaken the signal. "But—sweetest Superba—do not frown," Caldora implored. "The net is spread again. The day is set—the place. Jacques Bourbon is marked. He is living on borrowed time."

"You purposely let him go—you crawling thing. You were afraid to strike. You are afraid of Serjianni. Get out of my sight! Send Ottino to me."—but Ottino failed Joan too. Only Serjianni lived up, every whit, to her expectations of him. When Joan bade him produce Alopo, as promised, she was given only the head. The body was handed over to the commonality, who dragged it through the streets, chanting obscene, rhymed observations upon what the carcass had been to the Queen.

CHAPTER TEN

O N THE ROAD toward Nola, Duke Andria and the Princess
Maria so inflamed themselves and each other with looks,
and then by riding close together so their legs touched and rubbed
up and down, that they decided Her Majesty Marie-Luise was
overtired, and must sleep that night in Nola. When they went to
the litter to inform her of their thoughtfulness they found her
slumbering peacefully, but that did not dash them. They woke
her up to tell her she could sleep.

That night, with connivance of sister Caterina, the pretty
pair played at the wimble-timble, but only in an outward kind
of way, Guglielmo taking special care not to pierce the maiden-
head, out of respect for his expectations as Maria's husband. They
were still at it when their watch came to say that Riccardo and
the worthless chest had been taken on the road by the Marzanos
but—so far as could be seen in the dark—Serjianni's men were
not coming any closer to Nola.

Comforted, the cousins slept, after the Princess Maria
praised God in her prayers for allotting her a husband so con-
tinent, so self-controlled, because—she admitted—several times
that evening she had felt herself approaching the proximity of
sin.

Next morning the road was conned and scanned, and—no
pursuit appearing—the well armed cavalcade proceeded up the
valley to Avellino. But for his obligation to the ladies, Guglielmo
wistfully opined that he had army enough with him to take the

place. More than half the inhabitants of the city were of the Del Balzo persuasion, but the garrison was Caracciolo's and so the gates were closed in their faces.

"The next time I come this way will be another story," the baby-faced Duke told Maria, and for his bravery as well as his forbearance she loved him all the more.

After Avellino their way led through a considerable stretch of Caracciolo country, but in the absence of any specific command from Serjianni the locals shewed a sagacious respect for so much traveling strength, and all the while, by his insouciance, Andria continued to endear himself—head over heels and beyond computation—to the tender sensibilities of his bride-to-be.

Unaccustomed to concealing anything she felt, the Princess let her heart glow from her eyes, and so warmly that when the party went to sleep again the former Queen kept Maria in bed with her, thereby adding fuel to the flame.

About noon of the next day's riding—which was bringing them into Andria's titular domain—the rear guard announced overtaking horsemen, a small party spurring hard.

Once again, every move and gesture the Duke made toward outfacing their pursuers and providing their defense appeared to be superhuman, demigodlike, to the Princess Maria, and his Heavenly attributes were only a little dimmed by the chance which made battle unnecessary.

The newcomers were Riccardo and his company, released by Joan's grace, and now come to report events and get fresh orders. In a general way, everything that had passed shewed the cabal's cause in vigorous health, except in the one particular that applied to Andria and the performance of his Roman assignment. Braccio's forehandedness in overrunning The City before Del Balzo could do it threw a deep shadow athwart the future as the absent Taranto had planned it, and Sforza's release for the counterattack made for worse confusion. Guglielmo knew as well as any man that he was no match for either of those two veterans in the field, so Taranto's instruction to make friends with Sforza now appeared to apply. Accordingly, Andria commanded all haste straight on, to the speedier disposal of the Ladies and young Gabriel. Until he was shut of them he could do nothing.

Riccardo was sent back to Naples to cultivate his favor with Queen Joan and with Serjianni's Antonio. Before that small party was well out of sight another dust cloud approached from the direction of Naples, and under it a courier from Marino Marzano, summoning Andria in the names of both sovereigns to report in full force instanter to join the attack upon Rome.

Here, on a salver, was the brightest of opportunities to treat with Sforza for the future whilst serving under him, but it came too soon. Del Balzo's first obligation was to the soft-sided of Taranto's family, so the courier was returned with a promise of compliance, "at the earliest"—which looked to be in about a month—and the cavalcade entered Andria.

The Princess Maria had seen every stone of Andria times without number, but never before with the eyes of one who was to become its Duchess. That gave the place quite a new air. Actually, her marriage contract was not signed, or even drawn as yet, but that was a mere detail, and her child heart swelled in an access of supreme joy, the joy of female possessiveness (itself a transcendent emotion), augmented by the special attributes so recently discovered in the thing possessed. Maria, as the saying goes, was beside herself. Then, exactly at the climax and peak of Maria's happiness, Guglielmo's resident mistress came running out of the palace, with the Duke's son—*ae* 5—to kiss his magnificent father, and the woman kissed him too.

Like a tragically wronged Queen out of classic fable the Princess Maria drew herself up to her full—but negligible—height, and declared, "I shall take the veil!"

"Nonsense," her mother consoled her. "You will marry Guglielmo as intended, and be a good mother to his children."

"He never told me he had any children," the Princess wailed. "I shall take the veil."

The Princess Caterina could not move her sister's resolution either.

"How would *you* like it if Tristano Chiaramonte had made you a mother before he ever saw you?" sister sobbed.

"I'm sure he has," Caterina replied. "Every man does." The two mistresses of big brother Giovantonio were brought forward in evidence, but they were alike unable to stem the flow of Maria's tears or to heal the wound. Maria's sympathies were all with the Colonna girl. "In her place I would not marry even HIM," wailed the Princess. Some maids are so constituted.

Already sick with love and bedeviled by his Roman frustration, the fallen idol was fairly prostrated by this quirk in his intended bride. Puzzled beyond a mere male's capacity to assign reasons to a female's actions, he accepted Maria's new, low opinion of his worthlessness and took unto himself all culpability, not only in this one particular but in a broad, categorical and sweeping generality of self-abasement. "I have failed Giovantonio. I cannot take Rome. His sister has thrown me over. One more stroke and my cousin will disown me."

For relief he began driving the army furiously forward—on peaceful, friendly roads—as if lashing his men to an attack, but Maria rode no more beside him, and their sweet love games were ended.

Approaching Lecce, they were met by a festive party of townsfolk, come out to hail their Countess and her son with joy and rejoicing. Marie-Luise gave them Gabriel as her heir, here, and their new master, but because of his callow years the Lady Maria was left in Lecce with him. Gabriel was accustomed to obey her, as his former nurse, even more readily than he obeyed his mother, and the arrangement was accepted without demur.

Thus the Prince of Taranto's immediate family was early divided, and whilst the Lady Maria, with one daughter toddling and another forming in her womb, remained in Lecce, the pregnant Giovanna was carried to Taranto in the household of Marie-Luise and her daughters.

By the way, the Duke's army had been steadily growing and the call for volunteers spread wide, so that, entering Taranto, Andria was commanding twice as many men as had left Naples with him, and in Taranto he was joined by as many more. At the same time all their citadels were amply garrisoned for safety and ease of mind, so that he felt no trepidation at leaving the Ladies alone. In fact, Guglielmo was relieved to be escaping the hurt eyes of the Princess Maria, and he thought of pitched battle against either Braccio or Sforza as a lark by comparison to the ordeal of her silent recriminations.

At parting, Maria would not kiss him but hid behind her beads and gave him Christian blessings as if she were already an apprenticed religious.

Ettore Pappacoda was glad to get away too. He had been his own prisoner—so to speak—neighboring on two years, and of recent months the cabal itself had seemed to be running away from him. Sound information had ceased to arrive, and the rumors were mostly unhappy.

That Taranto had joined forces with Joan, Ettore found incredible. Had the *cousins and brothers* so soon forgotten what she had done to his father?—forgotten that Ettore remained a pauper-pensioner because of it? If Taranto had gone that way, how could a Pappacoda continue to accept his largesse and eat his food?

The end of Alopo, in the muck, was a bright spot, but credit for that must go to Serjianni, and the best evidence to hand indicated that Serjianni had now done away with Uncle Artuso!

Ettore knew that his uncle had been assigned to retrieve the Crown, and that he had not obeyed, but that was the last word of him even at second-hand. Artuso had not been named, neither as functionary nor as guest, at Queen Joan's wedding.

Even so, young Pappacoda had more to live for than Duke Andria, as the two rode side by side in the midst of their army, and to cheer his formerly gay companion the scrawny lad patted an invisible pot, complaining, "That lazy life in Taranto has made me fat. Let us stop by the way and take Avellino—for the exercise."

From the depths of his stygian funk the lovelorn croaked, "What does Avellino mean to me now? What are earthly possessions? Dross—nothing but dross."

"Hoo-hoo!" Ettore hooted. "Since you feel so—still let us attack—and if you are killed going over the wall Maria will cry her eyes out."

"You jest, but I am ready to die if I cannot win her back, and I call you to witness my behavior on oath. Never will I touch another woman—but only Maria in holy wedlock. Witness?"

"I witness that you are acting like a child. What you need is four or five women to make you forget her nonsense."

"Not one—if I live ten thousand years. I shall be as celibate as she."

"Well, then, you must do something for diversion. Let us take Avellino."

Foot, lance and horse, they numbered something over four hundred, but they lacked any manner of storming machines.

"We can build some."

"That will take months—and we must get to Rome."

A rugged strain of practicality ran through all Pappacodas, and Ettore drummed home the palpable truth that to march upon Rome—in Queen Joan's name—before the Avellino question was settled to Del Balzo satisfaction was a wanton waste of the most golden opportunity Andria was ever likely to have.

"The question is settled," Andria objected. "Giovantonio made agreement."

"An agreement under duress."

"I have accepted it," Andria shrugged, "and it has been confirmed by the King. We are to have the cash—the fruit—and Serjianni keeps the tree."

"But Serjianni has not paid over the fruit—and he never will unless you force him."

"What do I hear? I can remember the time you felt considerable obligation to Serjianni."

"I cannot wish him enough boils!" Ettore spat, and went on, solemnly, "Gugl, we owe it to Uncle Artuso's memory to take Avellino. Nothing would have pleased him more."

"Stop talking as if Artuso were dead," Andria snapped.

"Then stop acting as if you were! You haven't smiled since we left Taranto."

"I have nothing to smile about."

"You haven't said anything funny."

"I don't feel funny."

"Well, I do, and the only way I can keep from laughing is by mourning my uncle. You need a woman."

"I don't want a woman."

"You don't want a woman! You don't want Avellino!—but you're going to get both. I'm not going to let you make a fool of yourself."

"Am I too long about it? You can make a fool of me in half the time! I have lost Rome. I have lost Maria. Now Your Sagacity would have me fly into Taranto's teeth!"

"He would be the first to urge you."

"How can you say so? If I take Avellino without Joan's blessing, that will amount to an open declaration for Louis II d'Anjou. My title comes from Aunt Alix in Provence—along with Baux. The two are inseparable."

"But if you do *not* declare for Louis II, you lose Baux in the end. Louis will never let you have Baux unless you are on his side."

"And shall I declare for Louis while Taranto is hot after an Aragonese for King?"

"You are only guessing. We have no official word from Giovantonio—no word at all."

"Your uncle has."

"Alas, poor Uncle Artuso!" Ettore drew a long face again.

To avoid the well meant persecution Duke Andria spurred toward the head of their column, and—as much to satisfy himself as to stop Ettore's mouth—he sent one spy, at his swiftest, to Naples to learn the elder Pappacoda's whereabouts and bring back confirmation.

Ettore could not hear the instruction given, but when the lone soldier set off breakneck, he spoke aside to the Tarantine Commisseriat, commissioning him to supply—that night—the prettiest girl to be found, whether amongst those trailing with the foot, or seen in the fields, or picked up in the next town, she to be put into Duke Andria's bed before he retired.

Well satisfied with themselves, the two lads again rode together, somewhat more congenially. Guglielmo even smiled at his companion, and Ettore's pox-marked visage grinned back. "The farmers need rain," he said.

"You Pappacodas would argue your teeth out," said Andria.

"All right, they *don't* need rain," Ettore conceded, "but when the Prince left me in charge of Taranto, we were ALL for Louis II, as nearly as I can remember, and I've heard nothing to the contrary."

"You knew that Cardinal Colonna offered the Prince a wife."

"I taught Erri to say so—and sent him to Rome."

"And Giovantonio sent him on to Constance—accepting. Taranto wants the girl—especially if her father is to be Pope—but Colonna can't win the Election with Aragon against him, so the Prince has gone to Palermo to work on King Ferdinand through the Chiaramontes. Giovantonio is offering the King the Crown for Prince Juan if they will support Colonna."

"Suppose he fails?"

"Giovantonio is a man of Destiny. He will not fail—unless by some stupidity of ours."

"Stupidity yourself! Ferdinand the Just may object to betrothing his son to a Queen who already has a husband. That's pretty public connivance at murder."

"Murder yourself!" Andria retorted. "In the first place, Joan was not married when Giovantonio made this plan——"

"But she's married now! That should teach the Prince how far he can trust Joan II."

"Nobody trusts her. But you mistake. Joan is *not* married even now in the Eyes of God. She and Bourbon are cousins and cannot marry without Papal dispensation. Needless to say they obtained no dispensation, not knowing which of the Popes has God's Ear. But when Colonna is Elected, he merely discovers—in his Canon Law—that they are not married, and cannot wed, because of their blood ties, and there is no murder in that."

"Has the Cardinal agreed to it?"

"I should certainly suppose so, but who can say? Erri was to carry his answer straight to Palermo."

"How—straight? Straight from Constance to Palermo?"

"Aye, by sea."

"Erri knows the way?"

"He will meet with a mariner who knows the way—or has a needle."

"Nonsense!"

"What is nonsense?"

"What is a needle?"

"A mariner's needle. You rub it—and it floats on water— pointing the way."

"Pointing the way to Palermo? Tosh!"

"It is true. Every steersman has one."

"What will they think of next! You and I could use such a needle ashore."

"I need no needle. I am commissioned to hold Rome—on my own if I can, but if not, then by treaty with Sforza."

"Then you are reconciled to the loss of Baux—if Taranto brings back Juan d'Aragon for King."

"I shall have something better than Baux—right here in the Regno—and Avellino too—unless I turn Giovantonio against me by this insanity of yours. But if I take time out to feather my own nest, or any way embarrass Taranto's plans with Chiaramonte and Aragon, he will say that I acted in pique—because of Maria—and I shall lose everything—Baux, my wife, my friend and cousin, and, in the end, Avellino and Andria too."

"I should say that Cardinal Colonna is more likely to embarrass those plans than you or I. Can he get the Tiara without the votes of Louis II?"

"You will have to ask Cousin Raimondo about that," said Gugl wearily, mopping sweat from his brow. "I know as little about what is going on in Constance as you do. Perhaps if I were better informed I wouldn't make so many mistakes. But Raimondo is smarter than I am. He will keep Louis's ear open—and if Cardinal Colonna won't follow Taranto, then Taranto must follow the Cardinal."

"That's why I say you and I need a needle! We don't know which way the wind blows. That's why I say you should take Avellino now, while you can. We can do it in four days."

"Get thee behind me, Satan!"

"Write to Giovantonio and ask him!"

"It would take more than four days to get a reply."

"We'll be four days getting to Avellino with this troop. Write to him. Let me write to him."

As weary of debate as of this gloomy, brideless life, Andria agreed to that, and at the first halt each took up his pen. Both employed the same cipher, and wrote on the same subject, in theory, but that was scarcely discernible in the reading. Duke Andria bared his bruised heart, heaped ashes on his own head, told of Braccio's success and Sforza's release, *et al, et al,* and mentioned Avellino only between moans: but Ettore began by saying—*We are taking Avellino.* From that point his screed went on—in softer vein—to plead the cabal's crying need for closer communion and more direction from its leader. The writer disclaimed responsibility for any bad decisions he or Gugl might make as long as the Prince's ultimate goal remained shifting, nebulous and almost totally obscured. *We have had no word from my illustrious uncle since Your Highness sailed. If he is still alive he must be Serjianni's prisoner.*

Each writer chose his own courier, and the two left the camp together, but under direction to separate if apprehension threatened.

"Now, if we don't have an answer by the time we get to Avellino," the baby-faced Commander declared, "I don't want to hear any more about taking the place."

"Only this much," Ettore persisted, "while the ink is here and our pens are hot, let us write to Joan for her blessing. If Taranto is bringing her the husband of her choice, we must be her allies, and if we are—by my father's blood!—we should get something out of it. She never will forgive Serjianni for chopping up Alopo. She wants you to go against Rome. Point out that by serving her you lose Baux—and she will give you Avellino out of hand."

Simple, logical, probable—not even Andria's captiousness could invent any sensible objections to this innocent maneuver, and a faint interest in the earthly life began to stir in him once more. "But not by letter," he emended the procedure. "Serjianni will be intercepting all Joan's letters. Someone must speak to her, face to face. YOU, Milord, incog!"

"Not I," said Ettore. "That fellow, Riccardo. Where is he?"

"Probably in her bed."

"Send someone to him—and you will be Count of Avellino before they sleep again."

"By title, perhaps," the Del Balzo agreed, "but Serjianni will never evacuate the fortress simply because Joan tells him to, so we shall still have to drive out his garrison, and that will delay us just as long as if I had not the right."

Nonetheless, a pair of worthies was sent ahead to Naples to find the soldier Riccardo, or—themselves—to lay Andria's obedience at the Queen's feet if Riccardo could not be found.

Then the boys went to their beds.

"Allo, Gugl Highness," purred the pride of Gravina, batting her eyes in the manner approved for the seduction of Dukes. "I am Puccia."

"I see you are," said Andria churlishly. "Put on your clothes and get out of here."

Puccia deserved better treatment than that. Truly she was not at all bad, in any reasonable man's scale of romping values. By being short of stature and slightly wry-necked, she looked like a female gnome, but definitely a female one, with a luxuriant growth of black curls, where black curls should be, and a firm round figure, superior in symmetry to either the Princess Maria or the mother of Andria's child.

True, Puccia was brazen, but in a cute way: the Commisseriat had chosen well: and Guglielmo was only prolonging his agony by being high-chested about it. He wouldn't even look at her as she twisted and rolled and bounced up and down, pretending to weep because he didn't like her. As a matter of fact, her vanity was wounded, but it was merely her misfortune to be the first woman Ettore procured for this purpose. Not even Venus could have succeeded. Andria's resistance was at its peak.

"It isn't your fault, Puccia," Andria assured her. "I know—it's my traveling companion's idea of physic. Here. I pay you." He did that, generously, and spatted her bottom in congenial farewell.

Ettore had stationed himself to keep tabs on the outcome, and when Puccia came out, counting her money, he recovered what he could from the lost endeavor. "Thou'rt paid. Go to work!" said Pappacoda, pointing to his own bed, and for the next three nights he enjoyed the same favorable economic position with Puccia's three successors, taking his own medicine, so to speak, while Andria paid the apothecary.

On the march by day the celibate preened himself on his moral stamina, laughing at his volunteer physician and criticizing his prescriptions. "The second one was too tall, the third, too dirty, the fourth—well—her flesh did have an attractive quality.

If I were not on oath I should have enjoyed the fourth—didn't you?"

Far from taking his failure to heart, Ettore claimed the victory. "You are laughing, you are almost your old self. I expect you may say something witty soon. That's all I meant to accomplish. Keep your oath—if you will—but keep your balance too."

"I'll keep my balance," said Andria grimly, but in all conscience the strain was telling upon his constitution, and Ettore had not the eye to see his patient's deterioration within. Not alone the rigid continence, so contrary to his nature, and nightly tested beyond Saint Anthony's powers of endurance, but the continuing erosion of doubts, misgivings and—above all—his ignorance of events beyond the range of his vision, combined with Pappacoda's persistence in argument to undermine Guglielmo's normally equable disposition.

Andria's folly had been to hope—each day and night since leaving Taranto—that within another hour they would be overtaken by a courier, come express with the message that the Princess Maria had relented, and called him husband once more. That hope was not dead but it was failing, and no couriers arrived from other sources either. Not one spy or envoy had returned from his mission. Not one ray of light penetrated the murk of their quandaries. Yet, Ettore had the stubborn pertinacity to say, "Tomorrow we take Avellino!"

Bitterly Andria asked, "Will I find it in my bed?"

"It will be as easy as that."

"We shall not even halt in passing Avellino unless Taranto's sanction or Aunt Joan's blessing reaches us by tomorrow night."

"I took you for a reasonable man," Ettore countered.

"Sensible, at any rate, too level-headed to risk my future—and yours—on one mad pitch."

"Gugl ... For two days we have been riding through Caracciolo country. Right?"

"Right."

"We have seen scarcely one able-bodied man the entire breadth of it. All the work is being done by women. You have seen it yourself. Where are the men?"

The answer was not far to seek.

Fewer than half of all the Barons had responded to Marzano's call to arms. The times were too precarious. Numbers felt that the summons had no other purpose than to leave their estates defenseless so that the transalpine hangers-on of Bourbon could move into their towns and citadels. Others sat tight expecting a change in regime, either through Taranto, the Papal Election or an uprising of the commonality. Some who had served under Braccio were confident that he would defeat Sforza at Rome, and others were just too lazy to move.

To set a proper example for these dilatory, Serjianni had insisted upon all but all of his family taking the field, so that when Guglielmo and Ettore rode through the district, the only male Caracciolos remaining were lame, halt or bedridden with age.

"I call this to your level-headed attention," Pappacoda continued relentlessly, "so that you will realize what you are up against when you get to Rome and try to treat with Sforza. He is surrounded by Caracciolos."

"He will be all the more eager to greet a friend."

"Perhaps—if the Caracciolos will let you get near him. They will outnumber us—twenty to one. On the other hand, if we wished to turn aside a few miles—here and now—we could take Melfi. It is defenseless."

Duke Andria exploded, shouting, "Is there no limit to your madness? Take Melfi! Take Melfi and no Del Balzo, no Orsini, no Pappacoda—nor any of us ever again could draw an easy breath. Take Melfi—and every Baron in the Regno would turn against us. We should have Caldoras, Cantelmos, Sanseverinos, Carafas—and even Orsinis—even the Queen—on our tails unto the third and fourth generation! Take Melfi!"

"Your Highness has misunderstood me," Ettore hastened to make peace. "I said only that we *could*—that the Constable and his family could not stop us. How much easier, then, to take Avellino, where the Del Balzo right is well established and two-thirds of the citizens will hail Your Highness at sight!"

Only slightly mollified, Andria repeated his determination not to attack the city unless that move had been clearly approved by the Prince of Taranto or Joan.

"Well, damitall!" cried Ettore, himself incensed. "Will you not even knock at the gate and ask for the money that is your due by agreement? That will not delay your capture of Rome by more than a quarter of an hour!"

"Why waste our breath? They will simply tell us to go to Hell."

"But—will they? They know their own weakness—and they can see our strength. I think, if we sat down athwart the main road, blocking the gate, they might hand over the gold. Nobody inside knows how eager you are to get to Rome. You have already promised me to wait twenty-four hours for a reply from *somebody!* I ask you only to sit there."

Thus, little by little, and step by step, Ettore Pappacoda instituted the siege of Avellino by force of circumstance, not without Andria's awareness, how he was being manipulated, but by such interlocked and logical contingencies that by condoning the first move he made the next necessary, inescapable, and the next and the next.

Guglielmo felt himself sucked down in a quicksand, with nowhere a place for his feet to rest and nowhere a twig to cling to.

Still the roads remained as empty of guidance as the brazen sky, nor bird nor cloud nor pillar of fire appeared to point his way.

The troop of four hundred was mightily impressive to Serjianni's garrison, and when the boys knocked and said they had come for some ten years' accrued back taxes, they received a civil response. All the Governor asked was that they produce an order—a release—from Serjianni.

Recalling that the secretary Antonio had provided Riccardo with that certain seal—and some of the hairs from his head— Andria sent still another spy to Naples to seek out that soldier, thus condemning himself to three days of suspense instead of the promised one.

Ettore immediately passed the wink to the Tarantine soldiers, authorizing a game of fox-and-geese with the local rind who brought produce to the city. All eatables were confiscated, and several unwary petty officials were collared and held for ransom. A pity to deprive the energetic Captains of their little rewards.

The three days became four, and Guglielmo could no longer wrestle with his conscience or defy his own best judgment. He was talking to himself. He could no longer sleep without a fourth bottle. Every approaching hoofbeat sent him to the door of his tent, red eyed and frantically eager, but those arriving brought only more ignorance, and the Duke felt that if he remained another day without credible advice, he must certainly go mad. If Ettore should say, just one more time, *What you need is a woman!*—Gugl would strangle him without remorse.

As a blockade, theirs brought little discomfort to the inhabitants of Avellino, but it was a misery *par excellence* to Serjianni Caracciolo. It set him hopping, and he could not send an army to break it because he had not any to send. Instead, he gave out for publication, that Raimondo Orsini Count Nola had signed a contract to wed his sister Isabella. Raimondo was said to be on the way home from Constance to celebrate his nuptials, and Serjianni made sure that Duke Andria was among the first to hear about it.

The immediate effect was quite all that the Constable could have wished for, but he was not himself witness to it. Harried almost to frenzy by lack of information from any reliable source, the cherubic Duke had a veritable seizure. Catching Ettore by the throat, he shook him like a dice-box, screaming, "It is not true! I know it is not true! Tell me the truth—the truth—the truth! I've got to know the truth. I've got to know what is going on. That is a lie—but who knows? Who knows? Who knows?" He actually shook a first-rate idea out of Pappacoda, and then nearly lost it by strangling the man.

Their aides risked their own necks to pull the two Highnesses apart and put wine-spirits on Andria's temples. When he could hear, and Ettore could again speak, the Pappacoda said, "The Colonnas in Paliano should know the truth of that. They must know almost everything that happens in Constance—that concerns their brother Oddo."

"That is an inspiration," said Andria.

"The Cardinal couldn't commit them—and the rest of the Colonna family—to Louis II or Juan d'Aragon or anybody else without their sanction. They would know if the Cardinal has fallen out with Raimondo—or with the Prince."

Andria was relishing that discovery like the marrow of a bone. "The Colonnas will know—everything—everything we don't ... I'm sorry I went off my nut, Ettore. Please forgive me."

"O, sure," Pappacoda grinned. "What you need is a woman."

Guglielmo only closed his eyes.

"Shall I send a man to Paliano?" Ettore asked, massaging his Adam's apple.

"Send, Hell!" Andria burst out, springing to his feet. "Nobody we send ever comes back! Break camp. We'll go to Paliano ourselves for a council of War. If the Colonnas are still on our side— they'll help us take Rome. Break camp!"

"O, no-o-o," Ettore groaned. "I never meant that. Let's get your money out of Avellino first, and then to Paliano if you will."

"Not another day. Not another hour. Break camp. We march at dawn. Why didn't you think of Paliano before?"

"*Peste!* I'm sorry I thought of it now," Ettore wheezed, and stumbled, laggard, from the Duke's tent to give the unwelcome order.

To that point Serjianni's strategy was working in his favor, but exactly there it turned, because as Ettore stepped out of the tent—before he could speak his order—he saw the soldier Riccardo dismounting, that moment arrived from Naples.

"In the nick!" cried Ettore, running to embrace him. "Have you seen my uncle? Have you seen the Queen? Gugl! Gugl!"

Riccardo had seen Artuso, but access to Joan—public or private—simply was not to be had since the bungling of her plot with Caldora to assassinate Jacques Bourbon.

Only Joan was suspected, and not Caldora, so the weasel remained as her "guardian" for Serjianni, but on top of that her consort had set the entire body of French Courtiers to watching her so diligently that she could not use the stool without at least two of them retiring with her.

The two most avid to smell her droppings were the pair who hoped to have the taxing of Salerno and Celano, and Superba flattered them by applying those titles whenever she addressed them. That infuriated Serjianni, to be sure, but it had not got the Queen permission to speak with anyone alone, and so, perforce, Caldora's second attempt upon the King's life had been postponed several times.

Riccardo had his details from Serjianni's Antonio, and Ottino Caracciolo, but neither of them had access to Her Majesty, and none of the males could conceive a better way to surmount the impasse than by abiding the outcome of Caldora's second attempt, with its promise of beautiful finality. It was the Duchess of Sessa who cooked up the plot to free her "Baby" from Bourbon and Serjianni at one stroke.

At first Covella had to work without any manner of assistance from the Queen, because Joan never would trust Ottino again after Alopo's death, and would not even give herself the pleasure of peeping upon them when Ottino came to the Duchess' bed. That was well, however, because if Joan had peeped, the erstwhile "Salerno" and "Celano" would have come peeping too, and the loving pair never could have perfected their *coup*.

Artuso Pappacoda was in on it, and that explained the good Uncle's long silence. Success depended upon absolute secrecy, and Artuso was taking no chances, writing no letters, and trusting no man. He was hidden in Castel Capuano, in command there, strengthening its armament and defenses, letting in soldiers a few at a time, preparing for the siege they must expect when Joan escaped and came there to live.

Hardly any of the people who figured in Covella's scheme realized what they were being used for. Serjianni's Archbishop was one. Covella had preyed upon his sympathies and got him to ask permission from Jacques Bourbon and Serjianni for the Queen to attend a private banquet in honor of Cosimo de Medici, the Florentine banker, who was visiting Naples incognito. Neither did Cosimo de Medici know that they were using him.

Until this time the Medici had been backing a Pope of his own at the Council of Constance—in fact, his candidate was the same Pope whom Ladislaus had run out of Rome—but Cosimo was now willing to turn his support to Oddo Colonna upon certain terms.

Riccardo had been giving the Florentine plutocrat a good deal of special attention, and discovered that he was secretly plotting to overthrow Joan and Jacques and bring the Colonna and Louis II d'Anjou into power together. That was what really brought Riccardo to Andria's camp, but Covella and Ottino took no account of Cosimo's plots. Their only aim was to get Superba nestled under Pappacoda's wing in Castel Capuano. After that was accomplished they would dispose of the banker at their leisure.

The Archbishop represented to Serjianni and the King that Cosimo de Medici would not consent to a Colonna Pope until he had spoken to Joan alone, but her captors countered that Her Majesty was known to wish Bourbon's death and they durst not let her out. Whereupon the very nub and essence of Covella's cunning was revealed, and Joan herself was won over.

At the Duchess' instigation Joan called Jacques Bourbon to her side and whispered him the hour and the place where Giulio-Cesaro di Capua would be waiting to fall upon him for the second time, describing the arrangement so circumstantially that the King could not doubt her. Thus Her Majesty spared her own soul the smirch of her husband's blood by sacrificing a Captain who was simply obeying orders. She took special care not to implicate Caldora—not so much for fear of his counter-testimony against herself as because she would need him to make the *third* attempt—now that she was exposing the second.

"Why do you tell me this?" asked Jacques. "In two days you might have been free of me—to reign alone. What has changed your heart?"

"*You* have changed my heart," Joan murmured against his cheek. "Your gentle ways have taught me to love you. Ah, you doubt me now, but if Captain G-C is waiting—as I have said he will be—you will know that I have spoken the truth."

Not to draw the matter out, G-C was waiting, and he was apprehended red-handed. He was promptly beheaded, and the King—in gratitude—permitted Joan to dine with Cosimo de Medici.

Courteous as only a Florentine can be, Cosimo professed to be floored by Joan's charm and refused to discuss the Papal snarl at Constance until she had slaked his ardor.

"Go at once to the Archbishop's palace," Joan murmured against the Medici's cheek, "and I shall follow."

True to her word, the Queen did follow, and advertised it well, but when her coach—bearing only herself and Covella— reached the Archbishop's gate, the driver whipped his nags past the place like a Fury and did not stop until they were all safe inside Castel Capuano.

"In that case," said Duke Andria, "we shall not be breaking camp."

The Queen was free!—almost a sovereign again. The Del Balzo petition for Avellino would promptly find her now—and there was Artuso at her side, her chief defender, a virtual guarantee of Her Majesty's favorable response.

The boys sat down on either side of Riccardo with parchment, ink and pen, and on the basis of the key to Serjianni's cipher began laboriously to forge their order for release of the Avellino gold. What their fiction lacked of likeness to the Constable's style of composition must be compensated for by the authority of his seal and the hairs of Antonio's head.

In Naples, meanwhile, other affairs of State had taken precedency over Andria's petition. Joan's first free act was to open negotiations with her spouse for a treaty establishing a Commission—upon which Serjianni should NOT sit—to determine their individual prerogatives as co-rulers of the Regno. This letter had to be smuggled into Castel Nuovo to avoid the Strong Man's grasp, but it ran that gantlet easily because the Constable was trying to be in ten-several places at once.

Serjianni held his father-in-law responsible for the Queen's escape—as he had warned Caldora he would do if she ever got away—and he commanded Ottino, who was still nominally Castelan of San Vincenzo, to take Milord Prince of Capua into his custody. Appalled to consternation by so much authority, Ottino fled, first, to Castel Capuano, but Joan refused to admit "Alopo's murderer", despite his assistance in her release, and despite the prayerful wailing of Covella. The Queen also, orally, stripped the watchdog of his title to Nicastro, but that made him no poorer.

In panic, then, Ottino rode hey-go-mad to Andria's camp before Avellino, thereby not only revealing his own bias and complicity but implicating Andria and Ettore in a *coup* they had not touched, and only learned about at third-hand.

No matter!—said Andria to the quaking fugitive. "A show of colors is due all around and we are glad to have you."

"How are you at making cannons?" asked Ettore. He had not as much faith in their cipher forgery as the others and wished to back up their verbal assault with a force less open to doubt.

Ottino never had practiced the art of cannon-making, but he was willing to try. "You hollow out a log," he guessed, "and put copper bands around it to prevent splitting."

"Begin at once," Andria ordered grandly. "Make three. Let no expense be spared." Now that he was in this mess beyond any chance of withdrawal he meant to be inside the fortress, on the defensive, before Serjianni recovered his balance from the blows Fate was laying on.

You need waste no sympathy on the Constable, Milords, but his world was collapsing. His father-in-law, his cousin, his Archbishop and Pappacoda—all revealed as traitors in an hour: Avellino sorely threatened, and his signet and secret cipher in enemy hands, transferred by a traitorous secretary who was, as yet, unsuspected. A good many slings and arrows are required to bring a monster down.

Caldora had not been seen since Joan's escape, but he could hardly have left the city, and—after Ottino's panic flight—Serjianni named the elder Marzano his second choice to ferret out the weasel and put him into prison. Sooth, Duke Sessa was the only practicing Commander available, and even his personnel was reduced to a minuscule token army. His son Marino was in Salerno with a press-gang, recruiting sailors for a fleet against Rome, and—all-in-all—they were so short-handed that Serjianni himself led a company of the Palace Guard into the street in response to a rumor.

Caldora had started the rumor expressly for this purpose, and as soon as Serjianni had gone a safe distance, the Capuan arms—that same group which had succoured Joan out of her villa—converged upon the Lungo and filled the Mole. The drawbridge was up, so Caldora presented his compliments to the King by halloo across the moat, not asking protection but ready to dispense it. He asked lief to march these men into Castel Nuovo, to place them at Bourbon's disposal, to keep Serjianni out, thus ending forever Caracciolo tyranny over the sovereign.

That was music to Bourbon's taste, but such a large body of soldiers made him wary. He would like to hear more if the Prince of Capua would come in with no more than *four* of his men. That might have given Caldora pause, but he knew that the Palace Guard remaining within was honeycombed with disaffection and rotten with bribery. Several were in his pay, some in the Queen's, a few held over from Alopo's day, and many owed their places to Ottino. The person least likely to command their obedience was His Barbarian Majesty. So Caldora entered with a suite of only four, leaving in command of the troop on the Lungo a lieutenant who had been aide to the recently depolled Giulio-Cesaro. The lieutenant's only instruction was to wait, and to keep out Serjianni and Duke Sessa.

Of course, some busybody looking for a groat ran with the tale to the Constable, and he managed to meet up with Duke Sessa so they could return together. Their two companies, merged, almost matched man for man the Capuan chivalry, but battle is always shunned in Naples if any shifty dodge whatever can be found for alternative.

Trust Serjianni. He drew rein before the Church Incoronata, close enough to the Lungo to confirm the situation without provoking the Capuans either to attack or to bolt. There he left Marzano and his half-armored light-horse, and himself rode on—stern but not bellicose—into the midst of Caldora's common soldiers, attended by Antonio and perhaps ten Palace Guards.

The atmosphere was explosive. Serjianni always carried tension with him to these people of his father-in-law, and this day—although the order for Caldora's arrestation had not been published—the warrant could be read in the Constable's eyes.

That nameless but tough lieutenant, uncowed and unabashed by Caracciolo's High-and-mightiness, came to intercept his progress before the Constable could get near enough to the drawbridge—which had been raised again—to give a signal or in any wise communicate with the bridgeman through his slot on the far side of the moat. "We are shut out, Lordship," the lieutenant explained without respect. "This is not by Your Worship's order."

"Where is your master?" asked Serjianni evenly.

"The Lord Prince is inside with His Majesty the King, but His Majesty had a fright the other day—they say—and so wouldn't let us in. Now that Your Lordship is here—will it be all right for us to go in? Bourbon won't be afraid any more."

Serjianni did not reply, but continued to ride slowly forward, almost as if he were alone on the Lungo, until he could look straight across the moat and see the white blur of a face in the slot nearest the drawbridge, two smudges of eyes. The bridgeman was watching him.

That would be a creature just barely human, whom the Constable had looked at times beyond number but whom he never had really seen: a nobody, an ape who had learned the trick of grinding up a bridge at a signal, at another signal, grinding it down: but this day, a sigh—which the Strong Man could neither swallow nor quite utter—warned him from within himself not to give the signal. The man—the ape—would not obey it.

Serjianni did not test his premonition. Easier, safer, more comforting, to comprehend that the animal had his orders, given sensibly to protect the King's person. The drawbridge was not to be lowered for anyone. This was not discrimination against Serjianni particularly, but a wise provision against contingencies, seen and unseen, a defense which Milord Melfi would be the last to breach. Why, suppose he did stand upon his dignity and insist that the bridge be lowered for him. The Capuans would charge it—and then he must defend it—at what cost of life? No. That were vanity.

Serjianni turned his horse's head back toward Incoronata. The Capuan lieutenant nudged his mount to follow.

"Stay where you are," Caracciolo growled, concentrating in that short command all the loathing, venom and detestation which events had been storing up within him these many days. Tone and overtone, it stopped the soldier cold.

It also left Serjianni's mouth very dry, with a taste the color of dung.

Time had been when Barons, great Lords and Kings, Ladies and Queens, durst not oppose his will by a breath. Today—only flunkeys obeyed him, and not every one of them. How would it be tomorrow?

Inside, Caldora was lying, *staccato* as usual, trying to save his own neck by accusing Serjianni of God knows what, presenting himself as the Crown's protector, Bourbon's mainstay, the perfect intermediary betwixt the separated husband and wife. This situation wanted mending. The ultimate test between Bourbon's "authority" and Caracciolo's power, inevitable since the Count of Marche first arrived in the Regno, implicit in their anomalous relationship, could be postponed no longer. Caldora had forced finality upon them, and it was imminent. Once Serjianni recognized that—give the Devil his due—his measures toward self-preservation were ambitious, spirited and daring.

In front of the church Serjianni spoke very low to Duke Sessa. "Take your men beyond Uovo, and as fast as you can get them to San Vincenzo. I don't care how—but get there—commandeer everything that will float. Come through from inside—into the Castel—and take Caldora prisoner if you have to kill Jacques Bourbon to do it. After Caldora is in chains—come down and let me in. I'll amuse his men here meanwhile. Go!"

The concept of taking possession of Castel Nuovo by sending a force *through* the prison by that under-water, underground route, was bold enough and without precedent, but the far greater hazard lay in remaining to keep the Capuans "amused" upwards of two hours. Even if the Sessans met with no resistance, the feat could not be accomplished in much shorter space, and Marzano took more than two thirds of their joint fighting force with him. Serjianni was left with a baker's dozen, counting Antonio. He decided to send Antonio for re-enforcements, if any were to be found. "Get the men from my palace—the Arsenal—the city gates—the Customs." This was grasping at straws. The city Sergeants, catchpolls and Blacklegs could be summoned *en masse,* but their fighting value was nil. Of Barons commanding disciplined troops, the dearth was unexampled. Those who were not with Sforza at Rome were in their own bailiwicks strengthening their walls against his return.

"Try Malizia Carafa," said Serjianni. "Tell him the rabble is rising."

The head of the Carafa clan had troops, if he could be excited to use them, but the only threat that could unbend him and get the ancestral dust out of his nostrils was that of a popular uprising. In politics Malizia Carafa was a Queensman, but he had not participated in public affairs since Her Majesty had so far forgotten herself as to lie with the low-born Alopo. Mere people, as such, were anathema to this patrician of patricians.

Antonio quite understood his master's needs, and rode away, ostensibly to see them fulfilled.

Serjianni returned to the Capuan lieutenant and came straight to the point. "I am posting a bounty of two thousand ducats on the head of Duke Andria. You are the first I have told. If you march at once I shall also pay all expenses. You will have the two thousand clear."

To speak of 2000 ducats—clear—knocks the insolence out of a man. "Duke Andria is a cousin of the Queen," said the low-born fellow, pondering his chances.

"Duke Andria is besieging Avellino."

"I know."

"Two thousand ducats."

"My master told me to wait."

"When your master comes out, I shall make him the offer. He will send you to do the work—but he will keep the money."

"Still and all, the two thousand wouldn't do me no good if I went against my master. I'll have to leave the Regno."

"I will protect you. You have nothing to fear." The lifelong habit of supreme self-confidence made that assurance ripple easily off the tongue, but even as Serjianni heard his own words a pang of doubt struck sharply at his breast. Unless Duke Sessa's excursion were successful—unless Serjianni could get that drawbridge down—his ability to "protect" the guilty from punishment might be a little curtailed in the future. Luckily this dolt of a lieutenant did not comprehend his own present power, so difficult is it for a soldier to overcome habitual awe and know when to strike down his betters.

All the dolt said was, "Will Your Highness put that in writing?"

Only the exigencies of his defenseless situation held Serjianni's temper in check. "No pen," he choked, "no paper."

"Inside," the lieutenant suggested sweetly, indicating the Castel. "And I couldn't go to Avellino without earnest of the expense money. The men want to be paid."

"I have less than a hundred by me," said Serjianni.

"Inside," said the man again.

The disagreeable fellow appeared to be challenging the Constable's ability to get into the Castel, almost as if he were faintly aware of Caracciolo's own doubts. "How much earnest would you require?" asked Serjianni, not only to beguile the time but to open the bidding for a transfer of allegiance. This was a fine body of men.

"Five hundred—as earnest," the lieutenant hazarded.

"I will give you an order for five hundred. You can pick up the money at my palace—on your way to the gate."

"Your Highness has no pen," said the dolt, "no paper."

"We can go to my bank."

No bank in Naples had opened its doors since Superba's flight, and both men knew it, but this backing and filling did consume time.

"That ring is worth five hundred," said the Capuan, indicating a stone on the Constable's hand.

It was a carbuncle as big as a bird's egg, set in square gold with a diamond the size of a pea in each corner.

"You have not much experience of jewels," Caracciolo sniffed. "That ring is worth nearer five thousand."

"May I see it?" asked the soldier extending his palm.

Serjianni was beginning to like the man, or—at least—to think better of his capacities, but he did not take the ring off his finger. "You may see it—you may have it—if you march at once, and bring me Andria's head. Then we will speak of a permanent connection."

The Capuan withdrew his empty palm, and looked into it, then studied that hand's ringless back. Turning toward the Castel, he let his eyes cover its grim stone face, impenetrable, its narrow, lofty windows, the parapet. "His Highness told me to wait," he said again.

"You may wait a long time," said Serjianni ominously, trying a new tack.

"How long?" asked the Capuan.

"Forever ... I am afraid the Lord Prince is pleading with Bourbon for his life."

"And will Your Lordship not go in and save your father-in-law?" The lieutenant's face was as hard as the Castel walls.

The extraordinary spectacle of the Grand Constable sitting in mounted parly with a body of Capuan soldiery for more than an hour, in the hot sun, apparently shut out of Castel Nuovo, had drawn a curious and nasty-tongued crowd to the Lungo. The Queen's escape was well relished by all the low-born, and the minstrels were improvising ditties of mockery, scathing to all the males involved. No Sergeants came to quiet them either, because Antonio had not called them, and the Prefect of that civil department had his officers guarding the shuttered shops of the goldsmiths and silk-sellers, the banks and pawnbrokers. An innovation of the populace was long overdue, wanting nothing more than these small events to make it break with a roar.

When Duke Sessa's contingent put out into the Bay in such craft as lay available, a surge of rumor-babbling riffraff came rolling toward the Mole, the better to see the fun. On the beach, Sessa had left only a few grooms in charge of all his horses—more than forty—arousing the sin of covetousness in the breasts of thieving opportunists. Stones flew, and the horses bolted, each pursued by as many as seven vociferous potential owners. This increased the already swelling racket to such a pitch and tumult that it brought Jacques Bourbon and Caldora to a window of the Castel—but briefly. As they looked down, they saw Serjianni and the lieutenant looking up at them, and both drew back instantly—drew back without a sign.

That was the most ominous portent to date, an almost open rebuff, and it struck the former Strong Man an icy bolt to the heart. The look of the tableau, seen so briefly, had not indicated that Caldora was pleading for his life, and the lieutenant—full of his own thoughts—began picking his nose.

The time had come for action.

Serjianni—outwardly as confident as a boy of 15—raised his voice, calling over to the bridgeman, bidding him close the span.

"I may not, Sire. The King——"

"My compliments to the King—and I would speak with him, an he please. Fetch him to the bridge."

"O, God!" the bridgeman groaned, as if his doom lay equally in refusal or compliance, but his frightened face moved away from the aperture.

Benignantly, to the Capuan, Serjianni said, "We are in time."

The observation had a cryptic quality, to the lieutenant's military mind, but Your Worships ken that, whether Jacques Bourbon had the courage to face Caracciolo or not, the diversion created by the request would prevent His Majesty and the Castel staff from too close observation of the seaward panorama, would prevent too careful consideration of any other approaches to the Castel by concentrating attention upon this single one.

Indeed, the demand for admittance could not have been more timely. The guard on San Vincenzo had recognized the warrant for Caldora's arrest as a safe-conduct *cachet* for Duke Sessa's men to pass through the prison, so that even while the sometime Prince of Capua and Jacques Bourbon were debating their reply to Serjianni—hampered in their decision by the advice of those outland Lordships who had permitted Joan to give them the slip—the elder Marzano passed through the last of the heavily guarded doors into one of the Castel's main halls, tributary to the reception hall and within sight of the throne-room entrance. The jabbering French, with Caldora in their midst, were standing in that entrance.

Marzano and his troop—in no special order, none showing steel, but all primed and ready to draw if need be—were well advanced across the receiving room before their presence was noticed. Men-at-arms stood about, in their decorative way, at posted intervals along the walls, but in them was no defense for the Castel's current proprietor or for the Highness named in the warrant. Some of these statue-like creatures were surprised at the sudden influx of men who had long been their comrades, but none gave warning or sounded alarm. They merely looked on, grinning broadly.

Then Jacques Bourbon saw Duke Sessa, and stopped speaking, trying to recall who His Lordship was, and whether they had been friends at last meeting.

Caldora was quicker to recognize his own predicament, because Marzano was not smiling, and in his hand was a document with viciously dangling seals. This the Duke extended toward the King, as he made a most perfunctory obeisance, and spoke without lief. "If Your Majesty please, I am commanded to arrest Count Aversa, *alias* the Prince of Capua, as a traitor and an enemy of the Regno," and he continued, without a pause, to Caldora, "Your Highness will deliver me your sword."

Bourbon's Bedchamber was petrified, but Jacques's lower jaw worked spasmodically, opening and closing his mouth several times, silently save for the click of his teeth.

The weasel raised his sharp-bearded chin proudly, the only man of his group in full possession of his faculties. "The charge is false," he declared. "I refuse to surrender. I put myself under His Majesty's protection."

For any practical purposes, a newborn lambkin could have afforded protection on a par, but—to his credit—Bourbon tried. Anger, not fear, made him choke and sputter, but finally he spit out—"Go to! You and Serjianni too. Go to! You shall not—dare— arresting in my presence! *My* friend! No. Get out. I am King. I protect him. I protect the Prince of Capua."

The Bedchamber was cackling then too, and even moving to surround and shield Caldora physically, but no one drew.

"Guard, ho!" Jacques called. "Put these men out." The men-at-arms only grinned the broader, making no move, unless to shift their weight for the ease of their feet.

"Surrender, Highness," Duke Sessa lowered, again shewing his warrant which nobody wanted. "You are my prisoner. Must I take you by force?"

"Guard! Guard!" the quasi-King was shouting. "Drive them out. Stop them! *I* am King."

Marzano grasped the yawper by the velvet at his throat. "You are King by the Constable's sufferance," he barked. "This Caldora is your enemy. I'm locking him up for your good. Don't make me spill blood."

"Serjianni is no Constable! I have no Constable. Let me go. You dare——"

Some of the Courtiers tried to interfere, tried to loosen Marzano's grip, crying outrage, treason and blasphemy, but over their uproar Sessa called out, "Take him!"—in command to his men—and the scuffle was soon ended. Nobody was even scratched, which is a tribute to the astuteness of the outlanders if but little credit to their courage.

Caldora himself hardly struggled at all as he was pinioned and disarmed. He and his four retainers recognized the hopeless odds against them the moment Jacques Bourbon failed to get obedience from the men-at-arms. To the Capuans—and to almost everyone who witnessed that failure—it looked like the end of Jacques's reign. He was no better than a prisoner himself if the Castel staff defied him, and even permitted his sacred person to be manhandled by Covella's husband, but the Barbarian was learning Neapolitan ways and that preserved him a little while longer.

Marzano's men had brought gaolors in with them, bearing an amplitude of chains, and as these were decked upon the captives Jacques Bourbon saw the fix he was in with terrifying clarity. His only course lay in pretending to accept these moves as zealous loyalty, and so—as Caldora was led away—the King pitched himself upon Duke Sessa's chest, feigning tears as well as he was able and hailing him, "Deliverer!"

Marzano was more soldier than politician, and his field was only half won: he had still to rescue Serjianni from the midst of the Capuan horse on the Lungo: so he peeled the King off his breastplate without ceremony and dropped him into other arms. "Keep him away from the windows," he commanded, and climbed to the Castel's highest parapet to appraise the situation.

If the Capuans knew or even suspected that their Lord was taken, their first and best retaliation would be to fall upon the Constable and hold him hostage for Caldora's release. To lower the bridge and join battle were too dangerous, for—finding themselves attacked—the Capuans would chop down Serjianni and his little guard before relief could possibly reach him.

From the vantage point of the parapet Duke Sessa could see most of the city, and saw that nothing so like anarchy had prevailed in Naples since the night Ladislaus died. His own horses, driven mad by pursuit, were still flying through a score of streets. Looting was forward all over town and riots were boiling for possession of the city gates.

Directly below, Serjianni appeared to be handing over something to the Capuan lieutenant. The man studied it a moment—and then seemed to slip it on his own finger—like a ring. If Marzano had possessed his son's wit he would have said that this was a Hell of a time for Serjianni to be marrying a Capuan soldier.

In sober truth Serjianni was not happy. Only too obviously, Jacques Bourbon was not going to give him an Audience through the bridgeman's slot, and the bridgeman was afraid to come back and say so.

Time—that vaunted flier!—had broken both wings, and the longer the Constable and the lieutenant sat the more certain they became that nothing was going to happen as regarded the bridge.

The lieutenant spoke aside with his corporals, and an unmistakable pressure began to force the Palace Guardsmen closer together, too close to draw, too close to ride, too close for any defense.

Serjianni stood in his stirrups to look toward Incoronata, but only the rabble filled the way. Any succours Antonio might be bringing were not yet in sight.

As the Constable dropped back into his saddle, sodden, a fast-emptying sack, the Capuan's insolence reached a new peak. "Is Your Lordship expecting someone?" he asked. "Duke Sessa, perhaps?"

"Duke Sessa has gone to Avellino," Serjianni lied brazenly, "but he does not know about the bounty. Your chance is better than his."

"Yes, my chance is pretty good," the lieutenant laughed. "Let me see that ring."

No common man had spoken so rudely to the Constable in forty years.

As he handed over the jewel, Serjianni said, "If you ride at once I shall not publish the bounty for a full day. That will give you a better chance."

Admiring the ring on his own finger, the Capuan replied, "This is bounty enough for me, Lordship. Why should I go to Avellino?"

"To save your neck," Serjianni barked, incensed beyond caution. "I command you—now—to march these men to Avellino—to break Andria's siege."

"Save your throat, Lordship," the rude fellow taunted. "I hear Andria has an army of a thousand. Maybe he's put a bounty on your head, eh? Ever think of that? Maybe he's put a bounty on your head, Lordship. And what would you do, was I to put my sword to your throat right now?"

"I would bite off your hand," said Serjianni with more vigor than he had any right, the probabilities being what they were. "You are under arrest for theft, Messer Capuano. You are my prisoner."

That tickled the lieutenant's funny bone so that he laughed—like a horse—in Serjianni's face, and the Capuan was having such a good time withal that he did not hear the drawbridge start down. Everybody else heard it, however, because the chains were loud and the windlass needed grease. Practically every voice on the Lungo exclaimed at it, and every eye was fixed upon the heavy beams and sturdy planking, descending with a singular majesty and meaning which few who saw it ever had detected in such a commonplace sight before.

The lieutenant stopped laughing very abruptly. His bravado had been based upon a bridge immovable, by art or magic, yet, here it descended, and would settle into place directly under the hoofs of the Constable's mount.

Serjianni's horse, on the brink of the moat, was hardly closer than the lieutenant's own, and a lunge to push the Caracciolo over—under the bridge—could scarcely fail to carry him over too, into deep water, loaded with mail. Your armored knight dreads nothing else so much as the aqueous element, be it only knee deep, for once you are down, and the water run in, you never rise again—until Judgment Day, of course.

The lieutenant's delay was but momentary, his inner debate no longer, and his shouted order was as quickly voiced, but through each of those moments, without pause, the drawbridge continued to descend, so that by the time the common soldiers heard the command, "Keep them out of the Castel!"—the bridge was down, with a resounding *boom* for a period.

Then the mystery, how the bridge came to be lowered in defiance of logic, was redoubled, because not one living human was to be seen at the Castel end of the span. The arched aperture was no more than a great black grin, empty except for the fringe of spikes at the top, the elevated portcullis, which looked like a nasty set of upper teeth waiting for something to chew.

If a body of men had rushed out throwing javelins, or if a company of archers had knelt, bows taut—anything—the Capuans would have known what they were up against, but this way they had nothing to go on.

Serjianni—on the contrary—followed Marzano's reasoning to a nicety, and—assuming success and his own welcome—he was on the bridge before it stopped bouncing.

That planking had been laid for chariots, so it accommodated six horses abreast, in a pinch, but the outer two riders would have been in imminent danger of the drink. Serjianni aimed for a middle course, drawing as he moved, and one of his Guards was almost as fast, coming alongside on his right. The lieutenant moved faster, to make up for lost time, and caught hold of the Constable's left-hand rein, stopping the entire procession. Behind them, Palace Guards and Capuans jostled for the center of the bridge, shouting bad names and curses at each other, thwacking with the broad sides of their swords but drawing only horse blood.

"You can't go in!" the Capuan informed Serjianni. "No one is to enter!"

"Messer Capuano," said Caracciolo, "permit me to save your life again—and this is positively the last time."

"Talk your head off, you can't go in."

"I am going in—but if you follow me—nothing can save you."

"I'm not moving." The soldier put his beast broadside of the bridge, directly in Serjianni's path, his naked blade across his horse's neck. To his disadvantage, that position put the Castel gateway more or less behind him.

"I am patient only because I need men for Avellino," said the Constable wearily. "You are my prisoner—but I free you: you have stolen my ring—but I give it to you: on condition that you withdraw, outside the city: wait for me on the Nola road—and I will lead you to Avellino tomorrow morning myself."

"I obey no man but the Prince of Capua."

"The *former* Prince of Capua—your master Count Aversa—is now in a donjon of San Vincenzo, and will remain at my good pleasure." The statement had a clang of verity to it that received some support in an instant. Pikemen were emerging from the Castel in a solid phalanx, their pikes lowered to a horse's knees, and from the parapet above a rain of bolts banged down on the mail across the moat. The argument was convincing.

"I believe you," said the Capuan, moving his mount gingerly around the Constable. "Hold your fire. I withdraw. On the Nola road—tomorrow—Lordship. I will go."

Like a big fat fool, Serjianni let him go—ring and all! Needless to say the Capuan was not on the Nola road next day. He marched those soldiers straight to Aversa and spent the night blowing his own horn in the ear of Antonio Caldora.

Compared to the lieutenant, the King was no problem at all. He agreed! He agreed that Caldora and Del Balzo were traitors. "How can people be so wicked?" he asked. He agreed that Serjianni should take every available man from the Castel to break the siege of Avellino—"And at the Crown's expense! I agree! And don't hurry back. I know these things take time. Take your time! I'll manage—somehow—until you get back."

Joan's letter, looking toward treaty, was burning a hole in Jacques's pocket.

"Take Milord Sessa with you. I'll keep the bridge up. Nobody will get in," Jacques urged.

"I should be more concerned about people getting out," said Serjianni. "Milord Sessa will stay here to see to that."

"Admirable! Admirable!" the King repeated. He would have promised to hang by his heels for a fortnight to be rid of this pair. "Will Your Highness march tonight?"

"It will take me all night to get ready," said Serjianni. "I shall march at the fifteenth hour in the morning."

That too was *admirable,* and while Serjianni began his preparations for that march, the King wrote a letter to Sforza, as Grand Constable, reminding him that Caracciolo's fingers could not be loosed from their grip on the old baton, and describing the new one—very splendid!—in the making for him by the King's jeweler. The abuse of Caldora and the imposition of Marzano's guardianship were bitterly complained of. His Majesty hoped that the War upon Braccio could spare its genius long enough to set these matters right whilst *Duke Melfi* was engaged in private concerns at Avellino.

This missive was given to a page from Lorraine with instructions to mingle with the kitchen staff of Serjianni's army, to go with them only until opportunity afforded to get away toward Rome.

The Neapolitan Way was not hard to learn, and Jacques further congratulated himself upon his concurrence with Joan in her choice of Sforza for a new Chief Minister. That was a particularly happy augur for their first conference. At last Joan and Jacques had found one topic they agreed upon.

Neither King nor fading Constable could spare a moment from his private interests to consider the turbulent city, the looting, thievery, rapine and arson that were making the night a lurid Hell for honest householders.

Bourbon thought the streets were a little noisier than usual, because he was unable to sleep, but Serjianni—in the clangor of the armory, spurring the smiths at their sharpening, shafting and repairs—heard nothing of it until Antonio came in, bloody and spattered, only one jump ahead of a mob.

"Where the Devil have you been?" his master demanded. "I sent you for help."

"Highness—I have been in the Carafa palace—attending Duke Maddaloni. His Highness was not ready to see me. You know how the Carafas are. Only by the greatest persistence could I deliver your message."

Ah, Serjianni brightened, "but he did send help?"

"Not yet, Highness, but Milord Maddaloni begs you to endure the night, and he will answer for the city's tranquillity from the fifteenth hour tomorrow."

"That is very good of him," Serjianni snapped sarcastically.

"His Highness believes that the rabble will wear itself out tonight—and get very drunk," Antonio added.

"My opinion exactly."

"Great minds run in the same channel, Highness. Milord Maddaloni feels that the commonality is easier to handle with a headache—and vomiting——"

"Quite. Quite. A very wise man. But at the fifteenth hour we take the road to Avellino and I shall not give a Dominican damn whether Naples is quiet or not."

In sharpest contrast, on the topmost tower of Castel Capuano, three people were in tears for the city's suffering. Queen Joan, Covella, and Artuso Pappacoda were tormenting their sensitivities by counting fires. Eight blazed at once in various sections of the city, lighted by accident, arson or vengefulness, and threatening to lay waste the capital.

As Queens go, I think that Joan II was not a very good one, but in this extremity she found the grace to weep. "Ah, Naples, poor Naples," she mourned, "who is there to save you?"

"I will go," said Pappacoda. Vain though it was, the proffer was valiant, for the rabble was growing more vicious as wine and fire inflamed it, and Artuso's entire armed company would not have made more than two mouthfuls for that ravening multitude.

"You will not leave Covella and me here alone!" Her Majesty decreed, and, sharply to her Lady, "Stop that caterwaul! I know whom you're crying about, and I won't have it."

The Duchess of Sessa did not know that Ottino had gone to Avellino, and she pictured him trampled upon by the milling thousands of dirty, unworthy feet.

Some of the sharpest clashes had occurred directly in front of Castel Capuano and at the nearest gate, because partisans of Superba had massed in that area to cheer her and defend her. This portion of the populace wished only to celebrate Her Majesty's liberation, called all her detractors troublemakers, and essayed to reform them by cracking their skulls.

Hundreds had clamored for audience, as if this were a new regime, but none had been admitted until—by dogged persistence—the envoys of Andria got their mission announced. Wiser men would have known better than to force the Avellino question upon Joan's notice that night of nights. More tactful men would have chosen words of congratulation and flattery, and—above all—never would have used that harshest bisyllable—*demand!*—but these were simple fellows, rude and crude and worn out with waiting for Her Majesty's ear. They told Artuso that Andria "demanded" Avellino as the price for his march upon Rome, and Joan, listening just inside the next room, burst upon them in royal fury.

"*Rome!*" she screeched. "To march upon *Rome!* Here—get them *here*—here in Naples they are needed. *Demanding*—the fools! Go back—back to Avellino—FLY!—and tell His Highness that to have favors from me he must deserve them. I grant no *demands.* I reward those who love me—and love the Regno. Let him show it. Get him here. Let him quiet these streets. Let him kill my enemies. Let him earn Avellino. *Demand!*"

Both envoys were beaten to their knees before Joan's resentment of that one word was spent. Pappacoda ushered them out, and added his advice to the Queen's. "Tell my nephew, from me, that I advise him to come here—and Duke Andria too. They will be needed, and they will be rewarded, each according to his service. Do not spare your horses."

Then, again, Artuso sought permission to enter the street, to put out fires, to see that others were not started, but Joan would not let him go. She had been thinking. "If those boys have four hundred men—and come here to me—I won't have to make treaty with Jacques. He must settle on *my* terms. Was I too harsh with them—do you think? Have I frightened them away? Send after them! Say that Andria shall have Avellino if he brings his army within three days."

Even as that message was being put on the road, new and unexpected aid offered, and this, much nearer to hand. Malizia Carafa Duke Maddaloni, roused from his lassitude of three years' standing, by Antonio's visit that day, now sent his secretary in an escort of twenty plush knights to offer the elegant obedience of His Magnificence to Queen Joan, and to repeat the assurance he had sent to Serjianni. Municipal tranquillity would be restored by Carafa arms at the fifteenth hour of the morrow. You could tell that the secretary was imitating his master's turns of speech. Meanwhile, the twenty mounted sergeants-at-mace were at Her Majesty's command as a personal bodyguard, an earnest of Milord Maddaloni's good will.

"Send them up four at a time," said Joan, "but *you* are not to go into the street, Artuso. The more sovereign *we* get, the better I like you—and I'm sorry I killed your brother."

"Your Majesty is all kindness," said Pappacoda, bowing himself out.

That was such a sweet thing to say that, for a moment, Joan considered reforming her character sufficiently to merit the compliment. "If you stop that damned sniveling," she told Covella, "I'll give you one of Carafa's sergeants-at-mace. Aren't we coming up in the world? Mother of God!—this is the first time Malizia has ever spared me so much as a groom."

Unaccountably, the Duchess' snivel turned into a squirting flood. "I don't want you to think I'm ungrateful—Baby," she sobbed, "but I don't want anybody but Ottino."

"Don't want one of Carafa's knights! Covella, where's your good taste? Every one of them can read. I wonder if they can read aloud—while they're doing their duties."

"Ottino is the only man I want reading to me."

"I never heard such nonsense in my life. Quick! Find my Virgil."

"I'll just go without—until you forgive him."

"You'll wait a long time!"

"It wasn't his fault you lost Alopo. Nobody can stop Serjianni."

"I can stop Serjianni!"

"O let's not start *that* again. Here come the Carafas."

Four sergeants-at-mace were shewn in, an eye-filling spectacle even fully dressed. Malizia had designed their garb and the chasing on their armor, or had copied it from a most exclusive source not available to the vulgar.

Superba instructed them in their duties, and Covella assisted with stubbornly averted eyes. "Mm, mm, mm, MMM!" Joan applauded, weighing the components of a work of art she meant to compose herself. "Who likes Virgil?"

"Don't care if I do," one stalwart volunteered, accepting the work from his sovereign.

"Now, just lean back and start reading to us."

"Where shall I begin?"

"O, that doesn't matter. Just read," said Joan.

In all honesty one must admit that literature was not Joan's forte, and this touch of Virgil was sheer side to impress the elegant knights of Carafa. Her Majesty's gratification came from aesthetic labors with semi-plastic materials, the arrangement and rearrangement of masses, colors and forms. Superba never had enough of that. She had only just got the four men distributed to suit her, and the reader launched, when Artuso appeared in the door with a handsome newcomer—not a Carafa—only a boy, perhaps 17.

"It never rains but it pours," Pappacoda observed. "If Your Majesty isn't too busy, look who's here."

Joan rolled her eyes at the morsel offered before giving up what she had to speak. "I'm never too busy," said she, "undress him," and she returned to the Virgilian.

"Do you recognize this boy?" Artuso persisted.

"I never saw him before in my life. Who is he?" asked Joan.

"This is Urbano Origlia!" Artuso announced proudly. "And he came of his own accord."

O, the irony of that! After all the angling the Queen had done to lure Urbano Origlia within grappling distance, that he should arrive voluntarily while sixteen Carafa sergeants-at-mace were still waiting to come up in relays!

When Joan said she never had seen the lad before, she was mistaken. She had seen him as a baby. His father had been Grand Prothonotary of the Regno in the Council of Ladislaus, and young Origlia's position corresponded—in a general way—to Ettore Pappacoda's. That is to say, his Minister-father had been removed from her Council by Joan at the beginning of her reign. There the likeness between the youths stopped.

Origlia was as handsome as Apollo, which Ettore certainly was not, but the young god lacked such fine, rich friends as Ettore had. Urbano never had traveled with the Del Balzo-Orsini cousins, and his father's deprivation had thrown him among the people, despite his high birth. He had become very popular among the guilds-men and artisans, and more especially with their wives.

Joan had got wind of his prodigiousness from a cress-seller whose husband had been accidentally killed in the alum mines. Origlia had tried to get the widow a pension, and wound up with a home, rent free. Not a midwife in Naples but would gladly pay him to bring his business into her Seggi. Their name for him was "the Three-legged".

Naturally Joan was interested, but until this night Origlia had ignored her summonses, under the impression that she was interfering with his social work. He was organizing The Midwives Guild.

The cat, apparently, had Origlia's tongue. He could only stare at the amazingly complicated intertwinings of the arrangement before him. It looked like a giant squid.

Artuso attempted to break the ice. "Urbano has brought some Captains of the people, Majesty, to offer their services——"

The Virgil lover, rapidly approaching a climax, drowned out Artuso with the wounding of the stag in Book Seven, his voice rising shrilly and *tremolo* as—

"*Ascanius himself too—*
"*Fired with love of distinguished praise—*
"*From his bended bow aimed arrows—*
"*Nor was the god unaiding—*
"*To his hand which otherwise would have erred—*

"And with a loud whush the shaft impelled—
"Piercing his belly and his flanks.
"The wounded animal fled—"

The reader shuddered to a stop with a soft moan of ecstasy. Joan pushed him away. "Let Messer Origlia speak for himself," she said, as the second Carafa knight's back bent like a bow and and shot *his* arrow into the air.

"What's the matter, Messer Origlia?" the Queen laughed at him. "Haven't you ever heard Virgil before?"

Again Pappacoda tried to answer for the awe-struck youth, but Joan cut him short. "You may go to the fires now, Artuso! I feel much safer—and this room is getting close ... Come over here, Messer Origlia. Let me look at you."

Stunned, and slightly nauseated, the social-minded lad still dimly recollected his mission. Instead of obeying Her Majesty, he planted his feet, brushed Covella's hands away from his codpiece, and resolutely piped, "The French must go!"

"Why, bless your heart, son, *these* aren't Frenchmen," Joan assured him. "They're Knights of Maddaloni—Carafa's Order—and they'll go soon. How about it, boys? One, two, three, all together, for love of your Queen and country!"

"I don't mean them," said Origlia, but the two macemen who had Joan crushed between them were both shouting, "For Queen and country!"

Origlia's message had to wait. "My compliments to the Lord Duke," said Superba as the four stalwarts gathered up their armor. "His men do their duty well. You will dress outside. Help them, Covella. Now!—Messer Origlia—come and sit on my lap and tell me about the Frenchmen."

Pappacoda, trailing the knights toward the anteroom, paused to speak resignedly, "Will Your Majesty want any more Carafas?"

"Not right away," said Joan loftily. "Bring Origlia's friends."

"O, no!" gasped the sunny-faced lad. "Or—yes—but, if they're to come up—would Your Majesty put something on?"

"But I thought they wanted to see me!"

"They—aren't expecting—to see so much of you," Origlia gulped. "Just a scarf—or something?"

"The tyranny of the People!" the Queen complained: but when the two shuffled in—one a Seggi Captain, the other, President of the Dyers' Guild—she had put on something loose.

The spokesmen for the commonality let Origlia drive their bargain, speaking only in corroboration of his thesis, which boiled down to this: in the absence of any effective authority in Naples they were the only ones who could quieten the multitude and bring the unwashed to Her Majesty's support. This they would do, asking only—in return—that "the French", meaning Bourbon's oppressive Council, be removed from all Ministries and offices of public authority.

"I'll do better than that, Little Chicken," said Joan. "For you—I'll drive the French out of the Regno. Several women have told me how you touched their hearts."

"They exaggerate, Majesty," said Origlia modestly. "They don't know the difference between their hearts and their lungs."

"Even so," said Superba.

On that basis a co-operative movement began: the Queen and Origlia, at their anatomicals; Pappacoda and the leaders of the people entering the teeming streets to spread Joan's promise among the minor despots of the nether world, the bandit chieftains, the Presidents of the guilds, and other pseudo-Barons without titles.

By the fifteenth hour, when Malizia Carafa—true to his promise—sent out his soldiers, their work was already done. The streets were so quiet that even Blacklegs and Sergeants of the Watch were beginning to show themselves. A litter of dead, dead drunk, and other casualties had to be stepped over. Many shops yawned doorless, windows gaped, and charred skeletons of buildings still smouldered, but the city was quiet—and it was Joan's city at last.

Homing, with that consolation for his heavy heart, Artuso saw Serjianni march—out of Castel Nuovo, and out of the Constablecy. If Andria and Ettore were heeding Joan's summons, the two armies would meet on the road. Even allowing for Caracciolo's enormously greater experience, the boys' larger force would probably overwhelm him—and what would Serjianni do then? Why, call his family home from Rome, of course, and continue the selfish struggle, without regard for the cost to the Crown.

Artuso also saw the Lorrainer separate himself from the marching men and slip into an alley, afoot. Curious, he sent his groom to follow and find out where the man went. Then Artuso sought his bed and tried to get a little sleep before the conference with Jacques Bourbon, but Joan had been at the brandy—that cup for Generals—and she was in command.

Origlia had already been made Grand Prothonotary, and dear old kissless Pappacoda was routed out to become Acting Lord High Secretary of the Regno, a startling rise in the world for both, and Serjianni's Archbishop—who had taken refuge in Castel Capuano in the night—was made Her Majesty's Almoner.

"There won't be any *alms* for a while," Joan admitted, "but every Queen has an Almoner."

Pappacoda's first assignment as Secretary was to dictate command invitations to a select list of Superba's Barons and their wives with a view toward assembling a Court and a Bedchamber appropriate to her dignity.

With Taranto's cabal in her interest, Carafa back of her, the commonality at her feet and Andria's army coming, Joan saw no reason for hiding her light under a bushel like an ostrich.

Artuso let the weak spots in Joan's logic pass, by the way, until she should be sober: he did not even tell her that Serjianni had marched: so that she was still high in this uncompromising mood when the King's emissaries sneaked into Castel Capuano to settle all differences. Duke Sessa had refused to permit Bourbon to leave Castel Nuovo under any pretext, but four negotiators of Jacques's selection had escaped the ban. With his usual want of tact her husband had elected to send four of Joan's former gaolors, the presumptive "Salerno" and "Celano" among them. The Queen smiled at that pair like a cobra.

They made Jacques's excuses for not attending in person.

"We don't need the squirt," said Joan. "You can take him back to Marche with you."

Their Highnesses missed the allusion to their return to Marche in their eagerness to put Bourbon's best foot forward. They had even brought along the jeweler's drawing—the design for Sfora's new baton. "Serjianni is no longer Constable," said the aspirant to Salerno. "He is no longer in Naples. Attendola Sforza is Grand Constable of the Regno."

"You're damned right he is," said Joan, ripping the drawing in two, "by my appointment months ago. And he doesn't need any confirmation from that satchel-head you call King. Where has Serjianni gone?"

They told her, and Artuso bore them out.

"Trouble-boy!" Her Majesty exploded. "The bane of my existence! He can figure more ways to annoy me!"

"But no more," the pretender to Celano interposed. "His Majesty has summoned Sforza from Rome to protect the Throne. Serjianni will never annoy Your Majesty again."

Superba howled like a she-wolf. "Summoned!—from Rome! That infamous, stupid, double-crossing viper! How does he expect me to get Oil for my Crown? I've *got* to hold Rome.

"Milord Secretary! Send after this messenger. Stop that summons from reaching Sforza—or get to Sforza and countermand it."

"It is done, Majesty," said Pappacoda, considerably enlarging upon the fact, but getting on with the meeting.

"Don't ever leave me, Artuso," said Joan more calmly. "You are the only man alive I can trust. And now hear this, Milords. It is our will and decree that every appointment and title conferred by Jacques Bourbon since he came to Naples is rescinded as of this moment, and you four Highnesses— whatever your pretensions—are hereby banished the Regno for life. Get out!"

The men who had persecuted Her Majesty so long squealed like wounded leucrotas now that her heel was on their necks, but of mercy she had only this much: "I give you two weeks—to steal what you can before you go—on condition that you send Caldora—the Prince of Capua—to me within twenty-four hours. If he isn't here by this time tomorrow—Jacques Bourbon is banished too."

"Impossible!" the envoys gasped. "Caldora is not His Majesty's prisoner. He is held by Duke Sessa."

"Then we will banish Duke Sessa too. Caldora must be brought to me."

One Frenchman got the floor long enough to protest that the purpose of this meeting had been to effect accommodations but they found Her Majesty unwilling to compromise at a single point. They found her banishments unacceptable and her demand for Caldora's person utterly unreasonable.

"So it is," Joan admitted. She had been inspired while the frog croaked. "I will compromise on the subject of Prince Capua."

The outlanders hung upon the Queen's weighty silence as she tried to order the sequence of her own necessities in relation to the Caldoras, father and son.

Antonio Caldora had not joined Sforza's expedition against Braccio da Montone, as a loyal Baron should have done, but had been sitting tight upon Aversa and Capua, which was equivalent to keeping a muscular hand around Joan's throat. He would move now to break the trap that held the elder weasel, but without losing that grip upon her if he was man enough to hold it. Conciliation was indicated there. She must confer title to County Aversa upon Weasel II, as his father had been insisting.

"You need not send Prince Capua to me," said Joan.

The old man might rot in San Vincenzo for all Joan really cared, except that he had not yet divulged the hiding place of the bastard Rinaldo. She would like to get that out of him before he was released. One had to have an heir, and it might better be a reputed son of Ladislaus than either Bourbon or Louis II.

Joan measured the Archbishop with an eye to her need. Why should not the Churchman enter San Vincenzo in the name of the Holy Office of the Inquisition and put Caldora on the rack? Antonio Caldora would not blame the Queen for his father's ordeal if her envoy were standing before him—at that identical moment—presenting Antonio with his new title and urging him to liberate the sweet old thing.

"All I ask you and my husband to do," Joan told the *Bourbonois*, "is co-operate with Antonio Caldora as soon as he makes his plans known. He may lay siege to Castel Nuovo—or attack Serjianni—or burn the town of Sessa, since that's his nearest neighbor. No matter what the Lord Count Aversa does to free his father, it has our approval and you must help him."

The exiles *in petto* did not even need to submit such a point to Bourbon for approval. They replied in his name on the spot.

"His Majesty will be most happy to co-operate with the Lord Count Aversa, if Your Majesty will lift our banishments and co-operate with us."

"Your banishments stand!" the Queen said firmly, giving Origlia goose pimples of satisfaction, "but I concede this much authority to *Monsieur* my husband. He may conduct the conversations with Cosimo de Medici—as long as he does not fail to win that money over to Cardinal Oddo Colonna for Pope."

That was the only concession Jacques Bourbon obtained from the conference, and when messengers went to fetch the Florentine banker he had quietly taken his departure. Cosimo had done pretty well in politics, as that art was practiced in Florence, Constance and points north, but the Neapolitan brand was just a little too rich for his blood.

As soon as the outraged but impotent diplomatists had been put out of Castel Capuano, Joan gripped Pappacoda's arm. "Artuso! Get him back. You've got to get him back. How shall we do it?"

Serjianni was meant, of course. Joan could not reign, Naples was not Naples, without the Strong Man.

"Stop him before he fights with Andria," the Queen pleaded. "One of them might get hurt. We need them both—we need both armies."

Joan might have added that she needed that Avellino gold, too. Sforza's troops had received no sinews for their War in a long, long time.

"How can we get him back, Artuso?"

"I think he'll turn around if you tell him that Bourbon has called Sforza home—to become Constable and to take over the Castel from Duke Sessa. That's the best way I know."

"Put that on the road at once!"

That was a busy road. Not counting the ordinary traffic to and fro, at intervals were—first—Andria's two bunglers, and pursuing them—second—Joan's man with her softer message: third—Serjianni and army, and—fourth—his recall to wrestle with Sforza.

All unaware, before the walls of Avellino, Duke Andria, Ettore, Ottino and Riccardo made ready for the assault.

Ottino had finished two cannons by reaming tree boles and banding them with copper, and these potential destroyers of walls and men were stuffed with saltpeter, loaded with a boulder each, and pointed in the general direction of Avellino's citadel. No other engines of death and demolition had been made because Andria put all confidence in the forgery and in his swordsmen. The cannons—and a company of crossbow strategically placed— were no more than a kind of insurance against deception and trickery by the other side.

Ottino Count Nicastro was to carry the document. "They won't suspect me," Ottino boasted, "I have been through that gate a hundred times for Serjianni, but—I never tried to take an army in with me before. I'll have to explain that—I think."

"Nothing easier," said Ettore. "We are here to search for spies. That is why we took the Sheriff and the Baily prisoner. Serjianni has reason to suspect them."

The Sheriff and the Baily were two of the officials that the Governor of Avellino had not seen fit to ransom, but now they were trussed and set upon horses in Ottino's custody. Those three were to ride in the forefront of a brave company of Andrians, and the Duke was to follow with as many Tarantines as could squeeze through the gate before alarm was raised.

No hostility was to be shown until the hiding place of the gold had been revealed. Then—at a signal—each of the connivers was to turn upon the nearest Caracciolo soldier or partisan and slay him where he stood.

"Those who run won't run far," said Guglielmo with excusable self-satisfaction, "because the townsmen know we are coming and the streets will belong to us."

Ettore was not to enter the city but would remain with the bowmen and cannons, to keep the gate open and catch refugees, if any should get beyond the walls. He was also to be ready to rescue Guglielmo and Ottino if events turned against them, but that was the last thing to be expected, and when the conspirators parted they were still laughing about a contingency so remote.

As chanced, however, the Governor of Avellino recognized their document for a forgery on sight, for the simple reason that the mountain of gold had been moved by Serjianni a good while back.

The Governor, a portly man, was still in bed when the false document was brought to him, but he came out all-standing when he read it. "Ottino is renegade!" he discovered, truly shocked that the watchdog had found so much courage. "Where is he now?"

The understrapper who had brought in the letter had left Ottino in the street, flanked by the Sheriff and the Baily, and backed by Duke Andria and army. "The commonality are hailing Del Balzo as *Count,* Excellency," the incompetent added unhappily. "What does it mean?"

"It means revolution, numskull!" the Governor cried, sticking one fat leg into the sleeve of his doublet. "Tell the Castelan to keep the soldiers out—but get Ottino and Andria inside. Say that we are getting them the money. Run!"

The Governor's valet and even the wench in his bed were sent scurrying with commands for the citadel's defense whilst Messer Roly-poly struggled to dress himself, calling out other orders and instructions to servants who were not there.

In no time at all the bad faith of both sides was equally apparent to each, and—long before he had planned to do so—Andria was forced to give the signal for attack. Not more than ten of his own men were actually inside the fortress courtyard when the rush of the resident guard to cut off those few and prevent further ingress made instant battle imperative.

"For the Star of the East!" cried the *putto*-Duke, drawing, and that—the battle-cry of des Baux—was echoed and re-echoed all over the city, to the gates and beyond.

The fight was for the portcullis and the bridge over the dry moat, the source of all succours for Andria and company, their only hope. Powered thus by vital necessity and the immediate sense of personal righteousness in doing battle for his own, Del Balzo's arm was worth a score of the defenders'. They—hirelings and conscripts—had no reason to prolong the struggle other than to preserve what life was sacked up in their worthless hides.

Crash, crunch and groan, clang, bang and bawl, the issue never was in doubt after the first quarter hour. The ten Puglians—whether of Andria or Taranto—laid on for the Star of the East with zeal as hot as their master's, and even Ottino's normal sluggishness responded to the tempo of the occasion. "Kneel, dogs, kneel!" the Caracciolo kept crying in a sing-song rhythm as he swung a heavy falchion at the knee-joint of each man he faced, and cut them down one after another like a scytheman mowing grain. Four he felled in that fashion before the others found a simple salvation in obeying his command to kneel. Better to bruise the knee-cap by dropping on it than to have it splintered beyond repair, and down they went like so many pilgrims before the Sepulchre.

Riccardo was in command of the main body of troops, pressing hard to get inside, and every blow he struck was delivered in vengeance for the drowning of Aloys.

Not to revolt Your Worships with the blood and guts that spurted and puddled for another half hour, suffice it, that by the end of that space the citadel of Avellino was in Del Balzo possession, and the Governor was being dragged to the rack. None of the attackers believed that the gold was gone. "A turn of the screw," said Guglielmo, "and he'll tell where it is."

A sad mistake, but not the saddest of the day, I ween.

The uproar of the premature attack upon the citadel started exchanges between rival factions in many quarters, and one—especially—to close the city gates. A shower of bolts from Ettore's bowmen did not frighten the warders and—lest the gates be barred before he could get there for hand-to-hand assault—the Pappacoda touched off one of Ottino's cannons. O, gruesome, Milords. Some splinters of that tree were driven through and through men and armor, bone and brain of those who stood nearest, not the enemy. Heads were carried off—to a distance of a rod—and Ettore was among those felled. Ironically, the heavy rock projectile rolled only a few feet, hurting no one.

The first assumption was that Ettore was dead, when the largest remaining piece of him was found. Probably no man ever has survived with less face, but somehow he breathed through that hole, so he was carried into the citadel and stretched on a bed.

Guglielmo could spare his fallen comrade only one, short, weteyed moment, so much wanted doing. "Never—*never* did a man work so hard—toward his own destruction," said Andria, Signing himself. "God, save him." Ettore was left with a priest, and the priest summoned a surgeon. Andria proceeded with his conquest.

About half of the garrison had escaped, fleeing pell-mell toward Naples. A few had been killed or chopped off at the knees, and the rest were given their choice of swearing allegiance to the conqueror or confinement in the bowels of the place. Not many elected to go below, and the fealty oaths of the others were forward when two messages arrived from Joan II the Queen, coming arm-in-arm, so to speak.

Andria's envoys, who had left Naples first, brought Her Majesty's ban upon the operation which had just been accomplished, and the Queen's messenger, who had caught up with the others on the road, delivered their ray of hope that title to Avellino might be realized if Guglielmo would first restore order in Naples. Both emissaries agreed in the letter of that command. Andria and army must appear in the capital, in the Queen's defense "within three days". Neither of the speakers had any royal instructions appropriate to the situation as it existed. Neither of them knew that Serjianni was coming this way behind them, about four hours behind them, but on the double with his Palace Guards.

"I can't go to Naples," Guglielmo complained, thinking aloud to Ottino. "There's too much to be done here. We've gone too far to draw back now. I'm not going to lose what I've got."

"No, no. Don't go," the renegade watchdog agreed. His own daring of the past few days had drained his vitality severely. "Don't leave me here alone. Too many would jump me. You can't leave Ettore dying. Wait—wait until you hear from the Prince of Taranto."

Andria was beginning to doubt that he ever would hear from Giovantonio again, but—having made himself *de facto* Count Avellino—he decided to stay until at least the tax gatherers were all men of his own party.

Meanwhile, back on the busy road, the courier sent by Pappacoda in Joan's name to overtake and alarm Serjianni had fulfilled his mission brilliantly. The Palace Guard did a *volte face* in its tracks and marched back toward Naples, making that turn some hours before the swiftest of the fleeing garrison from Avellino had got that far.

Serjianni returned the Queen's courier to her, bearing his compliance, and in Castel Capuano elaborate preparations began for a love-feast between the classic rivals.

"Bring rats," Superba commanded, "hundreds and hundreds of rats. This is going to be an alliance that only death can break."

How many of the rodent-kind actually were gathered together for Joan's diplomacy is not recorded, but the floor of a certain passageway through which Serjianni must pass was well covered, two deep. All according to the Prince of Taranto's recommendation, every door on that passage—save one—was locked, and that one led straight to the Queen's bed. On the bed she spread her mellowed charms, covered only with a scent, and these preparations were no more than completed when the former Constable—with Antonio at his elbow—was let into that noisome, reeking, squealing corridor.

The result was every whit as satisfactory as Giovantonio had promised, even to the last detail. Nothing was wanting to complete the degradation of the man who had been too strong. One stride inside the door Serjianni felt his feet and legs assailed by the vicious pack of furred demons. Nay, had they been Devils he would have fought them, and—odds on—he'd have won, but being what they were made Serjianni spew like a fountain and quake in wall-eyed terror.

Antonio struck here and there, crying his master, *Courage!*— but the rats, as they will, went for the vomit, biting each other, and piling around Serjianni in a bloody, awful heap. Gasping, gagging, almost sightless, Serjianni groped and tottered from one door to the next, a pitiful sight, a Lord brought low, a thing without will or reason. "Mama," he babbled. "Mama, mama," and then touched the handle of his release. He was through that door like a streak, and he slammed it behind him without a thought for the fate of his secretary.

"Mama! Mama!" Serjianni sobbed to the Queen, who opened her legs to receive him, mail and all.

Covella softly slid the bolt against the rodents as Serjianni climbed on to the bed and buried his face in the bosom he had spurned for, lo! these thirty years. At the moment, one supposes, he was too overwrought to recognize whose teats those were, but the almost extinguished spark of his identity was fanned a little by Joan's breath, and fed a little by relief for the ratlessness of this place. He was saved, and as that awareness established itself, by degrees, the Caracciolo returned to the shell of its mortal clay, bringing with it a different horror, the desolating realization that this was the end.

No longer strong, no longer Constable, no longer Samson, but the merest Duke of Melfi, the man felt his buckles being loosed and knew that his time had come. The Duchess of Sessa was performing upon him, at last, the office she had practiced at least once upon every other male Joan ever had desired, and Serjianni had not the power to resist her. "Thou sow!" was all he said, as Covella piled his armor on the floor.

"Now! Now!" Joan yearned to him, kissing his face, his ears, and filling both her hands with what she never had touched before. "O, now, my love! My man! My mate! We shall rule—in ecstasy! Now! Now! Now and forever. Nothing shall break this tie. Do you not feel it? Do you not know it? Together we shall rule the Earth. Gian! Just thee and me. Say that you feel it. Say that you want it. You want me! You want me!"

"I want Avellino," said Serjianni, holding back and attempting to disengage her grip. "Swear that I shall have Avellino——"

"Anything! Anything!" Joan promised, panting. "Only fill me now!"

"Here—then!"

The world rocked. The bed rocked. "Home!" cried the Queen. "Drive it home!"

"Confirm me now. Repeat after me: I, Joan, by God's Divine Will Queen of Naples, the Two Sicilies, Jerusalem and Hungary, do hereby irrevocably confer and bestow upon Serjianni Caracciolo Duke Melfi——"

Et cetera.

That was how Serjianni got title to Avellino, about three hours after Gugl had put himself in possession.

MR. THAYER INTRUDES

You Probably Sympathize with Duke Andria and Ettore in their leaderless confusion. I know I did. Where *was* the cabal headed?—and why didn't Taranto send some word for their guidance?

It's a funny thing, but those questions are easier for you and me to answer today than they were for those fellows right on the spot. They could not see the myriad interlocking contingencies—world-wide—that prevented Taranto from reaching any firm or constructive decision, but we can fill them in without too much trouble by a glance at the contests raging elsewhere.

At the outset the cabal had leaned toward Louis II, and Count Nola had carried that leaning to Constance, where Cardinal Colonna responded favorably. Then, in the year of Taranto's imprisonment, subsequent events persuaded the Prince that alliance with Aragon was preferable, and he had conceived the grand strategy of reconciling the interests of King Ferdinand of Aragon with Colonna as Pope. At the time, the Prince had two strings to that bow, marriage between Joan and Juan d'Aragon, and the impending nuptials of his sister Caterina with Tristano Chiaramonte.

Joan had failed to hold up her end, when she married Jacques Bourbon, but no party to the negotiations had actually refused to hear more, and no principal had definitely rejected an offer. The project remained very close to the Prince's heart, very much alive, and the wedding of Chiaramonte and Caterina drew on apace.

Correspondence was continuous between Chiaramonte in Palermo and King Ferdinand in Perpignan, but Ferdinand also was holding all decisions in abeyance, induced to bide his time in the matter of Corsica *et al,* by the change in the fortunes of Louis II d'Anjou.

Louis had been virtually King of France, as the guardian of the addled Charles VI, so much so that the Duke of Burgundy had attempted his life time after time, but the energies of the British King Henry V at Agincourt indicated a new regime. Louis II had not himself fought in that battle, but his armies had, and lost so many men that—for the nonce—he was practically eliminated as a contender for the Crown of the Regno. Neither the Council at Constance nor the Faculty of the Sorbonne was afraid of Louis II any more. Duke Jean of Burgundy chased him out of Paris, to Angers in Anjou, and entered treaty—or conspiracy—with the Dauphin.

One might almost say that Burgundy and Henry V were already on Aragon's side. Every blow they struck was to his advantage. In order to cross the Channel from England, Henry V had sunk the only ships of War the French had—ships which had been provided by the Banca San Giorgio of Genoa. Those sunken vessels would never be used to keep Ferdinand out of Corsica.

So when the Emperor proposed that Ferdinand permit him to leave Perpignan to go a tour of Constance, Paris, Calais and London, bespeaking an understanding all around, to the exclusion of Louis II, what could Ferdinand do but comply—and wait upon the outcome of the Emperor's journey?

Benedict XIII did not resign, however, and that embarrassed Taranto's negotiations with Cardinal Colonna. So, too, did Serjianni 's proffer of a Caracciolo bride for Count Nola, and Braccio's entry into Rome. Why should the Cardinal give Taranto a wife if—in the end—he must buy the obedience of Naples and possession of the Vatican from two other fellows? Still their correspondence continued, direct from Constance to Palermo.

The Council itself was paralyzed until Sigismund should return. The Emperor's presence in Constance was necessary to make a ballot valid.

When you consider all the factors involved it is no mortal wonder that the Prince took his ease in Palermo. Things weren't going so badly, really. The Del Balzo Star of the East had ascended over Avellino—and one of the Caldoras might succeed in assassinating Bourbon any day, freeing Joan to marry Juan d'Aragon. One thing waited upon another.

CHAPTER ELEVEN

A MAN OF GREAT resilience, Serjianni arose from Joan's bed full of plans for their future. He put out of mind those past superstitions which had pointed to her sewer as the sluice that would wash away his career and fortune. He had hit bottom now and bounced. Thenceforward, instead of ruling Joan by fear and force, he would govern her (and thus her Kingdom) by the suasions of a lover, even as Alopo had done. Serjianni's confidence rested upon the quality of his premier performance, which he regarded with some pride. Her Majesty had not cried "Uncle", true, but twice in the course of the bout she had stopped speaking altogether, and once she had bitten his neck.

With his drawers in his hand, Duke Melfi—and "Count Avellino" if you please—said, "What has been done about Sforza?"

"I have commanded him to stay about his business in Rome," said the Queen. "It remains to be seen whether he will obey Bourbon or me. He cannot do both."

"You have reconfirmed him as your Constable …"

"I had to, dear."

"I understand. But Sforza will have more confidence in his appointment if he has confirmation of it from me. I shall send him my old baton—with a few pleasant words—assuring him of my friendship as long as he prosecutes the War upon Braccio in a loyal manner."

"You would do that for me! You orange blossom!"

"But to give my letter weight—so that Sforza cannot doubt that you and I are reconciled—I must sign as one of Your Majesty's Ministers of Council. It must look as if I had merely changed portfolios, and the new one must carry sufficient dignity to look as if it would content me. I must have a title more substantial than *orange blossom*."

"You ARE my orange blossom! What other title do you want?" asked Her Majesty, flushed with victory.

"Make me Seneschal," said Serjianni.

Joan might have expected that from one so cruel, but Melfi's manner had disarmed her. In fact, Alopo's executioner had not thought of the irony of his demand when he made it, but only of the pleasure he should have in dictating Sforza's place at table.

"Come back to bed," said Joan.

"Back——"

"You did only one side."

"I got only one County," the gallant retorted. He was not yet at home in this tender diplomatical medium.

"The rats are still there," Joan teased, crooking her finger coyly. "Come on, Serji."

"As Seneschal?"

"We'll see," said Joan, rolling over. "Submit your qualifications."

They were sufficient, as appears, because he got the post, but in the midst of that hurly-burly the fugitive Melfians arrived from Avellino in their breathlessly defeated condition. Serjianni's County, so hard won in bed, would have to be taken all over again, on the terrain.

Artuso Pappacoda stood by, expressionless, as the battered men—to explain their defeat—exaggerated the size of the attacking army and asserted that Ottino Caracciolo had been its chief Commander. The confusion of that had prevented the defenders from fighting their best, uncertain which side Melfi's cousin was on. Mistakenly, they reported Ettore Pappacoda dead, thus giving Serjianni the impression that his kinsman was now Duke Andria's greatest strength.

In the new Seneschal's view, that was no strength at all but only a poor sort of joke. The Queen appeared far angrier than he, and she turned upon Pappacoda railing, "It serves Ettore right! He disobeyed me. They all disobeyed me. I called them to Naples. Is this the kind of discipline we are to expect of Taranto's cabal? Are his cousins to play fast and loose with our Baronies? Are these our allies? Summon the Council!"

Mindful of his own altered status, now that Caracciolo was in the house, Artuso bowed meekly, and offered no defense for his kinsman or his allies, but Serjianni said, "Let us not be hasty. It would be most unwise to reveal our intentions toward the cabal in the presence of the Council. You will frighten people. The Del Balzo-Orsini cousins have many friends, have they not, Artuso?"

"Yes, Milord."

"We don't need the Council to tell us that, do we?"

"No, Milord."

"Could you advise Her Majesty to admit before the Council how the Prince of Taranto has been serving her with the Aragonese?"

"That shall not be mentioned," the Queen broke in. "The Prince of Taranto shall not be named, but Andria and Ottino must be taught a lesson. Artuso, you will summon the Council!"

To hear Her Majesty, one would have thought she had a Council worth summoning, but the poor thing was formless, and so explosive with dissensions that to seat it around a table for conference was to invite a whirlwind indoors.

Only to begin with, there were Pappacoda and Serjianni, the betrayer and the betrayed, who now found reconciliation expedient but were not yet reconciled.

Then, Serjianni and Origlia. The handsome young humanist was hardly aware of the thirty-years' accumulation of subtleties which underlay Joan's so-recent bedding of the Strong Man. The boy saw only the superfices, and so could not but regard the new Seneschal as his rival for their paramour's affections.

Throughout the previous night, and, indeed, up to the hour of Serjianni's return, Joan's ecstatic homage to Origlia's enormity had led the youth to fancy himself as the power behind the Throne, and Her Majesty had substantiated his position with the title of Grand Prothonotary. True, she had then put her Grand Prothonotary out of her boudoir, during the episode of the rats, but Origlia—in the pride of his proportions—looked upon that as no more than a temporary setback, and he was quite ready to match powers with Serjianni, man to man, on the Council table or anywhere else.

The prestige of Malizia Carafa would be one stabilizing influence, if Malizia could be persuaded to attend this session, a Minister without portfolio, but even he was a potential explosive in mixture with Origlia's humanities. Worse, Origlia had called back those two low-born companions, bellwethers of the city's guilds and the populace, and confidently expected them to have seats by his side.

On the high-born level, only one Baron in Joan's new levee had arrived so far, and that was Covella's brother Marino Ruffo, who shared his sister's low opinion of Serjianni as the son of a Sarda. Further, Marino Ruffo was pepper in Caracciolo's nostrils because he was currently guardian of Sforza's bastard Francesco, and the contract to marry that boy to Ruffo's daughter Polissena was already drawn and only awaited the *Condottiere's* return from Rome for signing.

Covella herself was to have a seat at the table, so that when noses were counted Serjianni was outnumbered *eight* to *one,* and that was his original reason for objecting to this conference. His only possible ally was the aristocrat Carafa, who could be depended upon to desert the Queen on any issue favoring the commonality, but even *two* so powerful against *seven*—if the seven had Sforza and the people behind them—were not in a position to dictate policy.

Nonetheless, Serjianni must face his colleagues in the new government sooner or later. The constituency of the Council was not likely to improve until he himself improved it. Accordingly, be acquiesced, and at the twenty-third hour before the confab began he sent Antonio to Castel Nuovo with messages for Marzano Duke Sessa.

The summons was oral, put into the mouth of the traitorous Antonio, calling Sessa to the conference for the better control of his wife and to keep her brother subdued. "But before His Highness leaves the Castel he must do three-several things for me," Serjianni directed. "First—and above all—he must make certain beyond peradventure that neither Caldora nor the King can possibly escape."

"O, certs, Milord," said the faithless.

"Then he must send an order to the town of Montalto—in Marino Ruffo's name-calling for Francesco Sforza's presence in Naples."

The old baton and a conciliatory letter signed by Serjianni had already gone to Attendola's camp outside Rome, but if that maneuver failed to hold off the great warrior, physical possession of his eldest son would not come amiss in subsequent diplomacies.

"When Sessa's men have the boy actually in hand, they are to take him secretly to my palace. On no account is he to be brought here to Castel Capuano."

"Your Excellency looks far into the future," Antonio flattered his master.

"Even farther than that," replied Serjianni. "Have Sessa also get off word to his son Marino, who is pressing conscripts in Salerno, commanding him to take all the men he has—toward Avellino."

"Only *toward* Avellino?"

"Marino is to hold back his attack, nor let his men be seen, until my doltish cousin marches his soldiers out of Avellino. Then he is to strike—and *fast!*"

"You expect Milord Ottino to come here—after all he has done?"

"I shall arrange that. Do not bother your head about it. Only be sure that Marino Marzano gets that message."

"Depend upon it, Highness, if I have to go to Salerno myself."

"But hurry back, Antonio. I need you here. You understand."

Antonio understood well enough to send a Tarantine to Montalto bewaring the Ruffos that the order requiring Francesco Sforza would be a forgery. Then Antonio sent still another of that ilk to Avellino, warning Andria not to divide his forces no matter what bait was offered.

As soon as the double-dealing secretary had left Castel Capuano, Serjianni contrived to catch Covella alone. "Sow," said he, "I'll make a bargain with you. Call Ottino to a rendezvous—and I will answer for Her Majesty's forgiveness of all his past offenses. Tell him that he shall have Nicastro—and somewhat more besides. Believe me, I bear my cousin no malice. I quite understand that all his failings are the result of his evil companions."

"You never spoke more truly," the irrepressible Duchess snapped, "because all the sins he ever committed are the result of associating with you."

"Call him home."

"Get Her Majesty's forgiveness first. In Maria's Holy Name, you didn't expect me to trust *you*, I hope. Get Nicastro for Ottino now—and I shall be very happy to call him home." From that position Covella was not to be budged, and so—when Superba's first Council sat, at last—Serjianni attempted to put Her Majesty's pardon for Ottino first in the order of business.

Nobody had questioned Serjianni's right—as Seneschal—to arrange their seating, but the docket was Artuso Pappacoda's prerogative, as Acting Lord High Secretary, and he had placed the Avellino question at the bottom of the list. If the Council remained in session long enough to reach that *item*, certainly some of the pseudo-Ministers would have been rendered *hors de combat*.

"Her Majesty's defense of Naples against a possible union of Sforza and Caldora forces had seemed of first importance to me," said Artuso mildly. He was determined to get along amiably with the former Strong Man as long as possible in the present emergency.

"The emergency is not so great as Your Lordship imagines," Serjianni argued politely, at first. "Her Majesty has just invested Antonio Caldora with County Aversa, and Milord Sessa has been treating the Prince of Capua very gently in his confinement. I do not think young Caldora will join with Sforza in rebellion— and if he does—that will hardly increase the danger to Naples, because my entire family and all my friends will have withdrawn from Sforza's command. Thus it is entirely fitting for Her Majesty to acknowledge her gratitude to the Caracciolos by lenience and generosity toward my cousin Ottino."

"Let Her Majesty decide," said Artuso, bowing toward Joan.

Superba was woolgathering at the moment, congratulating herself upon regaining Serjianni's sagacity and strong hand to guide her State affairs. A point in evidence of his superiority over herself in Statesmanship had just come out of his mouth, and her heart was humble before it. Serjianni had been wise enough to order gentle treatment for Caldora in prison, whereas she—giddy woman—had sent a Churchman to put him on the rack! This business of ruling required a man. She must do something fine for Serjianni at once, before he found out that the Archbishop was jerking Caldora apart.

"We will speak of Ottino—Count Nicastro—first," said Joan—but then another country was heard from.

The seat assigned to Origlia was at the foot of the table, as far away from the Queen, Carafa and Serjianni as the Seneschal could put him. There he was flanked by his common friends, isolated, a plague spot, Her Majesty's nethermost territory. Technically no objection could be raised: those three were the lowliest of those assembled: but Origlia's place contrasted so sharply with his proximity to the Crown a few hours back, he was not resigned to it without a struggle.

"Superba—dearest Majesty," said the boy winningly, "are we to consider distant affairs—the taxing of Avellino and Nicastro—before the welfare of the people of Naples? The French must go. That's the important thing," and, warmed by the sound of his own voice, he went on with more passion than tact, "These petty jealousies might wait upon the larger issue. You have promised me to send the French away—and I have promised the people——"

"The people be damned," growled the patrician Duke Maddaloni, and his ruff of wiry chestnut hair bristled like the neck of a fighting cock. "I am not here to advise with those who want concessions for *the people*. The French must go. I agree to that, but not because the filthy scum of *the people* say so. Give Nicastro to Ottino. Make him Captain of Naples. I am for order enforced by law and not by coming to terms with *the people*."

Origlia would have retorted hotly, but the President of the Dyers Guild—who had heard himself called names by patricians before this—put a restraining hand on his arm.

Joan—in her majesty—turned to Serjianni, saying, "We pardon and restore Count Nicastro, if he will sever his alliance with Andria. Send for your cousin at once."

Covella—who was seated directly across the table from her husband—gave her Lord a twitch of triumph, and, damp eyed, turned to Joan, saying, "Baby—Majesty—charge Milord Sessa with Ottino's safety. Let there be no 'accidents'." As if, before God, she suspected that Marzano would work Ottino some harm in jealousy over her.

"Let there be no 'accidents'," the Queen echoed, and smiled warmly down the length of the table to where Origlia smarted in defeat. "For you—my Little Chicken," she beamed upon him, "Artuso has already drawn the edict banishing every man Jacques Bourbon brought into the Regno. They must all be gone within eight days—and they may take with them only enough gold to get them back to Marche."

"And the King?" asked Serjianni, with a touch of nostalgia for the dream he had dreamed which was now being blasted. "Must the King leave Naples too?"

"Release Caldora," Joan said brightly. "*He* knows what to do with Jacques Bourbon—and this time, I beg of you, do not try to stop him."

Silence fell heavily around the table, for every Councillor there thought of himself as a good Christian, and your good Christian does not plot husband-murder with his Queen in mixed company. Carafa—especially—would as soon have pared his own toenails in public.

Taking the initiative, Duke Maddaloni set the convention of ignoring Joan's true meaning and confining his comment to the simple question, if Caldora should be released. Duke Maddaloni thought that he should be, and not only released but placed in supreme command of the Regno's armies, advanced over Sfora's head. In the Carafa code, Caldora must be the better soldier, by reason of his noble birth. Attendola Sforza had been born the crudest of peasants, and his present rebellion afforded the perfect opportunity to strip him of all titles and cut him back to size.

Covella, who sat next, had no scruples against regicide, having conspired toward it to the limits of her ability ever since Jacques's arrival in the Regno, but she had an even more pressing reason for favoring the weasel's release:—to protect Queen Joan from the effects of her "victory" over Serjianni. Covella never had understood why Baby cried so long for that particular rattle, and in her fat heart the Duchess had known that it would be an evil day for Joan and for the Regno when she finally got it. Overbearing and grasping as Sarda's son had ever been, now his ambition would acknowledge no bounds. Aye, free Caldora! Hail Sforza! Come Braccio and Taranto! The combined armies of the world would hardly suffice to keep Serjianni in check now that Joan had "defeated" him.

Pappacoda, with wonted practicality, held Bourbon in such small esteem that whether he lived or died was not of the least importance, but Artuso was with the majority in favor of a free Caldora, lest the cabal lose its landing place for invasion through Aversa.

Origlia's party was not bloodthirsty for Bourbon's life: sufficient for their purposes, to ship him back where he had come from. Their choice for General, however, was all for Sforza. How the People does love a winner!

Only Ruffo of Montalto was heart and soul for keeping Caldora in San Vincenzo, but he was too canny to defy the Queen *and* his sister, Serjianni *and* Carafa Duke Maddaloni. Ruffo spoke, rather, of wooing Sforza to Joan's persuasion, and volunteered himself to go and do it. His services in that way were not despised, neither. Joan thanked him kindly and mentioned her intentions in the way of a wedding present for little Polissena and Francesco Sforza.

Duke Sessa kept his face quite stony through discussion of the marriage, but he was all in favor of conciliating Attendola Sforza if that were possible. If it were not possible, then, certainly, Caldora must be released, because Sessa's own command was entirely inadequate to defend Joan's regime unless the towns of Aversa and Capua sustained their share of the shock.

Finally Serjianni, who assumed the right to sum up for all, brushed the conventions aside and laid down one edict as final. "No harm must come to Jacques Bourbon."

"Why not?" asked Joan. "I am Queen of the Regno—and will decree whose executions I please."

"You could," her Seneschal granted, "while you still held the Vatican, but you can't smear yourself with your husband's blood while Braccio has you off balance in Rome. You must look beyond the end of your nose—even as far as Constance. If an accident befalls Jacques Bourbon now, we shall lose the Papacy to some French friend of Louis II d'Anjou, and you your Throne along with it."

"What difference?" asked Joan, reverting at once to her old bickering habits with Serjianni. "I have already lost my Throne to Jacques Bourbon."

"You have not lost it!"

"He sits upon it. You gave it to him. You call him 'King' to my face."

"He cannot leave Castel Nuovo. He is your prisoner."

"Ah! Make him my prisoner, then, in fact. Release Caldora—and put Jacques in his cell."

The simplicity of that solution impressed several of the Council so much that they took the Queen's part, notably Ruffo of Montalto, but Duke Sessa raised his voice too, arguing that the silence of Aversa thus far was ominous. "Antonio Caldora may have marched to join Sforza already. You've got to let his father out—or get me help somewhere—more help than your cousin Ottino!"

"Let him out! Let him out!" Serjianni roared, "but you cannot shut up the King. The Churchmen will take it ill if you do. All these friends of Bourbon you are banishing will go straight to Constance screaming their heads off."

"Let them go where they will," piped up Origlia. "They cannot stay here."

That presumption was one goad too many for Serjianni's self-restraint and he stood up bellowing for Antonio, to throw the pretty lad out the window, quite forgetting that Antonio was on his way to Salerno. The only flunky in attendance upon the Seneschal was no more capable of executing that order than of finding the lost chord, so Serjianni took it on himself.

Many rose to restrain him, including Joan, who tugged at his arm screaming, "Listen to me, Orange Blossom! Listen to me!"

Caracciolo shoved her back into her chair with his old pre-rat abandon, booming, "Don't call me Orange Blossom!"

Then everybody was shouting at once, except Carafa and Artuso. The Acting Secretary was well content to let the outburst run its course, cutting short the order of business, but Malizia Carafa had a better idea and the presence to enforce it. Standing suddenly in Serjianni's path, he raised both arms high over his head and slowly turned from gabbler to gabbler, all around the table, with the air of an outraged Jove. Arbiter of elegance he always had been, and now he assumed the role of umpire in the debate upon national defense and foreign affairs.

The room fell silent to hear the oracle, but as soon as the noise stopped Duke Maddaloni put one arm around Serjianni's shoulder and whispered only to him, "Send Origlia to Constance with the news."

Comprehension dawned on the Seneschal's face like sunrise over a mountain, and he eyed Urbano Origlia as if his imbecility—although complicated by a foul personal odor—had been made endurable by the Carafa genius. "You love Naples, don't you?" Serjianni asked the handsome youth.

"More than my life," Origlia replied with fervor.

"You love your Queen."

"More than my soul."

Serjianni grinned broadly. "You are just the man to go to Constance—*before* the edict of banishment is published—before Jacques Bourbon is confined—and prepare the Council for what is coming. Lay Her Majesty's case before those Churchmen with your wonted eloquence and explain that she is acting in defense of the restored Church. Point out that Sforza—Bourbon's only defender—calls himself Duke of Benevento against Her Majesty's wishes. Say that together they plot against the Queen's life. You can do that, can't you? You are just the man for it."

"I can," Origlia replied, "if Her Majesty commands it."

"Her Majesty commands it," said Serjianni, without even looking at Joan: but he was thinking on his feet then, and he made a mistake. "I have had no real satisfaction out of Constance for months." The words were no sooner out than he realized his blunder. Everybody at the table had heard his hoot and hurrah about Count Nola signing to marry his sister. Either he had lied before or he was lying now, but—bullheaded—he pushed on to make his point. "My best men cannot get through. But—Messer Origlia!—you will be able—entirely unsuspected. Her Majesty expects great things of you."

Impetuously, the boy ran around the Council table and pitched himself at Superba's feet, covering her hands with kisses. "If you command me with your own lips, Majesty, I can bring you the moon," he gushed.

"O, that would be nice," said Joan.

"Bring her Raimondo Orsini with the Crown and you can keep the moon," growled the Seneschal. "The first thing you must learn when you get to Constance is whether Raimondo Orsini is still there. He was supposed to be on his way home to marry my sister, but these Orsinis and Del Balzos are so untrustworthy—I would not risk a white on it. If he is still on our side, he can do much for you in Constance. If he has changed sides we may never see you again. Isn't that the way of it, Milord Acting Secretary? Can you add a word for Messer Origlia's guidance?"

"There is no doubt of Count Nola's allegiance to Her Majesty," Artuso replied. "As soon as we have a Pope to bless her Crown, Nola will bring it and place it upon her head. That has long been our understanding with Her Majesty. If you, Milord, ally your family with the Orsinis by marriage—in good faith—we welcome you."

"Bravo!" cried the Queen, clapping her hands. "Artuso is always so calm."

Orange Blossom had to swallow that, but he had his retaliation. Still addressing Artuso directly, he said, "Then Your Highness has no objection to Messer Origlia's embassy to Constance? You will furnish him with signets and passports to carry him safely to Count Nola and Cardinal Colonna?"

"I shall do everything in my power to make Messer Origlia's journey pleasant and successful," Pappacoda promised.

"I too!" said Malizia Carafa with feeling. It had been his idea in the first place, and he could not get rid of *the people's* mouthpiece quickly enough.

Origlia and the Queen wet each other with their tears. To be parted so soon!

Ah, that was the tragedy of being born to a Crown. Always, always, the public good must be considered before self. "Don't any of you laugh, either," Joan sobbed. "You haven't seen what I'm giving up. Show them, Urbano."

"O, no!" said the hypersensitive Carafa. "We'll take your word for it."

"As a connoisseur, Milord, I should think you would wish to examine a masterpiece," Joan chided him: but Origlia also was opposed to the display in the presence of his companions from the lower orders, and so—in deference to all their censors—the pair withdrew to an anteroom for a parting memorabilium.

Then Origlia was off, and those other representatives of the people left Castel Capuano with him, assured and reassured that "the French" would be gone within eight days, Jacques Bourbon confined in San Vincenzo, Caldora released, Sforza placated before he could burn Naples, and the price of bread brought down.

Sessa was sent back to Castel Nuovo to curtail Caldora's torture at the Archbishop's hands, whether the secret of Rinaldo's whereabouts had been divulged or not, and to concert measures with the liberated weasel for the defense of Naples if Sforza should attack.

Marino Ruffo was entrusted with the Peace mission to Sforza himself, wherever he was to be met with by that time, and if he had started home he was to be presented with the County Ariano, to turn him back upon Braccio. Ariano belonged to the Carafas but Malizia relinquished it for this purpose.

Pappacoda appointed himself to carry the news of Caldora's release to his sons in Aversa and Capua, engaging—on his honor—to prevent them from joining Attendola in rebellion, and that brought the docket to the *item* Avellino, how Duke Andria was to be removed and what his punishment should be.

Artuso was gathering up his papers, quite prepared to ignore that unfinished business. Carafa Duke Maddaloni—the only remaining Councillor of those not resident in Castel Capuano—was taking his leave. He congratulated Serjianni on his statesmanship. "The crisis has been well met," he said. "I see no cause for immediate worry——"

"No," Caracciolo retorted, "but Your Highness has not lost the County Avellino. That is still of some concern to me."

"But of course it is," the money-man sympathized. "Would you like me to act as intermediary? I have always found the Del Balzos very reasonable—and, as I understand it, all Duke Andria wants is the cash. Wasn't that your agreement with Taranto?"

A denial of that agreement was on Serjianni's tongue but he swallowed it and embraced Duke Maddaloni as arbitrator with spurious, loud-voiced enthusiasm. "Would Your Highness undertake it? Would you learn how much money is wanted? My purse is at the Queen's command, but if Del Balzo's price is reasonable——"

"I shall address Milord Andria at once."

"How can I thank you? Arrange a meeting. Invite Duke Andria to Maddaloni and I shall join you there. Reasonable men can always reach agreement. Is it not so, Milord?"

Malizia thought it was so, and since this method of bargaining could save Serjianni a good part of the gold he had already confiscated, not only Carafa but Covella and Pappacoda too assumed that Caracciolo's intentions were honest, in that degree.

Joan promised to pardon Andria's offense as soon as Serjianni should be satisfied, and so—hot upon the heels of the Queen's forgiveness of Ottino—a second missive went to Avellino, inviting Duke Andria to confer in Maddaloni under Carafa's protection.

All these machinations did not meet with uniform success.

The first snag was struck by Duke Sessa when he went down into San Vincenzo to take Caldora off the pulleys. The Archbishop had not yet jerked either of the weasel's arms out of its shoulder socket, but he had made them both mighty sore without learning the first thing about little Rinaldo's hiding place.

When the dropping stopped and wine was brought, in the Queen's name, to the Lord Prince of Capua, by that title, Caldora sensed his advantage. Out in the world the political situation had changed and now his services were wanted. "To defend Joan from Sforza," Marzano of Sessa explained. "The Queen and Serjianni are lovey-dovey—and you are their pride and joy."

Taking a leaf from Sforza's book, the Lord of few words put his terms in a single *decemeter*. "I'll do it for the Duchy of Bari."

"You know?" said Sessa jovially, "that's why I'm a poor man. I never ask for enough—and so I don't get anything."

"Yes—Bari," Caldora repeated. "If I don't get Bari, my son Antonio will join our forces with Sforza's and sweep over the Regno—in Bourbon's name."

The second snag struck was Antonio Caldora, when Pappacoda spoke with him in Aversa. Weasel II praised Artuso for his flexible ethics, "now that Taranto's cabal has gone on the rocks," and suggested that one more right-angled crook in the Pappacoda conscience would permit Artuso to remain Lord High Secretary under Sforza and Bourbon.

"Taranto's cabal has not gone on the rocks," Artuso objected. "We are merely biding our time—and we look to Your Lordship for co-operation when the time comes—in line with your father's commitment."

Hard as glass, and twice as brittle, Antonio Caldora cut short that hope——"Until my father is freed I acknowledge no commitments. I am on Sforza's side—and Sforza will be here—in Aversa—within two days."

That was the first definite information anyone had concerning Sforza's actions, and if it were reliable Joan had not much leisure in which to haggle over price. Accordingly, the Duchy of Bari was conferred upon Caldora, but with deep royal reservations.

Lacking even the rudiments of bargaining power, Jacques Bourbon took flight—a few galley-lengths—holing up in Castel Uovo. The "exiles" all went with him too, and they were not inveigled to come out in any eight days. It took six times that long to move them, but—in the end—they were all packed off except Jacques and a few of his body servants, who went into the donjon Caldora had vacated. Serjianni told Joan she would live to rue that, but she was emboldened to it by the report that Sforza's marching banners were now embroidered with Her Majesty's crest and personal device—thanks to the gift of Ariano. Sforza came as Joan's Constable, not Bourbon's, and he had not abandoned the siege of Rome. He had left the CARACCIOLOS in charge of operations there!—and if they deserted their posts, the loss of Rome lay squarely in Serjianni's lap.

Sforza held himself obedient to Joan II in all things, and was returning to her side expressly to free her from corrupt and evil advisers. In keeping with this pose, Attendola instructed his Captains to greet the united armies of Sessa and the Caldoras as boon-fellows, and on no account to quarrel with them, and so it befell, not far from Capua, that all Joan's defenders sat down to eat and drink and roll dice on the drumhead together, but Sforza himself had not stayed to fraternize.

Together with Marino Ruffo, Sforza slipped off to Montalto to attend their children's nuptials. Thanks to the secretary Antonio, Serjianni's attempt to snatch Francesco Sforza before the marriage could be celebrated had fallen on its arse, and the impostors had been belabored out of town with cudgels, ax handles and vine props. That was the severest battle of this entire expedition, but it was not the end of Antonio's usefulness.

Riding to Salerno, ostensibly to send Marino Marzano *toward* Avellino, this perfidious—who had not yet received even one piece of silver for any of his treachery—deliberately set himself to win the gay lad over to the Tarantines.

Trading upon His Highness' childhood friendship with the Del Balzo-Orsini cousins, Antonio asked what Marino expected from life that would repay him for what he was losing. "Not to mention your mother."

"Losing my friends—and my mother too? You have come a long way to give me a lecture."

"You are breaking her heart."

"You are breaking mine."

"You can mend your ways."

"You can go to the Devil. My mother doesn't know from one day to the next where I am or what I'm doing."

"Every time you obey your father you drive a nail into her coffin."

"O, yes," Marino recalled, "you were in the courtyard the day we brought back Riccardo. You gave him and his men—a hundred ducats apiece."

"I wish it had been a thousand."

"You *are* a Tarantine."

"By choice, not by birth. May I ask why Your Lordship is not a Tarantine?"

"Why not? Nobody has ever asked me—and that's the plain truth of it."

"I ask you now—in the name of the Prince of Taranto, and for your mother too."

"She never sent you to me."

"Well—no—but she is in trouble."

"I should not know her else—but—what can I do for her?"

"Disobey your father."

"That will draw only one nail out of her coffin."

"It will draw a stake out of her heart—a stake that is being pounded in by Duke Melfi—who is now made Seneschal."

"No! Not Seneschal! Serjianni? How are the mighty fallen! But tell me all and never mind your riddles."

"You are commanded, by Serjianni and your father, to lead your conscripts to the Avellino road. You knew that Duke Andria and Ottino Caracciolo had taken Avellino."

"It is in the air. They say Ettore Pappacoda was blown to bits. Rest his soul."

Both men Signed themselves.

"You know, too, that your mother has a violent passion for Serjianni's cousin?"

"I am sorry for him, but it will do him no good to complain to me. All my mother's passions are violent—but there's nothing I can do about it."

"You can prevent—catastrophe."

"I hear you say so, but you do not tell me how. Will you not speak to the point?"

"Your Highness gives me no assurance that you will do the necessary."

"I should be a fool to promise until I know what is required of me."

"And if I tell you, the secret's out, and I shall be to hang."

"You have already said enough to hang yourself. Come—out with the rest. I give you immunity."

"Your Highness is commanded to wait—in a kind of ambush—until Ottino marches out of Avellino, leaving Duke Andria alone. Then you are to attack the citadel—not before. Every ruse will be attempted to draw away so many men that you will have no difficulty overcoming the rest.

"Ottino will be called to invest Nicastro—on his own behalf—to come to Naples and receive high honors—to go against Sforza. Serjianni will try everything—and I have already warned Duke Andria not to be taken in—but the one appeal Serjianni will bank upon is a call to rendezvous with your Highness Mother! Ottino will find that irresistible. He will believe any writing she signs—and so—"

"You invite me to refuse to attack."

"Quite the contrary. I shall now return to Naples and report Your Highness eager to attack, but—meanwhile—I invite you to parly with Duke Andria and Ottino. Warn them that no matter what the Duchess writes Ottino must not leave Avellino. If he never leaves—you never attack—and yet you obey implicitly."

"Simple, isn't it?" said Marino.

"The difficult part is always to leave the impression with Serjianni—and with your father—that you and I have acted in good faith. I need not point out to Your Highness that, since I cast in with Milord Taranto, waking and sleeping I have lived on the brink. One false step—no more than an unguarded word, perhaps—and in I go. No great loss, to be sure, and yet—as long as I am trusted—I am in a position to furkambulate the Lord

Seneschal's plans, such as this one. I put myself in Your Worship's hands. I cast myself upon your mercy."

"Bottoms up!" said Marino, raising his goblet. "I drink long life to you—long life on the brink."

"And I, to the Prince of Taranto," said Antonio, "who gains a strong arm in Your Lordship."

"Eh? Do you think so? Well, I fear nothing but danger, that's true. But you tell Taranto for me—when you report my conversion—that I should like to know where he's going. It's easy enough to see that we cannot go on with Bourbon and Joan canceling out each other's rule, and we all have our bellies full of Serjianni, but will the Prince break with the Queen now, and defend his Cousin Jacques—now that Joan and Serjianni are bedfellows? If I am to be of any use to the cabal I should know which way to jump. Do you?"

"I do not," said Antonio, with an amazing kind of pride in that confession of ignorance. "Your Worship may satisfy yourself in parly with Duke Andria, but I am the humblest of servants and spies. I do not know where we are going. It is enough for me to go with the Prince. He is a Man of Destiny."

Marino's natural inclination was to pass a jest upon their Destiny, but the simpler fellow's sincerity was too profound to abuse for fun. The implication was that the younger Marzano had been initiated into the service of a strange new god, but the capacity for such awe was not in his character, and he entered the new life chiefly to see what would happen next. What happened—after Antonio left Salerno to return to Naples—was strenuous but not exciting, being brought about by Marino's unwilling conscripts who had been rounded up for sea duty and now required to be coerced a second time to make them bear arms on land.

Still they reached a point of vantage on the Avellino road in two days—and Ottino had not left yet—so Marino and his body-servant blacked their faces for a nighttime sortie upon the citadel.

"We're just going to change our luck," he told his lieutenants at the camp, and arranged for horses to be waiting at dawn to bring them back.

Marino was very nearly of an age with Andria, and their pranks and japeries had accounted for much of the happiness shared in happier times, so that—despite their past political differences—a modicum of welcome was to be expected, and no danger whatever on the higher levels, once officious and self-important underlings had been bypassed.

Surprising, then, to meet a response so cold, hard and forbidding. The order was out from the citadel to bring all mysterious prowlers before Duke Andria promptly, since—even yet—no communication had been received from the Prince of Taranto, and messengers from Naples usually came with straw on their feet or in some other disguise invented by the way.

Facing Gugl and Ottino, young Marzano was certain they recognized him even through the soot besmearing his features, and he gave them their most secret countersign with a mocking flourish toward his blackness. *"Cousins and brothers!"* he laughed, grimacing, but Duke Andria's eyes remained stone. Rebuffed and uncomprehending, Marino turned to Ottino, saying, "Well, you and I are *brothers* in more ways than one! Will you not give me your hand?"

Caracciolo extended his, lifelessly, and Del Balzo put his into the pile, speaking solemnly as all their fingers intertwined. *"Cousins and brothers* is more than a sign. It is a pledge," said he.

"I take that pledge," Marino said gaily, "but have you two been bitten by this Man of Destiny bug too? I take your pledge with all my heart, but in the name of whifteen demons I mean to be cheerful about it! If revolution isn't good for a few laughs what in Hell is it good for?"

"Tomorrow," Andria whispered, smiling a little. "We will try to be cheerful tomorrow. Come and see—Ettore. The surgeon is changing the lint."

"Alive!?"

Ah, yes, a little, and barely. That explained the solemn air, and—O!—the explanation was clearer when Marino saw what lived, the jawless pulp, the skull exposed, the quivering eyeball which had no lid and no sight either. "Ola," Marzano groaned. "It were merciful to finish him."

"No, no." Andria would not hear of that, and drew Marino away from the bed: then—in memory of their former ways—he said wanly, "It only hurts him when he laughs. The leech says—if he gets through tonight we'll save him."

Getting Ettore through that night thus became the first common aim and endeavor of the augmented party, in its Avellino branch, and the wounded man was, ever after, the symbol of their unity. Guglielmo, Ottino, Riccardo and Marino talked all night, so that, by cock-crow, the heir to Sessa knew almost as much about Taranto's cabal as if he had been in it from the outset. He also remained as ignorant as the others of their leader's intentions. Andria could not say how the Prince would behave toward Joan when he learned that Serjianni was riding in her saddle. "So far as I know," Guglielmo admitted, "Artuso Pappacoda has had only two letters from Giovantonio since he left Naples, and *all* they said was—*wait*. Taranto will take my hide off when he finds out that I have not waited—and got Ettore almost killed in the bargain."

"That was my fault," Ottino volunteered mournfully. "I should have put more metal bands around those cannons."

"If you had put more metal bands around them they'd have cut off that many more heads. But that's beside the point. I was supposed to take Rome—not Avellino—and now I've got it, the place hangs on my neck like a goiter. I've GOT to get to Rome—to Paliano—to talk with the Colonnas. I've got to know the truth about Cousin Raimondo—if he's marrying Serjianni's sister!—but Ettore is down—and even if he lives he's in no condition to leave in command here. Ottino won't have the responsibility. The place is full of Melfians who would jump him from behind."

"Nobody will jump Your Lordship from behind while I am here," Riccardo boasted. "I can see four ways at once."

Although they spoke of the danger to Ottino from the rear, the real menace to his governance which all apprehended was the guile of Serjianni and the weakness of Covella. When that was mentioned—even by roundabout—Ottino bridled, furious. "Do you take me for a child? Well, then, I will stay. Put me in command and go to the Colonnas. Serjianni cannot fool me—and Covella would not try to."

In evidence of his own acumen, and of Covella's solicitude, Messer Wooly-wit cited the four letters already received from Naples.

Item—the Queen's forgiveness and summons to be invested, Nicastro.

Item—the Duchess' warning to beware the jealousy of Duke Sessa.

Item—the bid of Malizia Carafa, to Andria, for conference in Maddaloni.

Item—Serjianni's appointment of Ottino to the Captaincy of Naples, to begin upon his arrival in the capital.

Lumping the four *items* revealed Ottino's simplicity of mind, for they were not lumpable, and Marino painstakingly shredded out the fallacies in the other's logic. "My father feels no more jealousy of Your Highness than you can balance on the point of a pin," said he, "so that letter shews how readily my mother can deceive herself, and if she is deceived, she can deceive you—unwittingly—because of your faith in her.

"Secondly—the letter from Duke Maddaloni shews that he too can be made a dupe—because I will stake my life that Carafa would never enter a collusion against a Del Balzo. You know that, Gugl. The Del Balzos are one of the very few families the Carafas regard as their equals. Malizia spits upon us Marzanos—and squints down his nose at Caracciolos as Serjianni-come-latelies!

"Believe me, Maddaloni means Your Lordship no harm, but he is befooled by Serjianni. Now—hear me—for I have the solution that will let you start for Paliano tomorrow.

"I take it, Your Worships trust Antonio—Serjianni's secretary?"

They did, implicitly, and had many proofs of his fidelity. So Marino embellished that traitor's rede, enlarging it to fit the circumstances. "I am trusted in Naples—so far—and I am charged with the recovery of this place. My instructions are very specific. I am to wait until Ottino leaves and then attack. But if Andria leaves—and Ottino stays—my confusion will want new instructions. I have only to sit still, and as long as I have the city surrounded—and Ottino does *not* come to Naples—my father and Serjianni will rest on the assurance that I have the situation in hand.

"You, Guglielmo, take your best men—as many as you wish—and go to Rome. Slip out by night—and my men will all be looking the other way. But do go at once, because Sforza is now back in the Regno and when you reach Rome you will have only Braccio to contend with."

"*Only* Braccio!" Andria grunted, "and the Roman Orsinis!"

"I wish I could go with you—but that would spoil the show. We must not let my father and Serjianni know I am renegade—until the latest. No, my place is here, and you need not worry about Serjianni or Mother tricking Ottino, because I shall see their letters first, and we shall weigh them together. And if I am commanded to attack Ottino—after you are gone—he has only to offer a sham resistance. I move my men inside the walls and hold the citadel—ostensibly for Serjianni but in fact for you. I am a son-of-a-bitch, am I not?"

No one could have doubted Marino's sincerity, his frank, open manner, his eagerness or his logic, but still Duke Andria tried all he could to find flaws: the man had been an enemy until that hour: the decision to be made was momentous: but—twist it and shake it as he would—no holes appeared in the plan and no baseness in Marzano's motives.

O, workable! The opportunity to speak with the Colonnas could not be more propitious, and the expedition could be given a wondrous air of rectitude even in the eyes of Queen Joan. Selflessly heroic, it would say, in essence, *I bow to Your Majesty's will. I relinquish Avellino in the custody of a Caracciolo, and where your great General Sforza has failed you I step into the breach to preserve you Queen of Rome.*

That would please the Prince of Taranto, especially if Rome could be occupied without a treaty with Sforza, and—given a few hundred Colonna troops in aid—Guglielmo thought he could do it in—say—two months. No Pope was likely to be applying for Roman residence in less time than that. The Council had been sitting in Constance about three years and agreed upon nothing but the burning of John Hus. The chance of a ballot within the next sixty days was nil.

Only one question kept buzzing Andria, preventing his immediate decision to march. He could think of no reason why Marino Marzano should so suddenly put his extraordinary talents and resources at the disposal of the cabal, or why he should press so hard for action. What had Marino to gain?

Nothing, and there was the rub. As the eldest legitimate son, Marino stood to inherit Sessa, under Joan's regime, but the gay blade must see that Taranto never could support the same regime as Serjianni. If the Prince did not take Bourbon's part, he would call in Louis II—or even the Aragonese without Joan's connivance—and she must fall, carrying the Marzanos down with her. Marino, then, would be utterly dependent upon the largesse of Joan's successor for an estate to tax. Could a man in his senses take such a gamble simply because he preferred the company in the one camp to that in the other, which now included both his parents? The concept was stunning in its novelty, almost incredible, until—upon searching his own heart—Guglielmo was amazed to discover that he might do the same thing himself.

With a final, excruciating squeeze of his mental ventricles, Gugl gave birth to a monster ... Marino was single. Marino fancied himself as the spouse of Taranto's sister Maria. Marino was joining the cabal to ingratiate himself with the Prince, to gain a wife of royal blood and a dot to match. Marino was urging Andria to march—into an ambush—where he, Maria's quasi-betrothed, would be disposed of under cloak of War, leaving the Princess free to marry Marino.

"I cannot leave Avellino until Ettore is out of danger," said Messer Baby-face.

"Of course not," Marino agreed, and in a voice as tender as any mother's, ever, "Let us look in on Ettore again."

Andria's eyes fell away, to his own shoe-tips, unable to meet Marzano's, for he was ashamed to the core of his well-born being to have thought that other thought.

The four men moved silently to the door of the sick-room, but where are eyes sharp enough to detect the degree of another's suffering? Ettore still breathed—and dawn was come.

Over-weary, Marino returned to his command, but still said nothing to his officers about their new alliance, only passing some small jest upon the quality of Avellino tail. They laughed, as lieutenants always must whether the Commander's quips are funny or not, and mentioned a prisoner taken in the night for his persistence in attempting to enter the town after the gates were barred. "We had to take him away from the police," said one, wide eyed, angling for his master's praise.

"Any letters?" asked Marino.

"Not a scrap—but he had a lot of money—for a soldier."

"How much?"

"More than forty gold pieces—of Palermo."

Of Palermo! "Bring him in," said Marino without displaying his emotion, and submitted to his valet to be undressed and have the soot washed off his face. Both eyes were full of soap when the prisoner was brought, and both the prisoner's eyes were full of sleep. "Eh? What's your name?" asked Marzano.

"Quito," replied the other, but that meant nothing to the Commander. The only member of the fighting quartet whom Marino ever had met was Riccardo.

"Whose man are you?"

"The Queen's man, Sire."

"What were you doing in Palermo?"

"I had leave to visit my cousins and brothers."

Marino opened his eyes. "Leave us alone," he told his men, and, when they were gone, "I have spent the night with our cousins and brothers—in the citadel. How did you leave the Prince?"

"In excellent health—but low in spirit," Quito reported, beaming. "Is it true, Highness? You are one of us? O, Milord!" he dropped to one knee.

Marino pulled him up and embraced him. "Why is the Prince low in spirit? What message does he send?"

"By his order it is for Duke Andria only. I am not to speak it where another can hear. Your pardon, Highness?"

"I would not have it otherwise. You are a good man, Quito."

"Thank you, Highness."

"But I am not going to smear my face up again to go back into town with you—not until tonight. Can you not tell me, at least, why the Prince is despondent?"

"The King of Aragon is dead, for one thing, and everything's at sixes and sevens."

"Ferdinand dead! So soon after the Emperor's visit? That sounds like poison."

"Just what Milord Taranto said, but Milord Chiaramonte denies it."

"Eh? We'll never know, will we? But that should start the voting in Constance."

"Aye. Their Lordships agree on that, and I may tell you too, I think, that there is no longer any doubt that Cardinal Colonna will be Elected."

"Then waste no more time here. Go to Duke Andria at once, and say for me that I urge him to the move suggested last night. He will understand that, and I will visit him again tonight as soon as it is dark. Here." Marino gave the messenger a bag of gold pieces minted in Naples. "You should not be carrying money from Palermo. That was a dead giveaway—the only way I knew where you came from."

"I shall be more careful, Highness."

"Hurry!"

By the graciousness of that short passage and interchange Del Balzo's last doubts of Marino were dispelled, so that when the blacked-up heir to Sessa entered Avellino again, all that Guglielmo had, whether of wealth or information, belonged to the new ally without stint or reservation. The pith of the message from Taranto was recited first, in an atmosphere made more cheerful by the improvement in Ettore's condition. Their Lordships accepted the surgeon's word that his patient was sleeping, although nothing in Pappacoda's appearance indicated pleasant dreams.

The death of Ferdinand d'Aragon put an end to Taranto's plans to see Joan II marry Prince Juan. The principal reason was that Juan's elder brother, Alphonso, who succeeded to the throne, succeeded also to the throne of Island Sicily, and Alphonso was not inclined to pass that title to his brother without wearing it a while. Prince Juan without title to Sicily *ultra*Pharum lost half his charm as a consort for Joan, and the other half dropped off when it was known that no Aragonese arms would be available for defending Joan against her enemies.

Alphonso d'Aragon—a born fighter—had employment ready and waiting for every soldier and seaman who could be raised from one end of Aragon to the other. He had first to subdue Majorca and Sardinia, and after that, to take Corsica, and he was not asking any Pope's permission, or the Emperor's, or that of the Council of Constance. These islands were all his, and Alphonso's way was to bless himself in his own possessions.

While Alphonso was doing that, Prince Juan must act the King at home in his brother's stead, and so marriage with Joan was out of the question.

Alphonso was already married, so no use thinking of that, and the other two Aragonese Princes—Pedro and Herri—were the veriest chicken, not over 16 *ans*.

Quito had not been instructed to state in so many words that this turn of events automatically threw the cabal to the support of Louis II d'Anjou, but that inference was fairly implicit in Taranto's consent to the capture of Avellino. *Take your aunt's town if you can, dearest Cousin, as long as your campaign does not unduly delay your occupation of Rome. You may inform Aunt Alix in Baux when you have done, but I should not send her any of the revenues. We may need that money to pay soldiers to make her claim stick.*

Taranto also informed Andria that he had sanctioned the marriage of Count Nola to Serjianni's sister, expressly to bring her dowry into the Orsini family, and now that the Election of Cardinal Oddo Colonna was assured, Cousin Raimondo might return to Naples at his own discretion, to collect the rewards of a job well done.

The Prince himself was remaining in Palermo only to be present at the wedding of his sister Caterina and Tristano Chiaramonte. The money-man bridegroom had already sent his galleys to Taranto to fetch her. That unpaid portion of Caterina's dower, which could not be squeezed out of the Crown under present conditions, was being made up to Tristano by conceding to him the taxing of County Copertino, near Lecce. Queen Joan's approval of that transfer was being assumed.

Andria was not to worry about the Princess Maria's childish resentment of his mistress and the son he had by her, but was to put all his energies into chasing Braccio out of Rome.

"Every time Quito repeats that," Guglielmo groaned, "I break out in a cold sweat."

"Get into a saddle and make your horse do the sweating," Marino urged. "Your time is getting short now. We'll have a Pope within six months!"

Grinning, Del Balzo drew Marzano to a window, to look down on his massing troops. More than two hundred lances gleamed and shimmered in moonlight so bright that no torches were necessary. "I told Ettore—I was going," said Andria. "I'm not sure—but I think he understood."

"He will see them—when you come back," Marino said, offhand, to cover his own emotion. "You have done yourself proudly there. And the best part of it is, those men wish to go. I haven't commanded *willing* soldiers in years!"

"I hope your men are willing to let us pass," said Andria, "because—once we start—we're going through, no matter who tries to stop us."

"Trust me," said Marzano.

"I do," said Andria.

On that note they embraced and parted. Nobody tried to stop the troop, but only a few days later Ottino Caracciolo—by his singular perversity—gave Marino's trustworthiness a terrible black eye. Even with Quito and Riccardo both watching him inside the citadel, and Marzano's army outside the walls guarding him from himself, the sometime Count Nicastro sneaked off alone—to meet Covella—and the next time he was heard of he had been given residence in San Vincenzo, in a cell at no great distance from the King's.

CHAPTER TWELVE

G OING ONLY BY back roads, and as quietly as a large company of lance may move, avoiding Naples and all the larger walled towns, took Andria some eighteen days to reach Paliano, and when he got there nobody was at home. Domestics do not count, of course, but the gateman *said,* "Nobody is at home."

If I had been the gateman I should have said the same thing to such an army, but this fellow was promptly contradicted by a weak soprano from somewhere behind him. Guglielmo could not see its source through the porter's little Judas window.

"I am at home, and I will receive His Highness," the bodiless voice trilled, and—regardless of their unstable pitch—the words carried authority. Anna Colonna, going on 14, was accustomed to being obeyed, and especially when she was suffering one of her Headaches.

This day's Headache was an Act of God in disguise, because Anna always had wished to do the honors of Paliano as its untrammeled, unbridled mistress, and no Prince or Knight as angelic as this one had ever before applied. The run-of-the-mill guests at Paliano since Brother Antonio had gone to Constance had been a sorry and earthy lot, mostly relatives and beggars, sometimes the two in one.

The gateman excused himself from the window and turned to defend the short end of a lost debate. "We cannot admit so many strange soldiers, Highness. That would be the same as surrendering the castle. What would your mother say?"

"Mother would leave the castle in God's hands—and I shall do the same. You are not to argue with me, Antonio. Send the soldiers down to the farm, but I shall receive His Highness in the great hall. Admit him—but give me time to get there." Anna took off, lithe as a boy, across the courtyard and up the long stone stair-steps two at a time. You never would have guessed she had one of her Headaches, and but for her skirts you could hardly have guessed her sex. Anna was going to be a tall woman.

"Mistress Anna!" the gateman called after the child in futile appeal. She was already out of sight.

A lucky thing Mother was not at home, Anna congratulated herself. This visitor obviously came from Naples, and so must have come in connection with the odious plot to marry her to the Prince of Taranto. For all she knew, the pretty Prince at the gate might be her husband, arrived to claim her.

If that were the case—regardless of his beauty—he should hear directly from herself that he had nothing but his trouble for his pains. If Anna could not marry her brother Antonio, for first choice, or his comrade Raimondo Orsini Count Nola, second choice, then she renounced the world and would enter the Convent of Our Lady, becoming the Bride of Christ, Third Choice.

This battle had been forward at Paliano ever since "Uncle" Oddo's letter from Constance had peremptorily directed Mother to *train up Anna to become Princess of Taranto as the wife of Giovantonio Del Balzo-Orsini*—and the far-fetched argument, repeated to persuade her, was that this would assist God in making Uncle Oddo Pope.

Anna was perfectly and dreadfully aware of the multiform distinctions which set her apart from her brothers, sisters, cousins, and all little girls else, and seldom shunned the responsibility of setting those sinners a model of primmest austerity, but she never had presumed to give God a hand with Works He was capable of performing for Himself, and the suggestion coming from one's Cardinal Uncle had a mildly blasphemous odour.

No date had been set for the wedding, and Colonna women hardly ever married before age 15, so that Anna—heretofore—had expected to rectify Uncle Oddo's sacrilege at a face-to-face meeting which surely would occur in the course of two years. If this visitor were her proposed husband, however, Anna was ready to come to grips with the issue at once, and—the more to awe the Neapolitan and give her dictum weight—she seated herself in the Ducal Chair embroidered with the arms of Colonna-Paliano. Not even Mother was permitted to sit there.

"Now what?" asked Anna's nurse, a Roman gentelwoman—hight Maria—who bore a marked facial resemblance to the young Highness. "Your headache seems to be better."

"Much better, thank you," Anna panted. "Show His Highness in—as soon as he comes up. I think it's the Prince of Taranto—come to take me away—but I'm not going. I'll tell him so."

"Nonsense," said Maria. "Get off your father's Chair. You know better than to sit there."

Anna raised a stubborn chin. "In the absence of Their Highnesses—and my elder brothers—I am Duchess of Paliano—to all intents and purposes—and I shall receive the Neapolitan envoy in my father's Chair."

The "nurse"—who was in fact the mother of Anna, and of Antonio and Prospero Colonna too, by the fatherhood of Cardinal Oddo—never had won an argument with anyone, much less with her most formidable offspring, so the topic was still being wordily bandied when Duke Andria was announced, and entered the great hall hard upon the echo of his title, with a suite of only three. His soldiers had been sent to the farm.

Informed of the situation by gateman, Castelan and Major-domo, Guglielmo laid himself out to encourage Anna's humors, bowing low and humbly, kissing her hand, solemnly putting his person and his arms at Her Highness' command.

"I have no commands—right now," said Anna sedately, "but I might have some later. Will Your Lordship take refreshment? My preserves cook is putting up a persimmon compote which I find delicious."

The preserves cook had put Anna out of the kitchen about an hour before, refusing—in an unwonted and foolhardy burst of rebellion—to have her handiwork devoured before it was fairly stewed. Now, as always, Anna would have her way, and the cook would have to eat humble pie, because—of course—for the Duke of Andria, the best in the house must be lavishly spread. Over a bowl of the fruit, so sickening sweet that Guglielmo could scarcely swallow it, he made several remarkable discoveries about his hostess and the ways of her world.

Not the least of these was Anna's marvelous attachment to Raimondo Count Nola, which dated from the earliest times, when she had been no more than 6 years old. "We are secretly betrothed," the maid confessed, "and that is why I cannot obey Cardinal Uncle Oddo and marry the Prince of Taranto."

The Del Balzo was gratified to learn that the Cardinal had issued his instruction even though Anna had countermanded it. "You and I shall be cousins no matter whether you marry Count Nola or the Prince of Taranto," said the Duke, inevitably comparing the child with the Princess Maria who had renounced him. Until this time Guglielmo had kept his self-imposed oath not to touch a woman pending his forgiveness by Taranto's sister, and—truly—he apprehended no menace to that resolution in this cousin-to-be. Anna was not only flat, she was plain, not ugly, exactly, but pale, and burdened with a frowning seriousness that amounted to incipient grimness. In that censorious expression Guglielmo thought he saw the opportunity to disentangle some of the confusions his betrothed had caused him. Weighty questions seriously asked of Anna, he reasoned, should bring answers typical of the Princess Maria, but when he delved into the sources of babies, pre-marital, and this child's attitude toward them, he was taken aback by the revelation that all babies in Anna's world were found under cabbage plants, and this, notwithstanding that she had brothers and male cousins of almost her own age until you couldn't rest.

A more touching innocency than Anna's has still to be recorded. All "marriages" were made in Heaven, and hers with Raimondo Count Nola had been recorded On High the very next day after she was told that she could not marry her brother. It partook of nothing earthy. By "spouse" Anna understood only the outward show, the title, the honor, the management of the hosuehold: and the Nuptial Mass—in anticipation—was in the nature of a Divine License to prowl the cabbage rows together, and to hold in common any babies either party to the contract might find.

The nurse-Maria, who chaperoned these conversations, even sitting at table by Anna's gracious permission, batted her lids at the cherubic visitor, bespeaking his mature comprehension. The woman was almost twice Guglielmo's age, but this subtle communication tended to narrow the gap. Then she lowered her eyes in such a way that the Duke was forcibly reminded how long the Council of Constance had been in session, depriving this gentlewoman of Cardinal Oddo's comfort.

Anna's official "Mother"—that is, the Duchess Paliano—was attending a family conference in Marsi, where Uncle Giordano, the eldest living Colonna, was attempting to choose an heir from among the boys. Although a widower, Giordano's cabbage patch had failed him, and Mother hoped to see little Odoardo named successor to Marsi in the old man's will.

Anna's nurse sniffed audibly. "Your Lordship understands that His Serenity Cardinal Oddo Colonna has in mind something much finer than Marsi for the eldest boy, Antonio—much finer."

"O, that stands to reason," said Anna. "Look how much older Antonio is. My brother Odoardo is only one month older than I am."

"Don't say such things," Maria admonished, flustered and blushing, but Anna assured Cousin Guglielmo that it was perfectly true. "And Brother Prospero has nothing to worry about either," the maid continued. "He only went along to Marsi for the ride. No use piling titles on *him*—when he's going to enter the Church."

"O? I had not known that Milord Prospero was taking Holy Orders," said the Duke politely.

"He isn't," said Anna. "He'll start as a Cardinal. When Uncle Oddo becomes Pope he will turn over *his* church to Prospero."

"If only that wretched Council would get a wiggle on!" the nurse apostrophized. "I can't stand living in the country the year around. I'm a city girl, and I'm accustomed to a place of my own."

"The Vatican will want a new roof before anyone can live in it," Guglielmo recalled.

"Ah, don't I know it?" Maria warmed to him. "It's just a sin the way they've let everything run down."

The balloting had not begun "even yet" in Constance, according to the latest Colonna intelligence, then some days old. "We never open Father's letters—unless the temptation is too strong for us," said Anna. "Not that we're anxious. Uncle Oddo will certainly be Elected Pope, because that is the Will of God."

No Churchman in Duke Andria's experience, from the smallest priestling up, ever had expressed his certitude of conversance with God's Will more confidently than Anna. She could not always be prevailed upon to convey that Mystery to others, but—make no mistake—Anna always knew It. What is more, God's Will and Anna's developed—upon longer acquaintance—an amazing statistical record for coinciding. Her record for successful praying, too, was quite unmatched. Sooner or later—one way or another—all Anna's prayers were answered. That was because she never bothered Heaven with trivial importunities—like asking for letters. "Antonio has written to me only once since he went away," the maiden said with acerbity, "and is he going to catch it when I see him!"

All communications from the Cardinal were for Father—that is, for Lorenzo-Onofrio Colonna, Duke Paliano, the fighting hope of the brothers—and they were sent on to him, usually unopened, wherever he might be. With only token assistance from the rest of the family, Lorenzo-Onofrio had to protect all their improved real estate within the Eternal City from sack and ruin by either Braccio or Sforza, and at the same time be ready to relieve attacks by the Orsinis or other bandits upon the Colonnas' outlying estates.

"There is practically no connection between these Roman Orsinis and Raimondo's people," Anna hastened to explain. "They are two entirely separate branches of the family."

"My mother was an Orsini of the Neapolitan branch," Del Balzo boasted to increase his welcome.

"That must be a great comfort to you," said Anna.

Gugl conceded the comfort of that, but could find none in this picture of Duke Paliano cooped up inside some Colonna town-house. That offered little encouragement to his own brave plans. The look of it was that the Tarantine arms must first take

Rome, before they could so much as hold a Council of War with their Colonna allies. The ladies did not know how many men the Colonnas could put into the field, or where most of them were located that day. "That's the sort of question Father answers best," said Anna, with a very slight smile of apology.

Whom Uncle Oddo would anoint sovereign of the Regno was more in Anna's line, since that was the Will of God, pure and simple. The topic had been one of her daily lessons ever since they had begun to train her up to become Princess of Taranto.

"Not Joan II?" asked Andria.

"Indeed not!" the nurse-Maria interposed before Anna could answer. Like most of her sex and ilk, Oddo's neglected mistress called the Queen a grave sinner, but Anna was more lenient. Signorina Sobersides expected Her Majesty to find virtue and redemption through the Tears of the Virgin as soon as Uncle Oddo got the Tiara.

Feeling his way, Guglielmo asked Anna what she conceived Joan's sins to be, but the dear girl—spooning her sixth bowl of persimmon compote—refused, as a sinner, to sit in judgment, lest she herself be judged. "But I do wish I could just have a good heart-to-heart talk with Queen Joan," said Anna. "I think she might act differently."

"You are likely to have many opportunities," Andria choked, "after you are married. I should like to be a little fly on the wall at some of your meetings with Queen Joan."

"O, I should have to talk to her all alone—and pray with her—to get her to abdicate."

"Yes, you certainly would," Gugl agreed. "That would be a very severe test of Heaven's favor if you ever prayed for that."

"But she must—in the end. God in His Wisdom—after many years—has united the two Houses that each has its right to the Regno, and He has blessed that union with five children in whom the rival claims are joined at last. It is perfectly beautiful. It is so right. How can anybody fail to see it? Have you ever met the Duchess d'Anjou?"

Andria never had.

"Neither have I, but she must be a wonderful woman!" Anna was starry eyed.

Nobody in the Regno—leastwise, nobody in the cabal—had ever touched off red fire to the glorification of Louis d'Anjou's *wife,* or cared a great deal who she was. All the talk had been Louis II—Louis II—and of his sons, of course.

Guglielmo—as heir to Baux, and thus the nearest thing to a full-blown Angevin in the cabal—was a little ashamed to be reminded of this Heavenly union by a pale-faced chit in her teens. It made him look rather a monkey.

The Duchess d'Anjou was Yolande d'Aragon, a cousin of the lately entombed Ferdinand the Just, and her claim to the Throne of the Two Sicilies was based upon a drop or two of Hohenstauffen blood—much diluted by the passage of many generations. The Hohenstauffens had been German Emperors two centuries before, and held their seat of Empire in Naples until the House of Anjou drove them out—and drove them into marriage with the Aragonese.

This was the bootless "right" to rule the Regno about which Anna Colonna now made such to-do. It was a poor thing, hardly able to stand on its own feet. In fact, any of the Aragonese royal family could advance the same claim. It was the basis for Aragon's present possession of Sicily *ultra* Pharum, and if Joan II could have married Juan d'Aragon—as her inspiration had been—their union would have matched Yolande's with Louis II in every Heavenly particular except the children.

Duke Andria had to grant that those three boys Yolande had borne to Louis d'Anjou had a definite edge over all other contenders, in the absolute sense, which Anna attributed to the Will of God. It gave Gugl a new sense of righteousness to be on Anna's side. He always had been for Louis II, but for the more mundane considerations of Baux and Avellino. This twist put a halo on it. You might say his operation at Avellino had been a Holy Crusade, himself a Knight Templar, and—if Ettore died— *he* would probably be canonized—a martyr.

This Will of God gambit was not so childish as it had sounded at first. Anna had something there.

"Besides," said she, "Louis d'Anjou is a direct descendant of Saint Louis of France."

"Well, so is Jacques Bourbon—and so is Joan," Andria said humbly. "In fact, Queen Joan has the advantage on that point. She has *two* Saints in her family. Saint Louis of Toulouse was a son of Charles the Lame of Naples."

"Let us say no more about it," said Anna.

Another idiosyncrasy of the Cardinal's daughter came out before the castle of Paliano slept that night. When she was about to retire, one of her very rare smiles flashed on for Guglielmo, and she asked, "Do you know why I like you, Cousin?"

"I had not dared to infer so much," said he, like the Del Balzo that he was. "But if it is true—tell me why—for I so little deserve your esteem."

"You have been here almost all day," said Her Highness. "We have talked about everything under the sun, but never once have you said—*We can't have everything.* You are the first person I ever met who did not say it, sooner or later. When I meet a new person I *wait* for him to say it—but you didn't. Why can't we have every-thing—if God Wills it?"

"Ah-if God Wills it."

"My opinion exactly," said Anna, and bade Cousin Gugl have pleasant dreams.

Alone in the apartment assigned to him, Andria tried to decide if that parting constituted an invitation to visit Anna in her bed. His experience of females gave the highest likelihood to the chance that her saintliness was shamming, and—oath or no oath—a man had a duty to his hostess if that was what she had in mind.

"Why can't we have everything?" he repeated to himself, a dangerous kind of question, and no motto for a maid.

Still Andria held back, in deference to Taranto's ambition here, an ambition nowise canceled out by Anna's peccadillos upon her affianced state. Even though the Prince never had seen the child, that he remembered, and was not likely to be impressed when he did, he would not relish to receive her tampered and toyed with by Messer Cupido Mouth. On the other hand, probably the swiftest way to come into conference with Duke Paliano was by climbing into Anna's bed, events being so prone to run by contraries. Typical of virtually all human experience, Lorenzo-Onofrio would be moved—mystically, magically—to come home in the midst of it.

Thinking, then, unselfishly, to spare his men the pains of taking Rome unaided, Guglielmo stepped into the dark corridor, shoeless, and started in the direction his best estimate esteemed Anna's apartment to be. In no time at all—he had not moved the length of a string—a soft hand took his, and a whisper said, "*This* way." Thus Andria's oath of continence was shattered—not with Anna, to be sure, but with her mother who really needed it.

Heaven only knows what Anna would have understood by Andria's invasion if he ever had reached her boudoir. Her Guilelessness had fallen asleep telling her beads and praying for the return of Antonio and Count Nola out of the Switzer country.

Between times, that night, the Duke and the grateful nurse considered the problem of Anna, how she was to be convinced of those certain facts which most children half her age already knew. "Has she never watched a bull or a boar—never seen a stallion mount a mare?" asked Del Balzo.

"She has seen them—but calls their doings beastly—whilst she remains always on the side of the angels. I wish she might stay so pure forever."

"Now, that were against God and Nature. Would you condemn her to a life without pleasure?"

"She will learn soon enough what devils you men are."

"Are we so bad? I must say that you enjoy it."

"The more shame to me, but that is because my termps began young. Anna has not menstruated yet."

"Should she not?"

"It would ease her headaches."

"What says the surgeon?"

"What surgeon? She would die of the examination!"

"A midwife, then."

"She-panders! Would you have the child deflowered so young?"

"I would have her know that she is a woman—and what that means to a man. Right now she has her 'husbands' so mixed up that Taranto looks like an ogre to her. She is afraid of him—and will make a bad wife."

"It is none of my doing."

"Are you not her mother?"

"I am her mother only in fact. I have no voice in her marriage—or how to train her for it. That is the province of the Duchess Paliano—and *she* is too much concerned for her own children to give mine a second thought. You shall see, when she gets back from Marsi."

In justice to the Duchess—even before she returned with the other children from Marsi—Guglielmo correctly surmised that the charge of neglect was exaggerated, biased by Maria's self-conscious awareness of her position in the household, a position which she felt more keenly than any of the others. Comprehending that his attentions went far to alleviate the gentlewoman's sense of inferiority, Guglielmo breached his oath again—and then again—out of sheer Christian charity, but the exercise did not teach them how to overcome their awe for Anna, her virginity of mind, and so the cause of Colonna-Taranto amity was not advanced one tittle, nor the labors of the Council of Constance lightened.

Next day the Duchess and her brood came home, and Del Balzo observed at once that Anna's sway cut across all blood lines, extending to this "Mother" as well, and over the entire family. Her rule was soft, but nonetheless real, and even her full-brother Prospero, four years her senior, could scarcely decide which side of his bread to butter without Anna's advice.

Watching the technic of her power in action, Guglielmo saw that the little lady's ability always to be right was no mere bad habit of adolescence which she would be able to break. Inborn, and as much a part of her as the jib of her jaw, was the unerring sense of selection which permitted her—nay, forced her—to choose from any given set of circumstances only the data in support of what she wished to be true. That, then, and only that, became the truth: "Let us say no more about it."

Unquestionably, a bride so equipped would expect to rule her husband with the same firm righteousness, and Guglielmo was not sanguine that this would rhyme well with Giovantonio's disposition and habits of command. Worse still, Andria realized with a sinking heart that Anna could not recognize a jest as such even after the funny thing had walked up and nipped her, and Giovantonio loved his joke.

When Anna's two giddily infantine "sisters" made mock of her solemn airs, throwing themselves into spasms of glee uncontrollable by ordinary means, Anna knelt between them, a very martyr, and sacredly intoned, "The very next one of you who giggles—will be sent away to marry the Prince of Taranto."

They were not unimpressed by that, but clung to her, begging forgiveness, and—just for a fleeting moment—Guglielmo considered if that were not a solution of merit for Taranto's future. It was not a solution, of course, since both younglings were truly offspring of Duke Paliano: Colonnas, they were, but that was not the same thing at all as being the only daughter of the Pope.

Little Odoardo Colonna had not got Marsi as a result of the family conference. Uncle Giordano's gout was so much better that he had sent them all packing, damned if he would make a will with twenty more good years ahead of him.

"Never mind, Odito," Anna consoled him. "If Uncle Giordano dies without a will, Father will get Marsi and *he* will give it to you."

It was not the boy but his Duchess mother who wanted sympathy, and the more so when she saw Anna's nurse wearing the most satisfied smile that had sat on her face in three years. "Stop smirking," the Duchess commanded. "Anna is perfectly right. Lorenzo will get Marsi—and pass it on to Odoardo—so there's nothing for you to smirk about."

Maria's face was cleft from ear to ear in a drippy moon, "I'm not smirking, I'm smiling," she said. "I'm so happy that you went to Marsi—I'll kiss Odoardo's feet if you like, and call him Highness from now on."

The Duchess Paliano was utterly incapable of the retort memorable, but she did the best she could to prevent anyone from thinking she was a fool. "If you mean what I think you mean," said Her Highness, still addressing the nurse, but laying a dead-fish eye upon Duke Andria, "I'd rather not have my son associated with your memories."

"O, Mother, you are tired," Anna interposed. "Maria *loves* Odoardo,"—and, lest a test of that affection be called for, the maid hurried on, "Prospero! You must take Milord Andria to Father at once. His Highness is going to drive Braccio out of Rome."

Ah, that was more to the Duchess' taste. "Thank God!" she applauded. "Now we shall get some new clothes. Your Highness finds us threadbare—because Braccio has my favorite tailor under lock and key working for him. Prospero, you will show Cousin Guglielmo where Aranda has his shop, and bring him back with you—with plenty of materials."

The Duchess did not appear ragged to Andria, but that was her way of speaking. Her family—the Gaetani—never had lacked for anything, and it was her pride that the Colonna women all bowed to her taste in dress. She had not much more figure than Anna on which to display her tailor's skill, but by lacing her meagerness from the sides and below she managed to pinch up a roll of skin at the neckline of a gown that looked like the real thing to all but critical eyes.

As chanced, the Duchess had been christened Sveva, which was also the given name of Guglielmo's Orsini mother, and out of that coincidence Anna fashioned a fateful tie, joining their visiting cousin to the household as closely as two proximate links in a chain. Continuing in that vein, Anna extolled Cousin Gugl as one specially versed in the difference between Roman Orsinis and Neapolitan Orsinis. He was just the man to settle a delicate point currently at issue right there in Anna's family. Before she would tell him which side of the debate *she* was on, Anna would like his expert opinion on one big question. Were the Orsinis of

Tagliacozzo to be considered Romans or Neapolitans? That was the crux of the matter. The boundary between the Regno and the States of the Church had moved from one side of Tagliacozzo to the other so many times that the Orsinis who had possession could not answer for themselves from day to day.

"I think you are laying a trap for me," the Duke winked. "You would like to hear me say that Tagliacozzo properly belongs to the Colonnas."

No, no. Anna denied that intention, although Tagliacozzo had been Colonna property anciently, and they might someday take it back, but that was not the reason for her question, and she would like an honest answer.

Mother the Duchess and Maria the nurse exchanged weary glances of resignation, but neither remonstrated against pursuing the topic their daughter found so significant.

"Well then," said Gugl, "the Count of Tagliacozzo is a subject of the Regno, no question about that, and his Countess is the sister of Duke Sessa, the aunt of my dear comrade Marino Marzano."

Anna was pleased to hear Duke Andria say so, because her very favorite cousin—Caterina Appiani—had been brought all the way from Piombino not long before to marry Count Tagliacozzo's son Rinaldo Orsini, and the Colonna family was utterly divided, whether they should be proud or sorry. Some had felt the disgrace so much they stayed away from the wedding.

The Duchess Paliano spoke up promptly in her own defense. "We stayed away from the wedding because we had nothing to wear."

"Cousin Cat said our dresses and jewels were beautiful," said Anna severely. As appeared, the bride had stopped the night in Paliano on the way to her nuptials, and she and Anna had found more in common in those few hours than either child had ever before encountered in another mortal. These singular affinities are not to be explained by crude and clumsy reason, nor yet by outward appearance or intellectual attainments. Sublimate spirit—or an essence unknown—works these marvels of attraction between the most unlikely materials, holding them as one for a year or for a lifetime, as may fall out. Neither old nor young nor male nor female is immune from this intangible, unpredictable force, and no further light is to be shed upon its blind operation after one has said, "I love her. She is my friend."

"Cousin Cat gave me her tear-vase," Anna told Duke Andria. "Would you like to see it?"

Guglielmo never had seen a tear-vase, or known that a receptacle for the lachrymal juice ever had been invented, so the bottle was sent for, a delicate contrivance of crystal, with a bulbous base and stems so ingeniously interwoven that tears—once in—never could be poured out, despite that it had no stopper whatever.

"It was found in a tomb," said Anna.

A bit of liquid—not quite transparent—rolled about inside but could not be spilt. "Whose tears are those?" asked Gugl.

"Cousin Cat and I both cried into it—because I was not permitted to go to her wedding," said Anna, implying by personal, mystical extension, that this mingling of their tears made them something more than sisters. "But now that I *know* Rinaldo's family are Neapolitan Orsinis——"

Pretty clearly the unwary Del Balzo had been drawn into a family argument without the least inkling of its merits. "Hold on!" he demurred. "I shouldn't like to commit myself until I know the facts——"

The facts could be told on the fingers of one hand. Cousin Cat's mother was Anna's Aunty Paola Colonna, the sister of Duke Paliano and of Uncle Cardinal Oddo. Anna had no clear recollection of Aunty Paola because she had left Rome to marry the Prince of Piombino before Anna was born, but as the mother of Cousin Cat this kinswoman's status was hardly distinguishable from that of the Holy Virgin.

Now Aunty Paola was widowed, and her son—Giacomo II Appiani—was Prince of Piombino, but he was maintained in possession of his birthright only by the ceaseless vigilance of Aunty Paola. "The ceaseless vigilance," Anna repeated, "because her dead husband's brothers are a pair of Devils." She Crossed herself protectively. "Do you know the Appiani brothers—Varri and Emmanuel?"

"Only by hearsay," Andria was glad to report. "I never have met them."

"That's *good*," said Anna, "because they have been trying to take Piombino away from Cousin Giacomo II ever since his father died, and the only way Aunty Paola could save herself and her children was by putting Piombino under the protection of Florence. You know what *that* means."

"Ceaseless vigilance?" Andria guessed.

"Ceaseless vigilance," Anna said again, "and finding husbands for her daughters who will help protect Cousin Giacomo II. Life wouldn't be worth living if she had to go on forever depending upon Cosimo de Medici for protection. The Medici don't even want Uncle Oddo to be Pope. That's why Aunty Paola married Cousin Cat to Rinaldo Orsini."

If a few *ergos* had been elided along the course of Anna's logic, Maria the nurse did not miss them. "I've said right along it was the smartest thing the Appianis could do," she averred.

"Are you married, Cousin Gugl?" asked Anna disarmingly.

"I am betrothed," said he, in his heart wondering if he were, truly.

"That's too bad," said Anna, "because Cousin Cat has two sisters who have no contracts yet. Do you know any good catches— with armies ready to enter the field?"

"I shall have to think it over——"

"How about your comrade—who is Rinaldo Orsini's cousin?"

"Marino Marzano? I—I don't know. Matchmaking has not been one of my major accomplishments," Andria admitted ruefully.

"Marriages are made in Heaven," Anna conceded, "but the Saints need our help on Earth. Will you take me to Tagliacozzo for a visit, Cousin Gugl?"

"I—I am under obligation to take Rome," Andria floundered.

"After you take Rome?—and bring Mother's tailor—so we have something new to wear?"

"God willing, I shall," Andria promised.

Anna turned to her brother. "Prospero, you must take Cousin Gugl to Father at once."

"I don't know where Father is," said Prospero discouragingly. Any unusual demand upon him was too much trouble for this Churchman-in-embryo. He never knew where anything was or why he should look for it. In short, he was as lazy as a Cardinal should be, and he had a head for his destined vocation too. It was larger than his body seemed to warrant, more like a melon on stilts, but exactly the right shape to wear a Red Hat with tassels.

"Don't be difficult," Anna chided her brother. "You can find Father easily enough. If he isn't one place he's another."

"That's just it!" The boy's point was proved. "You have to keep looking around."

"It isn't going to hurt you," Anna wheedled. "If Father isn't guarding the wine pressers on Quirinale he is in Hotel Tordinona."

"He may be halfway to Naples by this time," said Master Melon-head, quite well aware that his hazard was explosive. "Serjianni has sent us an offer."

"How was that again?" asked Duke Andria rising, drawn out of his chair involuntarily by the implications of the lad's announcement.

"Serjianni wants Father to go after Sforza—Uncle Giordano says."

"But your father has not gone!"

"I don't know whether he has or not," said Prospero, enjoying that ignorance. "I can't go all the way to Naples looking for him."

Completely uninformed of recent military maneuvers beyond the bare fact of Sforza's return toward Naples, Andria had only rule-of-thumb for his estimations of the probabilities.

Marino Marzano's treachery to the Crown could have been discovered.

Serjianni must be aware of the movement of Andria's troops out of Avellino, and he would have correctly surmised their destination. By offering to hire the Colonnas, the Seneschal hoped to frustrate Guglielmo's occupation of Rome. Belike his negotiators were also primed to break up Taranto's marriage plans.

Fortunately, the former Constable never had been able to do business profitably with the Colonnas, but—obviously—he meant to keep trying.

Bowing sharply to the Duchess and Anna, Duke Andria said, "With Your Highness' leave I shall go on to Rome at once."

He was half way to the door when Anna cried, "Not dressed like that! You will ride to your death." She was blanched even whiter than her pale self. "Prospero has Franciscan habits. You must wear one, and he will go with you. Ride mules—and say that you come from Assisi," Anna directed.

The advice was sound, but Andria disliked to put Prospero in jeopardy. "If you will just lend me one habit—I know Rome fairly well——"

"Prospero will go with you," said Anna.

The two false monks paused at the farm only long enough for Andria to instruct his lieutenants how they must act if he had not returned in three days, and the long plod began. The way was lengthened by the quality of Prospero's conversation and further tormented by the furnace of misgivings raging in the other's bowels. Only one thing was clear from the nature of Serjianni's offer. The clash between the Titans was on. Both double-dealers—Sforza and Caracciolo—under guise of defending the Queen, were at each other's throats for supremacy over her. Beyond that, all was conjecture, but Andria's head would not stop churning simply for being told.

From the very personal question, what this alarm might imply to himself concerning Avellino, the quondam Count of that place forcibly wrenched his thought away. If Avellino was lost, it was lost, temporarily, and he must launch a Second Crusade at his leisure. The urgency was not behind, not in the past, but ahead, in Rome, in the future with the Colonnas. That was his hottest spur—to reach Duke Paliano's ear before any Colonnas could be seduced to their own and the cabal's destruction.

Milord Paliano was no stranger to Duke Andria, but neither was he a friend. Lorenzo-Onofrio Colonna was not a quick man with a ducat, on the one hand, and—on the other—Guglielmo had purposely given himself the reputation of a wastrel, on his previous essay into Rome. Their Lordships had met and parted on that basis, with no hard feelings, nor no respect neither, so a handle for his opening argument was wanting even if Duke Paliano had not already marched toward Naples.

"Tell me, Prospero, does your father ever mention me?"

"He thinks you're crazy," said the boy.

"He's right. Does he think the Prince of Taranto is crazy too?"

"I forget," said young hopeful.

"How about Count Nola?"

"He has a head on his shoulders."

"I am happy to hear that. What makes your father think so?"

"Because he's going to marry Serjianni's sister—but you're not to tell Anna. It would give her one of her Headaches."

Andria was glad to have held his tongue when that sad revelation had been so near to utterance the day before.

"How does Milord Paliano get along with Braccio? Are they friendly?

"Hnnph," the lad snorted. "Braccio doesn't bother the Colonnas—or the Orsinis either. He knows how many make six."

"How many do?"

"Why, Cardinal Giordano Orsini is President of the Council at Constance and Dean of the Sacred College—and Uncle Oddo is going to be Pope. I can go in and out of Rome any time I want to. We didn't have to dress up like this—only Anna said so."

"She was thinking of me. I'm not so well known as you are ... How is it when Sforza is here?"

"Same thing," Prospero shrugged. "Nobody bothers us unless they want their heads broken."

That was a pleasant thought, while it lasted, but this day was not quite normal.

Long before they could see any part of Rome the two spurious Franciscans passed the site of an evacuated camp, probably the place where Sforza had left the Caracciolos in charge, but they had gone away so long before this that the rubble no longer attracted scavengers, not even a crow. Every heap of ashes had been sifted again and again.

Approaching The City more closely, its appearance was much less Eternal than it had been three years before, and the crumbling had been well advanced then. Only just enough wall remained around the whole town to support the arches over the gates, still Braccio persisted in the convention of guarding those entries, and this day even religious were being stopped for questioning and perfunctory search.

"How now, Prospero?" asked Andria as they came to the tag end of a queue. "What happens when they find our swords? Do we just say, *Colonna,* and pass through—or claim the protection of the Church Militant?"

The waiting line was long enough so that a quiet withdrawal was still possible, others were going away as the nature of the stoppage was whispered. Another gate might be attempted, or any one of a thousand breaches in the walls.

"They're recruiting," said Prospero.

"O, fine!" said Gugl. "We'll go to Naples in your father's command."

"Those aren't Colonnas. They're Orsini officers."

"And Braccio lets them do this?"

"How could he stop them?"

"Well—I should think—in his place—I might find a way. What does it mean? Would you say your father has left Rome or not?"

"It's hard to tell."

"I find it so."

"What shall we do?"

"I asked you first."

"The Orsinis will make game of me in this habit."

"No more than that?"

"They will insult us. We must resent it. They will draw. We will draw. Somebody might get hurt."

"Then, let us climb over the wall."

Just then a Braccian officer, assisting the Orsinimen to keep the volubly resentful herd in line, rode near enough to hail. He was being abused by forty tongues, and replying to the loudest in kind, so that the merest semblance of deference to him set Frater Guglielmo apart.

"Messer Bracciano!" Andria called, putting on an air of comradely knowing, and kicking up his mule.

The soldier leaned over to take a whisper.

"From Assisi," said Andria, quoting Anna. "Can you get us to His Lordship without waiting?"

"Assisi?"

"Assisi."

"Come." Wheeling his mount toward the press at the gate, where the "queue" was spread quite across the road in no kind of order, the Braccian cut a path through for his wards, with his steed for a prow and his voice for power. "Way! Way! Way for Milord. Make way!"

It was as easy as that.

The Orsini officers barely turned their heads from the questioning of a luckless yokel who was going to see the world whether he wished to or not.

Andria and Prospero were through the gate, unrecognized, unquestioned, unsearched, but they were not quite free. Their cicerone whispered *Assisi* to another Braccian—of a group—and they found themselves escorted by four cuirassiers, two before and two behind.

"Your sister is most remarkable!" said Andria with feeling. "One has only to follow her advice—in everything."

The Colonna did not yet know how they had got inside the walls. Events had moved too swiftly for him. Sooth, his ears had not caught Anna's directive, to say that they came from Assisi. So Prospero could not understand what his sister was to be praised for—in this instance—but he would have listened gladly to her advice, how to get out of their predicament.

They were being taken to the headquarters of Braccio da Montone under the misapprehension that they brought him intelligence from one of the cities he had stolen from the Church. It was not a topic for jest or a field for prankery to be indulged in by a "nephew" of the man who would be requiring the return of Assisi in a very short time, and no more suitable to the Commander of an army fresh come to take back Rome. Braccio's wonted restraint in dealing with Colonnas was likely to be taxed beyond its limits if he already knew that a Tarantine army was quartered on the farm at Paliano.

Prospero tried to tell himself that this was not his headache, but he was mightily curious to hear what Messer the Wit Andria was going to say when they faced the tyrant.

Gugl was no better prepared for that ordeal than his brother Frater, and never meant to let their mask carry them so far. "Signore Corporal!" he sang out to the fellow in command. "We give you too much trouble. We know the way from here."

"No trouble at all," the jolt-head returned. "How are things in Assisi?"

"The farmers want rain," said Andria, looking here and there in the street for the means to give their escort the slip.

"Never knew one who didn't," said the Braccian.

"I'm dry myself," said Andria. "Let us stop at the first Bush."

"Hoo!" the corporal quaked before so much courage. "Would you stop to wet your whistle before you report?"

"If I don't get a drink I won't live to report," Andria alleged, spitting drily.

"Here," said the corporal, swinging his saddle flask into Andria's hand. "It's only Issue—but it's better than nothing."

"I'm under a vow not to touch Issue," said Andria, passing the flask to Prospero. "It eats out the lining of the stomach."

The corporal was suspicious, but of what, he did not know. He realized only that the elder of the false Fraters did not wish to go where they were going, and that the younger was definitely fearful. When Andria pretended that his saddle girth needed tightening, and dismounted to attend to that, the soldiers sat in a watchful ring, and when Andria got down again—to make water—the Braccians were no less attentive.

As appeared, the only way to extricate themselves from their too obliging escort was by confession and bribery, but when Andria arrived at that conclusion their party had just reached the end of the Bridge San Angelo, with obvious intent to cross over. Bravely, then, he postponed the proffer of ransom to acquire some bits of tactical intelligence for the future. If the way to Braccio's headquarters lay to the left, they must pass the outworks of the citadel itself, revealing the present state of Sforza's defenses, how they were altered since last observed, and so on. If their way on that side of Tiber turned right, they must soon pass Del Balzo's own establishment, out of which he had not heard a peep since Braccio came to town. Worthwhile, in itself, to learn where the tyrant's headquarters lay in relation to both San Angelo and the private brothel Gugl had set up with such high diplomatical hopes.

It would be a rum coincidence if Braccio had taken over the well-stocked palace for his own use! The cellars, the larder, the women and other furniture were exactly what a tired Commander would wish to come home to, and—of course—that is just what had happened.

The corporal led the way to the right, and Duke Andria found himself goggling up at the familiar facade, over which floated Braccio's banner. The *Condottiere's* artists had combined the arms of Montone with those of Perugia and worked in a kingly crown, indicating the ambition of His Lordship to make Perugia and its environs into a little Regno!

In that moment the need to escape their guard was obliterated in Andria's mind: nothing would do but he must go inside: but Prospero—entirely unaware of the secret drama—had grown paler than his sister Anna, and his knees were beating the ribs of his mule from both sides so cruelly that the beast turned a reproachful head and blasted him with a sudden *hee-haw* that loosened the Colonna bowels.

Soldiers were everywhere, about the entrance, in the courtyard—Adjutants, couriers, aides—but discipline was lax amidst the bustle, salutes perfunctory, no showing of passes, no special care to guard the budding Majesty's person.

"Perhaps His Highness is not at home," Prospero quavered hopefully.

"No matter," said Andria in a voice of authority, in complete command of himself and quite ready to command everybody else in sight. "If he isn't at home we'll wait. Signor Corporal, you are dismissed." Without waiting to see the effect of that order, Andria dismounted, handed his mule to a hostler and headed straightway for the main door as if the place belonged to him, as in fact it did.

In his short life, Prospero never had seen bravery to compare. O, overbold!—foolhardy!—this Lord from Naples was throwing their lives away!—but what could one do but follow? To stand gawking were to draw more attention. In fact, nobody paid the striding Franciscan the tribute of a single glance, except the man-at-arms, sentinel in the doorway, who pulled his forelock in obeisance and received a hasty blessing. Prospero pattered after.

Inside the palace, without a glance to either side or behind, Andria followed the well known corridor away from reception halls and master's parlors toward the office of the Major-domo in the domestics' quarters, where the household must be run by someone, and who more likely than the staff he had left here?

At a door Andria paused to let Prospero catch up. "Just keep your mouth shut," he commanded brusquely, "stay close to me, and follow wherever I go. Close this door behind us."

"Are you going *in?*"

For answer, Gugl went in, flinging the door wide to do so.

As chanced, the Major was at his desk surrounded by butlers, waiters and cooks—nine or ten—and all gave the intruder their full faces to inspect as they stared at him. Most, if not all, and especially the Major, had familiar features. The Duke tossed back his cowl and pulled up the skirt of his habit for access to his weapons. "If one of you pronounces my name I shall cut out his tongue," said their master. "Now, hear me and remember every word. You have all done well to remain here. Stay on—serve the Lord Braccio—and I shall reward you too. I am not come back yet—but I shall be near by. Sometimes I shall come and ask questions. Keep my secret. That's all that is required—that—and two horses—good ones. Now!"

Consternation, Milords! Those servants gaped, flushed, grinned, gripped each other, laughed, wept, knelt, stood up— each according to his own emotion and style—incredulous but convinced on the evidence.

"Make it *three* horses," Andria changed his mind. "And Braccio must not see us leaving. Now take me to Aranda the tailor."

Then the Duke must suffer himself to be touched and have his hands kissed. One cook whispered his willingness to poison Braccio's soup, but Andria put him off until another time.

While their horses were being made ready, the Major led the way to the wardrobe where Aranda supervised the seams being sewed by four men and two women assistants.

"If you speak my name I shall cut out your tongue," Gugl began again. "Signore Aranda, bring your scissors and come with me."

The tailor took up his scissors right enough—but he opened them like the beak of an eagle and started for Andria's belly as if to snip out his gullet. "Who speaks to the Great Aranda like a pig? I am an artist, thou beggar, thou bleater, thou bastard of Balaam! Nobody commands Aranda."

The Major stepped between the tailor and his target, hissing, "See who His Highness is before you call names!"

Aranda stood no taller than a demijohn but not even the Lord of Creation could tread on his coat with impunity. "Let him be who he will, he will not scissor me my scissors! I'll scissor him. I'll snip his tongue out—the filthy thing is too long for his mouth whoever he is!"

"Forgive me, Signor," the Duke apologized. "I see that you do not know me, but I know you for the greatest artist-tailor in Rome or in the world. I spoke as I did because time is short. Be so good as to come with me—and make your fortune." As he spoke Andria was taking off the Franciscan habit, and motioned Prospero to do likewise.

Aranda knew the Del Balzo then—and Prospero too—and took a softer tone, but he was bound to Braccio by contract and command. He begged to be excused from riding with their worships and from supplying their needs of the moment out of the *Condottiere's* wardrobe.

"It is no more than justice—and poetic too," Andria argued. "Milord Montone is paying me no rent here. I merely take these brocades on account."

"You will get me hanged!" the tailor protested. "His Lordship wants that jacket for tomorrow night."

"But you will not be here tomorrow night. You will be with me—" he leaned close to whisper,—"*in Paliano.*"

Aranda twisted up a sour face. "The Duchess sent you!"

Guglielmo admitted that. "Her Highness bids you bring all your finest stuffs—and sew for a month."

The artist's expression—as if he chewed aloes—did not change. "For that figure—not even Aranda can do anything. Braccio has—at least—a chest!"

Then Andria was inspired, once more, to invoke the *Erdegeist,* the Elemental, the Name of wonder-working Names. "We shall need a trousseau for Signorina Anna Colonna," he said.

"O?—then—for Anna I will come," said the little firebrand tamely, and rolled up his scissors and some other tools too.

So it befell that Andria and Prospero, who entered the palace as drab religious, rode out of it resplendent in beautiful new jackets and velvet caps which Braccio never had worn and probably never would see again. They rode fine horses too, instead of slow mules, but they were not pursued.

Whilst Aranda went to his shop for materials, the now veteran adventurers, comrades in daring, put their animals up the hill Quirinale, where they found Duke Paliano with a company of fifty, guarding his wine pressers, just like Anna said.

"Where did you get that hat—and coat?" the Colonna asked his putative son. "How much were they?" Only then did he spare a nod and *Milord* for Andria.

The boy was bubbling to tell exactly—and in detail—where the garments had come from, but Andria thought better of that. "They are a gift to His Highness—from me," he said. "I beg you to permit him to accept them."

Lorenzo-Onofrio fingered his own frayed surcoat. "A fool and his money!" he said.

They were standing in the sun—and still they stood—although a shady arbor was at hand, with chairs and a bare board, inviting ease if no pleasure. Terse preliminaries grew terser still when the older man learned that Andria's troop—to a grand total of almost 300 human stomachs, to say nothing of their mounts—was quartered upon him. "By whose permission?" the Colonna snapped. Like his Gaetani wife, he was spare in the face, very spare, as if in the fabrication of such an economical man his Maker had grudged him only enough skin to cover his bones by stretching.

"Your Highness' daughter, Anna, invited me," Guglielmo said, and waited for the transformation.

The change was not so marked as it had been in Aranda's case, but more like a sigh of resignation, and the Roman complained at large how few people realized that Cardinal Oddo had not received a *denaro* of income from his churches since King Ladislaus captured Rome. "I'm keeping him— my brother and I. We pay for that establishment of his in Constance. We're backing him—and I'd hate to tell you how deeply he's into us. He had better come back Pope—because a mere Cardinal's income wouldn't get us off the hook in ten years."

The bid was, obviously, to shame Andria into volunteering to pay for the fodder his army was eating, but Baby-face was not as innocent as he looked. "I will accept nothing for my services—or for my men—in clearing the way for His Serenity's homecoming," said Andria, thereby forcing the shoe on to Colonna's other foot. "Braccio wants Perugia. Sforza wants Benevento. I want nothing."

"Well, come and sit down," Paliano grunted. "You are Taranto's cousin—and he wants plenty." The Roman led the way to the arbor and produced a jug and mugs from beneath the table. Paliano poured for himself and his guest, but only pushed the jug toward Prospero for the boy to help himself.

"I do not know the terms of my cousin's contract," Andria said honestly, "but getting Anna to wife leaves very little more to ask for—in this world—and I know that the Prince already holds the Cardinal's interests closely to his heart. I am commissioned right now to take Rome and hold it until Uncle Oddo is Elected."

"To hold it—in whose name?"

Gugl had to answer, "In the name of Queen Joan," although the manner of Paliano's asking made perfectly plain that the question carried a sting in its tail.

"Do you trouble so much for her? Perhaps you have not heard that your precious Queen Joan has exiled the Prince of Taranto."

"Not *again!*" laughed Andria.

"You laugh."

"It is a jest. Her Majesty mocks Bourbon by calling him Prince of Taranto."

"This is no jest. I have it from Serjianni's man that Taranto is exiled in earnest."

"I have been away from Naples—so long," Andria puzzled.

"Serjianni sent to me for men—to pursue Sforza. That is typical of Neapolitans. While *you* bring your army here to take Rome—they have to send to Rome for men to save Naples! I can laugh at that," said Colonna.

"My arms are never available for Serjianni's use," Andria said soberly, and the other surprised him by clasping his hand with real enthusiasm. "There is one thing we can agree upon, then," Duke Paliano said. "I cannot deal with that fellow! I sent his envoy to Francesco Orsini—you must have seen him recruiting. That will make a merry War—with both sides running backwards!"

Lorenzo-Onofrio's laugh was truly gruesome, exposing every tooth left in his head, but Andria seized the occasion to develop their one point of accord, boasting of his success at

Avellino. "And I left Serjianni's poor abused cousin Ottino in command!"

The Colonna sobered instantly. "Then you had better get back there with your men as fast as you can go," he said. "This envoy told me that Ottino Caracciolo was taken prisoner—in Maddaloni—and lies in San Vincenzo now. You have lost your prize by coming here."

"Ah, well," Gugl snapped his fingers, "easy come, easy go. What is one little County? Did this man have nothing to say about the health of Ettore Pappacoda?"

"Health? No!" Duke Paliano strangled. The effect upon him of Andria's flippancy was the same as if he had seen a demented child pour a hatful of gold pieces into the sea. "Avellino must be worth—seventy thousand a year," he murmured, "and you ask after somebody's health?"

"I left my friend badly wounded," Andria explained. "I would gladly give Avellino to save his life. And now you disturb me about Ottino. You say he was taken in Maddaloni ... Does that mean that Malizia Carafa connived at it?"

"Quite the contrary. Carafa's confidence was abused—and he is so resentful he has withdrawn from Joan's Council, swearing never to return while she tolerates Serjianni. I must send my congratulations to Duke Maddaloni. He is a very rich man."

"Very rich," Andria smiled, "and a great loss to Queen Joan."

"Yet she continues to pamper that bully! Every Barony she took back from Bourbon's Council when she exiled them has been given to some member of Caracciolo's family—and he himself kept Salerno."

Until Salerno was mentioned—and mentioned specifically with malice prepense, as if Andria could do anything about it!—Gugl had felt that relations were improving. True, he and Paliano had not broken bread together, but that was only because the visitor had not brought his own. Even with Paliano's change of tone—and in spite of the warning glint in his eye—Andria tried to maintain the growth of understanding in their common concerns. "Joan consented?" he exclaimed. "I can hardly believe it. They have fought over Salerno for years. I never thought she would give it him."

"He boxed her ears—right in Court—the man said. You know, Milord, Cardinal Oddo expected the boy Antonio to have Salerno. I understood that the Prince of Taranto engaged to get it for him. But he won't be able to do that now, will he? I mean—as an exile—his aunt won't be inclined to listen to his wishes. Frankly, I doubt if Taranto can fulfill his part of the marriage contract."

Andria made a gesture of impatience. "Your Highness, we are not children. You are not depending upon Joan's gift to make Antonio Colonna Count of Salerno. If Antonio is to have that title it will come from Queen Joan's successor—and as your daughter Anna interprets God's Will that will be Louis II d'Anjou. If my cousin Taranto has guaranteed Antonio's possession of Salerno, that means by force of arms, should the present incumbent fail to relinquish it upon order. The Prince of Taranto will fulfill every obligation he has signed, to the last detail. You may depend upon it."

"I am glad to hear your assurances," said Colonna in a flat tone indicating no joy.

"Shall we not study the marriage contract—now—and see what is first to do?"

"The contract is not here."

"At Paliano, then."

"The Cardinal has the contract. I read it—and signed it—as Anna's father. But I made no copy—and it has gone back to the Cardinal—as the active head of our family."

Straight-faced, Andria bowed to that convention, and—with more dignity than ever was usual with him—said evenly, "The cabal's first engagement to the Cardinal was to get Sforza's garrisons out of San Angelo and Ostia. I was assigned to do that—but we have had many setbacks—and now Braccio has added his complications. I need your help. If you will not act in the name of Joan, then let us do it in the name of Colonna. As soon as Francesco Orsini marches after Sforza, let us strike."

Lorenzo-Onofrio took one slow, deliberate swallow of wine, but that was not meant as a toast to their enterprise. "Impossible," said he. Impossible to permit the Colonna arms to be associated with any attempt to dominate Rome at the present time, because the balloting had not yet begun in Constance, and all the French and Angevin votes depended upon the Holy See remaining in Avignon. "We Colonnas can't show any special interest in preparing to receive the new Pope in Rome. That would spoil Oddo's chances—perhaps forever."

"Even if Oddo promises to crown Louis II King of the Regno?" Andria expostulated.

"Even so. The French delegates are not eager to see Louis II become King of the Regno. He's too big a man for them already. They are content to let Jacques Bourbon keep the Crown—a weak sister they can handle. But all are agreed that the Curia must have its seat in Avignon."

"But you don't want that!"

"No more than I want the stone. Unless Oddo brings the Papacy back to Rome we Colonnas will all be better off dead. But he may have to set up in Avignon a year or two. That will mean more starvation for us—but we are used to it—we can wait them out. What we can't do is advertise our intention before the votes are counted."

"Meanwhile Sforza and Braccio will have planted themselves so firmly in Rome that you can never get them out," Andria argued.

"We will treat with them when the time comes."

"And lose Perugia, Assisi, Benevento—lose half the Church lands?"

"We gain the other half. That is better than losing all."

"Milord!" said Gugl sitting briskly forward, "I am here to take Rome—if not in Joan's name or in the name of Colonna, then in the name of the Prince of Taranto. I have not a great many men—but I have other means——"

"Your Lordship has a great deal of money."

"I was not boasting of wealth. I can show you Braccio da Montone a corpse in twenty-four hours, and the Commandant of San Angelo dead drunk in less time than that. I have enough men to rout the Braccians once their leader is down."

Paliano's eyes hardened from within, but his tight mouth twisted into a thin smile. "How are you going to keep them out of a city without walls? I can show you a hundred and seventy gaps in the masonry where an army could march in forty abreast. As fast as you drive the Braccians out through one hole they will come back in at another. You are a brave man—I do not question—but you are young, romantic. You have no interest in building walls. Devil-may-care, eh? All for swordplay—but no man for laying stone upon stone."

"I fancy I could lay stone—and my men too—if we had to, but perhaps Your Lordship could undertake that part. Surely the French delegates to the Council at Constance would not take offense at the Colonnas for repairing the walls of their native city. Let us divide the labor. You lay the stone and I shall dispose of Braccio."

The sun had completed its round for the day, and the wine pressers and soldiers knelt at Vespers, filling and overflowing the small chapel which was one of this villa's outbuildings at a little distance. Still the Cardinal's brother sat, too much absorbed in this conversation to notice the passage of time, apparently caring as little for religious observance as for food. No telling when he had eaten last, but Andria and Prospero had not had a morsel since their breakfast on the road, and this was no fast day neither. Prospero—despite that he was being gorged on mental food and rare training for his future in the Sacred College—was frankly fidgety from hunger, and the goneness in Andria's middle suggested that eating, too, was frowned upon by those French delegates at Constance.

Emptiness doth make the fumes of wine more potent, and this exchange of views between ostensible allies was taking on more aspects of a duel with every utterance. The deepening twilight was disquieting too. Here they must spend the night, sleeping on penitential boards, belike, and susceptible at any hour to attack by Braccio in pursuit of his coats or his tailor ... Where, in fact, was Aranda?

Fixing Gugl on the gimlet of his gaze, the stubborn Colonna said, "I could not permit you to take Rome in the name of Taranto. You and he would be harder to pry out of San Angelo than Sforza."

"I should take that as a great compliment, Milord, if you were not also implying my bad faith."

"Taranto is not articled to support Louis II. It is not mentioned in the contract."

"Articled or not, my cousin's actions make his position clear."

"Name one, Milord."

"I could name a thousand."

"Just one."

"He encouraged me to take Avellino—for my Aunt Alix—and to reserve the revenues to pay Louis's soldiers."

"But you have lost Avellino."

Willfully—for the second time—Andria held back the truth about Marino Marzano and the supposed "loss" of Avellino. Like the Prince, this cousin too was learning the advantage of knowing just a little bit more than one's friends. "My loss is my loss, dear Uncle, and it does not alter the Prince's attitude. He was willing to see me hoist the flag of Anjou over Avellino if we had been ready, and he is in treaty with the Caldoras for a landing at Aversa. How can you distrust your son-in-law? Help me take possession—and San Angelo is in the family."

"Your cousin is also in the Chiaramonte family. He has all their money back of him—*Aragonese* money."

"That is only partly true, Uncle. The Chiaramontes are as Angevin as the Del Balzos. They were Counts of Clermont in Provence."

"Clermonts they may be—in Provence—but Tristano Chiaramonte does not live in Provence. He lives in Palermo, and his heart is Aragonese. He belongs, body and soul, to Alphonso the Atheist. Yes! I call him so! Right in your teeth I tell you—this Alphonso who calls himself King of Aragon is nothing less than a blackguard, blaspheming Atheist!—flouting the Laws of God—taking Majorca, Sardinia, and CORSICA next—aye, CORSICA!—scoffing the Sacred Oil—asking no Pope's blessing for any of his crowns. That is Atheism—pure and simple.

"Why, do you know what the loss of Corsica will mean to us? You, who suffer so because the Church is losing Assisi and Benevento, do you know what we lose if Alphonso takes Corsica?" The Colonna paused, but no reply could have stopped the list of calamities impending. "First, Oddo will get no tithes out of Aragon, Catalugna, Valencia, Sardinia, Majorca, or Corsica itself—or Sicily *ultra* Pharum—because Alphonso is an Atheist, and will forbid his clergy to remit. Then the

Banca San Giorgio will say to the Pope, 'Until Your Holiness forces Alphonso to return Corsica to us—you will not collect one *soldo* of revenue from Genoa or Cyprus or any place else where the Banca is fiscal agent.' Milan, Anjou and France will back up the Genoese so that Oddo will not have a *sou* of income from those countries either.

"That's what will happen if Alphonso takes Corsica. That's why the petty demands of Braccio and Sforza do not impress me very much. That's why I won't help you and your cousin take Rome. Taranto has been running with these Atheist servants of Satan. He has given his sister to one of them in marriage. He has tarred himself with their brush. I tell you frankly, if I were Cardinal Oddo I would not give him Anna."

Andria's head had bent, lower and lower, as Paliano pounded his points home. He did not raise it to reply, but spoke as one overcome. "I am sorry to hear Your Highness say that. You take a very dark view."

"The future of my House is at stake—everything the Colonnas own."

"May I ask Your Lordship one question?"

"Certainly."

"When do we eat?"

It was not the sort of trick to play on one of Paliano's temperament, but Prospero Colonna loved it. The boy's burst of laughter drew the old man's ire and thus Gugl was saved from instant annihilation. Better still, they got some food. The villa was not poorly staffed or supplied, but when Lorenzo-Onofrio was living alone in this way, his frugal bent dictated a regimen more rugged than that of an army camp.

To appease his host, Andria insisted upon eating in the kitchen. At the table, lighted by only two candles—tallow, not wax—he reopened diplomacies as he filled his stomach.

The Aragonese association was most unfortunate, Andria agreed, but—begging Milord Paliano's pardon—Taranto's motives had been misunderstood. "That is the penalty a Prince must pay for greatness," said Andria. "My cousin has put the Cardinal's welfare above his own, ahead of all selfish considerations, and so he incurs your suspicion—and suffers exile by Joan—but in the end justice must prevail and Your Lordship will acknowledge your error. I pray you may see the light before it is too late. Cardinal Oddo sees the truth of it now, and that is why he has got you to sign Anna's contract. If your brother becomes Pope—as he certainly will—it will not be because of anything you or I do or do not do here in Rome. It will be due in the largest measure to what the Prince of Taranto has accomplished in Palermo. He has removed the objections of Chiaramonte—and Aragon—to a Colonna Pope. The Emperor could not do it—but the Prince has done it."

"Eh?" Paliano grunted. "Is Alphonso the Atheist applying to my brother for Sacred Oil?"

"He will apply when the oil in your brother's hands becomes Sacred—by Election. If Alphonso ever applies, it will be Taranto's doing. Alphonso has NOT applied to his father's Pope for Oil—as he certainly would have done but for my cousin. If your brother hopes—ever—to enjoy the tithing of Aragon and of Sicily *ultra* Pharum he is indeed well advised to give your daughter Anna to Taranto—because no other man can pick those plums for him. If Holy Church is ever to be healed and this Schism ended—it will be through my cousin's influence over Chiaramonte and Alphonso d'Aragon.

"Don't let me coerce you, Milord, but you will remember that my sister was Queen of Sicily *ultra* Pharum—God rest her soul—" Andria, Paliano and Prospero Colonna all Signed themselves—"and we Del Balzos still own a good bit of that island. I have not had occasion to count them recently—but we must have twenty churches on our properties. Nothing to compare with the Chiaramontes, of course, but there they are, each one bringing in its little mite, and your brother knew they were there when he assigned Anna to Taranto.

"Now—I no longer ask you to assist me against Braccio. I take your objections as valid. But—Uncle—don't try to interfere—don't try to stop me, because I don't think the Cardinal would like it."

"I shall send express to ask him," said Lorenzo-Onofrio. Andria's dissertation, although cogent, had not convinced the bullhead that the Prince was in Palermo so entirely in the Colonna interests or that this greatness was so manifest as his infatuated cousin expounded. Andria's reasons for fulfilling the alliance with Anna made a powerful argument, but—to a soldier—they did not justify turning over the capital of Christendom to another Commander. "Will Your Highness defer your action upon The City until we have a reply from the Cardinal? You see my position. This is a great responsibility. I would not willingly offend Your Highness or the Prince, but I must protect my family too. There is no need for haste. I ask you to wait until the Cardinal expresses himself—and I shall abide by his decision."

Andria smiled slily. "Is Your Highness *inviting* my men to remain at Paliano?"

The Colonna winced, but, yes, he would feed the army. "If you can keep them from raping and stealing and getting me in trouble with my neighbors."

"Soldiers will be soldiers," Gugl reminded his host. "How long do you ask me to wait?"

"We reckon twelve days, going and coming. Sometimes more, sometimes less."

"I shall wait twelve days," Andria conceded, "if Signorina Anna assures me that God Wills it so."

Paliano tugged at his own nose, but took care not to sniff, and sent for an Adjutant to address a cipher to Cardinal Oddo. Before the scrivener got to the kitchen, a guard came in to announce that the tailor Aranda with eight bales of stuffs was claiming hospitality for the night, "On his way to Paliano with the Lordship."

"Eight bales!—to Paliano?" The paterfamilias wagged his head, a fountain of negatives. "O, no. O, no. O, no. That is not in our contract, Milord Andria. And if my wife has put you up to this, be warned, she has spent her allowance for clothing and gowns five years in advance!"

"Ah, well," Andria consoled his host, "be thankful you are not the Grand Turk."

Lorenzo-Onofrio slept ill that night, and could eat no breakfast either. His, the responsibility to get his unwelcome colleague in arms, his putative son, and his wife's overladen tailor, safely out of the festering town, and under guard into Paliano. No less than twelve men-at-arms must be spared for it, against brigands outside the gates and Orsinis within. O, Councillors of Constance, what a world of anguish was caused by your so deliberate deliberations!

Francesco Orsini moved that day, toward Fragola, where Sforza was reported to be, but the Andria-Aranda expedition went a different way. They were not molested until they neared Cave, which is beyond Palestrina and no more than ten miles from the Colonna-Paliano farm. There they saw approaching—from the farm, in fact—a crowd or mob or concourse of men afoot, the strangest, most incomprehensible assemblage, a crawling column, waving branches and some kinds of tools, ringing bells, tooting bagpipes, singing lauds!

No festival was on the calendar to explain it, nor was their apparel festal. Many wore aprons of leather or such, many were nude to the waist, others barefoot. As Gugl said, "What the Hell have we here?"

"They look like frantic masons," said Aranda: and Prospero, "They look like your soldiers, Cousin Gugl!"

Both guesses were correct. The drab but motley parade comprised perhaps half of the Tarantine army, but instead of swords, lances or crossbows, the men carried sledges, chisels and trowels. One trowel in particular they carried in a reverential manner, borne aloft on a rough platform, cushioned upon a Bishop's stole bejeweled!

The Colonna chaplain—a greylock—was at the head of the band, striding beside a Captain of renowned sobriety, a hero veteran of Avellino. The chaplain was robed for the Highest Mass, but the Captain was armored only in sacking, and in his eyes was a Vision.

Oyez! Your Worships may believe this or not, as you choose, but Maria the Virgin Queen of Heaven had walked through the Tarantine camp in the night, plainly seen by scores of the soldiers, officers and men. She had been clothed in Her Glory, a shining thing, and She had carried That Trowel, and handed it to Giacomo—one formerly called "the Scald", for a birth mark, but now known to his comrades as "the Blest".

"And her Celestial Highness the Virgin said—in a voice I shall never forget—'Go, thou, and rebuild the walls of Rome!' Beppo heard Her, and Tony, and Pierdisenno. They were the first, and so they bear The Trowel. Then the whole farm was bathed in Her Light, and everybody woke up and saw Her. She walked near enough to touch—but nobody dared. That were a sacrilege to blast a man's arm. Saying—'Go, thou, and rebuild the walls of Rome!' It war a Visitation—a Command from Heaven—and so we go, Highness, and beg your leave, and conjure Your Lordship to come with us. This is our salvation. The priest goes with us."

"They are Masons for Christ!" said the chaplain, blessing to left and right.

Not so much taken aback as you may suppose, Duke Andria turned to Prospero Colonna, and keeping his voice low asked, "Does your sister Anna walk in her sleep?"

"I don't know," the boy admitted. His skin was prickling. About the wrapt conviction of the men was something compelling and infectious. "No!" said Prospero, on second thought. "She doesn't. It was the Virgin!"

"Go, thou, and rebuild the walls of Rome!" Fifty voices took up the mystic incantation in a musical chant that chilled Andria's spine.

Aranda Crossed himself, shaking like a reed. Even the horses were trembling. The soldiers from town—Paliano's guardsmen—looked on in frowning wonderment, but among them was not one scoffer. Like Prospero, they had the will to believe.

Neither convinced nor skeptic, Guglielmo observed that if Anna had done this she had builded well. This fanatic band could enter Rome under cover of its mission, better concealed by its sanctity than the Achaeans in the Trojan horse. Their example would attract thousands to assist them. Pious women would bring food and wine to the Masons for Christ. Here was a spiritual rebirth for Rome at the depths of her degradation. Arms could be smuggled to them and—when the time came—they would down trowels and lay Braccio in their mortar.

Andria raised both hands in a secular benediction, calling out, "Go, thou, and rebuild the walls of Rome!" He too was on the side of the angels.

In the few remaining miles of their journey, Andria could not decide whether Anna had impersonated the Virgin or—through her special Heavenly Connections—prevailed upon God's Mother to make this Personal Appearance. It was a brilliant achievement either way, but before Andria could prove it on her, Anna had scored again, and this was the most impressive demonstration of the efficacy of her prayers that anybody had observed up to that time.

Antonio Colonna and Raimondo Orsini Count Nola were back from Constance!—and with them, as *lagniappe,* Erri, the courier *extraordinaire,* whom Anna had not even mentioned to God.

Anna's cup was running over. Nothing to compare with this ever had occurred at Paliano before. It completely robbed Andria of his due for bringing home the tailor. Aranda—artist of artists—was almost lost in the shuffle.

The veterans of more than three years in Constance had only then arrived—since the departure of the Masons for Christ—and the entire village of Paliano, hoist to Seventh Heaven by two miracles in one day, had followed the young master into the castle, confident that they should hear from his own lips that Cardinal Oddo had won the Election.

The walls could not have held another person, and so must have bulged a little as Prospero, Andria and Aranda forced their way toward the dining hall where the heroes were being seated. No stinting here on comestibles, even Erri was being led to a plate, to eat, a gent among gents. A stranger would have taken all three travelers for soldiers, because Antonio and Raimondo still wore the leathers which had brought them incog across the Alps.

The family—down to Vittoria, the youngest—all hung upon one or another of the men, an arm, a leg, a belt, or whatever could be grasped—except Anna who was advising the Major where each was to sit.

Surrounding the table, even standing in the window embrasures and on chairs, to see over the press, were the household staff and *their* children, not to mention the village Podesta, the parish priest, the tinner, the tanner, the tiler, who—with flute, fiddle and tambor—made up the town band.

Andria had no more than a scant hunting acquaintance with Antonio Colonna until this time, and remembered him best from Raimondo's description, as an agreeable youth, the embodiment of assent, one who never had been heard to say "no" to anything. That two-edged characterization was borne out by the public clamor at the lad's homecoming and by his ready consent to sit beside his real mother, Maria, beside his putative mother, the Duchess, and beside Anna, all at the same time. The trick could not be done, but Antonio agreed to it, and—of course—Anna won.

In looks, Andria found Antonio an improvement over Prospero and Anna: undeniably, he had a profile: but it was the other well-born of these pseudo-Switzers who really fluttered the damsels' ruffles this day. Raimondo Orsini had become quite dazzling.

"You've washed your hair!" cousin Gugl accused him loudly by way of greeting, which was to say, *bleached,* and Count Nola could not deny it. Always the fairest of the cousins, he had, by art, lightened his dirty-taffy mop to a shade like the yolk of a duck egg, and wore it plaited in two braids, each as thick as your wrist. To complete his allure for unwary maidens he had grown a long, silky mustache which he tinted the same color as his hair and trained straight down the sides of his mouth, two fearsome, sulphurous handles.

"Say nothing about it!" Raimondo hooted back, and impertinent Baby-face replied, "No!—neither would I."

"Never mind," Nola bridled. "Anna likes it."

"That settles it," said Andria with a mock bow. Then Erri came bowing too. "I presume," he faltered. "I know I presume, Lordship, but it is not I who presume. Highness Anna said I must sit here. I would not forward myself."

"Trust in Anna," Duke Andria whispered, "and she will make your fortune."

Then Nola fell upon his cousin's neck, and—like a tow-headed bear—danced him in a circle, speaking the while. "What is this with ANNA? Anna this, Anna that, ever since we came in somebody has been giving me Anna! She walks like a Saint and talks like a seeress—and everybody trembles."

"She may be—Saint and seeress in one."

"She may be a spoiled little girl!"

"No. She is most remarkable," Andria insisted. "Watch her. You'll see. She is rebuilding the walls of Rome."

Nola held his head.

The nurse-Maria came to welcome back the youth whose oath she had broken, and with the touch of her hand Gugl realized that the image of his lost bride had not appeared to his inner eye for several days. "Did Anna leave her bed last night?" he asked.

"No!" said her mother, sharply, defensively. "Don't think that."

"Eh? Go and see if her feet are dirty."

"I will not. Come. Anna says I may sit beside you."

Nola turned away grimly to watch this new sun about which all else revolved.

Andria pushed the gentlewoman gently away. "Go and look at her feet," he said, and then, to Erri, "You have seen the Prince!"

"Four times, Highness. I have been from Constance to Palermo and back again so often I could swim it in the dark!"

"You have been for the last time I hope."

"I too. The Prince is coming to Nola. We are to meet him there."

"You know he is exiled. Beware."

"We know. He will not be taken again."

No more could be said at the moment. The Duchess Paliano had discovered Aranda and must kiss the man who had brought him. The tailor himself modestly tried to avoid dining with those above him, but Anna's authority was invoked to force his feet under the table.

Raimondo pensively twisted one silken mustache around and around his finger, as attentive to the problem of Anna Colonna as ever he had been to the machinations of the politicos of Constance. He realized shortly that the girl herself was not consciously grasping for the power her elders gave her. She was not domineering, but issued the orders only because she was asked. She was spoiled, no doubt of that, but not beyond reclaiming, if her family and the vassals of Colonna would cease paying homage and desist from shielding her innocence.

Anna's attitude toward himself was more strange than alarming, girls being girls and prone to attach themselves to fancies, but he had not the slightest recollection of any love talk between them.

All in all, Nola was ready to administer a much needed lesson here, should the occasion arise: he would take none of her nonsense: but he was flattered to find himself seated beside her, almost as much honored as Brother Antonio. Paragon, Nonesuch, that she was, to these others, she thus displayed discrimination in his case.

Prospero Colonna did not let go his brother's arm until Anna had spoken to him three times. "You must not monopolize Antonio," she reprimanded, and then called for silence in the room. She told the town dignitaries—for all to hear—that God still had not chosen His Vicar on Earth, but would certainly lay that Sacred Burden upon Cardinal Colonna very soon. Master Antonio and his colleagues—who remained nameless—were only passing through Paliano, on a secret mission for the public weal. Then she declared holiday—that they might retire and pray for the Cardinal and the Masons of Christ.

Some—especially the local priest—thought it passing strange that the Appearance of the Virgin was not mentioned, except thus obliquely, but Anna's dignity and presence forestalled any questions and left the commonality well satisfied, even proud of being put out of the castle. After them, Anna dismissed the household staff—saving waiters—with equal graciousness and no hard feelings, and—happier than ever before in her life—she took her own seat, demurely, between her dearest brother and her blond and secret spouse.

Anna might have smoothed the back of either loved one's hand simply by reaching out, but the impulse to do so never came, and when either of the men touched her—the one as brotherly as the other—the pleasurable contact was about the same as having a cat rub against one's leg. In her freedom from bodily cravings Anna stood at the opposite pole from Queen Joan, with all the world between.

Quite obviously, from her manner of sweet contentment, no hint or suspicion of Count Nola's coming marriage had reached the maiden yet, and several of the members—especially Prospero Colonna and both mothers—were more keenly aware of that than of any other circumstance attending. They were on needles.

"Now!—tell us all about it," said Anna when the family, so to speak, was at last alone. "If the Election is not over—what brings you home? When will it be over? What is this secret that takes you to Naples? Begin at the beginning!"

Everybody burst out laughing, which startled the girl a little, but the nurse-Maria quickly explained. "They can't tell you everything at once, dear."

"Well, I have come home to be married," Count Nola answered one question, and there the answer lay on the table like the head of John the Baptist.

Nobody spoke for an awful moment, but everybody in the ken made motions of distressful hush, hush, hush. Prospero—sitting almost directly opposite Nola, and, thus, almost directly opposite Anna—was even more inept than usual, so eager was he to spare his sister one of her Headaches. He put his fool finger across his lips and hissed "Shhhhhhh!" like forty serpents.

Anna could not fail to see the gesture, because she was smiling triumphantly across the table at Duke Andria, on Prospero's right. Anna could not fail to hear that sizzing, but her smile did not fade, and the message it conveyed was not altered by so much as a flicker. She assumed that the hero with the Swiss coiffure had come home to marry her, and her smile said to Cousin Gugl, *Your Lordship may remember that I told you this would happen.*

Not to rub it in to any one person too long, Anna smiled around the table, at Maria, Vittoria, Aranda, the Duchess, and so on, receiving in return from each a quickly adjusted grimace of encouragement, sympathy or embarrassment. You could not have looked at so many caricatures masking gasped consternation without realizing something had slipped, but Anna could. Her penchant for seeing only what she wished to see enabled her to clear at a bound all hurdles of doubt. Her family was making faces, so what? They were looking at the Countess of Nola!

The Count, on the other hand, strenuously resented their hushing and shushing. It called to mind, at last, his habitual embarrassment in the face of little children, his never knowing what to say to them, and the defense he still practiced. He asked ALL girls of 5 and 6 if they would not be his wife, and boys, if they wished to meet Incubo. Both sexes almost invariably said, *yes,* but this was the first time one of them had tried to hold him to it.

To Nola's mind these presumed adults were doing Anna an injury, and he decided to snap the thread of her dream then and there. "I cannot get to Naples soon enough," he said. "We shall leave tomorrow—and the wedding is Mercuriday."

Anna, still smiling, turned to Brother Antonio. "Begin at the beginning," she said.

The byplay had no meaning for Antonio, uninformed upon either point of view, and he was sure his sister would not understand why *he* was going to Naples, but—asked—he must comply, for he would disoblige anyone else sooner than Anna. "It began with Uncle Oddo's housekeeper," he said.

"What is she like?" asked his real mother.

Antonio was no mental heavyweight but he knew who Maria was, in relation to himself, whether Prospero and Anna were aware or not, and he understood the gentlewoman's curiosity in the Cardinal's Swiss housekeeper. In short, he had made a poor beginning and wished he could start anew, but no inspiration came and he looked appealingly at Count Nola. Whether conversing in earnest or in jest, Antonio Colonna fit more snugly and was more at home as the butt, goat or object of another man's plot, a born pawn. Luckily—through his younger years— Antonio did not resent this, because he could not have changed it. His own father was using him on this occasion but the boy was barely aware of it.

To his young friend's rescue, Nola replied to Maria's question, "She is not unlike yourself, Madonna—except, not so pretty—which argues a kind of fidelity to your image."

Andria might have been glad for this information if he had considered only the relief it could bring to his paramour's conscience, but because Anna was hearing it too he tried to frown down his glib cousin. "What have housekeepers to do with your mission to Naples?" asked Andria. "Are the Swiss *hausfraus* electing the Pope?"

"They are doing more for the Church than those damned delegates," the Orsini returned. "And Cardinal Oddo did not know what a prize he had in Antonio until the housekeeper and an upstairs maid had a face-scratching argument over him and Urbano Origlia."

Andria, who knew Origlia's fame, regarded Antonio Colonna with a new respect. "My compliments," said Gugl, making the favored youth a little bow.

"Thank you, Milord, but your compliments are premature," said Antonio wanly.

"Antonio had not approached the housekeeper in that way," Count Nola explained to Maria, "out of respect for your image, Madonna, but the upstairs maid did not resemble you in the least."

"The maid was only twenty," Antonio volunteered, in the thoughtlessness of his youth.

To offset the mal-gallantry of Maria's son, the Orsini hastened, "In all conscience, I found the housekeeper the more—eh, *gemütlich—of* the two."

"Me, too," said the uncommon soldier Erri, nodding his opinion firmly.

"What was the Cardinal's opinion?" asked Maria frigidly.

"O, he preferred the housekeeper—five nights out of seven," Nola assured her. "In fact, the only time the rest of us could find her free was on mornings when the Council was in session. But this argument started one Venusday night not long after Origlia got there. We all thought the Cardinal would be asleep on a fast day, so we were upstairs having a nightcap with the girls. I forget who started it, Tony."

"The housekeeper," said Antonio glumly. "She was sitting on Origlia's lap."

"That's right. I knew something put it into her head to start bragging him up. O, this Origlia, this male Matterhorn! Master Whangster, King of the Flues! Priapusissimo Elephantinius!—until the maid could take no more of it, and practically called the housekeeper a liar. Who would believe that two such could be blessing one Swiss chalet at the same time?

"The maid said, '*Meri*'—that's Swiss for Maria—'*Meri*, you vassn't nowhere yed, and you didn't seen nodding, until you haff been around it, *Mon Papa Hip-popper!*'—that was the maid's name for Antonio—and the fight was on.

"The housekeeper got out her measuring tape, and I was taking bets, but before we got down to the judging—one word led to another—and those crazy Switzers began pulling each other's hair."

"Uncle Oddo woke up," Antonio recalled lugubriously.

"He certainly did!" said Count Nola. "You never saw a man's eyes stand out like his did when he got a good look at Tony's asset."

"Antonio has more than one," Anna said proudly.

"He has only one of these," Count Nola corrected her, "but that is all he needs. And that is why Antonio has come with me to my wedding."

"I am supposed to work on Queen Joan's sympathy," said Antonio.

"You are to work on Queen Joan, period," the other emended.

"O, do have a good heart-to-heart talk with her," Anna besought her brother. "I'm sure Her Majesty will love you—and do anything you ask."

"Indeed we hope so," the Orsini concurred soberly, "and to improve Antonio's chances, the Cardinal is keeping Messer Origlia in Constance with him, so Aunt Joan won't be able to make the comparison direct."

"Sorry, old man," said Andria to Antonio. "I've always heard that Origlia is pretty stiff competition."

Antonio made a wry mouth, and shrugged. "We can't have everything," he said.

"We can if God Wills it," Anna encouraged him.

"God didn't Will it," her brother replied humbly, "but I'll do the best I can."

"I'm sorry too, dear," said the nurse-Maria.

"O, it isn't your fault, Maria," her son consoled her.

"We didn't lose by much," Count Nola put in boisterously. "And I'll tell you this—Antonio makes Serjianni look like a man with a wart."

Antonio smiled modestly. "Raimondo is very encouraging. He's trying to keep my spirits up."

"I don't think I quite understand what you are to ask from the Queen," Anna admitted. "Is that the secret?"

Far from a secret, Uncle Oddo's demand, fathered by the exiled French nobles and mothered by the Faculty of Theology at the Sorbonne in Paris, was for immediate release from prison of Jacques Bourbon, and that demand was being screeched from the housetops all up and down the world, especially in Constance.

"Uncle Oddo has the pledge of all the votes he needs to make him Pope—tomorrow—or as soon as the Emperor comes back from England—if they would let it come to a vote," Antonio explained to his sister. "But the French bloc is contingent."

"Contingent," Count Nola explained, "means that the French delegates are answerable to the Sorbonne, and they won't vote for

Uncle Oddo until Jacques Bourbon is free and Crowned. That is Antonio's little chore in Naples while I am being married."

"There must be some mistake," said Anna. "The Sorbonne cannot force Uncle Oddo to Crown Jacques Bourbon against the Will of God."

"Nothing can stand against the Will of God," Raimondo agreed, "but the Sorbonne can keep Uncle Oddo from becoming Pope." This was Orsini's first encounter with Anna's Will of God phase, and he was beginning to realize what a man was up against in dealing with her.

Anna turned her sternest gaze upon him. "Louis II d'Anjou is heir to the Regno—and Yolande—and their beautiful, beautiful children," she said.

"That may be," Nola conceded. "I do not deny it, and if Uncle Oddo has to Crown Jacques Bourbon—interim—he will keep his fingers crossed, as a sign to God that he doesn't really mean it. You see, dearest Cousin, Louis II is far too busy now to come to Naples and be King right away. Antonio and I haven't seen Louis II since before the battle of Agincourt—and a great many things have happened since then. If it weren't for Louis II, Burgundy and the British would have run off with the Most Christian King long before this. He isn't right in the head."

"You jest so much," Anna complained, "I do not know if you mean it. Is the Most Christian King of France truly frenzied?"

"Frenzied, mad—crazy as a bedbug—but his eldest son—the Dauphin—is not quite so far gone as his father. He never will be able to read, but he can count—on his fingers—and he has run off with Caboche, the president of the butchers' union in Paris, to join the Duke of Burgundy."

"O, wicked!" Anna scowled.

"Now Burgundy is offering to desert his British allies and help the Peers of France drive Henry V out—if the

Peers will make him Regent of the Dauphin and get rid of Louis II."

"Vile!" Anna decreed.

"Infamous—but that is Louis's situation—on top of all his other troubles."

"God is punishing the French for not making Uncle Oddo Pope at once," said Anna.

"I had not thought of it quite that way," Orsini admitted, "but perhaps He is."

"I know He is," said Anna, "and He will punish us if we do not see that Yolande's beautiful children succeed to their birthright in the Regno. We must pray for her."

"I don't know that prayer is what Yolande needs so much as a well armed militia," said Count Nola. "Yolande has been telling God what to do here lately."

"That is sacrilege!" said Anna.

"I know it's sacrilege, dear girl, but Yolande d'Aragon is a hard woman. She is as much responsible for holding up the balloting at Constance as the Sorbonne or the Emperor. Yolande has two counts against God, and she isn't going to let up on Him until He does something about them.

"I don't suppose you were big enough at the time to remember this, but only a little while before King Ladislaus died in Naples, the throne of Aragon fell vacant for want of a direct male heir, and the Catalan Cortes had a choice of four candidates—all co-equal kinsmen. Yolande d'Aragon was one, and Ferdinand the Just was another. I forget who the other two were—but it doesn't matter. Ferdinand won and Yolande lost, and that was God's First Mistake."

"God doesn't make mistakes," said Anna brashly.

"Yolande thinks He does. She says Ferdinand bribed the Cortes—and she never has relinquished her pretensions to the throne of Aragon. And now that Ferdinand the Just is dead, Yolande thinks God has made another mistake in letting that same Cortes crown Alphonso without any Papal sanction. Yolande wants Uncle Oddo to promise that as soon as he is Pope he will force the Catalan Cortes to disallow Alphonso's claims and make her Queen of Aragon."

"I think so too," said Anna. "Alphonso is an Atheist. May I, please, touch your mustache?"

"You may," said Count Nola, leaning toward her with dignity.

Anna pinched the flax gingerly. "Thank you," said she. "I never felt one before."

Nola turned toward Duke Andria. "Uncle Oddo—at the moment—is listening to Yolande with more sympathy than you might expect," he told his cousin. "He leans that way because Yolande would also be Queen of Corsica—and of Sicily *ultra* Pharum. Colonna would have no trouble then collecting the Holy See's incomes from any of those places—or from Aragon. He would have no trouble with the Banca San Giorgio or Genoa or Anjou. Even the part of France that the British have left under Louis II will be docile. Over against that, Oddo would have to charge off Burgundy and England—until Louis and Yolande could conquer them. The Emperor is the mustard seed that will tilt the balance either way—and he is still in London talking to Henry V.

"On the other hand," Raimondo turned back to Anna, "the Vatican would have to remain in Avignon—in Provence—and so Uncle Oddo would have no tithes from Rome, and the Colonna real estate in The City—all those stores and tenements, palaces and hotels—would stand vacant, eating up taxes. God doesn't want that, does he, Anna?"

"O, no!" said Anna. "Yolande is mistaken."

"I see that you consider both sides of the question. Only fancy all that Yolande and Louis II would have, if God should do everything Yolande tells him ... Aragon, Valencia, Catalugna, Majorca, Sardinia, Corsica, the TWO Sicilies, Hungary and Jerusalem, Anjou, Maine, Provence, and France.

"If God is so good to them, He will have to disappoint a lot of other people all over the world. A million prayers must go unanswered—even some of ours."

Nobody before Raimondo ever had presented these problems to Anna in quite this light, and her esteem for the Lord she would espouse increased accordingly. Poor God! So many people came to Him for the same crown—or the same Tiara!—the merits of each rival plea held so highly, so sacredly by the pleaders and their factions. It was no jolly wonder He took so long to answer her prayers sometimes.

"If Yolande asks too much she will be chastened," said Anna.

Ah, yes, Raimondo admitted, that was the largest question. "Shall Yolande be chastened—or Alphonso d'Aragon? Louis II— or Burgundy and Henry? I am commissioned by His Serenity the Cardinal to win your husband to Yolande's support, to stop Alphonso, if not by argument then by force. The Prince of Taranto and Count Copertino can keep Alphonso out of Sicily and Corsica. They can force the resignation of Benedict XIII—if they choose. They can raise the money and the arms Yolande needs. I don't know where else she is going to get them. Everyman in France is needed to hold on to what they have left. None of Yolande's boys is old enough to take the field. Truly—I do not see how Yolande and Louis can do anything without Taranto and the cabal. So, dearest Anna, tell me the Will of God—and I shall faithfully repeat it to your husband whom I shall see soon—in Naples."

"Do you mock me?" asked the maid. "Do you mock God?"

"No—never—neither the one nor the other."

"You call the Prince—my 'husband'. You?"

"And so he is—or must be soon."

"Do *you* tell me I must marry the Prince of Taranto?"

"It is not my place to tell——"

"It *is* your place. Woman's first duty is to obey her husband. THAT is God's Will. You have been my husband in God's Eyes since I was six years old. You, My Lord, must tell me what to do."

"Then you must marry Taranto," Nola jerked out angrily. "But I am not your husband. That is nothing but a childish fancy. I am on my way to marry Isabella Caracciolo now—as I have told you all along."

O, shame! A murmur of *shame* ran around the table, even Duke Andria joined it.

"Let us speak no more about it," said Anna.

MR. THAYER INTRUDES

ANNA COLONNA'S IDIOSYNCRASIES quite take the play away from the political situation in the table talk, don't they? If you or I had been in the boots of either of the cousins, Nola or Andria, only just re-met after a three-year separation, and so vitally concerned in our purses by the shifty doings in Paris, Constance, Aragon, Palermo, I think we should have spoken more to the point. If it had been my money I'd have beaten the matter out thin, twisting and turning the probable consequences of every possible course to be followed—and I'm sure Nola and Andria did that. They must have done it—but perhaps not at the table. We can assume they got together that night and told each other all they knew, but the MS does not mention it. The MS keeps its focus on Anna— and nothing could be more natural.

Anna Colonna, in her later life, was one of Villon's chief sources of information, and—although she did not put the same complexion on these events that he does—he follows her emphasis upon details. That is to say, he sees with different eyes but from the same angle, he hears with different ears, but from the same position in the room.

Anna and her brother Antonio are the only people at that table whom Villon ever meets. They alone survived until he came to Rome, but Villon's prejudice is such that we can almost invariably identify "facts" he derived from Antonio by a disparaging or skeptical tone in the writing, whereas Anna was second only to Lisa in the spy's esteem. In fact, Anna awed him considerably more than Lisa did—as you shall see, if we live so long.

Impossible now to fill all the gaps of the writer's omissions, but perhaps the issues are clear enough. The Faculty of Theology of the University of Paris—which I have translated as "the Sorbonne", for your convenience—never had acknowledged the supremacy of the Papacy over itself, and it was not now going to give its votes to Cardinal Colonna until and unless it had him hobbled.

What the minutes of the meeting—now received history—fail to give us is any insight into the "lobbies" such as Count Nola's, their conversations, coercions and bribes, but the essence of these may be deduced—as they concern the principal persons of the MS—from the subsequent actions of these people as they revolve about Anna.

Count Nola had done a bang-up job of preventing Cardinal Oddo from sharing Duke Paliano's suspicions of Taranto through this period when the Prince appeared to have lost his grip. The Prince had *not* removed Sforza from Rome, he had *not* prevented Joan's marriage to Bourbon, he had *not* caused the Aragonese to abandon Benedict XIII. Still Uncle Oddo's confidence had been kept propped up by Nola's reassurances.

We feel—without being told so much—that Colonna's present demands upon the cabal, to free Jacques Bourbon and to espouse the cause of Yolande over that of Alphonso in Aragon, were somewhat in the nature of an ultimatum, a final test of Taranto's good faith and his ability to perform. If the boys did not come through this time, I don't think the Cardinal would have trusted Giovantonio any further.

On the evidence of Antonio Colonna's journey into the Regno under Count Nola's wing, it looks as if the Cardinal trusted that one Orsini and approved his marriage into the Caracciolo family. As the MS states, the Colonnas never had enjoyed dealing with Serjianni, and it argues the supreme confidence of the Cardinal in Raimondo Orsini's diplomatical ability to get the better of the Strong Man, boring from within, that he entrusted Antonio to his sponsorship and sent him to the wedding.

Count Nola, from his vantage point, after long observation of those lobbies at Constance, expresses complete assurance of Cardinal Colonna's Election, so we must assume a rather fine understanding between Oddo and the Emperor, quite apart from any engagements Oddo had made to Louis II and Yolande or any accommodations arrvied at with the Sorbonne.

The Electors were to be six from the Germanic States, six from Britain, six from "France", and six of Colonna's fellow countrymen. The latter bloc was assured to him by Colonna's own recognizances, the French bloc rested upon the contingencies already noted, but the Germans would vote as Sigismund directed—and he was currently in London working on the British. The only way those Anglo-Saxons had raised their quota of ballots to par with their neighbors was by virtue of Henry V's success at Agincourt and after, and the only way the British delegates could be induced to vote for Oddo Colonna was by getting him to promise to crown Henry V King of France, eventually.

Burgundy's pledge—given to the Dauphin and the Peers—to break his British alliance, might turn out to be the purest gold in Oddo's reserve, especially if Colonna, as Pope, decided not to keep his promise to Henry V, exacted from Colonna as a mere Cardinal.

Raimondo Orsini knew all that and so he must have foreseen that Uncle Oddo was quite ready to forsake Yolande and Louis II if the Emperor came back from England and told him he could not get the Tiara any other way. Even if that shift became necessary—as seemed likely—it would not materially alter the stipulations being imposed upon Taranto. Colonna must still insist upon opposing Alphonso d'Aragon in Sardinia and Corsica, whether Yolande were abandoned or not, for the double purpose of placating the Banca San Giorgio and somehow, anyhow, disposing of that stubborn shanker Benedict XIII.

The gravest menace to Uncle Oddo's prospects, if he should abandon Yolande, was the loss of Anna's prayers and the Will of God, but I don't think he was aware of that.

CHAPTER THIRTEEN

T HAT WAS THE WORST headache Anna ever had, and it lasted many days. To outward appearances, unless aroused, she lay in a semi-stupor, but within, her mind was as lucid as ever it had been. Outwardly, too, she remained a young girl, but inwardly she felt ancient. Now she had suffered, *ergo*, now she was a woman: but Anna's "maturity" was a singular phantasm, a dream of strange growth, and slow to approach what others have called reality.

The convent, which had seemed to Anna (the child) to be an alternative from insoluble worldly quandary, was not to be sullied by a woman with TWO living husbands, a kind of virgin Magdalen. This was the Cross God had given her to bear in the world among men, and she must not flinch from it or faint beneath it. She lay abed to order her thoughts, to consult God's Will. The finding of that was primal to all her feeling, thinking and doing, but it was not easily come by—in its purity—amongst so many conflicting desires of men whose wills imposed duties upon her with almost equal authority, and all under Divine Sanction. Anna had not only two husbands, but two fathers as well. Please God—the four might agree!

Of the four, Anna found her first obedience to be to Raimondo Orsini Count Nola, as her first and true spouse. The supremacy of a husband's will over a father's was well established and known to all. That would change, of course, with Uncle Oddo's Coronation. As Pope he would dictate to everyone, bring order out of chaos, and set the world to rights. Until then, however, his authority was no greater than that of one's second husband, the Prince, and wherever their desires conflicted—as in the case of Yolande versus Alphonso the Atheist—one must pray for a sign from Heaven, to save one or both from error.

Fortunately, Father, Duke Paliano, fourth ranking authority, presented no problem. He never would have a wish or issue a command at variance with Uncle Oddo's will. To his credit, Anna recalled that Father was the one who had informed her of Alphonso's Atheism, thus clearly shewing the Prince of Taranto to be in the wrong for running with those Catalans.

That was the message for Taranto, then, to be carried to him by Count Nola. In obedience to her spouse's first command she had found out God's Will, that the Prince must help to blast the Atheist, and—sick as she felt—Anna was prepared to convey that word when Raimondo's yellow braids hung over her bed, come to take farewell.

Between her and Heaven was the perfect understanding that she was absolved of sin in accepting a second husband. Now that Count Nola had explained how the French were acting toward Uncle Oddo, Anna was ready to smooth his road to the Papacy. That road was rocky enough without her tripping him up. By marrying Taranto she obeyed her parents as a good daughter should, and performed a duty to her noble House. Inextricably— and as sacredly as any cloistered nun—she was thus dedicated. This, her contribution to the amity of States, to the rectification of Holy Church, to the Glory of God. By accepting her lot without demur she was doing a wifely service to her spouse of record On High.

Looking up at Raimondo from her fevered bolster, Anna's faculty for semi-blindness saw that he, like herself, was dedicated in this service. Like her he was marrying, against his own will and inclinations, for the weal of the cabal, and not because he wanted the Caracciolo's dower or because he thought that Serjianni's sister would make a better wife than she.

Hail Maria! Raimondo's sacrifice was greater than Anna's, and his path would be more thorny, because his alliance was with the family of the seven-headed Antichrist, the evil genius of the Regno. Anna always had pictured Serjianni as a double Cerberus with one face behind, all tusked, fanged and slavering poisons. Now Raimondo must live with that great beast in pretended friendliness, stroking those heads, scratching that back, as one caressed a favorite hound. Raimondo must live a daily sham, deceiving the arch-deceiver, embroiling himself in the schemes of Queen Joan's party in order to overcome the monster.

"I shall pray for you," said Anna to Count Nola.

The promise had not the significance to Raimondo that it had to Guglielmo, who had come to the sick-room with the others, although he was not leaving Paliano. As one who could testify, upon the repeated and present evidence of his own eyes, to the potency of Anna's supplications, Duke Andria felt an exaltation swell in his breast, as real as a flatulency and even more elevating. The maiden's willingness to bring Nola to the attention of her Heavenly Sponsors was tantamount to assuring him victory in all his undertakings. It was the kind of help the Orsini would be needing to get through his marriage and col-lect his wife's portion, without handing over the Crown to Joan or going into prison with Bourbon and Ottino. Andria never had regarded that marriage as anything but a trap to endonjon his cousin, and had spent half the night with the bridegroom working out safeguards, and circumventions of Serjianni's evil designs. Anna's prayers were exactly what Raimondo needed, but they were a gift far above his deserts after so cruelly abusing her gentle sensitivities.

Count Nola was in equally poor odour with the entire household for the nonce. Everybody knew that what he had done to Anna had long wanted doing but nobody loved him for it.

Andria was not standing near the head of the bed with Count Nola and Antonio Colonna, but near the foot, purposely holding back so that Anna might see his disapproval of his brutal cousin.

Anna's mother—the nurse-Maria—with a wise expression on her normally placid face, stood guard between Gugl and the bedcovers, and when one of his hands moved—perhaps to brush away a fly—she whispered fiercely, "Don't you dare!"

"Dare?" The Del Balzo innocence was outraged, but he kept his voice low.

"You were going to lift that sheet."

"*Mother!*" he admonished her. "I would no more uncover——"

"You want to see if her feet are dirty. Well, they *are*. They are always dirty except on Holy Jovisday. Now you keep your hands off."

At the head of the bed Antonio Colonna was saying, "Pray also for me, dearest Anna. Pray that I can get Jacques Bourbon out of prison. Nothing is more important than that."

"I shall," Anna promised, and closed her eyes. She felt his lips brush her face—Antonio's, then Raimondo's—and a third pair was pressed to the back of her hand. Curious, she looked, and saw Erri, the soldier, streamy-eyed, on both knees. "You too," said Anna, but—in the present state of her agitation—she could not call his name.

"Dearest Anna," said Raimondo, "do you forgive me?"

"There is nothing to forgive," she said.

"I did not mean to hurt you."

"Let us say no more about it. Yours is the harder task."

Ah, yes! He had almost forgotten ... Raimondo—completely misunderstanding Anna's allusion—recalled that he must learn the Sacred Word for Taranto. "What shall I tell the Prince?"

"The Prince will follow his conscience," said Anna, "fear God and smite the Atheist!"

"The Atheist?" That nickname for the Aragonese had no general currency as yet.

"Alphonso," Andria supplied.

Count Nola's grimace was almost concealed by the curve of his mustache. "If the King of Aragon be an Atheist," he said, "we must all pray for his redemption."

"I do," said Anna, again closing her eyes.

After they were gone, the sick girl tried to place her prayers in the sequence of their importance, but could not go beyond the release of Jacques Bourbon without prompting.

Out of that necessity a closer communion grew between Anna and Andria. Faithful as a sheepdog, he would sit beside her as long as she required, telling her what to pray for. In these conversations Erri was identified as one of four Heavenly Instruments dedicated to wreaking vengeance for the drowning of Aloys. Strength to their arms!—and repose to the page's soul.

Granting the paramountcy of Bourbon's release, Gugl endeared himself to Anna by naming Raimondo's general welfare second. Then—still unselfishly—Andria would have Anna require of Heaven, the health of Ettore Pappacoda, whom he described as "faceless", and thus the Colonna girl began to form images of many men she never had seen. That became an extraordinary menagerie in a short time.

To the seven-headed Serjianni, whom she was praying *against,* and the instrument to destroy him—which was Erri multiplied by four—was added the faceless Ettore, for whom

Anna begged a new set of features, and after him, Marino Marzano.

Anna pictured Marino as a deer-hound, because his capacities as a working dog had Guglielmo's highest praise. Marino could bring down game or chase away poachers with equal facility, and these were his pursuits in Avellino which the Heavenly Hosts were expected to assist.

Artuso Pappacoda was a good old ox.

Count Nola—a lion!

Brother Antonio—a sleek Arabian courser.

Sforza—a wild boar.

Braccio—a stingaree.

Alphonso the Atheist—an Atheist, scaly and slimy withal.

Louis II—an Archangel.

The only figure that Anna could not bring to mind in some such convenient form was that of the Prince of Taranto, Andria's reports of him being so contradictory to the facts inscribed on her heart.

The sheepdog Andria did not scruple to describe Giovantonio as an eagle, but by the time the Prince had been plucked in conformity with Anna's inner vision he looked more like a vulture, and that was the character he bore with her until Anna saw him in the flesh.

The walls of Rome had been under fanatical—and very uneven—reconstruction for about a month, and Guglielmo had begun to smuggle in arms for a surprise attack. The entire strategy centered about the stonework, temporarily, and Cardinal Oddo had blessed the effort, so long as the hand of Colonna did not show too plainly. His letter had only the best to say about the cousins, and bade Duke Paliano co-operate with their "reasonable" aims, most especially to urge them to assist in the liberation of Bourbon. Absolutely nothing could be accomplished in Constance until that Highness was free.

Others of Anna's prayers were being answered ahead of that one. Count Nola's marriage had gone off swimmingly. Ettore was well enough to enjoy the visit of a whore once a week. Sforza had the tar whaled out of him by Francesco Orsini, and that was about the size of it when the Prince of Taranto plowed into Anna's sitting room with Colonna servants dangling from every joint. Behind him, fending off a mass attack upon their rear, was Tomaso.

Andria was with the gentle maid that day, playing tric-trac until the hour to join his smugglers, and over their game they had been speaking about Anna's prayers, as usual. Not even Gugl recognized Taranto back of his week's growth of beard and under the none-too-clean patchwork of a bravo. No more could Andria link this tumultuous entrance to any of Anna's pending supplications. It looked like a benison intended for someone else, which would have to be returned. "What hath Heaven sent?" exclaimed Andria.

Anna had just rolled the dice. "Two fives," she said.

Then Gugl recognized Tomaso—and *ba-a-a-ed* like a goat. At the same time the Prince was shaking off Colonna domestics as if they were little bugs, and as they flew he executed a beautifully timed and graceful movement that flowed without pause, a single magnificent gesture which swept off his cap, laid his sword on the floor, took him down on one knee in the bow supreme and brought him up out of it with his stubble scratching Anna's chin and both his arms around her. "Wife!" he cried, like an impetuous lover, "I have waited too long for this hour. You are the most beautiful woman I ever have seen! Kiss me!"

Giovantonio had used the routine a good many times to bring it to this state of rhythmic perfection, and it never had failed him before. The best part, I ween, was where his knee just touched the floor and he came up off it as if his eagerness for her embrace had lifted him, given him wings. Alas, they were vulture's wings—bat wings—to Anna.

How many young girls—and older too—had entered into the spirit of that greeting, aye, despite that he needed a shave! Eh? Taranto was a magnificent animal, and the whiskers were a part of him. Why, even when the kiss had been refused out of coyness by normal Princesses, they always had laughed a little in the doing!—but it was no way to approach Anna. It set the cabal back two years.

Shocked, revolted, horrified, insulted, Anna drew her face away from that bristly contact. "Thou beast!" she gasped.

"Beast?" The Prince never had been called so before. The epithet fell like a club across the nose of a puppy who has nothing but fun in his heart. Such a bruise inflicted on a common cur sends it whimpering to a corner, but Taranto was a cub of another breed. As swiftly as he had enfolded her—and as gracefully too—he let her go and mounted his dignity, standing well apart from her and very erect. "A thousand pardons, Highness," said he, cutting his words to a rigid length. "It will be long e'er Your Ladyship has reason to complain of me again." Then turning to Andria, he continued in the same tone, "As soon as Your Lordship is free I should like a word with you." That was all, and he left the room, followed by Tomaso.

Duke Andria had not been able to utter a word, but only a bleat of recognition. Like the servants, he looked to Anna for her commands. "Leave me, please," she said.

In the corridor, the Prince faced a wall of scowls, the same scowls that had seen Count Nola off with low-born, muttered maledictions, and for a lesser crime. Men and women, young and old, presented this Highness—royal though he be—with a united front of animosity, and whereas Nola had fortuned to be *departing* under this sinister cloud, Taranto was only then arrived. He would have been more welcome in a wolf den. "Take me to your master," said Giovantonio to the nearest flunky, but the Major-domo stepped forward haughtily. "Perhaps Your Highness would like to freshen up. Will Your Highness be in residence long?"

Andria came through Anna's door then, and the cousins fell into each other's arms. A sight for sore eyes and how fat you have got! Where do you come from? I'll explain about Anna. Have you seen Raimondo? This way!—and Tomaso! The soldier was embraced too.

By this means the Major and his staff were put off their hauteur but not out of countenance. Andria they knew to be on Anna's side, and one who observed the amenities. Even as he led the ruffian newcomer to his apartment, Andria said aside to the Major, "The Lord Prince of Taranto sends his compliments to Her Highness the Duchess—and awaits her welcome."

"Is Duke Paliano not here?" asked Taranto. "Must I deal with *another* Colonna female?"

"The Duchess will like that bow of yours! Paliano is never here. Come."

Alone—for a moment, before the eager family began arriving to view their exalted new son and brother—Andria tried to prepare Taranto for his second and inevitable encounter with his bride. "Anna is in the clouds, granted, but she'll grow up, and when she does she will be beyond price. What Anna prays for— Anna *gets!* I've seen it happen time after time. It's like having a magician in the family. Handle her right and she'll be the biggest asset we could possibly have. We can't lose."

"I must say she has one ardent disciple," said the Prince suspiciously. "Is tric-trac the only game you play with Anna?"

"It's the only game she knows," Andria averred. "You must teach her the rest—but slowly. Forget all you know about romancing. Don't try to sweep her away with passion. You must woo her like a bird."

"Who the Hell wants a bird for a wife! I want an heir. Do you know that I have four children now—all girls?"

"Four! We must drink to each of them."

"One in Lecce I never have seen. Caterina—she is called."

"To Caterina!" Gugl toasted.

"And the youngest—Francesca—by a Lady to Tristano's mother. She is in Taranto with my mother now."

"To Francesca!"

"And Maria!"

"Maria!"

"And Giovanna!"

"Giovanna!"

"But I want a son."

"Anna will give you a son. She'll *pray* for it. That's the way it works with Anna. You can have anything you want."

"But I have to sneak up on her to get it!"

"Well, gently does it."

"Sing her serenades."

"No, no. No serenades. She wouldn't understand a serenade."

"What would she understand—gifts?"

"Mm—yes—"

"Poetry?"

"Mm—some——"

"Look! This is too damned complicated—and her father isn't even Pope yet. That's going to make her worse. Do I have to keep coming to you all my life—asking what to do next? I'd rather marry one of the Carafa girls and take all my prayers in cash. Did I tell you Maddaloni sent his son Diomede to Caterina's wedding?"

"Excellent! Did I tell you that Maddaloni has withdrawn from Joan's councils—absolutely death on Serjianni for abusing his confidence? They never would have captured Ottino if Malizia hadn't guaranteed his safety, but they won't fool that old fox Malizia a second time."

"No—they won't," said Taranto, with a smile overfreighted with knowing. "When Diomede Carafa left Palermo—after Caterina's wedding—he didn't go back to Naples. He went to Burgos—to Alphonso. He's with Alphonso at Sardinia now—in command of one of the biggest warships in the Aragonese fleet."

Andria's face fell almost to the floor. "On your life, don't mention that here," he warned. "You haven't spoken with Raimondo. You were supposed to meet him in Nola."

"I am going there—eventually."

"He will tell you that the Cardinal is now inclined to make Yolande—Louis's wife, remember her?—Queen of Aragon."

"Ho-ha!"

"And you are expected to bring Count Copertino around to that way of thinking."

"I could move Mount Etna to Angers sooner. Count Copertino's money built the fleet in which Diomede Carafa has his command."

Andria covered both ears with his hands. "Don't talk about it *here!*" Sagely he refrained from quoting God's Will to his cousin, refrained also from mentioning that Anna was praying for the destruction of the fleet at Sardinia. These little differences of opinion were better left to be adjusted between husband and wife. What Andria conceived his duty to be was to prevent this marriage from going asunder before the vows were taken, to smooth, grease and hasten its consummation before the pair realized that their views were utterly irreconcilable, and Gugl in his heart sincerely believed that by doing this he brought Heaven under Taranto's command.

"I beg of you, Gian, do not speak of these Aragonese connections where a Colonna can hear you. Duke Paliano taxed me with the Chiaramontes the first time I ever spoke with him, and I have given him to understand that you have been in Palermo for the sole purpose of winning the Aragonese for Cardinal Oddo."

The Prince rolled a mocking eye. "How can they distrust me?"

"They do. And—Cousin—the man who tries to ride two horses oft-times splits himself. If you drop one hint of sympathy for Alphonso d'Aragon—you will not marry Anna."

"A Carafa wife would bring me twice as much in dot."

"The Carafa money is already on our side. There's no need to marry it. Gian!—keep your contract and marry Anna."

"Marry an icicle? Her face was cold as stone."

"She is a child."

"I have kissed some hot children."

"And will again! But—Cousin—admit this is vanity. Anna has wounded your pride. Will you let that kick apart the work of three years—ruin the best plan you ever laid? You have sent Raimondo to marry for the good of the cabal—and he went like a lamb into the lion's den. His life isn't worth three ducats from one day to the next—nor Artuso Pappacoda's neither. The only thing that has preserved them so far has been Anna's prayers. Is all their bravery to be wasted and in vain—because Anna took fright of you today? If you want to know—that entrance of yours scared Hell out of *me*. I thought you were the ghost of Atra Bilis."

A gathering tenseness around Taranto's eyes, a compression of the lips, had warned Andria to turn the matter off upon a jest, if possible, but still a blast seemed imminent.

"We lost also Aloys," put in Tomaso of the long memory.

It was not self-evident to the Prince that he would be breaking faith with the cabal's heroes—or living or married or dead—by renouncing Anna Colonna in favor of a more congenial bride, but his acid retorts were interrupted by more Colonnas, the children coming first, to bob at the knees and stare in awe at their new Lord Brother.

"Would you like to dress for the Duchess?" Andria asked the Prince. "Aranda has made me some fine things—"

"No, I would not," snapped Taranto. "This is my exile's costume. I shall wear it until my banishment is lifted—or until I lift it."

"Would you care to be shaved?" asked Gugl with calculated mildness. "My barber has the touch of a dryad."

"No, I would not," said the Prince again, no less crisply, "but your barber may wash my face, if you wish. I never have felt the touch of a dryad."

"May we watch?" asked little Vittoria.

"Certainly," said Taranto. "Anything to please the Colonnas!"

The sting did not leave Giovantonio's wounded pride all that day, and at dinner time it was renewed, because Anna had her dinner served in her apartment, sending out humble regrets to the illustrious guest.

"Anna suffers terribly from headache," the Duchess Paliano explained stiffly. "Little-girl headaches."

"Because her termps haven't come on her yet," nurse-Maria added.

"Regrettable," said Taranto, disbelieving their excuses. That disbelief, more than Andria's logic, completely reinstated the marriage contract in the bridegroom's intentions. Actually he never had meant to break that troth, but only bandied the topic to make a show of his masculine independence. Then, when Anna renewed the insult by continuing to avoid him, the same male perversity inspired the resolution to tie the bond at once, the sooner to force his distasteful presence upon the saintly recluse.

That topic was not broached to the women, in fact, nobody at the table mentioned the institution of marriage in the course of the entire meal. After supper Guglielmo took the Prince aside to say that he should go about his smuggling—"Unless Your Highness wishes to postpone it?"

"Not at all! You have everything so well arranged here, I wouldn't interfere for the world. And to set your mind at rest—I shall marry the Signorina Anna at the earliest."

Overjoyed, Andria called him Solomon. "The wisest decision you ever made! Come along with me. I expect to see Duke Paliano tonight."

"Bring him back with you," said the Prince. "It's rather his place to come to me, don't you think?"

"Shall we stand on ceremony? I won't be back for thirty-six hours—and I'll tell you this—Paliano will have to write to the Cardinal to confirm the wedding date. Lorenzo-Onofrio doesn't break wind without checking with Oddo first."

"I think I prefer to have His Highness come to me. I've tried being impetuous with the Colonnas. They don't like it."

"As you wish, Gian. I only meant to save time—and I thought you might like to see how we run the arms through."

"I'm sure you do it perfectly—but I have traveled a long way. I am very tired. Bring Duke Paliano to me."

Gugl could not be sure how much of the change in Giovantonio was due to the Chiaramontes and how much to Anna, but the returned exile was a vastly different Prince from the one who had sailed to Palermo in a leaky tub full of gold. His authority was firmer, more stubborn, his self-regard considerably higher, and his pride on a par with the Carafas. That much was all to the good, the experience and competence, the dignity and assurance were what the cabal needed in its leader, but what had become of his humor?

Andria recalled the period in his own life when he had forgotten how to laugh, in the throes of despond over his lost bride. A woman could do that to a man. Happily, the effect was not permanent. Gugl felt himself quite recovered in that particular. He had not even mentioned the Princess Maria to Taranto in half a day's conversation, and—come to think of it—Gugl never had asked Anna to pray for a reconciliation. Amazing!

The two cases were hardly parallel, however, and if Taranto had lost the ability to laugh at himself, the rest of his new dynamic—unleavened—was likely to go hard with Anna and her world of dewy cobwebs.

Andria applied at Anna's door to leave her a word of encouragement, but her maids had the suite bolted and would not let in even him. Gugl went to join his men with a lump of dread in his throat. What might not happen before he returned!

What actually did happen was dreadful enough. Prospero sang solos, accompanied by the Duchess on the lute.

The other children sang duets, and played their instruments in consort.

When Taranto fell asleep in his chair, that was almost as great a relief to the two mothers as to him. They had not drawn an easy breath between them since his tumultuous arrival, not so much for fear of any bodily harm he might do them as of his sheer unpredictability. As the Duchess said, "He is a man of impulse."

They debated waking him, and decided to send the children to bed first.

"Suppose," said the Duchess pensively, studying the stretched-out figure in the chair, "suppose he wants a woman when he wakes up."

"Most men do," said Maria. "I mean—Oddo always did."

"Shall we call the Major?"

"O, the Prince wouldn't want the Major! His Highness is all man."

"Yes—isn't he?—but I didn't mean *that,* Maria. I was thinking of Anna. His Highness might attack her again——"

"Anna's door is bolted," said her mother. "I think you can take care of him."

"It's the hospitable thing to do," said his hostess. "How shall we wake him?"

"Shake him," Maria shrugged.

"O, no! He's a *Prince.*"

"Pour gold-water in his ears," said Maria sarcastically. "It's your problem. I'm going to bed."

"And leave me alone with him?!"

"Now, Sveva, stop. He'll be much easier to handle if you are alone with him. There's a brave girl! Just remember that you're doing it all for Anna."

"That was a catty remark."

"Forgive me, dear. I was only jesting … There's wine in the carafe. I'll dismiss the servants. Good luck," said Maria—and closed the door behind her.

It is to the Duchess' credit—for she had not tried anything like this in years and her hand was out—that she waked the Prince in the pleasantest way imaginable, more or less assuring herself that his mood would be predictable when he opened his eyes. In fact, her touch was so light that Giovantonio was in the mood before he opened his eyes, and, only half awake, murmured, "O, a dryad!"

Events would have progressed more swiftly if the Duchess had snuffed a few candles before Giovantonio saw who the playful sprite was, but that never would have occurred to a Gaetani, no matter how plain.

"Your Highness!" said Taranto. "Please forgive me. I'm afraid I dozed. We rode hard from Ostia—and the sea was rough our last night out. I slept very poorly." Talk, talk, talk!

"I was examining your poor—jerkin—or whatever you call it," the Duchess broke in. "You must let Aranda make you some new things—something to hunt in. He is an excellent tailor. Come! I'll show you some dresses he is making for me."

Where is the man brave enough to say in her teeth that he doesn't give a damn about a woman's wardrobe? So the Prince, carrying only one candle, went with the Duchess into the tailor's workroom, deserted for the night.

"You can't get a very good idea of it—on the hanger," said the Duchess. "I'll slip it on for you."

In order to slip it on, she had to slip off what she had on, and to slip is to slip is to slip. Giovantonio snuffed the candle, and that light became Her Highness beautifully.

"I shouldn't—I shouldn't——" Her Highness choked, after it was much too late to stop.

"Of course you should," said the Prince. "Even little bees do it."

"I don't mean that."

"Whatever you mean—save your tears for tomorrow."

"Tomorrow! Dear God, what have I done?"

"If you don't know—nobody else will."

"I shouldn't have brought you here."

"What's the matter with *here*. I'm very happy—if you'll stop moaning."

"I'll never forgive myself, never!"

"Yes you will."

"O, Milord, did you see it?"

"I did not look closely—but I'm sure it's beautiful."

"What do you speak of Milord?"

"What else but this pretty thing? I saw it well enough to find my way."

"O, no, not that."

"What, then?"

"Did you see—Anna's wedding dress—hanging—right beside mine?" The Duchess was in great mental anguish.

"That I did NOT see," said the Prince gallantly.

"Are you sure? It's the worst luck in the world for a groom to see his bride's gown before the Mass."

"I did not see it—and I won't look as I go out. Now, are you happy?"

"Yes—O, yes!—yes!—yes! You darling!"

That was how Taranto became such a favorite of the Duchess Paliano's, but he himself did not know whether he had seen Anna's gown or not.

The next morning the Prince continued his conquest of Colonna hearts by letting the youngsters hitch him to their goat cart. They took the goat into the cart with them—amidst screaming hilarity and squealed delight—and His Highness drew the lot of them around and around the garden paths, which—as chanced—lay under Anna's window.

Was this the beast who had come mauling and pawing her the day before? He was playing the animal, to be sure, but the sweetness of his big heart was quite apparent. Anna tried to be shocked by the Prince's frivolity. Such conduct in a man of parts shewed him irresponsible, lacking in proper appreciation of the world's grave condition and his duty to it—but the children were having such a good time that Anna's condemnation did not convince even herself. Her head was not aching very much either.

The Duchess was not in sight, but Maria appeared in the garden, and—seeing Anna in the window—made pantomime, beating Taranto over the back with a stick and smiling up at her daughter for approbation. Giovantonio followed the woman's gaze, but looked quickly away when he recognized the pale maiden, and galloped the children, cart and goat, out of her range of vision. The laughter continued, however, so Anna knew the fun went on, only she was out of it.

This was her fate, to be ever apart, to be engaged on a loftier plane while others made fools of themselves, but apparently nobody had impressed that upon her bristly spouse as yet. Anna motioned her mother upstairs to her, and solemnly conveyed her compliments to the Prince. "Tell him that I am going to my prayers, and await his commands, what I shall pray for."

In other words, she asked for it. She was showing off to attract Giovantonio's attention and make a big splash with him. Never, after that, could Anna blame anybody else if the Prince asked Heaven for the impossible or made demands that turned her conscience inside out.

"You had better come down and play in the cart with the others," said Maria. "It would be good for you."

"How can you suggest such a thing?—with Uncle Oddo uncrowned, the Church unhealed, the Atheist taking Sardinia——"

"O, Anna," her mother interrupted, "you don't know one ten-thousandth part of all the misery in the world, and if you did you couldn't do anything about it."

"I do what I can every day. I pray."

"You are a good girl, and I know Everybody in Heaven loves you—but you are making yourself ill. Come down into the garden. The Prince won't bite you."

"If he is the Prince he should be he will understand my message. Please take it to him—and bring me his answer right away. I wish to pray."

Needless to say, Maria did as she was told. Anna heard the laughter stop in the garden—but it began again, disconcertingly soon. His Highness could not have given the topic of his more serious desires much thought. Then Maria was back. "His Highness suggests that you pray for yourself, dear, and he said it kindly."

"Is that all he said?"

"That's all. He said, 'I don't suppose Anna ever thinks of herself, she is so busy praying for others.'"

"Then he did mean it kindly."

"O, yes. The Prince is the kindest man I ever met. I'm so happy for you, dear. He is going to make you a wonderful husband. Will you be all right now? I'm going back to the garden."

Giovantonio was laying himself out to be charming, and when he tried he was irresistible. By the time the family gathered to dine that night, he was deep under everybody's skin, even the goat adored him, and his sayings and exploits had been so well reported to Anna that she had the Devil's own time staying away from the table.

The Prince WAS the first person who ever had suggested that she pray for herself, at least, since earliest infancy, and the novelty of that made Anna dwell too long upon its meaning. After the twentieth or thirtieth time over it, the complete thought came out—Tell Anna to pray for herself, *she is going to need it!*

That was the discovery which held Anna in her room the second night, even in the face of the glowing presages for her glorious future as recited by the family and the servants. Anna forced her body to stay away from the now congenial board, but her thought was there, off the leash and beyond imprisonment, avid to absorb its own impressions, to learn all that was to be known of the man who was going to make her so happy as Princess of Taranto.

This preoccupation had such a grip upon Anna, as her waiter laid her lonely table, that she ejaculated, "Tomaso!"—although she knew perfectly well that the waiter's name was *Giacomo*. "The Prince's man!" she explained. "Bring him to me."

Was ever a patter compromise?

"Bring—Tomaso?" The waiter was flabbergasted.

"Bring Tomaso. I wish to question him."

"He speaks only one word at a time, Highness."

"I speak only one word at a time myself."

"Aye, but you string yours together."

"Bring him anyway, I shall understand him."

Still the waiter floundered in confused indecision.

"Why do you not go? Does Tomaso not eat with the servants?"

"He does, when he eats, Highness, but he attends his master at table."

"What? Does the Prince so distrust the Colonnas that he must be guarded at his bride's table? That is the crudest insult yet! He is unbearable!"

Anna's maids and the waiter tried to placate their mistress, saying that this was a Neapolitan custom, but Anna sent directly to say that she had a message which would not be entrusted to anyone but Tomaso.

The Prince, comprehending only that his affianced was being further troublesome, did not oppose her wishes but sent Tomaso to get this message so Saint and esoteric.

Anna was much surprised by his compliance—as Taranto had known she would be—but she was not overwhelmed beyond retaliation. Her table was laid for one, but she had not sat to it, and now she instructed the soldier to eat her dinner, and the waiter to serve him. Anna sat well back from the table to watch, thus consciously beginning her second conquest among the four comrades, the sworn avengers of Aloys. Riccardo and Quito, still in Avellino, Anna never had seen, but Erri had wet her hand with his tears as Count Nola and Brother Antonio took their leave for Naples.

Tomaso was too wise a buck to be flustered by a well-born virgin. Whatever the point of this jest, he enjoyed the eating part of it as any sensible man would, working a methodical demolition upon each dish set before him. His head bowed a little sidewise, and his smile was crooked too, as he chewed and chewed, and did not say even one word until he received the question direct.

"Will your master reprimand you for dining here?" asked Anna.

"I won't know until later, Highness."

"Is he strict with you? Does he strike you?"

"Only when I need it."

"The brute!"

"O, I haven't needed it yet, Highness."

"But now you have stayed away from your post."

"I have His Highness' permission, Signorina."

"What is your master afraid of—in my father's house—to keep you on guard behind him?"

"My master is not afraid of anything—in anybody's house—Highness."

"Then why does he make you stand there?"

"He humors me, Signorina. I *like* to stand there."

"It is entirely unnecessary here at Paliano."

Since that was not a question Tomaso made no reply.

"How long have you been in your master's service, Tomaso?"

"I was with his father before him."

"You don't mean the King?"

"No, Highness, I mean the Prince of Taranto. It is a greater honor to serve such a Prince than any King in the world, and now his son grows into a greater man than he."

"You love the Prince very much."

"He is a Man of Destiny, Highness."

"What is Destiny?"

"Ma'am?"

"What do you mean by—Destiny? What is a 'Man of Destiny'?"

"Why, Destiny is Destiny, ma'am, and you can't get away from that."

"Is His Highness devout?"

"Ma'am?"

"Devout. How many Masses does he hear a day?"

"One, ma'am, if be there's a church near by."

"He has no chaplain?"

"Not right now, Signorina. He's an exile now. But back in Taranto we've got any God's number of chaplains, almoners, confessors and all the rest of it. Your Highness needn't to think you're goin' to live with the Turk in Taranto. The chapel in the citadel is that golden beautiful I've yet to see its like anywhere. You'll have all the religion you want and to spare."

"Thank you. I am happy to know it. How many children has the Prince now?"

"Four."

"Boys or girls? Would you like more roast?"

"All girls. I thank Your Highness, I will take another spot of roast if I may." Giacomo supplied it.

"And are they in Taranto—with Queen Marie?" asked Anna.

"Two are, now. The other two are in Lecce."

"O, yes. The Prince's brother—Gabriel—is in Lecce. Does he have any children?"

"I don't rightly know, ma'am. He's pretty young."

"Do you have any children, Tomaso?"

"Not now any more, no."

"You have had."

"Yes, I had a boy."

"Where did you get him?"

"Ma'am?"

"Where did you find your boy?"

"O. Under a bridge, Signorina."

"Where? What bridge?"

"It's near Taranto—called the Devil's Bridge."

"Can you take me to it?"

"If we was both in Taranto I could. Anybody can tell you where the Devil's Bridge is."

"I shall wish to go there as soon as I reach Taranto. His Highness must have a son."

"Beg pardon, ma'am?"

"We must find a son for His Highness, Tomaso."

The last bite of his roast caused Tomaso to choke, but he got it down with a gulp of wine and then spoke with difficulty. "I'm thinking Your Highness won't be finding an heir to Taranto under the Devil's Bridge. I know three begotten there—all died on the gallows like mine."

"O, I'm sorry, Tomaso. May I pray for him?"

"Would you do that, Highness? For me? Your people say you are the best prayer in the world."

"I ask Heaven only to be merciful. God's Will be done."

They Signed themselves.

"Your Highness never asks—any harm to come to any-body?—even if they deserve it?" Tomaso pursued.

"No, Tomaso. I ask only that evil designs be averted, that wicked men be punished for their sins. One man—especially—I mention in my prayers, asking only that his foul wishes be turned back upon himself. That is no more than justice—is it, Tomaso?"

"No more. Your Highness, might I ask that man's name?"

"It is Serjianni Caracciolo—"

"THAT'S the son-of-a-bitch! Go get him, Highness."

"We must not be vindictive."

"Who's vindictive? If Your Highness please, would you pray that Serjianni's life be lengthened and preserved until I get back to Naples? That's not wishing anybody harm. He wants to live, doesn't he? Just keep him alive—for me—would you, Highness?"

"I shall try," said Anna, and Tomaso worshiped her.

By these several chances everybody in the castle at Paliano was reconciled except the two principals, Giovantonio and Anna.

Gugl got back late the next day, but he came without Lorenzo-Onofrio. "Duke Paliano could not come," the Del Balzo cousin confessed rather drag-tail. "He had to go to Marsi."

Since Duke Marsi was the eldest of the Colonna brothers, that seemed perfectly natural to the Prince, and he expected both Lordships to ride up next day with trumpets, banners, and the first instalment on Anna's marriage portion. Neither appeared or sent apologies, so Giovantonio wrote out a high-and-mighty summons, inscribed with all his dignities, fairly requiring their attendance upon him at Paliano at once.

That had the effect of relieving Duke Marsi's gout sufficiently for him to travel, but he went a secret course, which did not touch Paliano, and Lorenzo-Onofrio with him.

No further doubt or any charity could misinterpret the fact that the Colonnas—male—were avoiding encounter with the exiled Prince.

When Andria rode again—on schedule—to the smugglers' rendezvous, no Colonnas met him, and the arms intended for Rome had to be brought back to the farm.

The most probable explanation was that the lay brothers had sent to Cardinal Oddo for fresher advice and directions, and wished not to embarrass their inadequacy in discussion until their reply was back. Winter had closed upon the Alps and couriers required twice as long for the journey to and from Constance.

Duke Andria would have called Anna into the parly from the first, saying that a letter from her would find the brothers somewhere, and eventually get a response. "She could even write directly to Uncle Oddo," said Gugl, but the harder side of the Prince was uppermost, and getting crustier with each setback.

"Ask no favors of Anna," Taranto commanded. "I shall never make myself beholden to her."

"You must bid her to bed—eventually," Andria reminded him.

"As my wife she shall be put on my bed like a tick. I will never bid her," said Taranto crudely. "And when she has given me an heir—I shall have her removed from my bed—forever. I have seen enough of Anna Colonna to last me a lifetime."

As perversely as if she had heard him speak, Anna turned up at the family table that night, propped all around with pillows and fussed over by waiters, maids and butlers in a nauseating manner.

The Duchess Paliano made a formal presentation of their magnificent and illustrious guest to Her Highness—his—Princess of Taranto. Under the circumstances, this soundful gesture was equivalent to whistling among the tombs to keep the courage up, but Anna's confidence stemmed from an Unearthly Source. "When will it please Your Lordship to marry me?" she asked her spouse. "I shall tell my father and Uncle Duke Marsi by letter—tonight."

"On Christmas day," said Taranto, to be testy, but Anna would not presume upon the sanctity of the Nativity. "Any other day, Milord," said she meekly, "and I shall see your wish fulfilled."

"I should like to discuss that with Your Highness' father," Taranto frowned. "Some details of the financial settlement will require his attention, and—frankly—as an orphan, I should like to look upon my new father's face."

"You shall do so, Milord."

"By Christmas?"

"No later than Twelfth Night—I promise you. And if Your Lordship receives financial satisfaction, and the date for our Nuptial Mass is set, may I ask a favor of Your Highness?" Anna could not have spoken more diplomatically or sincerely.

"Anything within my power," Taranto replied.

"I should like you to go to Naples and release Jacques Bourbon. Our Cardinal Uncle has assigned my brother Antonio to it, but he seems unable."

Everything Anna said this night flowed from almost motionless—and utterly colorless—lips in a limpid, uninflected stream. She was dispensing miracles and demanded their equivalent without emphasis or change of expression, so that the Prince remained unaware what this admission of Antonio's insufficiency cost Anna in her sisterly pride. Neither was the Prince attuned to appreciate the quality or the depth of Anna's surrender. Perhaps only Anna's God ever will know the degree of the self-imposed torment that brought her to this pitch. She laid her immaculate self, her soul undefiled, on the butcher-block for bargaining—as on a sacrificial altar—to force Taranto, he of all people, to come to Heaven's aid.

Unaware of any consideration other than his own will and confidence, the Prince replied, "I undertake to free Jacques Bourbon for you, Highness, as soon as we are married. I could not leave Paliano before that—could I?"

The question caught the Vestal unprepared. Now that truce had been reached with her Lord, she wished not to join battle again. Her eyes fell. She moistened her lips with a tongue as pale as they. "No, Milord," said Anna.

CHAPTER FOURTEEN

CHRISTMAS LASTED TWELVE DAYS at Paliano, one of them Holy, eleven for revels, one day for Anna, eleven for her worldly kinsmen. On the second of the looser days, Duke Paliano, Duke Marsi, also Lodovico Colonna Count Palestrina, and Antonio (an elder one) Count Zagarolo, all turned up at Paliano with their families and army enough to protect them on the road.

"What did I tell you?" Andria gloated to the Prince. "Anna never fails."

Taranto was beginning to get that prickly feeling too, every time Anna spoke about the future. It was not as if she foretold events but more and more as if she controlled them.

The Colonnas had come at last, to do the Prince honor, and every one of them was dressed to kill. They wore jewels that had been in the family since before the Hohenstauffens, and some new and some borrowed ones too, but Giovantonio's vanity was to greet them in his exile's weeds. The only concession he made to their splendor was to permit his hair and beard to be crimped, at the insistence of the Duchess and under her direction. "I want them all to see how pretty you are," she whispered, and adopted such an exaggerated air of proprietorship over His Highness, to advertise her conquest, that no one believed it *bona fide,* least of all her husband.

Our Del Balzo cousin upheld the sartorial honor of the cabal by turning himself out fit for a coronation, but the nurse-Maria was none so eager to parade her relations with his elegant self. Only in private did she—and Anna too—declare that Gugl looked like an angel.

Impossible—as well as useless—to describe that gaudy brawl, but there were highlights. Lorenzo-Onofrio in velvet—and a necklace!—made Andria's eyes pop, and when the chronic poor-mouth presented Gugl with a pair of diamond studs, the recipient staggered in disbelief. A few hours later, when Duke Paliano discovered the tailor Aranda still on the premises, still snipping and stitching, he let out such a howl of anguish that Andria offered to return the studs, and—on my honor!—Colonna accepted them back.

The obvious reason for this massing of so much lordly Colonna manpower was to overawe Taranto and Andria, to keep them from riding too high a horse now that Duke Paliano professed himself ready to talk figures, to fix sums and dates beyond recall, but in that the effort failed. Hardly a male among the Colonnas left a mark on the memory of this meeting. No more were any of their women or children exceptional. It is a mortal wonder their husbands and fathers could tell them apart. Only Anna could call each one by name and recite their relationships without hesitation.

Early on, the party split into three—the youngsters, the Ladies, the men—each group making its own holiday, with scant commingling even at table and Mass. The Colonna males remained slippery and the New Year was hard upon them before the Prince and Gugl got all heads together, cornered beyond alibi, and reasonably sober.

Crash! Into Taranto's opening gambit rode Rinaldo Orsini from Tagliacozzo, the same who had married Anna's favorite Cousin Cat, her "tear-sister" who had given her the vase. Cousin Cat was not feeling weepy on this visit. Her spouse was riding to War and she with him, but the War they were riding to was not against Braccio in Rome, and they cried aloud their need for Colonna arms to help them. The Prince could not but suspect Colonna connivance, that this most annoying interruption had been arranged to defer his marriage settlement and postpone the attack upon Braccio. That collusion seemed so obvious and undeniable, through the first noise of the pair's arrival, that Taranto's rage temporarily blinded him to his own best interests. Andria made matters worse by chortling triumphantly, for the second time, "What did I tell you? What Anna prays for Anna gets."

"This is a fraud," Taranto growled.

"No fraud," said Andria. "This is Cousin Cat whom Anna loves above all people else. She has been after me to take her to visit Cousin Cat ever since I got here."

In support of Andria's assertion, the two girls were clinging together in supernal but unreasonable ecstasy, and in a moment—without leave or the slightest formality—they withdrew to be alone for confidences no others could comprehend or share. "To have a good cry in their tear bottle," Gugl guessed.

"Bosh," the Prince exploded. "Does a Commander carry his wife into the field—but no army?"

Rinaldo Orsini was wearing full armor—and a fine figure he made—but as far as could be seen he was attended by no more than eight or nine men. Speaking with tempestuous passion to his Colonna neighbors who were his wife's kinsmen, the youth's need explained Caterina's presence at his side. It was her mother—the sister of the Dukes Paliano and Marsi, sister also of Cardinal Oddo—who had called him to her defense, to save Piombino for her son Prince Giacomo II. Those satanic Appiani uncles of Giacomo were attacking—thus unseasonably—hoping to gain possession while the larger powers were too distracted to stop them, or—by their clangor—to divert Cosimo de Medici from support of Cardinal Oddo in Constance.

Varri and Emmanuel Appiani were desperate men, and the Colonna Dukes were not unaffected by Rinaldo Orsini's appeal. After all, it had been the Dowager Princess Paola their sister who—almost single-handed—had swung the Medici money and the Florentine ballot to Oddo's side. She had a vast claim upon them for aid if Piombino were now truly threatened.

"Do you doubt it, Milords?" Rinaldo Orsini whipped out a document purporting to be his mother-in-law's cipher. Anyone could see that it had been penned in frantic haste even if one could not read it.

"Is it not strange," Taranto put in, "that Her Highness Paola has not called upon her brothers directly?" His manner was openly scoffing, and he turned that skeptical eye upon the Colonnas as well.

"Our letters from Piombino are often intercepted," Duke Paliano lamented. "I do not doubt that Paola did write to us. This cipher is genuine—and urgent."

"How can you doubt me, Cousin?" Rinaldo Orsini faced the Prince squarely. "I pray your assistance too, in the name of the blood we share."

That claim was real enough, but not so proximate as to give Taranto a twinge, in the present state of his mind. "I could ask as much of you—against Braccio," he countered, "if you be a good Orsini. But where are your arms?"

"My army has marched ahead of me," said Rinaldo. "I plan to overtake it in Bracciano."

"Bracciano!" Duke Paliano winced at the sound.

"Bracciano!" the other Colonnas echoed sourly.

Bracciano was the seat of Carlo Orsini, a Roman of the Romans.

"Must you tie up with Carlo?" Paliano grimaced. "Is he going to Piombino with you?"

"Carlo has ships off Civitavecchia. It would take too long to negotiate free passage through Siena."

"But—*Carlo!*" The Colonnas screwed up their faces and shook their heads. "If you let Carlo Orsini into Piombino we'll never get him out."

"He is my cousin and my brother-in-law. I trust him," said Rinaldo simply.

"The greater fool you," growled old Duke Marsi. In Colonna eyes, the biggest mistake Count Tagliacozzo ever had made was in giving his eldest daughter to Carlo Orsini for wife. That was the real reason—and not lack of finery—that had kept Anna and the others from attending Cousin Cat's wedding. They had not gone to Carlo's wedding either.

"If Your Highnesses have ships to carry my troops——" young Rinaldo broke off significantly. He knew they had no ships. The Sforzans in Ostia had burned every Colonna bottom.

"Are you sure the Sforzans in Civitavecchia haven't burned Carlo's vessels too?"

"I am not sure," Rinaldo admitted, "but I am going to find out, and if there is no shipping for me I shall march through Siena without lief. Our Madonna Paola has called on me for help—and I am going to her any way I can get there and the fastest way I can get there. Will none of you come with me?"

Duke Andria—most touched of any there, perhaps because he knew it would please Anna—truly wished to volunteer, and he called for a word aside with Taranto to press a nearer relationship between Rinaldo Orsini and the cabal than the one already mentioned, aye, a closer kinship than Rinaldo knew. "He is Marino Marzano's first cousin—on his mother's side," said Gugl, and the Prince almost crushed the speaker's instep with his heel.

You ken the menace. Rinaldo Orsini knew well enough that Marino Marzano was his first cousin, but nobody outside the cabal was as yet aware of Marino's defection in the cabal's favor, and the Marzano Countess of Tagliacozzo—Rinaldo's mother— would be the first to denounce the convert if she learned he had switched sides on his father Duke Sessa.

"How-wow-wouch!" Gugl howled. "I wouldn't let it out!"

"Whoa-up," Taranto almost moaned, for this running down the Marzano line had brought to mind—at last and belatedly— still another enormously significant reason for keeping Rinaldo Orsini buttered up. "Do you know who he is?" the Prince whispered fiercely.

Foolish as the question sounds, Duke Andria answered, "No."

"He is my Archbishop's kid brother."

Gugl spatted his own forehead in punishment for having remained obtuse so long. "Of course he is!" he admonished himself, and to recover lost ground sang out, "Happy New Year, Cousin!"

Neither Taranto nor Andria ever had met this youngest of the Tagliacozzo Orsinis before this, but his elder brother—another Giovantonio—had been given the tithing of the Archepiscopal See of Taranto by King Ladislaus, to irritate one of the Popes and to hold the strongly fortified border town of Tagliacozzo loyal to the Regno. That was the importance of this bellicose boy to the cabal now. At the time of the Archbishop's appointment, he and Rinaldo had one brother older than they—Orsino Orsini, heir to their father's title—but Orsino had died interim, leaving the Churchman in direct line to inherit Tagliacozzo. It's a sad thing to say, but that circumstance made Cousin Cat's spouse very close indeed to the cabal's heart. Since man is mortal, and Canon Law forbids an ecclesiast to hold a worldly title simultaneously with Church dignities, the time must come when the elder Orsini brother would have to decide between his Archbishopric and his County. If he chose to keep the sweet thing he already had in Taranto, then this sprout, Rinaldo Orsini, was the next Count Tagliacozzo.

"Happy New Year, Cousin!" the Prince echoed, and went on, "You speak very nobly, Cousin Rinaldo, and your motives do you great credit, but let us consider the matter calmly. I do not think the Appiani brothers stand a chance. Florence is committed to the protection of Madonna Paola and Giacomo II in Piombino, and Cosimo de Medici is committed to Cardinal Oddo in Constance. This flurry of Varri and Emmanuel is not going to change anything. They will be put down."

"You're right they will, Cousin," Rinaldo flashed back, "for I shall put them down."

"More power to your arm! I wish you every advantage." The Prince smiled his most winning smile. "But you see how it is with us. We have to get Braccio out of Rome."

When one is young and eager and launched on a course, what is less welcome than sagacity to the contrary? Taranto never did entirely surmount the poor impression he left that night with one he had reason to woo, and the Colonnas shared in Rinaldo's malesteem by hiding behind their well worn objection to bearing arms by the side of Carlo Orsini. They would not go either. "Summon my wife," young Orsini commanded. "If you will not help us we must do it alone."

Cousin Cat and Anna appeared together, and added their impassioned appeals for aid to Piombino, but to no avail. So that—even in the dark of night—the brave young married pair rode off to their War alone, as they had come. The *status quo* at Paliano was in no way altered save that Anna's heart was annealed even more closely than before to that of Cousin Cat.

As Anna waved them out of sight she pictured herself in Cousin Cat's saddle, and determined to ride by the side of her spouse to *his* Wars, come a day, but her Lord in this vision kept the visor of his helmet closed so that Anna could not see his face, whether it was Taranto or Count Nola.

Too late that night—the Colonnas said—to take up the topics of money, dates and reciprocal commitments appertaining to Anna's marriage, but they agreed to meet with the Prince at the earliest next day, and by noon he had the four leaders assembled. Zagarolo and Palestrina might as well not have been there, but the childless, piratical Giordano Duke Marsi had several memorable features. He was older than Cardinal Oddo, actually, and so should have been head of the family, but Giordano always had been glad to let Oddo run things because the Cardinal did it so well. "Oddo got the brains and I got the gout!" he told Taranto, slicing a chunk from a new spice-sausage he had lately received from Venice. "I want you to taste that and tell me—I think the bulk of it is ground up Turks—but see if you can identify that seed they put into it."

As fast as his leeches could bake the pains out of him at one end, Duke Marsi could take it in faster at the other. All through this session, which lasted the rest of the day, he was nibbling, nibbling, nibbling. Politically that did not matter—his faculty of speech was scarcely missed—because Giovantonio did most of the talking.

Because of the icy condition of the Alps, the Prince would wait forty days for his bride.

Because of his exile and the difficulty of gaining access to his regular incomes, the Prince wanted the first payment of 3000 ducats in cash, to be handed over to him the day after the wedding. The balance—in four equal payments—might be half jewels, half gold, at the Colonna's discretion.

Giovantonio re-engaged himself to fulfill the contract as drawn, and further pledged them, that if Jacques Bourbon had not got out of San Vincenzo interim, he, Milord Taranto, would make that his first order of business after the wedding.

The session was utterly congenial, too congenial, in fact. Such questions about the Prince's Sicilian and Aragonese connections as might have been embarrassing were asked with apologies, and his standard answer of record—that it was all for Uncle Oddo—was accepted without cavil. If the Cardinal nursed any doubts along those lines, certainly he could resolve them within forty days.

Ah, that is where the boys were lax. They let those Colonnas get away from Paliano without any clear understanding—and no documentation—of what would happen if Cardinal Oddo had not replied in forty days.

Ten, twelve, fifteen of those days went by without sight or sound of a male Colonna. They might have gone *en masse* to Piombino for all the cousins knew. Andria brought the question to Giovantonio's attention as the two noble youths stood in the smithy on the farm, watching the swords and mail pile up. Hammers on anvils punctuated the problem.

"I shall marry Anna on fifteen February whether Oddo has replied or not," said Giovantonio.

"Big talk," said Gugl above the din of the armorers, "but I don't think you can. You couldn't make Anna kneel at swordpoint—and if you do—Paliano won't give you the money unless Oddo has said he should. What do we do then, carry off the furniture?—or hold the Duchess for ransom!"

Taranto puzzled a while. "You think they're stalling."

Del Balzo nodded. "The Colonnas are waiting to see whether Bourbon gets out of Joan's clutch in Naples before Alphonso d'Aragon takes Sardinia—or vice versa. It's a race.

They know you have a foot on each horse, so you'll be riding the winner—either way. You planned that, of course. I don't know how you could see so far ahead, but that's why you are the Man of Destiny and I'm just your stupid cousin."

"The smartest cousin of them all!" laughed the Prince, clapping Gugl on the shoulder. "And I'm not as wise as I look—I'm just lucky. I couldn't foresee this race, as you call it."

"You were wise enough to tie up with the Chiaramontes—you got Diomede Carafa into Alphonso's navy."

"O *that*," Giovantonio grinned, "that was just to protect your property in Sicily."

"Phttt! You were wise enough to plant Raimondo in Serjianni's family—and to send Antonio Colonna into Joan's bed."

"I didn't send him."

"You knew that Antonio Colonna would do anything Raimondo asked him to do."

"Well—yes. I didn't want to 'throw Raimondo to the lions'—as you once said—without a rope to climb out on. Serjianni won't treat Raimondo like he treated Ottino as long as Antonio Colonna is on hand reporting everything that happens to his father."

"That's what I'm saying. You have such a firm hook in both parties that it doesn't matter which wins. You win. And you sent me up here—into the Louis II camp—because of Aunt Alix and Baux."

"You came here of your own accord!"

"You are a genius. I have done nothing but stumble around."

"You brought Marino Marzano into the cabal—the greatest stroke of diplomacy since Ladislaus died!"

"I didn't do that. It was Serjianni's Antonio—and Quito."

"You were smart enough to trust Marino when he came to you. You captured Avellino. Your fanatics swarm upon the walls of Rome—and you have arms planted all over The City."

"Anna started the Masons for Christ."

"YOU won Anna for us!"

Guglielmo waved all praise away. "It's Anna we've got to talk about. How do we make sure you get her—on fifteen February? The Colonnas are making no preparations for the wedding."

"Anna's trousseau is ready," said Giovantonio wryly.

"She can wear that to the altar with any man."

"I don't think they could make her marry any man but me. Anna has very fixed opinions on the subject of marriage."

"She has indeed."

Nobody had told the Prince about Anna's childish wish to marry Raimondo Orsini. Nobody but Anna could have explained it fully, and she had not yet exchanged any confidences with her second spouse. The others—such as the Duchess—never discussed any disturbing topic that could be avoided, and Duke Andria was positively fearful of raising the issue. He—more than anyone else—was superstitiously and holily determined that nothing should interfere with their union.

"The only Colonna who could make Anna renounce you would be Oddo," said Andria. "If he spoke—with Heavenly authority—she would obey. That's why we have to get you two married *before* the Election. Oddo won't have Heaven's authority—with Anna—until he is actually Pope."

"He won't be Pope until Bourbon is freed. The Sorbonne won't cast their ballots."

"And that's why the Colonnas are stalling! They're breaking their necks—and Antonio's back—to get Bourbon out so that Oddo will be Pope before Alphonso takes Sardinia and Corsica.

You have them terrified that you will go over to Alphonso—taking Anna and her dower with you."

"Not so loud, Gugl. That's just what I mean to do." Taranto never had stated that in so may words before to any man.

"That's what I was afraid of," said Andria.

"Afraid? We cannot lose."

The Del Balzo could not swallow all his objections. "Gian, the Colonnas and the Council have read your heart. They know that you and the Chiaramontes are never going to defend Yolande against Alphonso, and so—they are not going to give you Anna and her dot unless we force them to. How do we do that?"

Waving both hands to either side around them at their armament, the Prince said, "By taking Rome."

"Without Colonna help?"

The weather, the holidays, and fading memory of the Virgin's Visitation, had slowed down the Masons for Christ. The repairs to the walls—although substantial—were not thorough enough to restrain a determined tomcat, and all the caches of arms inside The City were either on Colonna property or well known to the Colonnas.

"We might still surprise Braccio with an attack," Guglielmo grinned, "but it wouldn't come as a shock to Anna's folks. And they outnumber us—four to one."

"I wouldn't think of moving upon Rome without Colonna help," Giovantonio smirked, "unless we had—say—Sforza, or Carlo Orsini on our side."

"O, not the Orsinis," Andria pleaded. "Sforza, yes. I can treat with the Commandant of San Angelo, but Cardinal Oddo would ride a broom straight here from Constance if he found out you were dealing with the Orsinis."

"Or we might make Braccio an offer," Taranto suggested, and not in jest. "He'll be wanting strong allies—when the Pope comes home."

"We might."

"How much help could we bring up out of the Regno—in a month?"

"Let's find out."

In a week they found out that no help whatever was to be expected from Nola. That horse—of Taranto's double mount—was not running in very good form.

Erri came to Paliano with a groaning burden of warning and blackest prospects. On no account was the Prince to venture into the Regno to try to keep rendezvous. Traps were laid for him everywhere, and Count Nola's own household was a maggots' nest of Caracciolo spies. Only a token fragment of his wife's marriage portion had been paid to Raimondo, under plea of Serjianni 's poverty. True or not, the liar's rede ran that Francesco Orsini—being a Roman—had required payment in advance before he smashed Sforza.

Whoever had paid Francesco Orsini had got his money's worth. That was the only bright ray on the Regno's horizon. The blow to Sforza had been severe, especially in his stores, and Sforza had retired into the Ruffo country where he was organizing a cabal to murder Serjianni. Raimondo had not yet joined that movement, not only because his wife read all his letters but because—*I am using the Crown to help Antonio Colonna deal with Aunt Joan, and in that I have Serjianni for an ally. Serjianni would like to let Bourbon out, and bids me hold the Crown until Joan consents.*

Poor Antonio has NOT got Salerno yet, nor any other County to call his own, and he is losing weight so fast in the Royal Exercise, we may have to exchange him for Urbano Origlia or see him carried away by the next wind.

"I have also private conveyances for Her Highness the Princess Anna," said Erri hopefully, "if I may see Her Highness, please."

That was permitted, and Tomaso escorted his comrade to Anna's feet, attempting to act the sponsor.

"O, I remember Erri," said the maiden. "He is guarding my dear brother Antonio, are you not Erri?"

"I am—as I can, Highness. He is much with the Queen."

"Yes, I know. Do they have long talks?"

"All night, Highness."

"She listens to him?"

"Every night, Highness."

"All night, every night!—and still she will not give in? Such wickedness is beyond belief."

"He asks you to pray for him—a little harder—an it please you."

"O, I shall try."

Tears filled Erri's eyes. He seemed unable to visit Anna without crying. "The Lord Antonio is no thicker than two straws, Highness. He's a Christian martyr, that's what he is."

"You must see that he eats, Erri. I assign you to it."

"Yes, Highness, I'll do it, 'though I'm not much on cookery."

"When you go back I'll give you some persimmon compote to take to him. Antonio loves that. And do you see the Countess of Nola? Were you at the—wedding?"

"I was Captain of His Highness' Guard—and stood no farther off than *that*. I had a new costume with real gold on the shoulder and two——"

"Was it a beautiful wedding?"

"Beautiful, Highness, like I say. All the men had new costumes—but I had real gold—"

"What is she like?"

"The Countess?—she's a horse of a woman!"

Tomaso sunk his elbow into his comrade's ribs.

"What did I say? I said horse!"

"A big woman?" Anna interposed. "And do they have any children?"

"Well, not yet, Highness. They only been married a few months."

"I shall have four children on my wedding day!" said Anna proudly, as if, indeed, that should teach the Countess of Nola her place. "You must take Her Highness some compote too, with my compliments."

"Aye, Highness!" Erri encouraged his idol, fully expecting to carry back poison. "You had best give it me at once. I start back within the hour."

The next in, on the shuttle from the Regno, was Quito, out of Avellino, who brought the cousins more encouragement than Erri had. The citizens of Avellino were so content under the new government that Marino Marzano could spare Riccardo and 200 lance! Quito brought money too, the first of the tax-take under the present Del Balzo regime. It was not a great deal, because the astute Marino as Governor was reserving a dollop for Serjianni and Joan, to carry out the color of loyalty to their impoverished suzerainty.

"What a man, Marino!" the Prince exulted. "Didn't I tell you he was the best acquisition the cabal had made?"

"How is Ettore?" asked Gugl.

Quito winced. "It's a pity to watch him eat—but his head is clear. Can't chew—no jaw—no teeth. They make up a kind of mush—and poke it down his throat—like he was a goose."

"Can he make himself understood?"

"Riccardo understands him. I can't. It's a kind of wheeze and grunt. *Ughsh, ughsh*, like that—but he can write."

"See that he gets all the women he wants," said Andria sadly. "Pretty ones."

"Pretty ones, Highness? That's not so easy. Some girls—even not so pretty—get sick when they see him. And he can't see *them*, you know."

"I know. It doesn't matter whether he can see them or not. Ettore likes pretty girls—get them for him—as many as he wants. Tell Marino those are my wishes—and tell him to make Ettore Castelan of the citadel. That is an order."

Not to be outdone in generosity by his cousin, Giovantonio sniffed, "And tell Riccardo to stay there. You bring back the lance, Quito. A man has to have somebody to talk to."

Their plan at this time was to inform upon themselves, cagily, to Sforza's lieutenant in San Angelo telling him where the Colonnas had hidden a certain few of the caches of arms in readiness for an uprising, and to give the same information to Braccio too, thus precipitating a clash between those forces, calculated to draw the garrison out of San Angelo to battle in the streets. The Tarantine army was to lie in wait for that exodus, and—under Duke Andria's command—to rush the bridge and gate when the defense was at its weakest and much excited to preserve its soldiers already sent to the caches.

Reason dictated that the Braccians, outnumbering the Sforzans, would be able to drive them out of The City, and that the retreat would move toward Ostia as soon as the defeated found San Angelo closed against them.

As the Braccians pursued the fleeing Sforzans toward the sea, Taranto was to enter Rome from the north with the Avellino lance and occupy Braccio's headquarters, man the bridges, and eventually the gates. Whether the walls could then be held against the tricked and ousted would depend upon the temper of the Roman cits, including—most especially—the Colonnas and the Orsinis. Belike those classic rivals would lay into each other, leaving their properties a prey to Braccio, who would be quicker to that plunder than to waste himself at the impossible task of trying to take San Angelo.

As Tomaso always said, however, "We need more men." What was wanting was a force at Ostia to take advantage of the tides of battle there. If the Sforzans in the citadel at Ostia came out to the defense of their brothers, this wished-for force should attempt to occupy the place. If the Sforzans did not come out, then the dream-force should prevent the fugitives from entering, or cut off the Braccians from return to Rome, as that might fall out.

To provide themselves with at least that one more contingent from the Regno, the Prince had applied to Malizia Carafa Duke Maddaloni, his confrere and associate in love for the Aragonese.

No response had been received from Carafa by first February, two weeks before Gian's proposed wedding date, when Quito spoke so touchingly of Ettore's condition, and Quito's opinion was that Taranto's courier never had got as far as Maddaloni.

"Since Sforza's army was scattered, his officers are all over the place. You can't go to an inn or a Bush on any road without bumping into a little clutch of them. They're talking to the people—the commonality—telling them to arm, organizing a grassroots revolution. They came to Avellino—we caught some there. Ruffo sent them to waylay us because he still thinks Milord Marino Marzano is on Serjianni's side. There's Sforzans in Maddaloni too. And I'll bet your man ran afoul of some of them—going or coming. If Your Lordship wishes, I can stop at Maddaloni on my way back, and see if the Duke has your message."

"Do that," Giovantonio eagerly agreed. "Explain our plan to the Lord Malizia. Ideally his men should come by sea, landing by night on the south bank of Tiber. We'll wait for a sign that they are there before we trip the trap.

"Go, Quito! You are dear to me as a brother."

"Before you go," said Tomaso, "come with me and be blest by our Saint mistress—but mind your tongue. One damned curse out of you and I'll knock your muttaphurking head off."

Thus the third of the unholy quartet was initiated into Anna's charmed circle, and Quito, no less than Tomaso and Erri, was awed to the soul by this virgin in the flesh.

"It's Her Highness Anna's prayers that saved Milord Ettore," Tomaso boasted, but Anna chided him. "You must not say that, Tomaso. Everybody has been praying for Ettore. It would be vanity to think that my prayers had been singled out."

"All the same," said the soldier, "he's got a lot stronger since Your Highness took him up. He can hear a little now—if he can't see yet."

"Then we must all pray for his eyes," said Anna.

"O, Highness, no, please," Quito protested. "Please don't pray for his eyes back. If Milord Ettore could see what he looks like—he'd do away with himself."

"Is it so sad? You wring my heart."

"It's that sad Your Highness would puke to see him. Stronger stomachs than yours have turned at it. But we do all we can to keep him comfortable. There's one strumpet's got so used to him—she can sit for an hour fanning the flies off."

"Do you have many flies in Avellino?" asked Anna.

"Millions," Quito answered, and subsided under Tomaso's glare.

"Ask Her Highness to pray—about Maddaloni—to make your mission successful," the dictator directed.

"What is your mission to Maddaloni?" asked Anna.

"It's a secret, Highness," Quito apologized. "I don't think the Prince would like it to get out."

"Never mind, then," said Anna. "God knows all our secret wishes—and grants those that are good for us."

Anna was not yet aware of the newly forming campaign against Rome, which would force her family to buy its way back in, using herself as collateral, but after Quito had left

Paliano, Duke Andria paid Her Highness a call with a view toward enlisting her for the duration without letting her know exactly what she was getting into. He said merely that steps were being planned to insure the celebration of her Nuptial Mass on fifteen February, and her prayers for success were the last assurance needed.

Anna was genuinely surprised to hear the question raised. "Is there any reason to doubt——"

"Your father is making no preparations. He has not said where the Mass will be given—in the church at Paliano—the chapel here——"

"In the chapel—as I understood—the Prince desired a quiet wedding."

"But the village will celebrate. The people will feast—yet no stores are accumulating—and the Lord Duke is avoiding us. I have not seen your father since Twelfth Night."

"Why should Father avoid you?"

"Perhaps because he has no new advices from the Lord Cardinal."

All the sincerity that was in her pierced Andria in two shafts from her great brown eyes as Anna said, "What are you telling me, Cousin Gugl?"

"Only what I have said. The wedding day approaches and nothing is done. We do not hear from His Serenity—and your father avoids us. The Prince is disturbed—and we are taking steps to assure Your Highness' marriage on the date agreed."

"What steps—are you taking?"

"We are strengthening our armies—bringing in more men. We have still to take Rome."

"Would His Highness force me to the altar?"

"He would enforce his contract—with the Colonna family. We want your help. Will Your Highness take the vows—in the chapel—if your father and your uncles do not attend the Mass?"

"No, Cousin. I could not. I will take no vows without my father—without Uncle Oddo's approval of the date. You would not ask it. The Prince would not ask it. I shall send for Father at once."

Anna sent for Father, but—this time—Father did not come. He was not to be found in Rome, and he was not at Marsi either, and neither was Duke Marsi.

Giovantonio and Guglielmo rode, with a sufficient complement of men, to Palestrina and Zagarolo and a score places else belonging to the Colonnas, but no responsible member of the family was available to them anywhere. Nothing could have been clearer than that the Prince of Taranto was getting the Colonna run-around again.

On fifteen February, Quito was known to be only somewhere midway between Avellino and Paliano with his body of lance, and still no response had come from Duke Maddaloni, so Rome was spared a bloody broil that day. Battle was joined in the castle at Paliano, but there only words and tears were spilt. The mothers refused to coerce Anna or the priest to go through the ceremony under present circumstances, although the cousins made plain to their ladies that this was the end of their severally friendly and familiar relations. Tears fell aplenty, and recriminations, but the Duchess and the nurse-Maria presented a united front and held it.

Taranto desired Anna to admit him to her apartments, when all else had failed, and this was the first time he ever had done so. They had spoken together, at table sometimes, in the garden, politely, distantly, with rigid reserve, but not since he crashed through it to his romantic debacle had the Prince entered Anna's door.

The maiden did not debate a moment or give herself a qualm about admitting her disappointed spouse. "Certainly His Highness may come in," said she, supremely confident of the rectitude of her position, of God's Grace and of the Saints' protection. As a further defense, both mothers, the old chaplain, and Duke Andria trailed after the Prince into Anna's sitting room.

Taranto bowed, but bent no knee. "Signorina."

"Milord ... Please sit down."

"I shall not be long saying what I have to say."

"Stay a little—and we shall understand each other."

"Today is our wedding day."

"I am sorry for the delay. I do not understand it—but His Serenity must have some very good reason for not answering our messages. He will explain—as soon as he can."

"I ask you to come with me to the chapel and become my wife, as your father has articled. You, at least, may fulfill your part of the contract."

"My conscience forbids, Milord. It is not God's Will. And if we act contrary to God's Will we suffer for it all our lives. I beg you to excuse me. I am not disobedient. When I am Your Highness' wife you will never have occasion to complain of me. Your will shall be my law, your commands, my life. But in this I must obey the voice inside me which says, 'Wait—this is not the time. Wait for the Lord Cardinal's command.' I must wait, Milord."

"The voice you hear is the voice of Satan bidding God to wait upon his whim."

"Say not so, Milord."

"I do say so. Whilst you wait, your brother fails at his mission—and fails in his health. Whilst you wait—Bourbon waits in his cell—the Council upon him—and God upon the Council. Must the Lord God of Hosts remain without a Vicar on Earth because YOU are so willful, misguided and stubborn?"

"Gently, Cousin," Andria murmured. The rest of the witnesses all were in tears, but Anna needed none of their help.

"You cannot shake my faith, Highness," she said calmly. "I see now that God is keeping Jacques Bourbon in prison to thwart the evil designs of Serjianni. Antonio never should have tried to do anything that Serjianni also desired. I never should have offered my prayers for it—nor you your sword, Milord. When Serjianni is beaten and punished and stripped of his power, then Jacques Bourbon will go free."

"Marry me today and I make that my first mission. The one leads straight to the other."

"I cannot—without my father. I beg you to be patient."

"I have no more patience left, Highness. I call you to witness that I am here and ready to keep my engagement now. If I never return, no one shall ever take me to task for it."

"O, stay a little, please! I do witness it. I know that Your Highness keeps his every engagement. Do sit."

"I have other engagements to keep now. You will excuse me."

"If I must—then be excused. I had wished to ask about our future—where we will live—what it is like—"

Taranto had left the room.

His cruelty, the affront, the unanswered questions, were not the cause of Anna's quick, hot tears. She wept because she had displeased her Lord and knew no way to quiet his anger against her.

Paliano became a living tomb after that. The cousins went to the farm to sleep with their troops. Anna seldom saw them, but only—at rare intervals—Tomaso, and, later, Quito. Those two came without Taranto's knowledge, slipping away to receive

Anna's absolutions for sins they had not committed, to partake of her goodness as if it were truly the pure, sweet water of life.

Neither of them, I think, ever betrayed a secret of their master's to Anna, but through their goings and comings and unguarded remarks she knew when the seizure of Rome was imminent, and when it was postponed again, then hot, then cold, then off, then on. No other events of the spring so much concerned her, but most of the reasons for the ups and downs were purposely concealed.

Anna blamed the Masons for Christ—faithless noddles—for failing to complete their noble task, but Duke Maddaloni was more largely and more immediately responsible for the plan's failure. When Carafa finally was reached by Taranto's messenger, His Elegance decided not to send the requested army to Ostia, for good and sufficient reason.

A great deal more than assassination of Serjianni was comprehended in Sforza's flourishing cabal, and it got steadily worse. The rebel-Constable had perforce to attack the Queen's troops, commanded by Sessa and the Caldoras, because they were defending Serjianni by Joan's order. At the same time, the birth of a child by Polissena Ruffo to young Francesco Sforza was hailed by the insurgents as an augury of such significance that it split off all Covella's kinsmen from "Baby's" support.

The Caracciolos, under Serjianni's patronage, were then farming every monopoly in the Regno, methodically stripping the people of everything they owned, prying the gold out of the tradesmen's teeth, and still the Crown was pressed for funds to pay the armies of Sessa and the Caldoras. Day by day Serjianni must lay on heavier and heavier exactions, thereby fanning up revolution within Naples itself.

The ringleader, rabble-rouser who had Naples seething was one of those precious friends of Urbano Origlia, either the

President of the Dyers Guild or the Captain of the Latrine Seggi—by name, Mormile—and he was hand-in-glove with Sforza.

Mormile began by accusing Cardinal Oddo Colonna of holding Origlia prisoner in Constance, and—at a signal from the Sforza *cum* Ruffo forces—Mormile presented Her Majesty the Queen with a screed purporting to be three demands of the People which must be granted as the price of their obedience and civic tranquillity. *Item*—banishment for Serjianni! *Item*—the recall of Urbano Origlia from Constance, no part of him impaired. *Item*—immediate accommodations with the Council at Constance in regard to Jacques Bourbon. As warranty that these demands would be met, Mormile required physical possession of Antonio Colonna, who would not be harmed but only held as hostage and released in good health as soon as all *items* were fulfilled. Failing that, the People declared a Republic, with Attendola Sforza as their defender, and the city gates would be opened to Sforza's armies as soon as those armies could get there.

Sforza's demands were more reasonable. All he insisted upon was the exile of Serjianni and restitution, in the sum of 24,000 ducats, for the stores he had lost to the Roman Francesco Orsini.

Duke Maddaloni was not contributing one ducat toward that extortion and not wasting a solitary one of his plush knights in the line with the unpaid starvelings who were holding Sforza back. The Carafa armies were well distributed to protect the family's personal property, and would not be spared for the cabal's Roman venture until Mormile could be scotched and Sforza tamed.

Malizia advised the Prince to leave Braccio in possession of The City, and to use *his influence* with Cardinal Colonna to have Origlia sent in chains to Maddaloni.

Because of the threat to Antonio Colonna, all Anna's seniors attempted to keep that from her as long as possible, but Maria gave it away by a screaming nightmare in which the Neapolitan rabble parboiled her eldest son before her eyes.

If Anna had been asked again after that to go to the chapel alone with Giovantonio, she would have gone, to save her brother, but she was not asked. If Father had any letters from Constance that spring, they did not come through Paliano, and Lorenzo-Onofrio himself was not seen once in the months of March and April. It was as if Anna's importance to the fate of nations and the healing of the Schism had suddenly come to an end. This world would go its sinful way with greater ease—and swifter—if she never married Taranto. Her elders appeared as unmindful that Antonio was being carried to his destruction as that Anna never would have four little girls of her own to play with.

By first May, Paliano was a very Purgatory. The Duchess and Maria were almost as desolate as Anna, moping from room to room, not caring to hunt or to entertain, never mentioning new dresses. Aranda had escaped from Mother, anyway, early in Lent, and returned to Braccio with a hair-raising story of having been kidnaped.

This was the lot of Woman, then, to sit and wait and wait and wait for her menfolk to look in upon her, a day or two, from time to time, between their diplomacies and their Wars. The latest word from Cousin Cat was that she too had been relegated to this sterile manner of existence. She was cooped up in Piombino while Rinaldo Orsini and Giacomo II were in the field against the elder Appianis. No more was required of any Princess than vast, nay, limitless patience, to endure and to pray.

Then the courtyard at Paliano was filled with music, one day, and shouting! Certainly someone had reason to rejoice. Anna stepped on to the balcony, looking down, and Maria and the Duchess came running too—and beheld what must be a dream. The Prince and Father together!—the Dukes Andria and Marsi embracing! Several other Colonna uncles and cousins, Tomaso and Quito and the Paliano town band were there augmenting the cheers, crying, "Joy to the bride! Hail the Princess of Taranto!"

"What is it?" asked Anna, breathless to know how the stubborn-hearted men had been softened. "What has happened?"

Taranto, drunker than any of the rest, sailed his cap high-high—into the air and shouted, "Louis II Duke d'Anjou is DEAD! DEAD! DEAD!!!"

A rum thing to crow about in the bosom of the Colonna family, was it not, Milords?

The Colonnas did not like it either. The men with the Prince were celebrating the Cardinal's sanction of an immediate wedding, which had come in the same letter, but they stopped cheering, at Giovantonio's shout, and shook their heads uncomfortably. Anna's momentary flight of pleasure was shot down in midair. She Crossed herself, whispering, "Holy Mother, forgive him."

It was true, however. Louis II was dead, poisoned in Paris by the Duke of Burgundy, because Louis—twenty-five days previously-had poisoned the Dauphin.

"The night my stepfather died," the Prince went on increasing his unpopularity, "I heard him say—'Louis II will never be King of the Regno.' Ladislaus said that to my mother. And—he *won't!*"

The young man would have been more discreet if he had been more sober, but—conversely—if he had not been so pleased with the event, he would not have been so drunk.

"Yolande d'Aragon is Regent of Anjou. Louis III is barely fourteen years old!" The Prince turned to Duke Andria and slapped his back by way of congratulation. "It will be six years at least before we have to worry about poisoning HIM!"

Anna turned away, and silent as a wraith re-entered her apartment.

"What's the matter with her?" asked Taranto.

"You have offended her, Cousin. This is her wedding day—and you have come to her jubilating over the death of a Prince." Not even Andria knew that this Prince—now dead—had the figure of an Archangel in Anna's fancy.

"I apologize," said Giovantonio thickly, but Anna was not there to hear. Anna was praying for Louis III, now more than ever the true heir to the Regno.

In Taranto's defense, be it said, that Cardinal Oddo also was relieved by this turn of events. He was sorry for Yolande, and regretted his own loss corresponding to hers, but—undeniably—this simplified the life of the next Pope enormously. It removed Yolande as a contender for the crown of Aragon by depriving her of any fighting power, at least—as Giovantonio said—for the next six years. That left the formidable Alphonso undisputed in his sovereignty over Aragon, but the Cardinal was fortunate in having for son-in-law the man of all men best able to cope with this King's contentiousness.

Let the Nuptial Mass be celebrated instanter if not sooner.

Yolande's newly weakened position was further salubrious Colonna-wise in that it reduced the grand total of physical opposition to removal of the Curia from Avigon. Oddo would be coming home to Rome the sooner now, in fact, he might find it unnecessary to set up in Avignon at all.

Give the Prince of Taranto and Duke Andria every aid in ridding Rome of Braccio and Sforza at the earliest. Do not let the Colonnas be conspicuously in command, however, until Jacques Bourbon is freed.

Then came the one specific restriction upon Anna's marriage. The Mass was to be celebrated and the 3,000 paid, but Taranto was not to bed his bride, not to take her from her home, until Jacques Bourbon was freed and reigning in the Regno co-equally in harmony with Joan.

"That is to say, *never*," said Taranto, "but we'll have the wedding ceremony all the same."

The Duchess and Maria went to dress Anna in her gown upon which Aranda had lavished a fortune in pearls. Both mothers were weeping like cut vines, but Anna, dry eyed, asked, "Why do you cry?"

"It's just a shame—a sin and a shame," Maria sobbed, "that HE won't dress up! You so beautiful—and him in those rags! A fine memory for a bride!"

"We are exiles," said Anna, sharing her husband's ostracism for the first time. "Perhaps His Highness would prefer to see me—in something plainer. Will you ask him?"

"We'll ask him nothing! *You* are going to look like a bride!"

Anna submitted to that, but still the older women wept, and the Duchess attempted to explain what it was that Anna—by the Cardinal's benignity—would not have to do for some time. "You don't have to be afraid, dear."

"I am not afraid," said Anna. "If I were not so sad for the Duchess d'Anjou—and her children—I should be very happy."

"That's what I mean, dear," the Duchess floundered. "There isn't going to be anything to be happy about—until later on."

"What Mother is trying to tell you," Maria chimed in, "is that you are going to stay right here—in your own bed."

"Alone!" said the Duchess.

"He is not to touch you."

"You will be married—but not—*married*."

"Let us say no more about it," said Anna, and she walked through the ceremony like a woman of marble.

Taranto was rigid too by that time, and buzzing in his fuzzy head was the notion that his bride's gown was familiar. "Where in Hell have I seen that dress before?" He could not recall—and so fell asleep, quite alone, because Duke Paliano remained in the castle overnight for their conferences next day.

MR. THAYER INTRUDES

VILLON NEVER BURDENS his text with explanations or arguments that do not apply directly to the persons who lead him, eventually, to Lisa. Sometimes we could wish for a few words of evidence in support of his more controversial assertions, but they are not there. It is not his purpose to convince anybody of anything—except the sublime rectitude of the Signora *della*Gioconda, when he comes to her—so that every reader is at liberty to take or to leave his occasional, offhand, almost blithe, accusation of murder.

In a single sentence the poet-spy points the finger at Louis II d'Anjou for poisoning the Dauphin, and at Duke Jean of Burgundy for retaliating by poisoning Louis II. As a matter of fact nobody ever was brought to trial for either murder, much less convicted, so that what we have here is nothing more than the expression of well informed opinion.

God knows the writer has logic on his side, and Duke Burgundy openly and loudly amplified the charge against Louis II while that Prince was still alive. This Dauphin who died on 4 April was the second or third of the King's sons to be carried off in a manner called "premature", and Burgundy asserted that Louis II had arranged all those deaths to clear the way to the throne for the younger and only surviving son, who was betrothed to Marie d'Anjou, daughter of Louis and Yolande. The motive was there all right.

Moreover, the youngster who then became Dauphin—named Charles, like his father—had been living for several years in Anjou's household and remained in Yolande's possession.

When one considers the pressures upon Louis II, exerted by the understanding between the now defunct Dauphin, Burgundy, the Emperor and Henry V of Britain, who—aside from Anna Colonna—can doubt that Louis II struck down the Dauphin?

Guilty or not, Louis survived only 25 days, and so it was perfectly natural for popular bruit to blame, or to credit, Burgundy for striking.

The flurry over Cousin Cat and the Orsinis of Tagliacozzo puzzled me for a time. The incident recounted is so obviously portentous and significant, yet the mainstream of Anna's life which the narrative follows appears to flow away from her tear-sister for a number of years. It is only when the pattern of the whole is before you that the marvel of its intricate weavings is revealed in its wonderful unity, and—yes—its economy too. No scene, no word, is wasted, believe me. You will remember Cousin Cat and Rinaldo Orsini.

CHAPTER FIFTEEN

I<small>T WAS THE PRINCE</small> who had the larger headache in the morning, but his pride was to conceal it in a military manner, putting on a show of strength and competence to impress the Colonnas with his position as the new *de facto* head of their family. He called them into council to hear the master plan for occupying Rome, and let be known that he expected the 3,000 to be paid within 24 hours. If Duke Paliano had to ride into The City for the money, Taranto was determined to ride by his side lest Lorenzo-Onofrio disappear again.

Surprisingly, the gold lay on the table when the conference assembled next morning, thereby revealing that the castle of Paliano held hidden resources if one but knew where to look.

As men of the world are wont to do, they made a jest of this transaction, speaking not very far off the true thoughts of their minds, but exaggerating, burlesquing and laughing more loudly than their sallies warranted, each to convince the others of his genuine good heart, with a view toward disarming all suspicion in preparation for the kill to come at a date.

"You didn't expect us to give up that cash so easily, Milord, confess it!"

Ho-ho!

"Well, no, I did not, Your Highness. And I suppose if I reach for it now—you will chop off my hand."

Ha-ha!

"Reach for it. Take it. It is all yours. Every ducat is clipped—and those that are full weight are spurious."

Haw—haw—haw!

"O, I will not take it up at once. I know it is Milord Paliano's heart's blood. Let him look at it a little while longer."

Eventually they got down to business, and the cousins presented their strategy for recovering the Vatican, Ostia, *et al.*, revising their former plan only in those parts where the Colonnas were to have been stabbed in the back. Now—on the table at least—Paliano and his Captains all became unsung heroes.

Andria was granted absolute command, as pleasing to Uncle Oddo, and even the gouty Marsi took pleasure in accepting an active but obscure post. "There's twenty good years ahead of me, and I was born to die in the saddle!" he boasted. The spirit of aggression was that high in all Colonnas now, now that Oddo's homecoming was in sight.

The Prince, of course, was the keystone, capstone and cornerstone of the edifice they erected. His, to free Bourbon, to extricate Antonio—alike from Joan who was draining his life and from Mormile the Neapolitan demagogue—and, finally, to convert Alphonso the Atheist to Christianity.

"How many men will all that require?" the Prince asked Tomaso.

"Twenty," said the soldier.

"So many?" laughed Gugl. "I could do it with three!"

"The other seventeen are to take Antonio's place with Joan," Taranto countered, and sent Tomaso to the farm to select their company.

A bee might have gone straighter, but as Tomaso traveled it the route to the farm lay through Anna's apartment, now become the seat, Court and throne-room of the Princess of Taranto in exile. Hat in hand Tomaso knelt at her bedside, wishing her joy of her wedded state, pledging his life in defense of her happiness.

"You are my first defender, Tomaso. I shall never forget that." Anna gave him one slender hand. "And now you are off to save my brother!"

"Give yourself no concern for it, Highness. In Naples they have a saying, 'One revolution to eight earthquakes, and the quakes come five a day.' It's no real danger, Ma'am, as you'll see when you get there."

"Does the Prince say I shall be coming to live in the Regno soon?"

The Prince had not said, but Tomaso knew the terms laid down by the Cardinal. "On my honor, Ma'am, I'll get Bourbon out of gaol before we're a year older, so you can give His Highness an heir."

"O, yes! And you too must keep an eye out for a baby boy. Will you be in Taranto?"

"Soon or late. We go first to Maddaloni."

"Look for one wherever you go—and perhaps we can give His Highness a son before I come there to live."

"Does Your Highness say so?"

"That would surprise him."

"Aye. It would that."

"Look hard, Tomaso, and I shall pray for you as I never have before. And you must pray too. Pray for little Louis III d'Anjou to grow up and become a fine King!"

"Ma'am?"

"Louis III."

"Aye?"

"Pray for him."

"Must I, Ma'am?"

"O, yes, Tomaso. Has nobody explained to you? If my Uncle Oddo must Crown Jacques Bourbon, he is going to keep his fingers crossed so that God will know he doesn't mean it."

"Do I hear my ears!"

"Yes, Tomaso, because as soon as Louis III is old enough, the Pope must Crown him King of the Regno in accordance with God's Will."

Solemnly Tomaso Signed himself as he asked, "Has Your Highness told this to the Lord Prince?"

"Not yet," Anna admitted sadly. "His Highness won't sit still long enough for me to tell him anything. But you can tell him—on the road."

The old soldier scratched his head. "Coming from me—he'll never believe it."

"He must believe it—or he may make some terrible mistakes. His Highness must smite Alphonso the Atheist!"

"Smite?"

"He must blast him from the face of the earth!"

"O, Highness, you had better tell this to Milord Taranto before he leaves Paliano. He has *everything* twisted."

"Do you think His Highness will come—to me—before he leaves?"

"I'll answer for that, Highness!—if you'll bless me now—the Prince will be here before you know it."

"O, bless you, Tomaso, bless you. The Virgin have you in Her keeping!"

Tomaso stumbled back to the conference room. The Colonnas were just leaving. He waited through adieus and sallies that seemed interminable, trying the while to frame his revelation so as not to get Taranto's gorge up. No words safe or soft enough came to mind, and so—when the Prince and Duke Andria were at last alone—the soldier flung himself on his face, prone, crying forgiveness before he had offended.

"What the Devil—"

"I beg Your Lordship, go to Her Highness Anna before we leave Paliano. Great matters hang upon it. I should not presume—but do go—without fail."

"I never intended otherwise," Taranto frowned. "Get off your belly and go choose your men." If too many of his bride's well wishers undertook to teach him manners and the humanities as applicable to Anna, they were likely to defeat their high aims. Giovantonio already felt as sorry for the child as one feels for a kitten accidentally trodden. The overtures of warning in Tomaso's approach made no impression whatever.

"Come with me, Gugl. I feel safer with you in the room," said the Prince, walking Andria toward the stairs. "Every time I open my mouth I offend her."

"She forgives you."

"Yes, dammit. I don't want her forgiving me. But—there I go again. You have the hang of her. She trusts you. That may be a good thing, too. If everything doesn't go hottso-tottso between us and the Colonnas, we may have to move Her Highness to Taranto. I assign you to it—now."

"You honor me," said Andria drily. "Let us hope no disaster makes it necessary for me to snatch your wife away from her home. That would be a test of any man's diplomacy—and I'm not sure I could measure up. You aren't planning any surprises for me, are you, Cousin?"

"No. None. But I shall feel so confident of your ability to do the impossible—if I require it—that I shall not hesitate to ask."

"Whenever you flatter me I am filled with dread. What do you think might happen?"

"Eh? We needn't guard against what I think *might* happen, it's the unexpected we have to prepare for. Be ready—any time—if you will, please, to drop your Roman labors and bring Anna to me, if I should send for her. Hello!—the mothers!—and crying still."

Maria and the Duchess sat in Anna's anteroom with her wedding gown between them. They were laying it away, perhaps to be worn by Anna's eldest daughter, eighteen or twenty years hence, and their emotion made appear that they had not stopped weeping since they decked the Princess in the pearly thing the day before.

"And now you are going!" the Duchess bawled, dropping the dress to hang herself on Taranto. "I'll never see you again. I know I won't. A beautiful thing comes into a woman's life—for only an hour——"

Giovantonio's hands, one on each of the woman's upper arms, had contracted steadily as she spoke until the pain was agonizing, paralyzing. Indeed, in another moment the bones must have been crushed if she had not stopped speaking to gasp her pain.

"Control yourself, Highness," said the Prince calmly.

"You—are killing me," Sveva groaned. "O, please! I will say no more. Ooo!"

Giovantonio let go the Duchess' arms and bowed to Maria. "Will Her Highness the Princess see us?"

The Duchess' arms dangled, and—indeed—felt to her as if they had been chopped off. As was said, she bore the bruises of Taranto's fingers for more than a month. The experience left an even more indelible mark on her memory, not only because she never could decide whether that memento was a mark of love or of some rather opposite emotion but also because she so often thought of Anna caught in that awful grip.

Unaware how cruelly the Duchess was hurt, Maria—wiping her eyes—brought Anna's welcome to her Lord and their cousin. The men entered the bedroom with tread adjusted to sick and holy places.

The pallid face with its twin furrows of pain between the large brown eyes had not been changed by marriage. Anna looked the same but her voice betrayed an upheaval and overturning, out of sight, but strenuous and still in progress. "My Lord," she said distinctly. "Cousin Gugl."

Taranto bowed but did not take her hand. Andria did, and kissed it. "How is your head?" he asked.

"Let us not speak of it. I wish to know My Lord's commands, how I am to address him. Will you not, please, Highness, sit this once in my room?—if only for a moment? I beg you. I wish to please you. O!" The Prince had sat. "Thank you, My Lord."

Guglielmo sat too. "If either of you wishes to send me away, you will have to tell me to go in so many words. I do not understand hints."

"Stay," said Anna. "You are my friend and you must help me to please my husband. I do not know how—and he is so strong."

"I am flattered by your concern—to please me," said Giovantonio. "It is not necessary to try so hard. Tell me how Your Highness wishes to be addressed."

"You may call me Anna except on formal occasions or in the presence of titled strangers, if it please you, My Lord."

"Thank you—Anna—that sounds like a friendly arrangement. Do you wish to call me *Gian?*"

"O, I couldn't, My Lord!"

"Then please yourself. The way you say 'My Lord' makes me feel very distinguished. But we shan't have the opportunity to address each other very frequently for some time to come, shall we?"

"How long, My Lord?"

Taranto tried to make a sensible estimate of the time his engagements would consume—but gave it up. "I cannot even guess. Perhaps two years."

"So long? I am so eager to see our children. I have gifts for them there——" In a row on the table, four ribanded boxes. "If Your Highness will be so kind as to take them. Tomaso can make room in his saddlebags. I put the name on each package."

Both men were speechless. They stared—and waited to be stunned again. They had only a breath's delay.

"I have taken the liberty of praying that our next child will be a son. Is that not right, My Lord?"

"You could not please me more, Anna. Your Highness is very good."

"And let me tell you," Andria put in once again, "what Anna prays for she *gets!*"

"Cousin Gugl embarrasses me, but it is true, My Lord—if I know what I am praying for. Right now I wish very much to help my brother Antonio, but I do not know what to ask for. Can you guide me, My Lord?"

"You must ask that he be delivered from his enemies."

"O, that I have done, but the Saints are so busy—it saves their time if I know his enemies' names and what they are plotting against him. Will you not tell me?"

"I shall have to find out first—in Naples—and write Your Highness a letter."

"Will YOU write me letters, My Lord?" The gift from him of the sun, moon and stars could have made Anna no happier.

"I shall write to Your Highness whenever I need Heaven's help against my enemies."

"If Antonio would only do that!"

"Perhaps I can induce him."

"You will see him, of course."

"I shall see him unless my enemies see me first."

"Serjianni!"

"To name but one."

"You will take greatest care, My Lord. You will not go to Nola?"

"If I must go to Nola, I shall take all the care I know how. And may I trust Your Highness will be praying for my safety?"

"Every hour, My Lord."

"Thank you, Anna," said the Prince tenderly. "As it seems to me, you and I are already working together, toward the same ends, as man and wife should."

A faint glow of color tinted Anna's cheeks in an area no larger than a cherry under each eye. "O, yes!" said she, tremulous. "Yes, My Lord—we are working together to see God's Will performed. I shall always tell you what Our Heavenly Father ordains—and you will execute it."

A finer working arrangement or a fairer division of their labors could hardly have been arrived at if they had been married ten years—still, Taranto sought to improve upon it. He arose and took up his wife's hand, saying gently, "And I shall always tell you what to pray for—in great affairs—and you, in strictest obedience, will convey my desires to Heaven."

"Until death us do part!" swore Anna, and pressed the Prince's powerful hand to her thin, chill lips in a kiss symbolic of her soul's devotion. "My Lord," she said.

Taranto was either so touched by Anna's pledge or so eager to get on a horse that he forgot the four gifts for their children, but Andria—to whom they were more significant, in contrast to his own sad experience with the Princess Maria—gathered them up in his arms, like a lackey, and followed his cousin out.

Thus the really knotty problem of succession in the Regno—under God's Will—was not even touched upon at their farewell interview, and Their Highnesses of Taranto parted with hopes high for the future they must share.

That night Anna began to menstruate for the first time, the thinnest trace of a trickle, amidst abdominal agonies that would have splintered an oak but did not bend her boyish frame. From then on her truly classical Headaches came only at the waning gibbous of each moon, between times, her health—her color—improved. The saying among her women was that marriage agreed with Anna.

They saw very little of Cousin Gugl at Paliano for many weeks after that. The troops moved off the farm quietly, going nearer to The City, strategically, and only a small garrison of Tarantines was planted in the castle to provide against Braccio's reprisals when the action against him should begin in Rome. That action was slow getting off the ground, and when it was started it stuttered, going by limps and halts.

For one thing, Braccio had executed most of his household staff after Aranda's return, so that Duke Andria could not introduce poison into the *Condottiere's* soup. Then, the Sforza Lieutenants of San Angelo and Ostia laughed at Andria's overtures for an understanding. They were feeling their oats because of their master's sensational recovery in the Regno, and could foresee no reason for reaching accommodations with any other Commander.

Their high and mighty attitude was well borne out by the frantic appeals the Colonnas were receiving from Serjianni and from Joan herself, pleading for troops and money to hold Sforza back. Only Sessa and the Caldoras stood between the raging rebel-Constable and the city gates, and he was coming closer all the time. The supplicants made their appeal trenchantly personal, plainly stating that if Sforza were not stopped, they would have no other recourse than to hand over Antonio Colonna to the mob.

That stopped the Tarantine-Colonna action against Braccio dead in its tracks. Old Duke Marsi was for sending—at least—Duke Andria and the Avellino lances to Joan's succour, and, incidentally, to Antonio's.

Guglielmo, of course, refused to go to prop up the tottering Strong Man. Besides—although this was not voiced in their wrangles—Cousin Gugl had to stay in the vicinity and keep an eye on Anna, in case her husband sent for her.

Duke Paliano tried to remain neutral, but—as always—his heart was only in home defense, and that was tantamount to agreeing with Andria, so nothing whatever was done. Marsi went back to Marsi and wrote Joan a sympathetic letter, and Guglielmo came out to Paliano, for the first visit in a long time.

He found the ladies exercised beyond reason by the imaginary menace to Antonio if he should fall into Mormile's hands, a menace which Andria always discounted in argument with the male Colonnas, but these soft-sided would not be convinced. They were not only praying for the boy's deliverance out of the Neapolitan cesspool-in-maelstrom but they had written a letter—a petition, rather, signed by Anna, Maria and the Duchess—to Cardinal Oddo, beseeching him to return Origlia to the Queen in exchange for their dearly beloved.

They pounced upon Gugl with their fears and fantasies the moment he was out of the saddle and would not let up.

"So much animation, Anna!" he exclaimed, truly rejoicing at the change in her. "You are a new woman."

"I wish I were a man," she retorted, "so I could ride to my brother's aid."

"Nobody is going to harm Antonio! He is every Neapolitan's most precious possession ... You are dressed for hunting, Anna. I am delighted. May I go with you? The Prince will be overjoyed to hear how well you are looking."

The older women had the grace to accept Andria's compliments to them, and Maria basked in his praise of Anna, but the Princess herself said only, "You too look well, Cousin. You have letters from My Lord? Has he seen Antonio?"

Andria had no letters from Taranto, he was forced to admit, and that information drained the color from Anna's cheeks. "We are frantic with worry about them both—in that terrible country—that awful War. Is there nothing you can do, dear Gugl? Does the fighting come near to Maddaloni? My Lord promised to write ..."

As last reported, the battle line was much nearer to the walls of Naples than to Maddaloni, but the women took little comfort from that. Asked Maria: "In what sort of place would a man like Mormile shut up Antonio—as hostage? If Antonio is so precious to them, they should treat him well, give him a house—and proper servants——"

"Antonio never will be handed over to Mormile, sweetest Maria," the Duke argued. "He is too valuable an asset to the Queen and Serjianni in their dealings with the Cardinal. They never will part with him."

"Then Sforza will capture him!" wailed the Duchess, and so it went, on and on, as they flew their hawks, as they played their tric-trac, as they dined, and even after they were in bed.

The night was hot. Nobody could sleep, and Anna had already wearied Heaven on these terrible subjects. Still they would not leave her mind. The first hungry or vindictive creature who recognized Taranto in the Regno would turn him in, sell him to Serjianni's executioners, and who but the headsman would know he was dead? If it happened in Nola, Raimondo would know. Perhaps the Countess of Nola would be Taranto's betrayer. Would either of them ever admit the truth of that to the Princess of Taranto?—or even to Cousin Guglielmo? One could only write to them and see.

The propriety of addressing her first spouse an inquiry after her second was itself questionable—Raimondo would be derisive—and yet, where else could one turn for a reliable word upon the fate of either husband or brother?

Anna slipped out of bed and—going softly, not to disturb her maids—sought Cousin Gugl's advice. His door was open, but he was not in his bed, nor was his man in the room. Ah, her elders —as usual—were continuing their conference on a subject so vital in her absence, behind her back, lest the hard facts give her a headache, but the day for such coddling was past. They were mistaken to shield her longer. As a married woman who had suffered much, she could bear the truth as well as any.

So thinking, Anna entered Maria's suite boldly, and thus for the first time caught her mother and Guglielmo peeling the onion. Moreover, Maria was groaning.

"Why do you do that?" Anna asked. "Why do you keep on if it hurts you?"

Neither party to the ding-dong replied for several moments. No more did they ease their hurt by stopping, or cover their heads in shame. They stuck to their knitting without dropping a stitch.

The light was dim, but Anna saw much more than she wished to, and turned away pensive, starting back to her own apartment.

Far from sorry for their object lesson, although it had been given inadvertently, Maria called out, "Your husband will make you know why—one day."

Anna turned, nonplused. "You were groaning."

"Aye, the Prince will make you groan."

"I shall never be so foolish," Anna contradicted. "Why should I?"

"The Prince will show you."

Anna realized that the threat was not empty. All these things the Prince would do, beastlike, as he had once rushed upon her with his bristling chin—if the Prince was still alive.

Again she started away, walking slowly.

"Anna!"

Again she stopped.

"You must never tell your Uncle Oddo that you saw us. Promise?"

Ah!—just as Anna had suspected, Maria was ashamed to be frittering away precious time while death stalked the Prince, untold dangers hovered over Antonio, Serjianni remained unpunished, Jacques Bourbon still in prison and Holy Church unhealed.

"I promise," said Anna, and left the room, drawing her robe tightly about her against the caress of the soft, warm air.

Someone was pounding at the barred gates—pounding and shouting with authority. Not Father—indeed—the voice could be Antonio's, and that was who it turned out to be.

Antonio in mail. Antonio with 40 horse. Antonio escaped from the Regno!—no, not *escaped,* exactly—come on a mission—but, O!—was this Antonio? What a change was here! Not only was he gone gaunt from the Exercise—that, everybody had been warned to expect—but whence his Lordly manner?

The castle was ablaze with light in no time—the entire household came flocking—but Anna did not tell her brother where to sit. He sat at the head of the table on his own initiative. "I am come to lead back every available man," said Antonio sternly, addressing Duke Andria most directly but taking the women-folk into this confidence with a beetled brow fearsome enough to still their objections. Actually he was practicing this speech and manner, since he must repeat the performance for his "father" and Duke Marsi.

"Sforza has Naples virtually under siege. The Colonnas—and their friends—must raise it."

"That is as startling a statement as any I ever heard," said Gugl. "In whose name is Sforza's siege to be raised?"

"In the name of Queen Joan II. I am happy to find you here, Milord Andria, for I bring you Her Majesty's pardon."

"Curiouser and curiouser," said the Duke, no more impressed by his pardon than by Antonio's vaulting airs. "Aunt Joan must really be up against it."

"Naples cannot stand a month. Unless our aid arrives before that, Mormile and Sforza will set up a Republic. All past animosities must be wiped out to save the Regno—to save the Throne." Antonio stood up and spread the fingers of both hands like fans, their tips touching the table before him. "To save MY Throne!" he said loudly, and waited for the gasp to go around the room. "Her Majesty Queen Joan is adopting me. I am to be her heir."

Naturally, the servants cheered, the children too. Not many Colonna boys ever had come home in the middle of the night—sober—with an announcement like that.

Andria did not cheer, for he saw that Joan's desperation had been pushed to the last extremity when she was willing to give away her Crown for an army. Antonio did not owe these fine prospects to the mark he had made as entered apprentice upon his kingly duties, nor yet to his father's imminent Papacy, but to the clutch of the People's hand at Superba's throat.

The mothers—notoriously unable to see beyond the length of their noses—ran from their places to kiss and embrace their preternaturally favored son. "King! Think of it! Antonio, King!"

Prospero proposed the toast. "To His Majesty Antonio I, of the Two Sicilies, Naples, Hungary and Jerusalem!"

Anna did not touch her goblet. "Does Uncle Oddo know?" she asked.

"Envoys are on their way to Constance with an articled agreement," Antonio replied. "Her Majesty promises to release Jacques Bourbon instantly Uncle Oddo blesses the Crown only unto her, not to them jointly, and—as Pope—he will also confirm my adoption, cutting out Louis III and all other pretenders."

Anna turned to a waiter. "Run to my bed and bring my rosary," she commanded. "It is under my bolster."

"Use mine," said the chaplain, removing his beads from around his neck, but Anna pushed them back. "You pray too, Father. This is going to take both of us."

Antonio's chin came up in an unaccustomed manner, for he never had quarreled with Anna, and to do so now was going to require all the kingly material in him. "Are you going to pray—for me—Anna?"

"I am going to pray for your soul, Antonio. Thou canst not touch pitch without being defiled."

Both mothers said something in the boy's defense but only Maria was understood. "O, Anna, Antonio will be a good King! Don't say defiled, dear."

Anna looked at their mother seated at the table, but saw her, instead, as she had been half an hour before, at grapple with Cousin Gugl, in that ludicrous position, groaning at their undignified gymnastic common to the lower animals. "Defiled," the maiden repeated, and turned back to Antonio. "Is Count Nola defending Serjianni too? Is he in arms?"

"Raimondo is in arms for the Queen. It is entirely incidental that Serjianni is her Minister."

"Do you—my brother—say so? What says the Prince my husband to all this?"

Antonio was not speaking like a brother but like the heir to the Regno, and Anna's unexpected opposition to his new role made the lad crueler than he was. "I have not seen the Prince of Taranto," he said, and went on with more heat than the accusations warranted, and getting hotter all the time, "He skulked around outside Naples a few days but never came inside the city, and now he has returned to his seraglio of concubines in Lecce and Taranto."

O!—what a prayer went up to Heaven then, from the Princess' heart of hearts! *Holy Father, do not place Antonio and My Lord in opposite camps!* Bad enough to have the brother she loved presume to the Throne of little Louis III d'Anjou, but worse—beyond measure—to separate her flesh and blood from the Prince to whom she owed every wifely duty. *Spare me that choice, Holy Virgin!* To take that decision, and then to live with it in all its consequences, Anna felt must be the end of her by physical dismemberment.

Oblivious of her suffering, unaware of its cause, Antonio was poking a hole in the air with a trembling, denunciatory finger. "We published his pardon—lifted his banishment—on condition that he return and fight for his country, just as we have forgiven Count Nola and Duke Andria, but your husband continues rebellious, and runs off to learn how many bastards he has accounted for. He does not even know."

Such words could have had no other intention than to hurt her, but Anna said softly, "A good father's first duty is to his family. I fear that the Queen has put a spell upon you, dear brother. I never saw you so before."

"You are sheltered here, Anna. You don't know what is going on."

"I am willing to learn—if you can tell me without shouting and without denouncing my husband to whom I owe every devotion. I know that the Queen is using you to get an army to save Serjianni. I know that if the Prince returned to Naples now his head would be chopped off."

"That is not true."

"Do not make yourself surety for it, Antonio. It would grieve me as much to lose you."

"Where is my father?" Antonio flung out. "I waste my time talking to women. Milord Andria, will you march with me?"

Gugl pursed his cupid's bow, and "No" came out distinctly.

"And do you say it is I who am under a spell?" Antonio flashed. "My sister Anna has you all trembling for Hell-fire! Well, her prayers do not frighten me. Prospero! Take me to Father."

"I don't know where he is," mumbled Master Melon-head.

That was simply Prospero's way. It did not indicate opposition to Antonio's regal pretensions. In fact, among Colonnas, Anna was quite alone in her stand against her brother's worldly aims, alone and very lonely. The picture of Antonio as Joan's heir was just too attractive for the others to relinquish, and they would not give it up in spite of Anna's warning that they were flying in God's Face. Both mothers said it was nonsense for her to pray for Louis III—a child nobody knew—when the Colonnas might have the Crown in the family in addition to the Tiara. If Anna could not make practical use of her religious gifts she was forbidden to pray at all.

In that, Anna was disobedient, continuing her supplications for the granting of other people's unknown desires, a singular medley of the carnal, the political and the sublime: but she had no letters from her Lord to give her prayers direction, no commands to execute for either of her spouses. They both had fallen away from her even before her blood kin. Her sisters, brothers and cousins in residence mocked her, even the servants grudged Anna their wonted attentions, and only Cousin Gugl—among persons she saw—remained on her side. Lamentably, he—once so firmly trusted for details of what to ask for—had lost credit in her sight for the swinish spectacle he had presented that night, just before Antonio came home, and Guglielmo knew not how to make amends. The subject never was mentioned between them, but it would not leave either of their heads, and so the innocent intimacy they formerly had shared was tarnished, corroded, if not destroyed.

One would think that events, as they followed swiftly—the trials and setbacks suffered by Antonio, his sponsors and associates—would have convinced the most stubborn of them that Anna was right, that they were combating the Will of God, but still they persisted in that mad course.

Antonio rode to Marsi first, confident of Uncle Giordano's support because of that friendly letter he had written to Queen Joan. Uncle Giordano did not disappoint, and together they approached Duke Paliano, but he refused to enter the race for the Regno without the clearest directive from Oddo.

Rather than return, a failure, to Superba, Antonio pushed on to Constance in person, leaving his family shaken if not shattered by divisions, and leaving Naples in such state that Serjianni had to be "banished".

Oyez! Joan's necessities could not wait upon such a long delay, and the only way she could save herself was by capitulation and compromise.

The ousted Seneschal went no farther away than island Procida, which lies in the Bay of Naples, and from that stronghold he continued to guide Joan's unsteady hand. By Serjianni's cunning, Joan herself—and not Mormile—admitted Sforza and his troops into Naples, and she paid her

Constable his 24,000 indemnity, so that he lost all his former interest in a Republican government. His troops restored the People to order.

To appease Mormile, the Queen swore, on her honor, that she had *sent* Antonio Colonna to Constance in exchange for Origlia, and that the outsized humanist might be expected to step off the next galley that arrived from the north.

One who never had shewn any aptitude for politics, or any interest in that art to speak of, that is, the Duchess Paliano, took an active hand in Antonio's cause, as his reputed mother. She went a journey to her kinsmen in Gaeta and Fondi—in the Regno—with the avowed intention of speaking with the Queen if possible, but Anna was not asked to go along, not asked for her prayers, so far was her fame decayed.

Alone as she was, isolated, ostracized, Anna did not feel sorry for herself but only for her family, running with such pertinacious blindness toward the pit of retribution. Not even when Uncle Oddo was Elected Pope at last could Anna believe that Heaven had relented, and—as appears—she was right. The Sorbonne had directed its delegates to vote, and the ballot was taken on Saint Martin's Day—whereupon Oddo chose to be called P. P. Martin V—but God's Hand still lay heavily upon the presumptuous, overweening Colonnas, because the Faculty forbade the Gallican clergy to remit one *sou* to His Holiness before Jacques Bourbon was liberated.

Nevertheless, the rest of the family considered that partial victory worthy of celebration, and every Colonna able to sit a horse foregathered at Paliano. To hear Maria you would have thought she was returning to Roman residence the next day, to be mistress of the Papal household, but Anna told her plainly that dream was vain. "Not even Uncle Oddo can live in Rome as long as he keeps trying to make Antonio King," declared the

Princess of Taranto, and she refused to leave her suite to dine with the family or to join in their merrymaking.

Duke Paliano thought this was the time to put an end to Anna's nonsense. She, after all, was the star of the occasion. Numbers of their relatives attributed Oddo's success to her prayers and her marriage, in combination, and—even more pointedly—looked to her and her husband to speed the Papal return to Rome and the restoration of Church revenues in full. They wanted to toast Anna for the past, advise her for the present, and make themselves agreeable in the hope of future favors.

Lorenzo-Onofrio did not, himself, credit Her Highness or the Prince with so large a part in progress to date, but he appreciated their importance to the Pontificate just beginning.

If Anna's prayers had been what they were cracked up to be, Alphonso the Atheist would not be—at that hour—making himself at home in Sardinia. The Aragonese were in full possession and the King had announced that he was moving upon Corsica at his own convenience.

If Anna's husband had been such a great man of his word as was pretended, he would have fulfilled his obligation in the matter of liberating Jacques Bourbon, so that the coarse sugar from France would already be rolling into Oddo's Apostolic Camera.

As Duke Paliano approached the familiar door to what had been the nursery but now was the Court of a Princess in exile, he hoped he could keep his temper and get Anna to the table without resorting to those recriminations, because both points remained at issue and his son-in-law was still the world's best and likeliest means of resolving them.

"Your head aches," Paliano began tactfully.

"Not my head, Father, my heart—and I fear it never will stop."

"You are a great Lady now—a great Highness."

"I shall always be your most obedient daughter."

"You will find—as you grow up—in Taranto or in Naples—that great Highnesses have often to do things they do not wish to do. No matter how your head aches or your heart aches, if the Prince tells you to join his guests—you must join them—and laugh and dance and sing, if need be. You must learn the responsibilities of your position."

"I know, Father."

"You must grow up."

"Yes, Father."

"Your illustrious family is here—and wishes to see you—your aunts and uncles and cousins. They have reason to rejoice and be happy. They wish to—to *thank* you—and to offer their good wishes."

"Those who love me have come here to my apartment. I have saluted twenty I never saw before."

"That is not the same thing. Everyone is asking—'What is troubling Anna? Is she too ill to eat?' I cannot go on making apologies. If you are my most obedient daughter, you will show that you appreciate your position and know how to be a Princess. Take my arm and let me show them that this house is not divided."

"This house is divided, Father," said Anna quietly. "That is what aches my heart. I cannot drink the toasts they are drinking. I can smile through pain—and have—many times—but I cannot celebrate blackest sin simply because I am a Colonna."

"What sin?"

"*What* sin! Ten thousand sins rolled into one—and you know them as well as I!"

"I know no sin that is being done here and I will not argue about it. I command you to do your duty—and leave these matters you do not understand to your elders—to your uncle who is Pope. Do you set yourself up to criticize the head of Holy Church?—and *me*, your father?"

"I ask only to be left alone—to make my peace with God as I may."

"No. I will not leave you alone. You must come with me— and *smiling*. You must tell your kinsmen that the Prince will free Bourbon—and bring the Atheist to obedience."

"I cannot."

"Cannot? You mean you *will* not."

"Cannot—will not—I make no distinction. I only know that I obey God's Will. God Wills that Jacques Bourbon shall remain in prison—and even that the Atheist shall have Corsica—to punish us for putting Antonio forward in the place of Louis III d'Anjou!"

There it was, Anna's message to the Colonnas. Lorenzo-Onofrio decided not to carry his daughter to the dining hall by force lest she shout that vicious dictum within the hearing of some who could not cope with it. He himself was able. "Do you turn against your own kind to excuse your husband's failure? Do you not know that he has cheated us? Luckily we have preserved you *intacta*. We have lost only three thousand—and that is all Taranto ever will get out of us!"

"What do you say?"

"I say that we will marry you to someone else—to a Commander who *can* free Bourbon and stop the Atheist—someone who has the will to do it!"

"I will not take still *another* husband, Father. You would condemn my soul eternally."

"Rot!" said Paliano. "You will marry whom you're told."

Anna did not reply, but she did not join the family celebration either, and the Colonna troubles continued.

What part of the Roman walls had been repaired by the Masons for Christ was knocked down again, by Andria and

Paliano driving Braccians out or by the same Braccians returning next day.

When Martin V tried to leave Switzerland, he started out
of Constance with a noble procession, as if to go to Avignon,
as he had promised Yolande Regent of Anjou and many others
that he would do. His plan was to turn left into a mountain pass
which would lead him eventually into Lombardy and the Duchy
of Milan, but his bad faith was smelled out and the Emperor
Sigismund escorted the Papal procession gently but firmly to
Geneva. There the Holy See was forced to set up housekeeping
temporarily.

Antonio Colonna was with the Pope in Geneva, and from that
base Urbano Origlia was sent to Naples, ostensibly to ship back
Jacques Bourbon. Neither Yolande nor the Sorbonne would permit Martin V to move another step until that was accomplished.

To His Holiness, in Geneva, Yolande brought Louis III to
be Crowned King of the Regno, and—by putting her off—Uncle
Oddo sacrificed the opportunity to be reconciled with Anna in
this life and to walk golden streets in the next. Cite all the eccle-
siastical authority you will to prove that Martin V eventually
ascended into Heaven, I give you his daughter Anna who said,
"Impossible!"

Came also to Geneva, the Genoese envoys of the Banca San
Giorgio, not only to plead their case as proprietors of Corsica
but to bid against the bank of Cosimo de Medici, the Florentine,
for Holy Church's business. No other account in the whole wide
world is so much to be desired by a bank, since even in the depths
of its poverty and degradation the Church has more money than
anybody else, magnate or King, Christian or Grand Turk. Even
without usury—which Canon Law condemned—the collecting
and forwarding of Holy Church's funds is the most profitable
work a bank can do if it has offices in many States and foreign

places, because in all those outland areas the Universal Church has its bottomless "poor" boxes and unfillable collection plates going like mad, and the changing of one State's money into the money of another State pays the bank a piece of every coin, no matter how small or large.

One of the many promises Uncle Oddo had to make in order to become Martin V was to give this money-changing business to the Medici, but the Banca San Giorgio could be much more troublesome than Cosimo, if it were cut out of the gravy entirely, and—beset as he was—the Pope decided to listen to the Banca's proposition.

No half-measures about them, these Genoese magnates offered to bring the Eastern Church—estranged for four hundred years—back under the tithing of the Roman Pontiff, and pointed to the Banca's strength upon Island Cyprus and in many other Eastern capitals as evidence that they and no other institution could possibly do this.

Just listening to all their arguments consumed a lot of time, and thus Martin V spent the winter in Geneva, waiting for Bourbon to arrive from Naples, and playing off one Orator against another.

The best offer the Pope had came from Visconti Duke of Milan, a plan devised to permit His Holiness to have his cake and eat it too.

Item—a Milanese army large enough to see the Papal household in safety across the Alps would be made instantly available, if—

Item—the Pope would bless Visconti in his ambition to absorb Genoa. Once Genoa was absorbed by him, the Banca San Giorgio would become automatically a Milanese institution, so that—

Item—the Pope might enjoy all the benefits currently being offered by those magnates without the necessity of defending the Banca against its sundry enemies, such as Alphonso d'Aragon.

Item—Visconti engaged to take over the protection of the Banca in all its outland possessions, Corsica, Cyprus and the East, without exception, the world over (and Visconti was the man who could do it), if—

Item—Martin V would make Milan the seat of Christendom, home of the Curia, his Vatican city, and Visconti offered to build Uncle Oddo a palace for his residence which should outshine anything that Rome had seen even in the days of the Caesars.

It sounded almost too good to be true, as—in fact—it was, but that did not stop Martin V from accepting the portions of it which were especially to his need, such as the army to escort him to Milan, where His Holiness and Duke Visconti could discuss the rest of those details at their leisure and convenience.

Visconti fell for that, and nothing remained but to await the spring thaws. The transfer from Geneva to Milan was scheduled to take place as soon as the roads became passable.

Martin V informed Duke Paliano to instruct the Prince of Taranto accordingly. If the Prince obtained Bourbon's release before May first, Bourbon should be brought to Geneva, if after that, to Milan.

Meanwhile, nothing that Taranto was doing appeared to have the slightest connection with Bourbon's liberation. From Maddaloni—where Giovantonio and Malizia Carafa understood each other very well—the Prince went on to Avellino, to strengthen old ties with the cabal's star convert, Marino Marzano. The renegade from Joan's communion learned, at last, from Taranto's own mouth, where the cabal was going, and was happy to be assured that he would lose nothing by going with it.

Although several persons who had seen Ettore, his wounds, and e'en lived with them, had attempted to prepare Giovantonio for his first beholding, still the actuality left the Prince incredulous, not only that a man so marred could continue to live but, more, that he should wish to. The Pappacoda recognized his Lord, however, from the tone of his voice, and gurgled—as you might say, "happily"—in greeting.

"What did he say?" the Prince asked Riccardo.

He said, 'Sire, I kiss your hand.'"

"Kiss!"

"It is his jest."

"Ho-ho," the Prince managed a strained guffaw, but took both Ettore's pale hands in his own. "By the gods, I kiss yours," said Taranto, and did so with much feeling.

Then, by stealth, and in defiance of all warnings, Taranto visited Nola, where he found Raimondo fast gaining the upper hand over his Caracciolo wife. The exile of Serjianni—although no farther off than Procida—had taken much wind out of the Countess, and the yellow-haired cousin had so far reduced the number of spies in his household that the Prince had already gone on to Andria before Joan was informed that he was in the Regno.

At each place their leader stopped, new cipher codes and signals were established for the cabal's secret communications, minute was made of the fighting strength, the stores and the gold, all things necessary for quick mobilization and sudden War.

In Guglielmo's capital, the Duke's mistress was lonely but uncomplaining, and she permitted Taranto to pleasure her because she knew that her master would be disappointed in her if she did not. The bastard—Francesco Del Balzo—had acquired a little sister from somewhere, but the Prince was too tactful to inquire closely into that. It was, after all, the Tarantine service that kept Gugl so long away.

Your son is a credit to you, Giovantonio wrote to his cousin. *Tall for his age, a swordsman already. I wish that I had fathered ten like him—or even one half so fine.*

In Lecce, Giovantonio found his brother Gabriel taking good care of their nurse, the Lady Maria. Leastwise, she was again pregnant, since being delivered of the Prince's daughter Caterina, and Gabe accepted the credit for the Lady's condition. Between them they were maintaining the heel of the Boot peaceful—if not very prosperous—exercising gentle dominion over Otranto, Castro, Nardi and Copertino. They shewed Gian their ledgers, how meticulously they forwarded the take from Copertino to Chiaramonte in Palermo, and presented to His Highness the richest local di Castro—a man in middle life—who was much smitten of the Lady and begged the Prince to make her his wife.

"Why, certs!" said Gian. "You could not make me happier. If you marry at once Gabe's offspring will be born in wedlock." For dower, the magnate's taxes were waived, which made him very happy, and that night the Lady Maria spent with the Prince for old times' sake.

The two little girls—Maria and Caterina—did not know their father from the ashman, but they kissed him obediently and accepted their presents "from your mother" with solemn gratitude. The gifts were bracelets from Anna's own babyhood.

"When shall we have the honor to welcome Her Highness?" the Lady Maria asked, but her guess was as good as the Prince's, he said.

At last and at length Giovantonio arrived home, letting the Tarantines know beforehand that he was coming, and for their delight he wore some fine things, and jewels borrowed from his brother. Old men wept and young girls sang, and their Lord's path was strewn with flowers. His "exile" was the subject of elaborate jest. Effigies of Serjianni and Joan were burned, singly and coupled, for Giovantonio's amusement. It were a shame to deprive the lower orders of their pleasure for the sake of secrecy. The royal arm never would be long enough to reach His Highness here.

The Princess Maria, attended by Taranto's two relict mistresses—the former *femme de chambre* and the Lady from Palermo—rode a mile outside the gates to greet him, with nurses to carry their babies, and a cheering multitude of cits and town dignitaries dressed in their holiday best.

The former Queen Marie-Luise by request of the Podesta, mounted a platform in the piazza and waited to greet her son there, with ceremony. It was all very pretty, and very sincere. In Taranto their Prince was already called Pope-maker, credited also with Serjianni's exile, and generally thought of as having renounced the Throne to spare the people of Taranto a War-tax. The public frivolities lasted a week.

In private, the Lady of Palermo—mother of Francesca—presented something of a problem. Half Catalan, half Sicilian, her blood was hot, and—unlike any of Taranto's other mistresses—she wanted him all to herself. She spit on Giovanna and found fault with Giovanna's child. When the bracelets were presented, she flung the one assigned to her offspring across the room, saying Francesca never should wear it, and threatened to scratch Anna's eyes out if she ever crossed her path.

Whether these idiosyncrasies endeared her to the Prince above his other mistresses is dubious, but they certainly got her the most attention. She was as jealous of the Princess Maria as of any other female and could not bear to leave her alone with her brother for a moment. Every time the Prince did get Maria aside to discuss her broken betrothal, in would pop La Palerma. In the end that nuisance served Giovantonio as an object lesson for his sister. "Do you see? Jealous people are all unhappy. You just make yourself miserable. Guglielmo loves you. He is dying for you. Will you not forgive him?"

"Yes, I forgive him," said Maria, as if she had done so long before, "but must I live in Andria with that woman?"

"Well, now, *that woman* is a very pleasant person—when you get to know her. I spent a day with her, coming through, and time just flew."

"What did you talk about?" asked the Princess. "The price of eggs?"

"So-ho! *There* you are hiding!" the Lady of Palermo burst in, and carried the Prince away.

Interruptions notwithstanding, a notary was commanded to draw up Maria's marriage contract, and Duke Andria was rebetrothed—*in absentia* and—when he least expected it.

The former Queen Marie-Luise had been badgered almost as much as the Councillors at Constance to get Bourbon out of San Vincenzo. She gave Giovantonio a great heap of letters to read from those ousted "French" Courtiers, all calling upon her blood-tie to Jacques as his last resource. "I suppose we ought to do something for him," said Marie-Luise.

"We shall," her son agreed, as if he acted solely at his mother's suggestion. He addressed the Pope in Geneva, stating that Bourbon's delivery was imminent, and that Jacques might walk out, a free man, if Anna—together with the balance of her dowry—were sent at once to the city of Taranto.

The reply, out of Geneva, was a good while on the way, and meantime the Prince shopped the Tarantine quayside for the fastest ships to be had. He held matched contests, and finally bought three vessels which could not be overtaken by anything else afloat (in those waters). These were manned and outfitted in pirate style, and the training of cutthroat crews was Giovantonio's occupation when—at last—the Pope's refusal came. Anna was not to move—and not another ducat would be paid—until Taranto had performed his share of the bargain.

With no more justification than that, the Prince sent express to Duke Andria, calling him back to the *Regno* with Anna and any part of her marriage portion that could be picked up. Then Taranto carried the Crown aboard the fleetest of his three corsairs, and sailed toward Sardinia for a heart-to-heart talk with his dear friend Diomede Carafa, and—mayhap—with Alphonso, Anna's dread "Atheist".

MR. THAYER INTRUDES

WAIT Now. It may be only my suspicious nature, but it seems highly probable at this distance—and in view of later events— that the plot to put Antonio Colonna on the Throne of the *Regno* must have begun earlier than this. Logic alone indicates that the concept originated with Cardinal Oddo in Constance, and that this was one of his chief reasons for sending Antonio to Naples and detaining Urbano Origlia in the north.

If that is true, the aim, the ambition, must have been in Antonio Colonna's head when he passed through Paliano heading south, but the MS does not even hint at it. I have tried, in my own mind, to rationalize Villon's arrangement of the disclosures, and I find at least three possible reasons why that motivation was ignored in its natural chronological sequence.

First, Anna received no hint of it at that time, and the narrative at this point is all Anna. The reader does in fact learn of Antonio's advancement simultaneously with Anna, somewhat dramatically, and it is her reactions to the intelligence that concern the writer.

Second, any insight Villon may have gained, at a much later date, into the authorship of the design to make Antonio King, and into the machinations toward that end, must have come largely from Antonio himself, who would—in nature—spare his father's memory the onus of originating the greedy grab. It would be much more like Antonio Colonna—and especially as he aged—to attribute the inspiration to Joan's love for him, but Villon will have none of that nonsense. The MS states that the proposed adoption was precipitated by Joan's necessity to defend herself from Sforza and the rabble, and I find no reason to question that, in the letter. It was indeed that necessity which brought Joan around to the Colonna point of view. Nothing in the text prohibits us from understanding that the question was already moot and much debated when the grip of the People's hand forced Joan to make the concession.

A third reason for Villon to pass over the plot at the time that Antonio and Count Nola were traveling together lies in the author's palpable liking for that gallant Orsini. As you must have observed, and will further, Raimondo Orsini is very nearly as large a hero in the writer's eyes as the Prince of Taranto himself, and it would not look at all well for that golden head to admit that the Colonnas had started diplomacies which Count Nola had not penetrated. That would be tantamount to saying that Antonio Colonna was the smarter of the two, and such an implication could not have been forced out of Villon on the rack.

The extra-dry personality of the poet comes up strongly in the wry, almost sardonic way he slips in the announcement of Cardinal Colonna's Election. If the reader is not paying strict attention he is likely to miss it entirely, and here again, the event—epochal as it was to the rest of the world—comes to us through the censorious eyes of Anna, colored by Villon's prejudices.

Those eyes and those prejudices may have been guilty of more distortions than I am aware of. I see the possibility that

Anna may have exaggerated the colossal stature of Yolande nee Aragon, Dowager Duchess d'Anjou, at the time of Oddo Colonna's triumph at Constance, and Villon may have blown up the part played by the Sorbonne, he being an old grad. You'll find other evidence in the MS that his alma mater was dear to him, and as a veteran of street broils between that student body and rival authorities of both Church and State, he adhered to the theory of supremacy for the Faculty. Naturally he would take this opportunity to add to its prestige.

Any number of experts will know more than I about Yolande's part in it. Did *you* ever hear that she was such a power in either French or Church politics after Louis II died? The only women who stand out in French versions of current transactions are the beautiful Bavarian wife of Charles VI—Ysabeau, called "the Queen"—and the Lady of Giac, another mistress to Jean Duke of Burgundy.

Ysabeau wants no introduction. If she, as Queen of France, missed any of the delights that Joan II enjoyed, as Queen of Naples, that is only because there were no French Carafas. The subtlest difference I am able to discern in their approach to their responsibilities is that Joan was a nymphomaniac and Ysabeau was merely an eager pushover, and giddy in the head. If Ysabeau ever had preferred one man above another, that was the Due d'Orléans, her husband's brother, and so, as Orléans left her bed one night, Jean Duke of Burgundy cut him down. That was some years back, but the deed was kept green by Charles Due d'Orléans, the orphan of Burgundy's victim. The boy had married a daughter of Bernard VII Count d'Armagnac, the Constable of France, and those two led a vicious party pledged to vengeance upon Jean the Fearless, but he was hard to catch.

More recently Ysabeau had amused herself with the son of that Salligny who had been taken to Naples as Jacques Bourbon's

"Constable". Now, the father was back, of course, one of Joan's exiles.

Where is the end of these interminglings? The widowed Duchess d'Orléans was Valentina nee Visconti, sister of Flip Duke of Milan: and the Lord High Advocate of the crazy Charles VI was Juvenal Orsini. I do not know Juvenal's blood kinship to Cardinal Orsini, Dean of the Sacred College and President of the Council of Constance, but it is hardly possible that he favored a Colonna for Pope.

As I say, any number of people can give me cards and spades in these French details, and I am only asking if Anna Colonna had built up Yolande d'Aragon's importance larger than it actually was. The French chronicles I have seen do not even name Yolande as the guardian of Charles VI, or of the Dauphin Charles, after the death of Louis II d'Anjou. Monstrelet, for instance, names the Constable d'Armagnac as the damnable reprobate in charge.

I should be inclined to accept the authority of the MS over that of Monstrelet in this particular, not only because Monstrelet is known to nod very frequently, but because Yolande d'Aragon was Count d'Armagnac's niece, as well as mother of the Dauphiness, and as such she might very well be attending to the domestic and maternal side of the guardianship whilst Count d'Armagnac was outdoors, on horseback, getting all the publicity. Monstrelet and Villon could both be correct on that point.

Naturally the Constable d'Armagnac is named. He and Charles d'Orléans had pushed Burgundy out of Paris and banished Ysabeau, in the name of the Dauphin, setting him up in the Louvre as Regent for his father. They sent Charles VI to live in a hotel.

That much is old hat and would not be worth repeating but for the fact that when Monstrelet does mention Yolande he opens to us a new reason for accepting her significance in Holy Oddo's Election.

The chronicler begins with one of his blunders, but he goes on to a rousing and sterling conclusion. He calls Yolande d'Aragon the "sister" of the Cardinal Duke of Bar, but he is mistaken. It is a very natural mistake, because the Cardinal Duke did have a sister named Yolande, and Yolande of Bar became the *second* wife of Yolande d'Aragon's father, thereby attaining the legal name *Yolande d'Aragon.*

Anna's Yolande, however, was borne by her father's first wife, Marta nee d'Armagnac, a sister of the notorious Constable. Marta died whilst Yolande d'Aragon was in earliest infancy, perhaps as a result of the birth, and Yolande of Bar reared Yolande d'Aragon with greatest love, a stepmother to be proud of.

Meeting a "Cardinal Duke" so soon after Villon has explained the quandary facing Archbishop Orsini, heir to Tagliacozzo, raises the question how Louis of Bar was getting away with it, and the answer is that he was one of Benedict XIII's Cardinals, Created at a time when his elder brother Edouard III was Duke of Bar. Edouard III fell at Agincourt, and Louis acceded to Bar unhampered by Churchly honors so nebulous. It was hardly worthwhile to resign a Hat which never had brought him a *peseta* from his Catalan parishioners.

The title had nuisance value, however, in dealing with Cardinal Colonna, because the voices of any Pope's Cardinals were pertinent to the Election, and the question, if the individual Cardinals should remain in the Sacred College after the Schism was healed was more often than not the price of their support. How much more had Oddo and Louis of Bar to say to each other concerning the throne of Aragon (if it be Yolande's throne?) and the so-greatly-desired resignation of Benedict XIII.

The doting stepmother of Yolande, long since widowed, was living with her brother in Bar, and to evidence their love, both drew wills naming Yolande's second son, Rene d'Anjou, heir to Bar.

As evidence of Oddo Colonna's satisfaction with the behavior of Louis of Bar at all points, Louis remained a Cardinal after the Election, and the elder Yolande was assigned the income of Bar for the rest of her life.

So, there we have Anna Colonna's Yolande—stepdaughter to the old, old Duchess of Bar, stepniece to a Cardinal who had just helped to heal the Schism, blood niece to the current Constable of France, mother to the next Queen, and mother to Louis III King of Sicily. She was in residence at the Louvre with the Dauphin and Dauphiness, and if she was not actually mistress of the household, who was?

If Anna was not justified in holding that Majesty so highly, her error is at least understandable.

What makes me doubt that either Yolande or the Sorbonne was so potent in the final ballot at Constance as Villon would have us believe is the certainty that the Emperor, back from Britain, had made clear to Cardinal Colonna that he must guarantee the Regency of France to Henry V and Duke Burgundy jointly. That was the agreement that removed the last obstacle to balloting.

Oddo's concession probably pleased the Lady of Giac very well, and even Queen Ysabeau, but it meant no good to Yolande—unless I have missed something.

CHAPTER SIXTEEN

T HE SUMMONS TO JOIN her husband found Anna in mourning for her official mother. The Duchess of Paliano had succumbed in Gaeta, of a malady unstated, and had been entombed there, or in Fondi. Nobody could say that the Duchess' death was another manifestation of God's displeasure with the Colonna family. It was no punishment to Lorenzo-Onofrio but only a vast relief, and Anna was as much hurt by their loss as any of Sveva's own children.

"I cannot go to Taranto until my mourning is over," was Anna's first excuse for postponement, and Duke Andria accepted it heartily. A month's delay would give him a fair chance to find some portion of the 12,000 ducats still due Taranto on his bride. It did seem a shame to appear before the Prince with only this reed of a girl singing Psalms to show for all their work, and Gugl recalled very vividly how 3,000 in gold had turned up there at Paliano, as if by magic, in the middle of a conference table. No doubt of it, the money was on the premises if one could but find the hidden spring.

Open negotiations with Duke Paliano for even a partial settlement, and for his free lief for Anna to depart, were utterly out of the question. Since the Colonnas had acquired the Papacy, and put one of their boys in line for Joan's Crown, they felt quite capable of carrying on from there without further concessions to the Del Balzo-Orsinis. Armed raids upon Rome had practically stopped, because their sole accomplishment was to make honest householders furious with the Colonnas. As a matter of fact, the widowed Duke Paliano had all but asked outright what Gugl was hanging around for.

"Believe it or not," said Baby-face, "I am waiting for an earthquake."

The nurse-Maria was not consulted at first, neither upon the location of the Colonna strongboxes nor upon the question of leaving Paliano in her daughter's company. While their mourning was deepest Maria must needs act full mother to the entire family, and that responsibility plus Anna's withdrawal from her confidence tended to make Maria a very poor ally for the work in hand: but no man can long keep such a secret from the woman he is sleeping with, and—besides—Maria several times caught her lover tapping walls, sounding wells, prying behind panels and trying the locks of chests.

"What have you lost?" Maria asked. "There's nothing in *there* but old candlesticks."

"Hmm. Gold ones? I may be reduced to that if I can't find the family coffers." Naturally, that led to full confession, to which Maria's objections were three: to take money would be stealing, even if it was owing; she did not know where any secret trove was; and SHE was not leaving Paliano if Anna did go, with or without her dot.

"O, yes, you will."

"O, no, I won't."

Debate had gone no farther than that when word came that the Pope had talked his way out of Switzerland by forbidding Alphonso to attack Corsica under pain of excommunication, and had actually crossed the Alps into Milan under Visconti's protection.

"If he has got that far he will soon be home," said Anna. "Let us wait a little. I have much to say to Uncle Oddo." No official expression had yet come from the Pope on the subject which had cut Anna off from her family, whether Antonio were to be King or not, and she hoped—with the help of Heavenly logic—to sway that pronouncement for the right.

They waited, but the Princess' expectations of a prompt arrival were much too sanguine. The Pope's promises which had got him his lift across the Alps were none of them in writing, and so the Duke of Milan—a very direct fellow—took the only sure means of collecting on his investment. He kept His Holiness surrounded with Milanese soldiers, for Oddo's "protection" of course, but with the clearest intention of detaining him in Milan until the Republic of Genoa and its soul—the Banca—had been brought to heel by Visconti's arms. The attack was already forward.

On his side, Martin V was in no particular hurry to leave Milan. Even if he could get away he had no place to go: Rome was in no better condition to receive him than it had been a year or two before his Election: and in Milan Visconti was paying the bills.

That is not to say that Oddo was idle. He spent four hours every day just cursing Serjianni. I hardly need tell you that Origlia had been unable to send Jacques Bourbon to Geneva, but he had sent a mincing kind of apology for himself, and for Mormile and Sforza, laying all blame to the charge of the exile on Procida. The suggestion was that Martin V deal directly with Sforza, since his was the power that prevented Serjianni from returning to Naples.

All very well, but Serjianni was still writing the Queen's letters for her, and in them he told with supreme confidence what he would cause both Joan and Sforza to do for His Holiness.

Sforza would be caused to evacuate San Angelo, Ostia and Civitavecchia, and to withdraw his claim to Benevento.

Joan would deliver Rome free and clear.

Sforza—at the Crown's expense—would be caused to force Braccio da Montone to disgorge Perugia, Assisi and all the other towns he had taken, back into Church's Holy Lap.

Joan would—further—confer upon old Giordano Colonna Duke Marsi, the Duchy of Amalfi and the County of Venosa, in the Regno, and adopt Antonio Colonna as heir, but ONLY after Martin V had sprinkled her Crown with his Holy Oil, and proclaimed her sole and only sovereign of the Regno.

Bourbon, his disposal, was not specifically mentioned in these despatches, any more than if he were already buried, and—indeed—interment might be necessary to clear the way for Antonio's adoption. No matter, the Pope agreed to everything, and sent Antonio by sea to Procida to say so, with only the one small proviso, that Joan sign Antonio's articles of adoption before her Coronation.

"Blasphemy!" cried Anna when these details reached Paliano. "That is not God's Will. That is infamous opportunism. Greed!—and all seven of the scarlet sins. Martin V is no Pope. Oddo Colonna is not my uncle nor any kin to me. I will not be a Colonna! I disown them all. Take me to my husband. I am ready to go."

If only Andria had been able to lay finger to 12,000 Colonna ducats, he too would have been ready to go—even without Maria—but the trove still eluded him, and so, in his turn, he asked Anna to wait a little.

"For money—yes!" said Anna. "I will help you look, because after I am gone they never will pay it—not the Colonnas."

They fairly took the castle apart, and Maria joined the search too, but with no luck. The look of it was that either the former Duchess had carried the liquid assets of Paliano to Gaeta (as she had her jewels) or Lorenzo-Onofrio had got very poor.

Then the "earthquake" Gugl had said he was waiting for struck Milan very close to Holy Oddo's head. That is to say, the envoys of the Banca San Giorgio got to comparing notes with Cosimo de Medici and Visconti Duke of Milan, discounting each other's paper from the Pope. So many promises to pay so much were in such patent conflict that His Eternity Martin V had to run for it, and only barely got to Mantua whole. From Mantua he thundered back his loudest condemnation of Visconti's attack upon Genoa, completely repudiating his agreement with the man who had carried him across the Alps.

Now, Mantua is nearer to Rome than is Milan, by a giant stride, and when Oddo took that step—bringing him closer by that much, also, to Maria—that set her quaking too. You'll excuse it, please, but a little bug was working inside the gentlewoman, one of Cousin Gugl's bugs, and while Martin V stayed in Mantua, it worked and it worked, and it grew and it grew, until there was no concealing from anyone but Anna that her mother was with child.

The greater Maria grew, the closer came the Pope. The Gonzagas of Mantua protected Martin V until he got his lies straightened out with Cosimo de Medici, then the Holy See moved on to Florence.

"That does it," said Maria. "Let's go."—but even then, her joining with the runaways did not bring illumination on that all-important point, where the Colonnas hid their money at Paliano. The three sadly prepared to leave without Anna's dot.

Little by little the women packed secretly as Andria gathered together what was left of the Tarantine army. It was no contemptible force, with Quito for lieutenant, and the Avellino lances; the danger was that so many men in motion would advertise their intention.

The ordeal of tearing up lifelong roots was especially hard on Anna. She never had known any other home and believed in her heart that she never would see this one again, never again see Cousin Cat, but she held pluckily to her resolution, and never blamed her decision upon God's Will. In fact, Anna was fearful that running away would not bring her favor in Heaven, and she trembled for herself in denying the sanctity of an Elected Pope: but whether she was following the Holy Spirit or not, It had departed this place, that much was certain.

They were ready to go, ready to fight their way out if need be, when Anna asked Maria, "Did you pack my wedding dress?"

Well, no, as befell. Maria had meant to—and so on—but it was not packed.

Unthinkable to leave without it, the horses must chomp their bits and paw the road while another chest was found to receive the garment, and more horses commandeered. The departure had been nicely timed to make the minimum uproar, to escape farewells, avoid alarm and delay pursuit. Special care had been exercised to send Prospero on an errand—lest, in weakness, his mother take him along—and the rest of the household was at siesta: but all these plans were like to be frustrate and set at naught by the getting of the gown.

It was folded in a box made of Eastern spicewood, on a rank of shelves deep in the late Duchess' wardrobe, where the two mothers had laid it by, the day after the wedding. All the more costly jeweled dresses had been kept there formerly, locked away from thieves. Maria shewed Gugl the box, and remarked, "If Sveva hadn't taken all her best things with her we might have collected some of Anna's portion right here."

That minded Andria to tug at the shelves, outwards, and that was the secret. Behind the shelves was a windowless, airless room full of gold. Luckily, Paliano had done his storing with method, and marked the stacks and tiers, for Your Worships know how long it takes to count out 12,000 ducats, even by tens! Siesta would have been over, Prospero returned, and the Hell to pay.

Bad enough, as it was. They were held up an hour, and one of the hostlers had ridden off to Genazzano or Palestrina to report the flight. Speed was of the essence, and yet more speed, because no defensible position could be reached before fall of darkness. Any clash that pursuit might precipitate must be a running fight, and for that kind of warfare Andria felt himself better prepared than any Colonna who could come after them.

The one paramount dread was that the enemy would be astute enough to hit upon the fugitive party's great tactical weakness. Between themselves and their nearest haven under cabal sympathy were vast stretches of the hostile Regno, to say nothing of the guards at the old border. All that Duke Paliano need do to bring disaster upon Anna and company was come up close behind and dog the party's steps without striking until some of Joan's customs officers or a body of Queensmen appeared ahead. What could delight Her Majesty more than to take the Princess of Taranto prisoner!

Three or four routes ran alternatively through Andria's head, to be chosen as necessity dictated, but all required that the border be reached and crossed in the night, and before pursuit had caught up.

Never flagging in his urgency for a faster and ever faster pace, regardless how it killed horses, Andria plotted every contingency and how to meet it, from hiding in the hills, to shipping out of Gaeta to Taranto itself, not forgetting that to encounter a force under one of the Caldoras might not come amiss.

As befell, the first Colonna to take after them was no Colonna at all but the mere lieutenant of Palestrina with about fifteen men who came only to confirm the hostler's unbelievable tale, and not even he caught up until the heavier gaited troop had passed by

Frosinone. Enough daylight was left to estimate well the small-ness of the overtaking contingent, and Duke Andria's maneuver was to halt ten of his hardiest at the roadside, leaving them there while the rest pushed on. The order to the ten was to prevent any of the Colonna men from either following or returning to Paliano with their information. The order was not obeyed to the letter. Two got away to return, but they did not get back in time to stir up further pursuit until it was futile, and the confusion of the Paliano household as it discovered its loss was so profound and absolute that no really dangerous body of Colonnas took horse until the next morning. By that time Andria's army had made camp, deep in the Regno, off the mainway to Naples, easterly, not far from Venafro, and Anna and her mother were asleep.

By that happy chance, the party was able to continue a little less swiftly but more carefully, bearing always eastward away from Naples, past Benevento at last, and into the Caracciolo coun-try. Knowing this way so well, the Duke brought his charges into Andria without another encounter worth mentioning, and the first person of note who was presented to the Princess of Taranto was the bastard Francesco Del Balzo.

I wish I might say that they hit it off, but the admiration was a little one-sided. Anna loved the lad, in Anna's way, but he stood in awe of her, perhaps because Andria would not let Francesco's mother eat at the table with these guests.

Anna stood the hasty journey beautifully, and Maria too, except, as the gravid lady said aside to Gugl, "If you had made me ride any faster Anna would have found out where babies come from right on the road!"

The child was still alive, however; they could feel it kicking, and Maria had another two months to go.

They were all well satisfied with their feat, getting away with the full sum of the contract, and the best part of it was that the

Pope could not afford to let Duke Paliano air the story or kick up a row. Too many people knew Maria's relationship to Oddo's children. It was just too scandalous—and laughable—for His Holiness to let it get out on him in those parlous times.

At their first dinner in Andria, the guests were introduced to a custom of Guglielmo's which Anna resolved to adopt when she become mistress of her own household. "What's new?" Gugl asked his Major, and the man would recite events of interest from all over the world. Some were none too fresh, but it's all news if you haven't heart it.

Item—Polissena Ruffo, wife of Francesco Sforza, and their infant child had been murdered. Serjianni claimed that Covella Duchess of Sessa had done it in revenge upon the Sforzas for leading the Ruffo family away from Joan. On the other hand, Covella accused Serjianni of doing it in revenge for being cooped up on Procida.

Andria's Major had no choice between the contenders, one was as capable of the deed as the other.

"That isn't a very cheerful introduction into the life of the Regno," Andria apologized to Anna. "I'm sorry that the first thing you had to hear was so—cruel."

"How were they murdered?" asked Anna.

"By poison, Highness," said the Major, "but Francesco Sforza, who survives, was mysteriously wounded."

"Haven't you something more cheerful?" the Duke prompted. "Where is the Prince of Taranto now?"

"The Prince is now at sea, Milord, reported to be returning the Crown for Joan's Coronation. He is supposed to be restored in his estates for this service."

Laughing, to divert Anna from the Coronation itself, Gugl said, "This is a wonderful country! Now, in Milan or Venice, if a man is exiled, the government takes over his estates and keeps his taxes and emoluments for itself or gives them to the exile's fortunate successor, but here in the Regno, the exile remains in possession, enjoys all his incomes, paying nothing to the Crown. The Queen has to 'restore' her exiles if she wishes to come into her fees as suzerain and sovereign! Isn't that a perfect arrangement? Anna—you are going to like it here!" Andria laughed boisterously.

"When is the Coronation to be?" asked Anna.

No date had been set, inasmuch as His Holiness had said that the articles of adoption—"making Your Highness' brother heir, must be signed first, and the Queen has not yet signed them, if my information is correct. Antonio Colonna is on Procida now with Serjianni, and I am told that they are going together to Florence to hand over the keys and passwords for San Angelo, Ostia and Civitavecchia to the Pope."

"My brother chooses excellent company," Anna murmured sarcastically, but her mother made no comment. The topic was moot, and if ten million words were spent upon it, Maria never would see eye-to-eye with Anna on the moral issues of Antonio's case: and since her son—HER son—appeared to be coming ever nearer to the Throne, she could not still the palpitation in her breast. No other gentlewoman *she* ever had known had given birth to a King! Maria did not voice it, but her resentment burned high against the strumpet Joan for not signing those articles of adoption, and Oddo was perfectly right in not sending Oil until the Queen had set her hand and seal. Oddo always had been the brains of the Colonna family.

"Will My Lord be delivering the Crown in Naples while Serjianni and my brother are at their Audience with Martin V in Florence?" asked Anna.

"Highness," said the Major, extending his arms and hands to express the unknown and unknowable, "as may be, the Lord

Prince of Taranto will not deliver the Crown at all." The news dispenser looked at Andria for approbation, and went on tentatively, "Some members of the family say that the Crown will not be handed over until Jacques Bourbon is released."

The Duke nodded to his man and smiled at Anna. "That will be Count Nola, Anna. Do you see? Gian and Raimondo have a hen setting, a little plan afoot. It is better if you don't know all the details, perhaps, but I shall ride over to Nola tomorrow and see how I fit in. Doubtless Raimondo can reach the Prince, and I shall send him word of your arrival. He will be happy to know you are safe—and so near to home."

"Yes," Anna smiled, "they would do that, My Lord and Raimondo!" Color rose in her cheeks, a sparkle came in her eye. "And you will go and help them, Cousin Gugl. O, do be careful. And I shall pray for you all! Maria, isn't it wonderful?"

Maria could not sit on both sides of the fence at once, but neither could she tell Anna that her husband was a meddling busybody who would do well to mind his own business. "Wonderful!" said Maria.

"May I ride with you to Nola, Father?" asked not-so-little Francesco. "I can ride very fast—on a good horse."

"But I leave you in charge of these ladies, Cecco. You must do the honors of our House."

The former prospect had been more pleasing, but the scion of Del Balzo accepted the inevitable. "Will Your Highnesses hunt tomorrow?" he asked. "Did you bring your hawks?"

"Damn!" said his father. "I knew there was something we had forgotten."

"Never mind," the lad consoled them. "I have enough for all."

Rather than hunt the next day, after the Duke was gone, Anna suggested a tour of the castle and grounds. Andria was so much larger and more splendid than Paliano, and the city ten times as large. Anna was more of a child than Francesco in the novelty of such a big world, and that made them better friends. The original castle had been built by the Emperor Frederick II Hohenstauffen—from whom, Anna recalled, Louis III d'Anjou had one-half of his right to the Regno—but the Del Balzos had added to it. Francesco knew, almost stone by stone, the history of every castle in the Duchy, and Anna drank in every word, picture and prospect, hungry—that first day—to take in all at a gulp, before she went on to Taranto and her children.

As fell out, she had more leisure than she knew, and eventually saw all the traces of Hohenstauffen fifty times apiece, because external circumstance, the affairs of men, were at variance with Anna's desires, perversely defying her prayers.

Anna was not discarded by blind Fate, not cast off to vegetate, an irrelevancy. Far from it. She—and especially her husband—and the Cousin who had saved her, were often prominently mentioned and roundly cursed by the Lords of Creation and even by God's Vicar, and for those very reasons her spouse and his kinsmen thought best to leave her where she was safe.

At the Papal Audience of Antonio Colonna and Serjianni in Florence, Anna's name was third on the agenda. Martin V asked first to see the signed articles of adoption. Joan had not signed because the Orators from France and Anjou had threatened to call back the Councillors to Constance and declare the Pope's Election null and void if she did. She would sign in secret, Serjianni promised, that must be understood between themselves. The steal simply would not bear publication.

Then His Holiness asked, "What good are these keys and passwords to me? Sforza sits still in Naples, he has not commanded his men to move out of any of these places in Rome—and I don't think you can make him."

Serjianni admitted that Sforza was a hard man to deal with, but Martin V was not justified in saying the keys and passwords would not work until he had tried them. "Let Antonio carry these talismans to Milord Paliano. I am confident his men will be put in possession of all three citadels. Let Antonio also carry the Blessed Oil—and if the strongholds are turned over to the Colonnas—let Milord Marsi come with Antonio to Naples to be invested with Amalfi and Venosa as promised. Appoint your brother Legate, with the power to Crown Her Majesty at his discretion. You can trust your own brother."

"Humph!" the Pope snorted, but Serjianni continued. "Her Majesty will have signed the articles and her last will and testament—in Antonio's favor—and when those documents are put into your brother's hands he will proceed with the Coronation."

Oddo did not see how they could squeak out of that, so he agreed, and then mentioned Anna, speaking to Antonio. "Have you seen your sister yet? She is in the Regno? Del Balzo carried her off."

"Anna?!"

"*Anna?!*" the Pope mimicked him. "Del Balzo also rifled the treasury of Paliano, and carried along Anna's nurse, whom he raped, bound hand and foot! That's your cabal for you. Those are *your* friends. That's what I get for taking in an Orsini! Don't tell me he's of the *Neapolitan branch*. All Orsinis are alike—and the Bel Balzo-Orsinis are the worst of the lot. Have you seen this so-called Prince of Taranto? Where is he? Why doesn't he get Bourbon out for me—as he said he would? You know, I wouldn't have to make all these concessions to Messer Serjianni if Bourbon were free."

Serjianni agreed at every point in Oddo's harangue, and suggested excommunication for the Del Balzo-Orsini cousins one and all, but defended Antonio and himself as laborers in Bourbon's vineyard. "It's that damned Castelan of Nuovo," Caracciolo complained. "Joan has a man in there who hates me, and I can't get him out."

"Excuses!" sneered His Serenity. "All I hear is excuses."

"I tried to get her to name me Castelan," said Antonio wistfully, "but she wouldn't."

"Pha!" said his father in disgust. "Big hammer, little head. What are we going to do about your sister? Can you get her back? I can't excommunicate the cousins under the circumstances. That's impossible."

"We can invite Anna to the Coronation," Antonio suggested. "Taranto is bringing the Crown, Raimondo says."

"Yes," Serjianni mused, "if Your Holiness would absolve me—now—we might take them all in one bag—at the Coronation."

"Absolve? Hold on! I don't want Taranto done away with. He's the strongest voice I have with Aragon. All I want is the whip-hand over him so he has to keep his promises. Don't you lay a finger on Taranto in violence—or Alphonso will keep the Schism going another ten years. Just get Anna back to Paliano—or into a convent somewhere—so I have some bargaining power. Their marriage hasn't been consummated, has it? Anna isn't pregnant? You wouldn't know—but find out! Ask in Paliano. I expressly forbade him to bed her."

Sometimes in those early days, Oddo must have asked himself if the Papacy was worth the trouble it took to get it and hang on to it.

Antonio Colonna took the Holy Oil, the keys and passwords from Florence to Paliano, and Duke Paliano assembled a troop to march into Rome and do the opening. At The City gates they assured Braccio that this expedition did not concern him, no attack upon his men was contemplated, all the Colonnas wished to do was cross Rome peaceably and try their keys.

The *Condottiere* laughed in their faces, just as Gugl and Gian had warned the Colonnas he would do when the time came. "Sorry," said Braccio when his mirth subsided, "but I am not yet crowned King of Perugia, and the boundaries of my domain are not defined. Until those details are attended to I cannot permit any Colonna to try keys in Sforza's locks."

Braccio and Sforza understood each other, to be sure, but no bad faith could be proved on Serjianni in this incident, so old Duke Marsi went on to Naples with Antonio and the Holy Oil, determined not to sprinkle Joan's Crown until every last article had been fulfilled.

Meantime, Serjianni had been homing from Pisa by sea, and he put in at Gaeta to smell out his welcome, whether he durst enter Naples or must still guide Joan's ship of State from Procida. At Gaeta he found out that Sforza had a very warm reception planned for him, so Serjianni wrote a letter to Joan, saying how sick he was. The only known cure for his malady was for Sforza to go in person to Rome and drive Braccio out of the Colonnas' way so they could use those keys.

Joan commanded Sforza to go, and—somewhat surprisingly—he bowed to the combined pressures of the Colonnas and Caracciolos and marched his army in a more or less northerly direction, leaving one of the Ruffo brothers behind to represent him at Joan's Council Table. Whether Sforza actually meant to strike at Braccio is dubious—their futures in relation to the Holy See could be settled more easily over a bottle—but for the nonce Sforza's own interests were best served by outward obedience to the Queen's will.

As soon as Sforza was out of sight, Serjianni landed at Naples amidst mingled hisses and jeers, but by moving swiftly he reached Joan's side with no bones broken. They went into executive session almost at once with the newly arrived Colonnas and a hastily summoned Council, and—lo!—there was Artuso Pappacoda, still Acting Lord High Secretary, and there was Raimondo Orsini Count Nola—with his hair in two braids—restored as Lord High Chamberlain, but "restored" with reservations. Those two notoriously Tarantine of heart were not seated beside each other. Count Nola's place at the table was between Sessa and the elder, much-titled Caldora—Prince of Capua, Duke of Bari, *et al, et aland* nobody tried to gloss over the symbolism of that. Orsini was at the table—he was in the Regno—under sufferance, always expected to be on his best behavior, and there was the military on either side of him to see that he stayed in line. Antonio Caldora—now Count Aversa—sat next to the elder weasel to strengthen that flank. Standing behind the Caldoras were their aides, to a total of six or eight, and no Baron at the table so poor that he sported less than three such in his suite. Only Raimondo Orsini was limited in this way. He was permitted but a single armed attendant. This day, however, he had been followed into the Chamber by a figure who appeared to be a Franciscan. That was Duke Andria who had got himself up in this way and stuck his baby lips together with some dirty beeswax or other, flattening them out. He could not speak with that stuff in his mouth, but the tacit assumption was that the pseudo religious was under vow of silence.

Seventeen persons, in all, sat at this Council Table, but most of them were not worth naming. Joan was the only woman, Covella had been barred for interrupting every meeting with imprecations for Ottino's release. One Ruffo representing Sforza was there, however, not the father of the poisoned Polissena but another brother hight Nicolo. His place was far down the table, next to the Archbishop-Almoner.

Urbano Origlia was not there, and neither was any other representative of the People.

Carafa Duke Maddaloni was not there, be assured.

Serjianni sat on the Queen's right, and Antonio Colonna on her left. Next to Antonio was old Duke Marsi, Papal Legate to the Regno, and now designate Duke Amalfi and Count Venosa. He hated conferences, and especially this one, because he had a speech to make that was going to be mighty unpopular. He was first on Artuso's *tapis,* so he had not long to fidget, and once he started speaking, he was not long in finishing, either. The pith of it was that—although he had the Oil in his duffle, and the Book of Ceremonials, with the place marked for him to read out the Coronation—the Colonnas did not yet hold Rome. With all due respect to Milord Catanzaro—Nicolo Ruffo—as Sforza's representative, there was an African in the woodpile, and the patience of P. P. Martin V had now run out. "There will be no Coronation," Marsi finished, "until Sforza and Braccio are out of Rome and not until His Highness Jacques Bourbon is privileged to sit at this table with us, a free man."

Of all who heard the Legate's demands, the two to whom that snapper was most unwelcome were Artuso Pappacoda and Count Nola, but they did not permit themselves even so much as an exchange of glances. You weet that the cabal's plan for springing Bourbon was already far advanced, and the plotters relied upon its success to restore the Prince of Taranto with credit in the bosom of his Papal father-in-law. Unthinkable that the Colonnas should turn the trick for themselves, and at no greater cost than the firmness of Giordano's elocutionary tones.

Artuso called up his severest dignity to say, "Let us dispose of these two propositions separately. Her Majesty will have done all that she, as Queen, can do—all that you can in reason require of her—when she repeats her commands to Sforza, as her Grand Constable, to drive Braccio out of Rome and then to withdraw his own troops. Even if that command left Naples today, the operation may take a month or two. You would not ask Her Majesty to wait so long for the Papal blessing.

"Milord Catanzaro, will you guarantee—with your person and your estate—that the Sforzas will obey Her Majesty's command? Will you help us to frame the order so that—this time—it will not fail of execution?"

Now, Catanzaro, Covella's other brother, never had been active in the cabal, but he had some parsnips of his own to butter. "I will, Milord," he promised readily. "I will do more. I will so bind myself to the Colonna welfare that there can be no doubt of my sincerity. I have the honor to propose the union of our Houses. If it meets with His Highness Antonio Colonna's approval—and with Her Majesty's—I shall give my daughter Giovanella-Maria to Milord Antonio Colonna for wife, with the Marchesate of Cotrone for immediate dowry and my County of Catanzaro in my will."

Ruffo had stolen the show—temporarily.

"A very interesting proposal," Serjianni smirked, trying to get the Coronation back in hand. "Doubtless the Colonnas will wish to take it under advisement. But you will immediately join us in the command to the Sforzas, as our good Secretary suggested."

"With all my heart," said the Ruffo.

"Will that satisfy your requirements, Milord *Amalfi?*" Serjianni gave Uncle Giordano's new title a slightly rancorous emphasis. He had wanted Amalfi—next after Salerno—for himself, as far back as he could remember.

Amalfi-Marsi tried to confer with his nephew *sotto voce,* but Antonio was too much affected by this marriage proposal to reply intelligently. *Count Catanzaro and Marchese Cotrone* sounded very well, but would these titles interfere with his prospects of becoming King?

"Stop fizzing, Antonio," said Joan sharply. "We have lots of work to do here. Nicolo's daughter is just a little girl. You wouldn't be able to put that weapon of yours into her for years to come."

"We accept!" said Amalfi-Marsi. "That is—we accept Her Majesty's order to Sforza as earnest of her fair intentions. That will be satisfactory, and our thanks to Count Catanzaro for his most generous co-operation."

"Now—if only we had the Crown to put the Oil on!" said Joan, looking steadily at Raimondo Orsini. "When may we expect to see it again, my dear Lord Chamberlain?"

Until then, Count Nola had been predicating the return of the Crown upon several reciprocal favors from Joan, that the Prince of Taranto be recalled from his banishment, restored in his estates, and given possession of his cousin Jacques, and—for bargaining purposes—the Queen had agreed orally to those demands.

Neither Nola nor Pappacoda put any more confidence in the Queen's promises than she in theirs, and—accordingly—they had still to trick Superba into keeping her word, but how?

Two fresh, unconsidered elements now wanted assimilation into their forming plan—perhaps three: *Item*—the presence of Serjianni in Naples, at the Queen's side. The plotters had assumed that he would remain holed up on Procida, an exile, but here he was, back in circulation like the proverbial bad *denaro,* and to be reckoned with. *Item*—on the positive side—the presence of Duke Andria and the availability of his considerable army, aid not to be despised, but—*item*—the presence in the Regno of Anna Colonna was a dubious quantity.

So that, when Joan asked, *When may we expect to see the Crown again?* Artuso's first impulse was to draw the Queenly fire upon himself by declaring the question out of the order of business, but the next *item* in the order of business would then be the second half of Amalfi-Marsi's demands, equally disastrous to the cabal's plans. In the absence of any brighter inspiration Pappacoda simply waited to hear how the lad with the Swiss haircut would try to salvage their scheme.

When may we expect to see the Crown again?

"Tonight, an it please Your Majesty," Raimondo replied boldly. "The Prince of Taranto awaits only the signal to bring it in."

"Then give the signal," Joan commanded. "We are ready."

Relief came from a strange quarter, and most unexpectedly. "We are not quite ready, Superba," Antonio Colonna objected, mindful what his father had said about preserving Taranto unharmed. No need to mention Serjianni by name, but, "The Prince has enemies. He—he must have safeguards—as my brother-in-law."

Joan missed—or decided to ignore—the veiled allusion to her Orange Blossom. "That he is your brother-in-law is safeguard enough," said she. "Let the signal be given. What is the signal, Count Nola?"

"I beg lief not to say, Majesty. I cannot give the signal without first speaking to Jacques Bourbon."

"You shall speak to him sooner than you expect!" Joan flared. "You may talk to him all night in the bowels of San Vincenzo if you do not obey me. Go at once and give the signal."

"No," said Serjianni. "First give Bourbon to the Colonnas. Then Count Nola will give the signal."

"He will give it *now!*" Joan screamed. "You—Milords Capua and Aversa—arrest Count Nola. I will not be defied."

The Caldoras sat impassive, staring at their sovereign as if they had not heard.

"Superba! Superba!" Antonio Colonna pleaded. "Do not send Raimondo to the donjon. He is my best friend. He is the only one

I can look to—the only one who can bring Anna to us! Listen to me, Superba!"

Joan had not failed to hear what Antonio said, but her rage at being balked and disobeyed had to have vent before she would take cognizance, and—since Count Nola had so many uses—Her Majesty found expedient to shift her spleen to spray upon the Caldoras. "I told you to arrest Count Nola. Do you refuse?"

The Caldoras said nothing, but a chorus of *No's* whipped around the table. Heedless of all opposition, the Queen continued addressing the weasels in a key that fairly opened the ceiling. "You are both banished! You are stripped, degraded and deprived of all titles, honors and rights whatsoever. Get out of my sight—both of you!"

That was a fine time to throw away two-thirds of her military support, but Joan had ever been unreasonable, and she persisted in this stand, against all argument.

Softly, under the Queen's screams, Artuso told the Caldoras, "If Your Highnesses will be good enough to make yourselves comfortable in my office—it will help us to get on with essential business."

"Very well," said Weasel I. "Come, Son." They left the Council Chamber, to a slight ripple of applause.

"I saw every one who clapped his hands," said Joan, "and I'll get even. Now! Antonio? What were you saying about your sister—and Count Nola?"

"Only this, that if Anna were here—perhaps in Your Majesty's Bedchamber—a Lady—we should have some control over her husband's actions." The young Colonna did not give his father credit for conceiving that piece of skulduggery, but everybody in the room knew that such cogency was beyond the speaker's capacities. "I think that Raimondo—Count

Nola—would be the ideal person to carry Your Majesty's appointment to my sister, and to bring her back. Anna trusts him—obeys him—implicitly."

"Thou Judas!" Nola cursed. "Thou double Judas! To do this to a Saint—and your sister."

"I think it is a splendid idea," said Joan. "Don't you dare give the signal until Anna is here with me. Then we shall see how our high-chested nephew behaves."

"I cannot bring the Princess here, Majesty," said Count Nola. "Antonio exaggerates my powers. Anna would not come with me."

"You will go and try. We mean her no harm," Superba crouted like a cormorant.

"No," Serjianni chimed in, "and we mean Taranto no harm. We simply want a check upon Taranto's headstrong antics."

"I refuse to go," said Raimondo.

"Well, now, I wouldn't say, *refuse*," Artuso suggested suavely. "You might go and talk it over with Princess Anna. Perhaps she would like to be a Lady in Waiting."

"She would!" said Antonio. "I have heard her say a hundred times that she wanted nothing so much as a heart-to-heart talk with the Queen."

"Isn't that sweet?" Joan cooed. "You hear that, Raimondo? Anna loves me. Go at once and bring her here. If you refuse— you are no Chamberlain of mine. I shall make Uncle Giordano my Chamberlain." She leaned over to pat the hand of Amalfi-Marsi. "Would you like to be our Lord High Chamberlain, Duke Amalfi?"

"Can't say that I should mind at all, Majesty. There *are* emoluments?"

"You Colonnas! Yes, Highness, there are emoluments. When there's money in the treasury the Chamberlain has eight thousand a year, and whether there is money or not he has his cut on all purchases for the royal households except food and clothing."

"That might amount to a pretty thing," the Papal Legate allowed.

"A very pretty thing," said Joan, "but our cousin doesn't appreciate it. Count Nola!—I command you to go to Andria, and Duke Amalfi will go with you. The one who returns with the Princess of Taranto shall be our Lord High Chamberlain thenceforward. *Selah!*"

"O, well, now," the blooming diplomatist from Marsi was suffering qualms. "We're getting a little off the subject, aren't we? It's a long ride to Andria—and a long ride back. I don't mind going—and I'd like very much to have that cut Your Majesty mentioned, but we'll have to get Jacques Bourbon out before I go. We got to talking about other things, but that was the point of my speech."

"You are a perfectly horrid old shit," said Superba, "and I will not let Bourbon out!"

"Then you won't be Crowned, you old bag," the Colonna retaliated.

"Shall we take a short recess?" asked Artuso Pappacoda.

"Yes," said Serjianni. "I want a word with Her Majesty."

"You stay near me, Antonio," the Queen commanded. "He'll slap me if you don't."

"I ought to slap your head off," the Seneschal retorted—but Artuso the peacemaker was on his way to patch up the wounds of the Caldoras.

Disconcertingly—the Caldoras had not waited. The look of it was that they had taken their "banishment" seriously and got out of reach of Joan's Castelan before the elder weasel could be put on the rack again. Perhaps they were joining Sforza. Leastwise, they had not gone to Aversa to prepare for Taranto's landing.

Pappacoda was mulling the meaning of the Caldoras' flight when Nola caught up with him, the Orsini also in a study called brown, twisting one mustache as if he would pull it out. "What do you think, Pappa? Had I better ride for it?"

"She'll give Colonna your baton if you run off now."

"She's going to do that anyway. She's trying to buy him off."

"But she can't. He has his orders from Oddo, and dare not disobey. Bourbon is coming out—and soon. That's what worries me. If the Colonnas get him out without our help, the Prince will look blacker than ever to the Pope."

"The Colonnas won't bother to spring Ottino either," Raimondo added. "Serjianni won't let them."

The door to the corridor stood ajar to guard against eavesdroppers, and the conspirators commanded a view of the Councillors milling outside the Chamber. As many as four or five of them—friends and foes intermingled—were coming for a private word with the Secretary but he forestalled them with a gesture to his own bodyguard.

"Suppose you did give Taranto the signal," Artuso said tentatively, "what would our chances be?"

"Nil. We are not ready. I was bluffing when I said I could deliver the Crown tonight. I do not know where Taranto is—or if he is near enough to see our signal."

"Where is Andria?"

"Did you not recognize him? He stood behind my chair."

"In there? The Franciscan! What a mad thing to do!—facing the Queen—and Serjianni——"

"Eh? *You* face the Queen and Serjianni—every day."

"That's different."

"It's not so very different, old friend, and we couldn't get along without you. Take care."

"You tell *me* to take care—"

Both men peered into the corridor, where the masquerading Guglielmo was attempting to efface himself by melting into the wall.

"Where are his men?" asked Artuso in a whisper.

"Coming into town—in small groups to escape notice. It will take three days to assemble them in any kind of order."

"We are badly off balance," Artuso observed wryly.

"That is why I thought I had better get out of sight."

"Aye, and take Gugl with you."

"I'll go to Salerno—and send someone to sea to bring Gian there."

"I'll tell the Queen you have gone to Andria to fetch the Princess. I won you over. Go!"

Alas, they had talked too long. Even as Count Nola stepped into the corridor the false Franciscan—hard pressed and recognized-picked up the skirts of his monk's weeds and set off at a dead run for the stair to the courtyard, toward his horse and liberty. Joan's Archbishop-Almoner sang out to stop him, but quite as many were disposed to let him go. Confusion was the essence of the contretemps, and the few halberdiers who lowered their weapons across Guglielmo's path were nowise determined.

Andria spat the waxy stuff into his palm and flung it into the face of one, knocked down a second with a forearm blow, and by the time he reached a third he had got his sword out from beneath the folds of his habit. Full voiced then, Andria's command froze another, and Count Nola with his solitary aide was following close behind.

In a sense, the cousins "fought" their way out of Castel Nuovo, but they left no dead or wounded in their wake. Raimondo banged about a bit whilst Guglielmo got into the saddle, but the Archbishop-Almoner's authority was no match for the prestige of the royal cousins, who certainly had as much right to depart at will as the so recently flown Caldoras.

The noise and hurrah reached the Council Chamber quickly. As Joan was assisted back into her chair at the head of the table she said, "We won't wait for Count Nola. He won't be back. You, Milord Amalfi, will be entered on the rolls for his emoluments as Chamberlain. Artuso will look to it and inform you of your duties."

Pappacoda, back in his wonted place, said nothing, which was the safer way.

The new Chamberlain would have knelt to pour out his gratitude, but Joan stopped him with her hand. "Don't thank me. I hate you. Jacques Bourbon is being brought here—now. Serjianni will preside over the balance of your deliberations. I cannot stand the sight of this worm they are bringing in—so I spare myself." She arose. "Good day, Milords. Come, Antonio." Her Majesty swept away, and the *double* Judas followed her out.

Artuso sat without change of expression, without apparent interest in the debacle he was helpless to prevent. He was pondering—savouring—the pleasant words of appreciation that Raimondo had given him, and thinking how finely the boys had treated Ettore since his accident.

Duke Sessa, equally impassive outwardly, let his gaze lie heavily on his colleague of the opposition. "You're old enough to know better," said the Commander cryptically. "What can be in your head?"

"I was just thinking—one of these days—I shall retire," Artuso replied wearily. "I should have done so long ago if I had ever got caught up on my work. There is always so much unfinished business."

"You'll never retire," said Sessa. "The Queen couldn't get along without you."

Then Serjianni and Bourbon were there, but no Ottino, of course. The former King had put on weight. In fact, he showed no ravages whatever from his long confinement. He was shaved and decently covered. He never had been cleanly. He had not been dropped or racked. His cell had been above the water line, but still he could describe rats big enough to saddle, and he knew Serjianni's failing. "One had blue eyes, and the longest lashes you ever have seen on a rat," he said, "longer than yours."

Perfectly aware of his status, and of the utmost he could expect to gain as a by-product of the Colonna Pope's necessities, Jacques still tried to get more, applying his arguments to the Papal Legate with heat and an endless contortion of Gallic gestures. First, he demanded to be Crowned above Joan, then, at least, equally with her, and—in a last spasm, tearing his hair—he cried out, "Take me back to your donjon! Take me back! If I am deprived of my birthright—let me die in a cell!"

If Jacques had persisted in that strain, he might have improved his position in the end: the Sorbonne would have been pleased to uphold him: but he changed this tune, demanding to speak with the French Orator. That diplomat was not in the Castel. This sudden release had caught everyone unprepared, but one point of substantial value Bourbon won. Mindful how Castel Capuano had sheltered Joan from him on occasion, he designated that defensible pile for his residence, and got it.

Artuso helped Bourbon put that over, and made note of the freedman's selection of Castelan, Major, *et al*, promising to assemble them. Serjianni's objections were all overridden by Colonna's insistence that no vestige of durance, restraint or espionage was to be carried over from one Castel to the other, and—as soon as darkness was deep enough to shroud the identity of the new tenant—Jacques was escorted to Castel Capuano.

Weary as he was from a full day of calm restraint in a caldron aboil with emotion, Artuso—with only his page in attendance-crossed the city to a public stable opposite the Posilippo gate. The place was asleep, save for the proprietor who opened a door before the caller could knock. By night Your Worships would not have recognized this horse dealer, but—in the sun—despite alterations of color, a beard, dress and carriage, if you be sharpeyed you might have seen in him the former secretary-bravo Antonio, who had survived that post in Serjianni's household only by relinquishing it.

Up to the time of Ottino Caracciolo's capture—and even some months thereafter—this Antonio had been able to push off his multiple treasons upon the broad back of Serjianni's cousin, largely because his master wished to think Ottino guilty and his secretary innocent: but the water got hotter after the luckless cannon-builder was shut up. Serjianni's secrets continued to be exposed, secrets that only Antonio knew.

The denouement had come when—after Nola's wedding— the former Castelan of San Vincenzo, he who had negotiated the marriage contract in Constance, claimed his reward. By Serjianni's promise this well-born, glorified gaolor was to have been made Castelan of the Citadel at Avellino, and Caracciolo kept that promise, in the letter if not in fact. Tax collections at Avellino under the governance of Marino Marzano had been something sad to see, and Serjianni looked for improvement in that quarter as soon as the new Castelan could snoop out the leaks.

With exposure of the entire Avellino fraud so imminent, Antonio had seen no alternative to cutting off the appointee's career, and so he had cut—and then run.

The stable and horse-auction had been bought with Papacoda's money but by Antonio's hand, and so far nothing untoward had occurred there. The nature of the establishment made it a blameless, innocuous rendezvous for all classes intermingled, a perfect point for the exchange of intelligence, the despatch of ciphers and many other transactions in surreptitious Statecraft.

"Ride after Count Nola, if you will, please, Antonio," Artuso directed. "He is on the road to Salerno. Tell him that Bourbon will be living in Castel Capuano, and I shall have limited access. Say that I shall try to join the boys in conference if I can. Find out where and when the Prince will land. Say—also—that the Caldoras have gone God knows where, and that a ruse is planned to trick Anna Colonna into the Queen's custody."

"Your Highness has spoken!" Antonio replied cheerfully. "I am already saddled."

Summing up next day, the only question found remaining at issue between Joan and the Colonnas was whether to Crown first or adopt first, and Joan won the debate by again pointing to the French Orator. He had spent the night with Bourbon in Castel Capuano, and a petition was already circulating in the city for a double Coronation. The sensible way to prevent that agitation from reanimating the Sorbonne and causing another six months' delay of Oddo's income from France was by conducting the solo ceremony at once.

Agreed!

All that was wanting, then, was the Crown, and Anna. Separate efforts to obtain both went forward simultaneously. Joan's ultimatum followed Raimondo Orsini to Salerno and then to Nola, threatening confiscation of his ancestral estates if he did not produce that bejeweled circlet within three days. Joan would have liked to see Anna's Uncle Giordano carry her command-invitation to the Princess in Andria, but he refused to go unless Antonio Colonna were invested with Salerno first. Fat chance of that while Serjianni had his health, so Duke Marsi-Amalfi sat down with Nicolo Ruffo to negotiate for Antonio's bride. To the Colonna maws, any taxing was good, and they were delighted to gobble up Cotrone while waiting for the bigger pieces.

Duke Sessa—of all people—was sent after Anna. He took along an empty litter, the Queen's own, for the Princess to ride in, and a select troop of the Palace Guard in parade dress to dazzle the country maid.

The bolder outlines of her family's advancement had reached Anna in Andria through the Major's recitals, which continued to enliven their dinners. Maria-Paliano would have preferred to receive the news hot, as it arrived in the course of the day, and then have the joculator get off his wheezes with the meat, but the Del Balzo clown was a bawdy fellow and Anna remained austere. She laughed enough on her rounds with Francesco, laughed because he could climb a tree faster than a cat, laughed at the goblin faces the Hohenstauffens had carved on their palaces, laughed because she slipped in the mud, but the buffooneries of the professional jester, turning upon Maria's ever-growing plumpness, were not funny to Anna, only most indelicate.

One night Maria came to the table after the children were seated, and announced with animation, "There's the nicest woman living here! I met her today. Do you know the one I mean, Francesco? Tall—with beautiful hair?"

"No, Highness," said Francesco, who knew very well. That was, perhaps, the first time anyone ever had addressed Maria as *Highness.*

The Major was not yet come into the dining hall this evening, but the butler glared at the waiters—for rattling plates.

"So well-spoken and genteel," Maria went on. "She seems to be more than a housekeeper—but she can't be a kinswoman, the Duke would have presented her."

"She was my nurse," said Francesco. "I used to eat with her—until—until Your Highnesses—came."

"O," said Maria.

"'O', what?" asked Anna.

"O dear," said Maria, and—taking a page from her daughter's book—"Let us speak no more about it."

"Your nurse may eat with us still if you wish," the Princess told her playmate. "Would you like that?"

"Father said she couldn't," Francesco admitted, downcast.

"That was very considerate," said Anna, "but we shouldn't mind. I'll send for her."

"Perhaps we'd better not," Maria worried, fully aware by that time who her new acquaintance was. "And yet, she was such a pleasant person. So agreeable—to *me*."

The resident mistress—whose name, I am sorry, was Maria—was at least fifteen years younger than the gentlewoman at the table, and—perhaps for that reason—had shewn no sense of rivalry or resentment of their juxtaposition.

"We shall have her up," Anna decreed, and just then the Major bowed in. "We should like a place laid for Francesco's nurse—and will you ask her to join us, please? What is her name?"

"Her name is Maria," said the Major and Francesco together.

"What else?" said Maria-Paliano.

The Major spoke to the butler, aside, saying, "See if she'll come." Then he gave Their Highnesses, as the first *item* for that day a solemn warning from Duke Andria to beware of gifts from Joan. "The Queen is expected to make Your Highness a Lady of Her Bedchamber, but this is only a ruse to trap you—and hold you—as a threat upon the Prince. We are required not to let Your Highness leave Andria under any circumstances."

"I hope I shall not be a burden to anyone," said Anna. "Is there no more cheerful news?"

There was the proposal to marry Antonio Colonna to Giovanella-Maria Ruffo, the little cousin of the poisoned Polissena.

"And how soon will someone poison Giovanella?" asked Anna. "Poor Antonio."

The nurse—Maria-Andria—presented herself smiling, and lifted the gloom by sheer radiance. Of poison, she had to say, that far more people got married than ever were poisoned, that nine out of ten people allegedly poisoned had died of a fish-bone stuck in their throats or something of that kind, and that lightning never struck twice in the same place.

"O, I think it does," said Maria-Paliano, folding her hands across her condition. "Where was Francesco born?"

"Here in the castle," his mother replied without rancor. "You may use the same bed if you wish. But that's really aiming the lightning, isn't it? You must call me to help you."

"Thank you," said the more expectant Maria. "I shall—and it won't be long now."

"*Madame* will begin lying-in tonight, Major," said the nurse easily, and turned to Anna. "Your Highness is eager to get to Taranto. I cannot blame you, with such a handsome husband."

"You know the Prince?"

"*Ah, oui!* The Prince is the last Highness whose conversation I have enjoyed. He is a very brilliant man. You are going to be very happy, dear Princess. Be not cold to him."

"O, no," said Anna. "I was afraid of him at first, but now I know he is very gentle."

"Very gentle," the younger Maria echoed, "but very strong too. He can flatten a horseshoe with either hand."

"He *can?*" Anna saw no immediate use for this singular ability, but she was proud that her husband could perform the feat if called upon, and Francesco's mother continued to unfold wonders. "An Egyptian fortune teller once told *me—The best man is like the trunk of an elephant—which can pick up a pin or break the back of a tiger.* Your husband is like that."

Anna felt the compliment more through the woman's tone than from her words. "I have seen a tiger," said Anna, "but what is an ephalent?"

Maria-Andria tried her best to convey an image of the beast, but it did not sound at all like the Taranto whom Anna knew.

"With your help, there is nothing His Highness cannot do," the resident mistress assured the virgin. "His cousins would give their lives for him—and may have to! But, forgive me! I see nothing but the best ahead for us all, now that we have such a magnificent Pope. Your Highness must be very proud and happy."

"We are," said the elder Maria, with a touch of belligerency. She sensed a reflection upon herself in this common person's knowing.

"I am not proud," said Anna, but the hopelessness of explaining Uncle Oddo's remissness to one outside the family, even to one so sympathetic and understanding as Francesco's nurse, kept her from going on. "Pride is a sin," Anna murmured lamely.

They spoke of sin, but never got down to cases. They spoke of a thousand things, great and small, and continued congenial from day to day in spite of Maria-Paliano's bridling, and occasional waspishness, in spite of Anna's growing reticence upon matters closest to her inmost heart and soul.

Time after time, in discussion, when Anna might have resolved a question by disclosing the Will of God, she held her tongue lest her new friend find her presumptuous, holier-than-thou. Isolated there in Andria, far separated from the world's affairs and the pushing political traffic, entirely unaware of the phenomenon, Anna began to grow up. She did not learn then how curiously she and the two Marias were interlinked by the masculinity of the cousins Giovantonio and Guglielmo, did not know that the embryo her mother was carrying was half-brother to Francesco Del Balzo, or that Francesco's mother was carrying the embryo of her husband's fifth daughter. Still, Anna was growing up.

When Maria-Paliano's baby was born, Anna and Francesco Del Balzo were swimming, without a stitch on, and—although Anna's body offered little or nothing by way of provocation—the gristly difference between their anatomies could not be hid, unless by hiding it where the difference was greatest, and that was what Francesco tried to do. This was that same old piglike poking which her brothers and cousins at Paliano had—in early times—tried to convince her was a "game", but Anna had thought better of Francesco. Finding the common clay in him almost broke her heart. She did not cry, but pushed him off with scorn so scalding that the lad felt it melt his bones. "That is what *pigs* do," said Anna, and that made Francesco cry.

Dressed, they were silent, until a passing slavey told them that a baby boy was come to Maria in the lying-in room.

"It's MINE!" screamed Anna, jubilant. "My prayer is answered! My prayer is answered!"—and she streaked for the bedside to claim her own, obviously the heir to Taranto.

At first they would not let her in, and when they did, the heir was disappointing. It looked more like a skinned squirrel than a little Prince, but Maria-Andria assured Anna that he would grow hair in time. "But why do you call him 'the Prince'?" The woman's curiosity was understandable.

"Because he is," said Anna, creating new confusions. "He is My Lord's heir! I have prayed and prayed." Then she ran to kiss the face of Maria-Paliano on the bolster, crying, "*Where* did you find him?"

Wearily, O, so wearily, her mother sighed, "That nonsense again? Anna, Anna, Anna. I found him between my legs. Will you not be sensible? He is not your baby—he is *mine*."

That was the cruelest thing Maria ever had said to Anna. It revealed a selfish streak in the woman that the Princess never had suspected before, a depth of treachery beyond sounding, beyond belief. That Maria should attempt to appropriate for her own, the son the Prince yearned for——

"Yours!?" Anna burst out. "You know God sent him to me. Even if you did find him in bed with you—God meant him for *me*."

"No, Anna, not this baby. God will send you another baby, but this one is mine."

"How do you know?"

"Because he grew in my belly!"

"A likely story!" said Anna. "Who will believe anything so preposterous? I pray God may forgive you for such a low lie—but I will have my son!"

"I give up," said Maria, closing her eyes. "Take him. He's yours."

Hardly able to credit what she had seen and heard, the other Maria, who was holding the child, stammered, "Perhaps—Your Highness—perhaps you will permit—Maria will nurse him for you."

"That will be quite satisfactory," said Anna with dignity. "I shall not be selfish with him. You may nurse him, Maria. I must go now and inform My Lord that his son is born."

First, however, before writing her letter to Taranto, Anna knelt in the Del Balzo chapel and offered up her thanks to Heaven. She was still praying when Duke Sessa arrived to carry her to Naples.

The resplendent Palace Guard, intended to impress the Princess, had been halted at the distance of the outermost city walls. The Governor of Andria refused to permit the Queensmen to so much as bring in the litter without specific orders from the castle. In view of his high source, however, and the importance of his mission, Marzano was granted the dignity of a large suite. Twelve of his officers attended him, but well surrounded by Andrian men-at-arms, up to the castle gate. There the Castelan and the Major studied Duke Sessa's credentials, and sent to learn the Princess' will in the matter of an interview. Anna could not leave the castle, that was understood, but she might receive her appointment to the Bedchamber from Duke Sessa's hand, if she so desired.

It pleased Her Highness—next only to having a son—to see so much regality at her feet, and, to let the Queen's envoy know that she esteemed the honor, and knew his quality, she said, "I trust Your Lordship will excuse me for not wearing my coronet. My titular jewels are in Taranto."

Childish though it was, the boast carried a fine overgloss of defiant confidence, for it disposed of the question of "exile" by ignoring it. That put Sessa at an instant disadvantage, because his preamble—which he went through anyway—had all to do with the lifting of Taranto's banishment, how Her Majesty was persuaded to leniency by the supernal recognizances of the Princess and her illustrious family.

Sessa read off the list of incomes, titles and honors already conferred upon the Colonnas, building up to Anna's own designation as the finest of them all. Most of this good fortune had already been reported at Andria, but a few windfalls were new.

That Uncle Giordano had succeeded Anna's spiritual spouse as Lord High Chamberlain looked bad for the cabal. It removed Raimondo from a place of trust in favor of one who supported Brother Antonio for King. What Duke Sessa put forward as a gain for her House and a source of pleasure to her was in fact a great loss and cause for alarm.

"May I inquire if Count Nola suffers some disgrace?" asked Anna, really wishing to know if he were in gaol.

"His Highness is out of favor," said Sessa, and hurried on, recollecting that Nola had fallen for refusing to do the onerous errand upon which he himself was engaged. "Your Highness' father, Duke Paliano, is to become also Count Alba. Her Majesty requests that Your Highness will stand as his proxy at the ceremony of investiture. The Queen's Graciousness also requests that Your Highness stand proxy for your brother, Odoardo, who is to be invested Count Celano. Her Majesty also confirms the Highness Odoardo as heir to Marsi."

Spontaneously Anna clapped her hands. "She remembered little Odi! I could kiss her."

Sessa thought he was making hay. "Yes, Highness, our Superba is the most generous of women, as I have reason to know. My own dear Duchess has been Chief Lady of the Bedchamber many years, and Her Majesty stood Godmother to our first son."

Upon that note they discovered their quasi-kinship, for Duke Sessa's "first son" was Marino Marzano the deer-hound who kept poachers off Cousin Gugl's preserves. Then the Countess Tagliacozza was Duke Sessa's sister, and the Duke was blood-uncle to Rinaldo Orsini, the spouse of dearest Cousin Cat. A small world indeed!

At length Marzano read out the proclamation making the Princess a Lady, and added—on Covella's behalf—that she was a mother to all the Bedchamber and would take Anna to her bosom.

For a fighter, Sessa thought he had carried this off damned well, so that Anna's reply was not unexpected, to a point.

"I am honored beyond expression," quoth the Princess. "I accept, humbly, with all my heart, but I cannot return to Naples with Your Highness because of my little son, born only an hour ago. As a mother, the Duchess of Sessa will understand that I could not leave him so soon, and I beg her to intercede for me with the Queen, and say that I shall come as soon as possible." Anna arose from her chair to indicate that the interview was ended, and it certainly was.

Duke Sessa bolted the castle, sped out of Andria, and himself rode to Naples with only such halts as were necessary to provide live horses for the two which died under him. This intelligence was too rare to be spoken by a courier. Marzano delivered it himself, and the Court was set on its ear.

O, many said *incredible*, but the doubt and suspicion of truth remained. The report was sent express to Oddo in his Florentine Vatican, and, all over Naples, even those who disbelieved the statement said that the Prince of Taranto had a wife to be proud of, a Princess worthy of him, for conceiving that sublime lie.

Giovantonio, the putative father, received the announcement in Salerno. He had it by word of mouth, as a rumor current in Naples, and by letter from Anna later the same day. On both occasions he laid his handsome head well back, and laughed and laughed and laughed.

MR. THAYER INTRUDES

CHECKING UP on Villon's facts concerning relations between Martin V and Visconti of Milan, one finds that Visconti had his wife beheaded on an allegation of adultery, either while the Pope was in residence there or soon after he fled.

Far be it from me to imply any connection between the two events, but if some modern newsman stationed in Milan can gain access to day-by-day records he may find a story there.

www.ingramcontent.com/pod-product-compliance
Lightning Source LLC
Chambersburg PA
CBHW031025030726
47497CB00004B/1010